THE
Italians

FRANCO, DOMINIC & VALENTINO

THE
Italians
COLLECTION

August 2015

September 2015

October 2015

November 2015

December 2015

January 2016

THE
Italians
Franco, Dominic & Valentino

MICHELLE REID
KATHERINE GARBERA
AMY ANDREWS

Published in Great Britain 2015
by Mills & Boon, an imprint of Harlequin (UK) Limited,
Eton House, 18-24 Paradise Road, Richmond, Surrey, TW9 1SR

THE ITALIANS: FRANCO, DOMINIC & VALENTINO
© 2015 Harlequin Books S.A.

The Man Who Risked It All © 2012 Michelle Reid
The Moretti Arrangement © 2009 Katherine Garbera
Valentino's Pregnancy Bombshell © 2010 Amy Andrews

ISBN: 978-0-263-91772-7

026-0116

THE MAN WHO
RISKED IT ALL

MICHELLE REID

Michelle Reid grew up on the southern edges of Manchester, the youngest in a family of five lively children. Now she lives in the beautiful county of Cheshire, with her busy executive husband and two grown-up daughters. She loves reading, the ballet, and playing tennis when she gets the chance. She hates cooking, cleaning, and despises ironing! Sleep she can do without and produces some of her best written work during the early hours of the morning.

PROLOGUE

A FEVER of hopeful expectancy had spread through the crowds waiting to see if the race would begin. Suited up and ready to go, Franco Tolle stood inside the *White Streak* team marquee with his safety helmet held in the crook of his arm and his eyes fixed on the monitor, watching for the race organisers' decision to show up on the screen. The wind had picked up, whipping the glass-smooth surface of the Mediterranean into a turbulent boil—not ideal conditions in which to race notoriously temperamental powerboats at sixty metres per second.

'What do you think?' Marco Clemente, his co-driver, came up beside him.

Franco offered a shrug in response. The truth was he wasn't worried so much by the racing conditions as he was by Marco's determination to race with him today.

'Are you sure you are up for this?' he questioned, keeping his voice level and his eyes fixed on the monitor screen.

Marco hissed out an impatient breath. 'If you don't want me in the boat with you, Franco, then just damn well say so.'

And there was the reason why Franco had asked the question in the first place. Marco was on edge, uptight, volatile. He'd spent the last hour pacing the marquee, snapping at anyone who spoke to him, and now he was snapping at Franco. It was not the best frame of mind for him to be in control of the boat's powerful throttle.

'In case you have forgotten, Franco, half of *White Streak* belongs to me—even if you are the one with the design and build genius.'

The petulance in his tone made Franco set his teeth together to stop him saying something he might regret. So they co-owned *White Streak*. So they'd raced both her and her sister boat across Europe under the co-owned White Streak company name for the last five years. But this would be the first time in three of those years that they would be climbing into the same boat together. This was the first time that Franco had given into the pressure and agreed to let Marco take the seat next to him.

And why had he done that? Because the championship hung in the balance with this one last race of the season and his usual co-driver had gone down with the flu yesterday. Marco was, without question, the best man to have sitting in Angelo's place when the stakes were this high, so he'd convinced himself that despite the rift in their friendship the two of them could be professional about this. What he had not known until he'd turned up here today was that Marco was not behaving like the laid-back guy everyone was used to seeing around the place.

'We used to be good friends,' Marco husked with low-voiced intensity. 'For almost all our lives we were the closest of friends. Then I made one small mistake and you—'

'Sleeping with my wife was not a small mistake.'

As if the wind outside had found its way into the tent, the chill of Franco's voice struck through his own protective clothing to his skin.

Marco seemed to breathe that chill in deep. 'Lexi was not your wife back then.'

'No.' Franco turned his head to look at Marco for the first time since the conversation had begun. They stood the same height, shared the same lean athletic build, the same age and the same nationality—but there the similarities ended. For where Marco was fair-haired, with blue eyes, Franco was dark: dark hair, dark eyes, a darker demeanour altogether. 'You, however, were my closest friend.'

Marco tried to hold his gaze. Remorse and frustration vied inside him for a couple of seconds before he sighed and looked away.

'What if I told you it never happened?' he posed abruptly. 'What if I said I made up the whole thing to break the two of you up?'

'Why would you want to?'

'Why would you want to throw your life away on a teenager?' Marco hit back, and revealed that frustration had won out over remorse. 'You still married her anyway, and left me feeling like the worse bastard alive. And Lexi did not even know I'd said anything to you, did she? You didn't tell her.'

As grim and silent as a corpse, Franco looked back at the monitor screen, the naturally sensual shape to his mouth clamping into a hard straight line.

'She can't have known,' Marco muttered, as if he was talking to himself. 'She was too nice to me.'

'Is there a purpose in this conversation?' Franco asked with a sudden flash of irritation. 'We have a race to attend to, and it must be obvious that I have no wish to discuss the past with you.'

'OK, *signori*, we have the go!' As if on cue, the shout from their team manager across the tent broke through the tension eddying around the two men.

Franco began to walk away, but Marco grabbed his arm to hold him still.

'For God's sake, Franco,' he murmured urgently. 'I'm sorry if I messed things up between you and Lexi, but she has been out of your life for over three years now! Can't we put the whole stupid incident behind us and go back to how we—?'

'Shall I tell you why you've decided to drag all of this up?' Franco swung back to him, icy contempt contorting his face now. 'You are in debt to White Streak to the tune of millions. You are scared because you know you need my goodwill to keep that ugly truth under wraps. You have heard the rumours that I am thinking of pulling the plug on powerboat racing and it is scaring you to death—because you know the whole financial mess you've placed us in is likely to blow up in your face. And just for the record,' he concluded icily, 'your lousy attempt at an apology for what you did has come three and a half years too damn late.'

Tugging his arm free, Franco turned away from Marco's frozen expression. In truth, he hadn't expected Marco to drag this up—and it didn't help the way he was feeling to know that back in his apartment divorce papers from Lexi sat waiting for him to find the stomach to read them.

He strode out of the marquee into the hot sunlight, cold anger fizzing like iced nitrogen in his blood. This was Livorno; his home crowd was out there. But he barely heard their rousing cheer. A red mist had risen across his eyes, in the centre of that his once closest friend lay entwined in the heaving throes of passion with the only woman he had ever loved. He had lived with that image ever since Marco had planted it in his head almost four years ago. He had taken it with him into his brief marriage to Lexi. It had coloured the way he had treated her and even made him suspect that the child she had carried was not his. It had changed the pattern of his life. It had embittered him until there was nothing left of the man he'd used to be, and when Lexi had miscarried the baby that image had shadowed the way he had reacted to the loss.

And the hell of it was that Marco was right: Lexi had never known why he'd behaved that way. The one small salve to his own wounded pride was that she'd never known how her betrayal of him with his best friend had broken his damn stupid, gullible heart.

Like a nemesis he could not shake off, Marco appeared at his shoulder again. 'Franco, *amico*, I need you to listen—'

'Don't speak to me about the past,' Franco cut in harshly, before Marco could say any more. 'Focus instead on the job in hand, or I will take the decision to fold up the White Streak company. And the financial mess you've placed it in will come out.'

'But you will ruin me,' Marco breathed hoarsely. 'My family's reputation will be—'

'Precisely.'

He watched Marco go pale, aware of the reason behind his terror. The famous Clemente name was synonymous with fine wines, honesty and charity. It headed some of the biggest charitable organisations in Italy alongside the Tolle name. Their two families had been close for as far back as he could remember—which was the reason he'd kept his rift with Marco so low-key. They still shared a business relationship. They met often at charitable and social events. He'd allowed Marco to laugh off rumours about the cooling of their friendship, and he knew he'd let him get away with it because it was less cutting to his ego than to let anyone learn the real truth.

'Hey you guys, wave to the crowd,' their team manager prompted from behind them.

Like an obedient puppet Franco raised his arm and waved while beside him Marco did the same thing, switching on his famously brilliant smile and charming everyone as he always did. Franco put on his helmet to give his hands something else to do. The moment he did so he lost his own smile. The two of them climbed into the boat's open cockpit. They strapped themselves in. Their race advisor was droning the usual information into his earpiece about wind speeds, the predicted height and length of the ocean swell. They did their pre-start checks, working with the unison of two people used to knowing what the other was thinking all the time. They had been childhood friends, through adolescence and into adulthood together. He would have staked his life on Marco always being there as a deeply loyal friend through to his dotage. Growing old together, kids, grandkids… Warm summer evenings spent watching the sun go down while drinking the best wine the Clemente cellars had to offer and reminiscing about the good old times.

The twin engines fired, their throaty roar a sweet song to Franco's marine engineer's ears. They took her out towards the start line—a streak of bright white amongst the dozen other powerboats splashing the glistening ocean with bright primary colours and bold sponsor logos, all of them holding back on the throttle like crouching dragons, ready to roar into action the split second they were given the go.

He glanced sideways at Marco. Franco didn't know why he did it—the old sixth sense they'd used to share making him do it. Marco had turned his head and was looking at him. There was something written in his eyes…a stark desperation that clutched like a giant fist at Franco's chest.

Marco broke the contact by turning away again, then Franco heard the low sound of Marco's voice in his ear. *'Sono spiacente, il mio amico.'*

Franco was still fighting to grasp what Marco had said to him as the engines gave a throaty roar and they shot forward. It took all of Franco's concentration to keep them on a straight line.

Too fast, his brain was registering starkly. Marco had just said he was sorry, and he was taking them out much too fast…

CHAPTER ONE

LEXI was in a meeting when the door to Bruce's office suddenly flew open and Suzy, the very new junior assistant, burst in.

'Sorry to interrupt,' she rushed out breathlessly, 'but Lexi has just got to see this—'

Her riot of blonde curls bouncing around a pretty face flushed with excitement, Suzy snatched up the television remote from where it lay next to the coffee machine and aimed it at the television. Everyone else gaped at her, wondering where she'd got the nerve to barge in here like this.

'A friend sent this news link to my Twitter,' she explained, hurriedly flicking through channels. 'I'm seriously not into mega crashes, so I almost stopped watching, but then your face flashed up on the screen, Lexi, and they mentioned your name!'

Crystal blue waters topped by deep azure skies suddenly filled the fifty-inch flat screen. A second later half a dozen long streaks of raw engine power suddenly shot across the water, flying like majestic arrows and kicking up huge plumes of foaming white spray in their wake. Before anyone else had even clicked on what was happening, an icy chill of recognition made Lexi jerk to her feet.

High-speed powerboat racing was for the super-rich and reckless only—the whole sleek, surging, testosterone-packed spectacle was a breathtaking display of excess. Excess money, excess power, excess ego—and an excessive flouting of the risks and the dangers that held most people awestruck. But for Lexi it was like watching her worst nightmare play out in front of her eyes, for she knew what was about to happen next.

'No,' she whispered tautly. 'Please switch it off.'

But no one was listening to her, and, anyway, it was already too late. Even as she spoke the nose of the leading craft hit turbulence and began to lift into the air. For a few broken heartbeats the glistening white craft stood on its end and hovered like a beautiful white swan rising up from sea.

'Keep watching.' Suzy was almost dancing on the spot in anticipation.

Lexi grabbed hold of the edge of the table as the mighty powerboat performed the most shockingly graceful pirouette, then began flipping over and over, as if it was performing some wildly exciting acrobatic trick.

But this was no trick, and two very human bodies were visible inside the boat's open cockpit. Two reckless males, revelling in sleek supercharged power that had now turned into a violent death trap as shards of debris were hurled out in all directions, spinning like lethal weapons through the air.

'This highly dangerous sport suffers at least one fatality each season,' some faceless narrator informed them. 'Due to choppy conditions off the coast of Livorno there had been disputes as to whether this race should begin. The leading boat had reached top speed when it hit turbulence. Francesco Tolle can be seen being thrown clear.'

'Oh, my God, that's a body!' somebody gasped out in horror.

'His co-driver Marco Clemente remained trapped underwater for several minutes before divers were able to release him. Both men have been airlifted to hospital. As yet unconfirmed reports say that one man is dead and the other is in a grave condition.'

'Catch her, someone.' Lexi heard Bruce's sharp command as her legs gave way beneath her.

'Here…' Someone leapt up and took hold of her arm to guide her back down onto her chair.

'Put her head between her knees,' another voice advised, while someone else—Bruce again—ground out curses at Suzy for being such a stupid, insensitive idiot.

Lexi felt her head being thrust downwards but she knew even as she let them manhandle her that it wasn't going to help. So she just sat there, slumped forward, with her hair streaming down in front of her like a rippling river of burnished copper, and listened to the newsreader map out Francesco's twenty-eight years as if he was reading out his obituary.

'Born into one of Italy's wealthiest families, the only son of ship-building giant Salvatore Tolle, Francesco Tolle left his playboy ways behind him after his brief marriage to child star Lexi Hamilton broke down…'

The ripple of murmurs in the room made Lexi shiver, because she knew a photograph of her with Franco must have flashed up on the screen. Young—he would look young, and carelessly happy, because that was how—

'Tolle concentrates his energies on the family business these days, though he continues to race for the White Streak powerboat team—a company he set up five years ago with his co-driver Marco Clemente, from one of Italy's major wine-making families. The two men are lifelong friends, who…'

'Lexi, try and drink some of this.'

Bruce gently pushed her hair back from her face so he could press a glass of water to her lips. She wanted to tell him to leave her alone so she could just listen, but her lips felt too numb to move. Locked in a fight between herself, Bruce and the sickening horror she had just witnessed, suddenly she saw Franco.

Her Franco, dressed in low riding cut-offs and a white T-shirt that moulded to every toned muscle in his long, bronzed frame. He was standing at the controls of a slightly less insane kind of speedboat, his darkly attractive face turned towards her and laughing, because he was scaring the life out of her as he skimmed them across the water at breakneck speed.

'Don't be such a wimp, Lexi. Come over here to me and just feel the power…'

'I'm going to be sick,' Lexi whispered.

Squatting down in front of her, the oh-so-elegant and super-cool Bruce Dayton almost tumbled onto his backside in an effort to get out of the way of the threat. Stumbling to her feet, Lexi stepped around him and moved like a drunk across the room, a trembling hand clamped across her mouth. Someone opened the door for her and she staggered through it, making it into the cloakroom only just in time.

Franco was dead. Her dizzy head kept on chanting it over and over. His beautiful body all battered and broken, his insatiable lust for danger brutally snuffed out.

'No…' she groaned, closing her eyes and slumping back against the cold tiled wall of the toilet cubicle.

'Not I, *bella mia*. I am invincible…'

Almost choking on a startled gasp—because she felt as if Franco had whispered those words directly into her ear— Lexi opened her eyes, their rich blue-green depths turned black with shock. He was not there, of course. She was alone in her white-walled prison of agony.

Invincible.

A strangled laugh broke free from her throat. No one was invincible! Hadn't he already proved that to himself once before?

A tentative knock sounded on the cubicle door. 'You OK, Lexi?'

It was Suzy, sounding anxious. Making an effort to pull herself together, Lexi ran icy cold trembling fingers down the sides of her turquoise skirt. Turquoise like the ocean, she thought hazily. Franco liked her to wear turquoise. He said it did unforgivably sexy things to her eyes…

'Lexi…?' Suzy knocked on the cubicle door again.

'Y-yes,' she managed to push out. 'I'm all right.'

But she wasn't all right. She was never going to be all right again. For the last three and a half years she had fought to keep Franco pushed into the darkest place inside her head, but now a door had opened and he was right here, confronting her when it was too late for her to—

Oh, dear God, what are you thinking? You don't know he's dead! It might be Marco—

It might be Marco.

Was that any better?

Yes, a weak, cruel, wicked voice inside her head whispered, and she hated herself for letting it.

Suzy was waiting for her when Lexi stepped out of the toilet cubicle, her pretty face clouded by discomfort and guilt. 'I'm so sorry, Lexi,' she burst out. 'I just saw your face and—'

'It doesn't matter,' Lexi cut in quickly, because the other girl looked so upset and young.

The same age Lexi had been when she'd first met Franco, she realised. Why was it that, at only twenty-three now, she suddenly felt so old?

'Bruce is threatening to sack me,' Suzy groaned, while Lexi stood at a basin washing her hands without being aware that she was doing it. 'He said he doesn't need a stupid person working here because we have enough of those, what with the wannabe starlets we…'

Lexi stopped listening. She was staring in the mirror at

the small triangle of her face framed by her rippling mane of copper-brown hair.

'It catches fire in the sunset,' Franco had whispered once as he ran his long fingers through its silken length. 'Hair the colour of finely spun toffee, skin like whipped cream, and lips…mmm…lips like delicious crushed strawberries.'

'That's so corny, Francesco Tolle. I thought you had more style that that.'

'I do where it counts, *bella mia*. See—I will show you…'

No crushed strawberries colouring her lips now, Lexi noticed. They looked colourless and faded.

'And you haven't been with him for years, so it never entered my head that you might still care about him.'

Lexi watched her eyelids fold down over her eyes then lift up again. 'He's a human being, Suzy, not an inanimate object.'

'Yes…' The younger girl sounded guilty again. 'Oh, but he's so gorgeous, Lexi.' She sighed dreamily. 'All that dark, brooding sexiness… He could be one of the actors we have on our…'

Lexi tuned the younger girl out again. She knew Suzy had no idea what she was talking about. She didn't mean to hurt, prattling on like that; she was just doing a really bad job of making amends for the huge gaffe she had made, but—

She turned and walked out of the cloakroom, leaving Suzy chatting to an empty space. Her legs felt weak and seriously unwilling to do what she wanted them to do. After she'd shut herself into her own office she just stood there, staring out at nothing. She felt hollow inside from the neck down, except for the tight little fizz of sensation currently clustering around the walls of her heart, which she knew was slowly eating away at her self-control.

'Lexi…'

The door behind her had opened without her hearing it. She turned that unblinking stare on Bruce, lean and sleek, very good-looking in a fair-skinned and sharp-featured kind of way. The grim expression on his face sent a wave of knee-knocking alarm shunting down through her whole frame.

'Wh—What?' she jerked out, knowing that something else truly devastating was about to come at her.

Stepping fully into the room, Bruce closed the door, then came to take hold of her arm. Without saying a word he led her to the nearest chair. As she sank down into it Lexi felt tears start to sting the backs of her eyelids and her mouth wobbled.

'You…you'd better tell me before I have hysterics,' she warned unsteadily.

Leaning back against her desk, Bruce folded his arms. 'There is a telephone call for you. It's Salvatore Tolle.'

Franco's father? Twisting her fingers together on her lap, Lexi closed her eyes again—tight. There was only one reason she could think of that would force Salvatore Tolle to speak to her. Salvatore hated her. He claimed she had ruined his son's life.

'A cunning little starlet willing to prostitute her body to you for the pot of gold.'

She'd overheard Salvatore slicing those cutting words at Franco. She did not know what Franco had said in response because she'd fled in a flood of wild, wretched tears.

'I asked him to hold,' said the indomitable Bruce, who bowed to no one—not even a heavyweight like Salvatore Tolle. 'I thought you could do with a few minutes to…to get your act together before you listened to what he has to say.'

'Thanks,' she mumbled, opening her eyes to stare down at her tensely twined fingers. 'Did…did he tell you wh—why he was calling?'

'He wouldn't open up to me.'

Attempting to moisten the inside of her dry mouth, Lexi nodded, then made an effort to pull herself together yet again.

'OK.' She managed to stand up somehow. 'I had better talk to him then.'

'Do you want me to stay?'

Well, did she? The truth was she didn't have an answer to that question. In her life to date, first as a fifteen-year-old thrust into fame by the starring role she'd taken in a low-budget movie that had surprised everyone by taking the world by storm, Bruce had already played a big part—working alongside her actress mother, Grace, as her agent. Later, when Lexi had gone off the rails and walked away from her shining career to be with her handsome Italian boyfriend, Bruce had not allowed her to lose touch with him. When her mother had died suddenly, Bruce had been ready to offer her his support. But back then she'd still had Franco. Or she'd believed she still had Franco. It had taken months of pain and heartache before she'd finally given in and flown home to Bruce in a storm of heartbreak and tears.

Now she worked for him at his theatrical agency. The two of them worked well together: she understood the minds of his temperamental clients and he had years of rock solid theatrical experience. Somewhere along the way they had become very close.

'I'd better do this on my own.' Lexi made the decision with the knowledge that this was something Bruce could not fix for her.

He remained silent for a moment, his expression revealing not a single thing. Then he gave a nod of his head and straightened up from the desk. Lexi knew she'd hurt his feelings, knew he must feel shut out; but he'd also understand why she had refused his offer to stay. For the phone call involved Franco, and where he was concerned not even Bruce was going to be able to catch her when she fell apart if the news was bad. So she preferred to fall apart on her own.

'Line three,' was all he said, indicating the phone on her desk before he strode back across her office.

Lexi waited until the door shut behind him and then turned to stare down at the phone for a few seconds, before tugging in a breath and reaching out with a trembling hand.

'Buongiorno, signor,' she murmured unsteadily.

Across hundreds of miles of fibre-optic line a pause developed that made her heart pump that bit more heavily and her fingers clench around the telephone receiver so tightly they hurt. Then the emotionally thickened voice of Salvatore Tolle sounded in her ear.

'It is not a good day, Alexia,' he countered heavily. 'Indeed, it is a very bad day. I assume you have heard the news about Francesco?'

Lexi closed her eyes as a wave of dizziness broke over her. 'Yes,' she breathed.

'Then I can keep this conversation brief. I have made arrangements for you to travel to Livorno. A car will collect you from your apartment in an hour. My plane will fly you to Pisa and someone will collect you from there. When you reach the hospital you will need to show proof of who you are before you will be allowed to see my son, so make sure you have the relevant—'

'Francesco is—alive?' she shrilled on a thick intake of air, feeling as if someone had hit her hard in the solar plexus.

Another pause on the line pounded and thumped in Lexi's head for a couple of seconds before she heard a softly uttered curse.

'You believed he was dead. My apologies,' Franco's father offered brusquely. 'In the concern and confusion since the accident it had not occurred to me that reports have been confused about… *Si.*' His voice sank low and thickened again as he gave her the confirmation she was waiting so desperately to hear. 'Francesco is alive. I must warn you, however, that he has sustained some serious injuries. Though how the hell he…'

He stopped again, and Lexi could feel the fight he was having with his emotions. Trapped in a spinning swirl of aching relief and fresh alarm due to those injuries he'd mentioned, she recognised that Franco's father must be suffering from a huge shock himself. Francesco was his only child. His adored, his precious, thoroughly spoiled son and heir.

'I'm—sorry you've been put through this,' she managed to whisper.

'I don't need your sympathy.' His voice hardening, Salvatore fired the words at her like a whip.

If she'd had it in her Lexi would have smiled, for she could understand why this man did not want sympathy from her. Loathing the likes of which Salvatore felt for her did not fade away with the passage of time.

'I simply expect you to do what must be done,' he continued more calmly. 'You are needed here. My son is asking for you, therefore you will come to him.'

Go—to Franco? For the first time since the news had tossed her into a dark pit of shock, Lexi blinked and saw daylight. It was one thing to know that Franco had finally taken one wild risk too many, and even to stand here experiencing the full horror of the result, but—go to him?

'I'm sorry, I can't do that.' It felt as if the words had peeled themselves off the walls of her throat, they were so difficult to utter.

'What do you mean, you cannot?' Salvatore ground out. 'You are his wife. It is your duty to come here!'

His wife. How very odd that sounded, Lexi thought as she twisted around to face the window, her eyes taking on a bleak blue glint. Her duty to Franco as his wife had ended three and a half years ago, when he—

'His estranged wife,' she corrected. 'I'm sorry that Francesco has been injured, *signor*. But I am no longer a part of his life.'

'Where is your charity, woman?' her father-in-law hissed in an icy tone that was more in keeping with the man Lexi remembered. 'He is bleeding and broken! He has just lost his closest friend!'

'M-Marco is…dead?' It was yet another shock that held Lexi frozen as the shattering chill of loss seemed to crystallise her flesh.

She stared blindly at the grey skies beyond her office window and saw the handsome laughing face of Marco Clemente. Her heart squeezed with aching grief and the sheer unfairness of it. Marco had never done a bad thing to anyone. He'd been the easygoing one of the two lifelong friends. Where Franco had always been the high charged extrovert, the reckless daredevil, Marco had tagged along because, he'd once told her, he was lazy. It was easier to go with Franco's flow than waste energy trying to swim against it.

Knowing Franco as she did, he was probably crucifying himself right now for involving Marco in his thirst for danger and speed. He would be blaming himself for Marco's death.

'I'm so very sorry,' she whispered across the fresh ache in her throat.

'Si,' Salvatore Tolle acknowledged. 'It is good to know that you feel sadness for Marco. Now I ask you again—will you come to my son?'

'Yes.' Lexi said it without thought or hesitation this time, for no matter how hurt and bitter she felt about Franco, his losing Marco had just changed everything.

Marco and Franco… One without the other was like day without night.

Lowering the phone back onto its rest, Lexi began to shiver again. She just could not stop herself. Lifting a hand to her eyes, she covered the threat of tears stinging there and wished she knew if she was feeling like this because she was relieved that Franco was alive or because poor Marco was…not.

'He's alive, then?'

Spinning around to find that once again Bruce had entered

the room without her hearing him, Lexi pressed her quivering lips together and nodded her head.

Bruce's slender lips twisted into a grimace. 'I thought the lucky swine would be.'

'There is no luck involved in being flung through the air with a load of lethal debris, Bruce!' Lexi reacted fiercely.

'And the other one—Marco Clemente?'

Wrapping her arms tightly around her body, she gestured a mute negative.

'Poor devil,' he murmured.

At least that comment conveyed no sarcasm, she noticed. She pulled in a deep, fortifying breath of air. 'I am going to have to take some time off.'

Bruce stood regarding her through narrowed eyes and Lexi could tell that he was not impressed by that announcement. 'So the Tolle effect still holds strong with you, then?' he said eventually. 'You're going to go to him.'

'It would be wrong of me not to.'

'Even though you are in the process of divorcing him?'

Flushing in response to that challenging question, Lexi half wished that she had not told Bruce that the papers had gone out to Francesco's lawyers two weeks ago.

'That isn't relevant in this situation,' she defended. 'Marco and Franco were like twin brothers. It's only right and fitting that we put our differences aside at a time of tragedy like this.'

'That's just bull, Lexi,' Bruce denounced. 'I'm the guy you ran to when your lousy marriage blew up in your face,' he reminded her with sardonic bite. 'I saw what he did to you. I mopped up the tears. So if you think I am going to stand by in silence and watch you walk back into that poisonous relationship then you can just think again.'

Raising her chin, she turned back to face him. 'I'm not about to walk into a relationship with Franco.'

'Then what *are* you doing?'

'Visiting a grieving and seriously injured man!'

'For what purpose?'

Opening her lips to let fly with a heated answer, Lexi flailed for a second and closed her lips again.

'You still love him,' Bruce stated contemptuously.

'I don't love him.' Walking around her desk, she found herself making hard work of hunting through drawers for her bag.

'You still lust after him, then.'

'I do not!' She found the bag and pulled it out of the drawer.

'Then why are you going?' Bruce persisted doggedly as he prowled towards her, reminding her of a sleek hunting dog gnawing on a particularly tough bone.

'I'm only taking a couple of days off, for goodness' sake!' Lexi breathed out heavily.

'Did he find time to come to *your* bedside when you were losing his baby?' Bruce thrust the words at her like a fisted punch. 'No. Did he give a damn that you were heartbroken, frightened and alone? No,' he punched again. 'He was too busy rolling around in a bed somewhere with his latest bit of skirt. It took him twenty-four hours to turn up, and by then the well-laid bitch had made sure you knew where he'd been. You owe him nothing, Lexi!'

'None of that means that I have to behave as badly as he did!' Lexi cried out, pale as parchment now, because everything he had just said was so painfully true. 'He's hurt, Bruce, and I liked Marco. Please try to understand that I would not be able to live with myself if I didn't go!'

'At the expense of us?'

The *us* held Lexi trapped as she stared at the sharply attractive man standing in front of her desk, looking the epitome of sartorial elegance in a cool grey suit, and she felt the ache of wretched tears return to her throat. Bruce was thirty-five years old to her twenty-three, and the glossy patina of his maturity and sophistication sometimes threatened to drown her in intimidating waves. The cold anger glinting in his pale blue eyes, the cynical edge to his grimly held mouth…Bruce rarely showed this side of himself to her, and in truth she'd never dreamed he would do this—bring out into the open what the two of them had been carefully skirting around for months. Bruce was her mentor, her saviour, her closest friend, and she loved him so much—in a very special way she reserved just for him.

But not in the way she knew he wanted her to love him, though she so desperately wished that she could.

'No, forget I said that.' He sighed suddenly, throwing out a hand as if he was tossing the explosive challenge aside. 'I'm angry because the—' He stopped to utter a softly bitten curse before he continued, 'Franco has raised his handsome head again just at the point when you were…' A short sigh censored the next words too. 'Go,' he sanctioned in the end, turning away to stride back to the door. 'Perhaps seeing him again after this length of time will make you recognise that you've grown up, while he's still the… I just hope you find closure on your feelings for him and when you get back you will finally be able to get on with the rest of your life without that bastard in it!'

Standing behind her desk, clutching her bag to her front and fighting the urge to run after him and beg him to understand, Lexi knew right then, in that struggling moment, that something else had just been brought to a close: her long relationship with Bruce. Tears burned hot as she took on board what that revelation truly meant. She'd been a fool—unfair, selfish. She'd known how he felt about her but had crushed the knowledge down so she didn't have to face up to it and deal with it. In the last few months she'd even started to convince herself that an intimate relationship between them would be possible—they worked so well together and liked each other so much.

But liking wasn't enough, and she knew it—had probably always known it. She had not been playing fair with Bruce from the moment she'd recognised how his feelings towards her had changed from good friend and mentor to prospective lover.

With her tongue cleaving tautly to the roof of her mouth and her lips pinned tightly together in an effort to stop them from trembling, Lexi dragged on her coat. She didn't have the time right now, but when she got back from Italy she knew that she and Bruce were going to have to have a long talk about where their relationship was heading.

Or not heading, she amended bleakly. If today's shock had done anything, it had made her take a hard look at herself. She was only twenty-three years old, and already she'd fallen in love with a rich, irresponsible playboy, become pregnant with his child, become his wife, learned how to hate him for using her, learned how much he'd resented her for turning him into a husband, lost their baby and lost him.

So why are you walking back into his life?

Lexi was still grappling with that question late that afternoon as she made her way out onto Pisa's busy airport concourse, a long delicately built figure of medium height, wearing skinny stretch blue jeans and a soft grey jacket, with a scarf looped loosely around her throat. Her hair was loose, floating around her strained, pale face; and her tense blue-green eyes were scanning the crowds in front of her for a sign to tell her who would be there to pick her up. Almost immediately she spotted a familiar face.

Pietro, a short, dapper man with a shock of silver hair and smooth olive skin stood waiting for her by the barrier. Pietro was Salvatore's personal chauffeur, and his wife Zeta was housekeeper at the fabulous Castello Monfalcone, the Tolle private estate situated just outside their home town of Livorno. Both Pietro and Zeta had always been coolly polite to Lexi; that had been a small something in a place filled with animosity and resentment.

Striding forward, Pietro greeted her sombrely. 'It is good to see you again, *signora*, though not so good the circumstances.'

'No,' Lexi agreed.

Taking charge of her small bag, he indicated that she follow him. Ten minutes later he was driving her towards Livorno in the kind of luxury car she had once turned her back on without a single pang of regret. Strange, really, she pondered as she stared out at the familiar sights sliding by the car window. She had come to love Livorno itself during her brief stay there, even if she'd hated everything else.

Her escape, she recalled, from tension and disapproval. A nineteen-year-old pregnant married woman—still just a girl, really—made to feel like an interloper and an outcast at the same time. Salvatore hadn't been able to stand looking at her. Francesco had reminded her of a beautiful golden eagle who'd had his fabulous wings clipped and his freedom to fly wherever he wanted to ripped away. He'd snapped at anyone who dared to approach him, picked fights—with his father most of all. He'd resented Salvatore's attitude towards Lexi, to his marriage, to their coming child. He'd hated it that he couldn't defend her because he had never been certain that she hadn't set him up in a baby trap as his father had accused her of doing.

'Why did you bother to marry me?'

Lexi moved with a jolt as her own shrill voice echoed inside her head.

'What else was I supposed to do with you? Leave you and the baby to starve on the streets?'

When true love turns bad, Lexi thought bleakly. She was still able to recall the aching throb of raw hurt she'd carried around with her for long lonely months until…

Oh, bring on the violins, Lexi, she told herself impatiently. So you had this amazing love affair with this amazingly sexy and gorgeous playboy and you got yourself pregnant? So you married the playboy and lived to regret it and lost your baby—which, to most people, was a huge relief? Grieve for your baby, but don't grieve for a marriage that should never have happened in the first place. And *don't*, she warned herself sternly, go all self-pitying again, because it earned you nothing back then and will earn you even less now.

The car slowed down and she focused back on her surroundings as they turned in through the hospital gates. It was a bright white, very modern, very exclusive place, set in the seclusion of its own private grounds.

It was the same hospital she had been rushed to three and a half years ago. As she climbed out of the car and looked at the building a whole rush of old emotions erupted inside. She did not want to walk back in there. She felt herself go cold at the thought. Her baby... her tiny baby...had been stillborn within those walls, those whisper-quiet corridors, that luxury accommodation.

'Signor Salvatore asked me to accompany you, *signora*.' Pietro's arrival at her side made Lexi jump. She blinked, fighting—*fighting*—to push back the memories, the strangling agony of old feelings, of painful emptiness and grief.

'It is this way...'

Somehow she placed one foot in front of the other. A security man guarding the front doors asked to see her passport before he would allow her to step inside. Her lips and her mouth felt paper dry as she rummaged in her bag to find it while Pietro became angrily animated, insisting that the precaution was not necessary when he could vouch for *la signora's* authenticity.

Lexi just wished he would leave the guard to do his job. This was all beginning to be too much for her. Francesco didn't need her. It wasn't as if he was alone in the world. He had a huge network of family and friends who had to be more than willing to gather around him. If she had an ounce of good sense she would turn around and walk right back out of there.

But she didn't turn and walk away. She followed Pietro across the hospital lobby and into a waiting lift that carried them up. Yet another walk down a hushed white corridor and Pietro was opening a door and standing back to allow Lexi to precede him inside. Beginning to feel as if she was floating on a current of icy air now, Lexi filled up her lungs and stepped into the room.

It took a couple of foggy seconds for her to realise that this was an anteroom. Comfortable chairs stood grouped around a low table topped by a small stack of thick glossy magazines. The aroma of fresh coffee permeated the air. A pretty nurse with her ebony hair neatly contained beneath a white cap sat at a desk behind a computer monitor.

She looked up at Lexi and smiled, 'Ah, *buona sera*, Signora Tolle.' She surprised Lexi by recognising her on sight. 'Your husband is sleeping but you must go in and sit with him,' she invited. 'He will be more comfortable once he knows you are here.'

Lexi walked across the room towards the door the nurse had indicated. Her heart was thumping, beating like a drum in her ears. She pushed open the door, stepped through it, then swiftly closed it behind her so she could lean back against it, light-headed with fear of what she was about to see.

The room was bigger than the one she'd stayed in. A large white cube of space, shrouded by soft striped shadows cast by the slatted blinds angled against the golden light of the afternoon sun. And she could feel every pore absorbing the hush of perfect stillness as she stood glued to the spot by the sight of the drips and tubes leading to a monitor alive with graphs and numbers that silently flickered and pulsed.

'You can come closer, Lexi. I won't bite.'

CHAPTER TWO

THE sound of that dry, slightly hoarse voice ran through Lexi in shivering stings of sharp recognition and she dropped her gaze to the bed, unaware that she'd been avoiding it in fear of what she was going to see.

She discovered that she could not see anything other than a swathe of starched white linen. She saw no pillows, and a cage had been erected over his legs. Her wildly skipping heart suddenly felt all curled up in her chest, cowering, as if something was threatening it. For when someone was forced to lie flat it usually meant a back injury. A cage usually meant broken legs. And whatever those tubes were feeding into him made her squirm, because she hadn't bothered to ask anyone what his injuries were. Not the nurse, not Pietro… Perhaps she should go back out there and—

'Lexi…' Franco murmured impatiently when she took too long to answer him. 'If you are thinking of making a quick exit—don't.'

'H-how did you know it was me?' she asked.

'You still wear the same perfume.'

She was surprised he remembered, bearing in mind the trail of different perfumes that had passed through his life since her. Dozens of women listed in celebrity magazines. All smooth, sleek, sophisticated, with—

'Since I cannot move, have some pity on me, *cara*. Come over here where I can see you, *per favore*.'

Curling taut fingers around the shoulder strap of her bag, Lexi peeled herself free of the door and walked forward on limbs that shook. Pulling to a halt at the foot of the bed, she felt her hectic breathing dry up altogether when she got her first glimpse of Franco's powerful length, laid out flat on the bed like a corpse. A white linen sheet covered three-quarters of him—his upper torso left uncovered to reveal the muscled solidity of his wide shoulders and arms like a splash of polished bronze against the starched white. White bandaging formed heavy strapping around his left shoulder and bound his ribs, and she gulped as a wave of distress broke through her when she caught sight of the dark, inky bruising spreading out from beneath the edges of the strapping.

'*Ciao,*' he murmured, in a husky low tone that sounded scraped.

Lexi gave a helpless shake of her head as her eyes began to sting with hot aching tears. 'Just look at the state of you,' she whispered.

Franco did not care that he was really pleased to see the evidence of those tears appear like deep pools in her beautiful eyes. He *wanted* Lexi to be upset. He even wanted her to pity him—was in fact ready and willing to push her sympathy buttons for all they were worth.

Dio mio, she looked good, he thought as he lay there waiting for her to look directly into his face. Her hair floated around her slender shoulders like a burnished halo, framing the exquisite triangle of her face with its wide spaced eyes and cute little nose and pointed chin. He did not care that she was pressing her soft lips together in a failed attempt to stop them from trembling, or that the grey patterned scarf she wore looped around her neck was as unflatteringly drab as the grey jacket she was wearing, which hid away from him all that he knew was softly curvy and gracefully sleek. For him she was still his first glimmer of sunlight in the darkest days of his life.

'Look at me,' he urged, feeling her fierce tension throb between them like an extra heartbeat. He could feel the fight she was waging with herself over allowing her eyes to make contact with his, and he understood why it was a fight. Once upon a time they hadn't been able to look at each other without wanting to devour each other. When they'd stopped looking their whole fated relationship had gone into an acute downward slide.

'Please, *cara*,' he husked, then watched as her eyelashes fluttered, the long dusky crescents rising upwards to reveal the depth of the ocean swirled by a hundred different emotions; that caused a clutch of agony so deep inside him the machine behind him started bleeping like mad.

Lexi shot a startled look at it, her breath lurching free from her strangled throat. Things were happening. She hadn't a clue what a normal pulse or blood pressure should read, but the flickering numbers on that machine were rising fast, and it scared her enough to send her shooting round the edge of the bed.

'What's wrong?' She reached for his hand where it lay on the bed, only to stare down in horror when she found herself clutching hold of a plastic shunt with tubes coming out of it. But before she could snatch her hand away Franco turned his hand over and imprisoned hers inside his warm, surprisingly strong grip.

'I'm OK,' he said, without enough strength to convey confidence.

The door suddenly flew open and the nurse swept in. With a brief vague smile at Lexi, she went around to the other side of the bed and began checking things.

'I think your wife must have surprised you.'

Lexi translated the nurse's smiling tease from Italian to English.

'She did *something* to me anyway,' Franco returned ruefully.

Catching onto his meaning, Lexi tried to reclaim her fingers but Franco just tightened his grip, and after a second or so compassion took over and she let her fingers relax in his. The moment she did so he closed his eyes and inched out a very controlled sigh. Almost immediately the number readings began to ease downwards. Flanking each side of the bed, the nurse and Lexi watched the monitor—the nurse with her fingers lightly circling his wrist, Lexi with her fingers still enclosed by his.

By the time everything seemed to have gone back to normal Lexi felt so weak she reached out with her free hand for the chair positioned to her right, drew it closer to the bed and sat down.

Franco didn't move or open his eyes, and as the room slowly settled back into quiet stillness, Lexi let herself look at his face again. She was instantly drenched by the old fierce magnetism that had always been her downfall where Franco was concerned.

He was, quite simply, breathtakingly handsome. There wasn't even a cut or a bruise to distort the sheer quality of masculine perfection stamped into that face. Working at a theatrical agency had, she'd thought, made her immune to so much male beauty, because she dealt with handsome men on a day-to-day basis. But everything about this man set her own blood pressure rising, she acknowledged helplessly—soaking up every small detail while he lay there, unaware of her scrutiny. The smooth, high and intelligent brow below ebony hair cropped short to tame its desire to curl. The subtle arch of his eyebrows above heavy eyelids tipped with eyelashes so long they rested against the slanting planes of his cheekbones. Half of his blood was pure Roman on his mother's side, and the line of his long, only slightly hooked nose, gave credence to that; while the wide, sensual contours of his well shaped mouth belonged to his proud Ligurian father.

Though right now that mouth was pressed shut and the corners turned down a little due to the pain he must be suffering, the agony of overwhelming grief.

'I'm so very sorry about Marco,' she murmured painfully.

Instantly the machine started beeping again. The nurse sent Lexi a sharp frowning glance, then added a faint shake of her head to convey the message that Franco was not ready to talk about Marco.

Her own lips pinching together in an effort to control a painful surge of understanding, Lexi looked back at Franco. A stark greyish tint had settled like a veil across his face, and she knew he was looking that way because he was blaming himself for Marco's death. Where Franco led Marco always followed. Anyone who knew the two friends knew that. But the slavelike loyalty Marco had bestowed on Franco had been both flattering and a burden—as Lexi knew only too well, since she had enslaved herself to him in the same way. And look at the burden *she* had become.

Was that the reason she had come here? Because she knew her slavish love and total dependency on him had become a terrible burden and she now felt guilty about that?

Right there, Lexi fell back in to that long summer four years ago when, at nineteen years old, she had finally done something all by herself after years of being sheltered by her over protective mother, Grace—beautiful Grace Hamilton, who'd sacrificed her own acting career to manage her daughter's surprise rise to fame.

But the year Lexi was nineteen Grace had fallen in love for the first time in her life and married Philippe Reynard, a French entrepreneur with all the outward trappings of celebrity and wealth so yearned for by Grace. He'd owned a fancy apartment in Paris and a rambling château in Bordeaux; and a yacht on which he'd spent most of his summers. He'd made

Grace feel like a princess, and encouraged her to loosen the chains on her daughter so that the two of them could enjoy an extended honeymoon sailing around the Greek Islands on his yacht.

Lexi had been allowed to travel to the Cannes Film Festival without her mother playing strict chaperone.

Excited about striking out on her own for the first time in her life, she had let the freedom go straight to her head and she had become sucked into the glamorous high life. She had proceeded to live it with the destructive blindness of a junkie—until it had been over her ability to think straight about anything…especially what she was doing to herself.

From Cannes to Nice, Cap Ferrat, Monte Carlo, San Remo—

San Remo…

Lexi closed her eyes and saw the same radiant blue skies and glistening waters she'd seen on the television screen. She saw the rows of fancy yachts berthed in exclusive marinas, the stylish boulevards lined with fashionable designer shops, and the pavement café bars frequented by the spoiled offspring of outrageous wealth. Places for the golden people to hang out, with their golden skins and golden smiles and glittering golden futures already mapped out for them. She could hear the golden ring of their laughter—feel the wildly seductive tug of their totally unflappable self-belief. When they'd allowed her entry into their select assembly she'd truly believed that she was one of them—the current golden girl of movie fame.

And of course there'd been Franco, the most golden of them all. The one possessed of all the male beauty his richly aristocratic Italian heritage could bestow. Older than her, so much more experienced than her, the leader of the pack of those super-exclusives. And she'd caught him. She, little Miss Totally-Naïve-and-Sheltered, had won the jewel in the crown without bothering to question how she had done it. Not once had it occurred to her that her new friends had found her naivety hilarious—a novelty worthy of turning into a highly entertaining game.

Lexi shivered as the cold, cold truth of her complete humiliation simultaneously creeped up her and chilled her to the bone.

Six months after it had all started it was over—the wreck of her life floundering amongst the wreckage of so much more destruction. Her mother and her new stepfather killed in a freak car accident. The shattering discovery that Philippe Reynard had lived his whole life in hock and, during his short marriage to her mother, had neatly and cleanly stripped Grace of all the money Lexi had earned until there was none of it left.

He'd called it 'investing in Lexi's future.' What a sick joke.

And even all that was not what had dropped her into the lowest, darkest place to which she had ever sunk. No. Her pale face was pinched as she stared at the man who had taken over her life. Lexi recalled the other damning piece of information that had really shattered her. She'd finally learned about the bet her new friends had placed to see which male ego would relieve her of her so obvious innocence before the end of that golden summer. She'd learned about the way all those people she'd stupidly called friends had watched and wagered and eventually laughed their exclusive heads off when Franco had won the prize. If she lived to be a hundred she would never be able to blank out the video someone had sent to her phone of Franco collecting his winnings. She still saw the date, the time and his lazily complacent smile. The only thing missing had been photographic evidence that he had actually bedded her. But that did not mean such evidence had not been around. Once the veils had been ripped from her eyes about Franco, she'd been able to believe him capable of anything. She'd been nothing but a big joke to him, and when the joke had backfired he had not known how the hell to cope.

In the way fate had of balancing things out, Francesco Tolle, golden boy of Europe's glittering society, had found himself punished for his callous treatment of her when she'd found herself orphaned, pregnant and broke.

Lexi blinked back to the present as a door closed, and she realised the nurse had left them alone. Looking back at the monitor, she saw that everything had settled back down again while she'd been taking a walk down memory lane.

Franco still did not open his eyes, and Lexi began to wonder if he'd fallen asleep. She looked down at their hands still clasped together, his long strong fingers totally engulfing hers in the same way they'd used to do—only without the worrying shunt piercing the back of his hand, feeding liquids and drugs into his veins.

Hands that knew her more intimately than any other pair of hands, she thought, shifting on the chair when the thought became a physical memory that skittered across the surface of her skin. Lexi frowned, annoyed with herself for being so susceptible to a mere memory. It wasn't as though he had the smooth caressing hands of an office dweller. His were firm, slightly callused capable hands, because Franco was at his happiest when he was hauling sail ropes on his yacht, *Miranda*, which he'd lived on that summer—or covered in grease and grime taking a boat engine to bits before he painstakingly put it back together again. Franco was a mariner through to his soul. Sailboats, powerboats, natty fast speedboats—even the giant supertankers and cruise liners the Tolle shipyard constructed near Livorno. As a qualified marine engineer Franco was in his element, no matter what size the craft. That he could also be successful at the business end of the Tolle empire was an extra string to his talented bow.

Then there was his well documented success with women. And why not? Lexi thought, unable to stop drifting her eyes over his powerful form, most of which was now hidden beneath the sheet. Leonardo da Vinci would have loved to

meet Franco, she decided, for he *was* his 'Vitruvian Man.'
Everything about him was in perfect proportion—even the
strength reflected in his squared chin. He badly needed a
shave, she noticed, feeling her fingers start to tingle with an
urge to run them over the rough shadow that gave him the
look of a reckless buccaneer. That he was—reckless, anyway; or he would not enjoy racing a supercharged powerboat
at such dangerous speeds.

It was no wonder she'd fallen for him like an adolescent,
dazzled by his larger than life personality. Physically he was
every woman's secret fantasy man, complete with that other
vital ingredient—a powerfully magnetic sexual virility. It radiated from him even as he lay there, bruised and weakened.

Lexi tugged in a small breath, overcome by the desire to
stroke her fingers over the rest of him, let her senses reconnect with all that glorious male beauty laid out in front of her
like a sacrifice. As a lover he'd been wildly exciting—the
kind of lover who loved to be stroked and petted as much as
he loved to do both. As a companion he'd possessed enough
lazy charm and captivating charisma to blind her to all his
faults.

He was kind to old ladies and animals. He could laugh
without constraint at the absurd, and—all the more potent—
he could laugh at himself. He had a brilliant technical brain
that had allowed him to design and build his first sailing
yacht at the age of thirteen. He was super-confident and totally fearless when it came to any sport that took place on
water. And he could lie in the sun for hours without moving.
Relaxing for Franco was as important as competing in some
crazy sport or his other favoured pastime: sex. Long after-
noons and nights of deeply sensual, stunningly uninhibited
loving was the sweet honey that gave him his boundless energy.

And he could be cruel enough and ruthless enough to
take on a bet to seduce the naive interloper in his circle of

elite friends because he liked to be challenged and he liked to win—to hell with the cost to the targeted victim.

Something else swept through Lexi. It was the rumbling of a hurt she had buried so deep it still had not worked its way back to the surface—though she was letting herself remember all the things she had shut away with that hurt. Things like the hard clench of dismay on his face when she'd broken the news to him that she was pregnant. The change in his eyes, as if someone had splashed the warm brown iris with a glaze of ice. Then there was the quiet sombre way he'd taken responsibility for his mistake and ultimately taken responsibility for her.

Where had her pride been when she'd let him do that? Smothered, by blind love and the desperate fear of losing him. Lexi was ashamed of that. But she felt more ashamed knowing that, for all the unforgivable things Franco had done to her all those years ago, she'd more or less walked into marriage with him to punish him for that ugly, humiliating bet.

And maybe that was the reason why she had come here—because she'd always known deep down that she had behaved no better than Franco had.

Looking up, she collided full on with a pair of stunning dark eyes the multicolours of tiger's-eye quartz. Yet another heated flush flared through her body, leaving her feeling stripped bare and exposed. Because she knew him. She knew by his carefully impassive expression that he'd been lying there so still because he had been reading her every thought as it had passed across her face.

Pulling her hand free of his grasp, she sat back in her chair, tense now and skittish. 'I don't know why I've come here,' she confessed in a helpless rush, laying something else bare for him: the battles she'd been having with herself.

Franco wished he did not feel so damn weak. There were tears in her eyes again, though she was trying her best to fight them. And her hair was catching the sunlight streaming in through the slatted blinds, setting it on fire with a thousand different shades of gold and red.

'I had this h-horrible premonition you were going to die, and if I didn't come I would always regret being so m-mean to you.'

'Would it help you to feel better if I complied with your premonition, *cara*?' he offered flatly. 'It would make you a rich widow, at all events.'

'Don't talk like that.' Lexi speared him with a pained look. 'I never wished you dead and I don't want your money.'

'I know you don't—which makes this situation all the more ironic.'

Ironic? 'Where is the irony in you lying here all battered and broken?'

'I am not in as bad a condition as I look.' The quiet assurance sent her restless gaze tracking over him once again.

'Explain your definition of a not bad condition.' She waved a trembling hand to encompass all the evidence in front of her, including the computerised machine monitoring him as well as feeding all sorts of drugs into him via the shunt in the back of his hand. 'You're lying fl—flat on your back and you've got a cage over your legs.'

'I am lying flat as a mere precaution, because I wrenched a couple of vertebra and the only thing wrong with my legs is a gash to my left thigh, which had to be stitched up.'

Her restless eyes moved to his bound chest. 'And all that strapping?'

'A couple of cracked ribs and a dislocated shoulder they had a fight manipulating back into place.'

She went pale as her tummy churned squeamishly at the image he'd just placed in her head. 'Anything else?' she squeezed out.

'A sore head?' he offered up.

A sore head... No broken bones, then. No crushing brain damage. No life-threatening injury to justify his father's insistence that she come here... Lexi lurched out from the strains of anxiety to embrace the sting of annoyance in the single release of her breath. 'You're supposed to be seriously ill,' she said accusingly.

'You don't see these injuries as serious?'

'No.' The summer she'd met Franco he had been cruising the Mediterranean while convalescing after breaking a leg so badly he'd required several surgeries and countless metal pins to get the leg to mend. 'Your father gave me the impression that you—'

'Wanted to see you?'

'Bleeding and broken and asking for me!' She quoted Salvatore. 'That implied you were in a coma or s-something.'

'People in comas don't speak—'

'Oh, shut up.' Jumping to her feet, Lexi paced restlessly away from the bed—only to swing right back again. 'Why did you want to see me?'

The heavy veil of his eyelids lowered to screen his thoughts. 'Lose the bag and take the jacket and scarf off before you roast.'

'I'm not stopping,' Lexi countered edgily.

'You're stopping,' he contended, 'because you took one look at me and now you can't help yourself staying around to keep on looking.'

She dragged in a strangled breath. 'Of all the conceited—' Fiercely she breathed out again.

'*Dio mio,*' he ground out. 'Even as I am lying here injured and in pain, and pretty damn helpless, you could not resist mentally stripping me of the covers so you could reacquaint yourself with what I look like.'

'That's not true!' Lexi denied hotly.

He just smiled the smile of a cat who'd cornered the mouse. 'I might be physically flattened, but all my other faculties are in good working order. I know when I'm being lusted after.

You look sensational too, *bella mia*,' he diverted smoothly. 'Even trussed up in all those clothes you've got on.'

'It's cold in England.' Why she'd said that Lexi didn't have a single clue.

'Glad I didn't make it there, then,' Franco responded. 'September should be a glorious month. English weather has lost its good taste…'

He closed his eyelids all the way now, as if he didn't have the strength to hold them up any longer. Lexi chewed on her bottom lip for a few seconds, wondering what she should do next.

'You're tired,' she murmured. 'You should rest…'

'I am resting.'

'Yes, but…' She slid a restless glance over him again. 'I should leave you to do it in peace.'

Irritation tightened his facial muscles. 'You have only just arrived here.'

'I know…' She was uncomfortably aware that she had moved back to the side of the bed. 'But you know you don't really need me here, Franco. It's just—'

'I was going to come to London to see you after the race, then—this happened.' The impatient flick of his unencumbered hand adequately relayed what *this* was. 'There are things we need to talk about.'

None that Lexi could bring to mind, except— A sound of thickened horror broke free from her throat. 'Are you saying it was because I sent you divorce papers that you crashed your boat?'

'No, I am not saying that,' he snapped, then let out a groan, as if even getting angry hurt him.

Lexi's eyes went straight to the monitor. 'You OK?'

'Si,' he muttered, but she could see that his breathing had gone shallow, his beautifully shaped mouth drooping with tension. 'Damn ribs kill me every time I breathe.'

'And you look ready to pass out,' Lexi said anxiously, watching the grey pallor wash across his face again.

'It's the drugs. I will be free of them by tomorrow, then I can get out of here.'

About to remark on that overconfident statement, she held back because she could tell he was only voicing wishful thoughts.

A silence fell between them. After shifting from one foot to the other a couple of times, Lexi gave in to what she really wanted to do, but didn't really want to do, sit down again. It was exhausting to be locked in this constant battle with herself, she admitted as she sat watching his breathing become less shallow and the tension in his face relax.

She just wished he didn't look so achingly vulnerable, because that didn't help her at all. Nor did it help when an old memory slunk into her head, showing her a moment—a short space in time in their hostile marriage—when Franco had sat beside her bed all night long. They'd had a horrid row, she recalled. Just another one of many rows—but this one had ended with her spinning away to walk out of the room, only to end up dropping at his feet in a faint. She must have been out for ages, because when she'd eventually come round she'd been in her bed and a doctor was leaning over her, gravely viewing the blood pressure band he had strapped around her arm.

Glancing up at the flashy screen that was monitoring Franco's vital statistics, she grimaced. His must be scoring an OK blood pressure because the thing wasn't beeping, whereas the old fashioned version she'd felt squeezing her arm had given her no clue at all that her pressure was a cause for concern.

She looked back at Franco. His hair had gone curly, she noticed for the first time. If he knew he would be mad. Franco went to great expense to make sure his hair didn't show its natural tendency to curl. His hair had been curly the night she'd fainted. He'd stood like some brooding dark statue at the end of her bed but it was only now, looking back, that she remembered the ruffled curly hair and the same grey cast to his face that had been swimming over it today.

'Your wife needs rest and no stress, Signor Tolle,' the doctor had informed him. 'I will come back in the morning.' He'd then spoken to Lexi herself. 'If your blood pressure has not fallen by then you will be going into hospital.' It had been both a warning and a threat.

'I'm sorry.'

Lexi blinked, because that gruff apology had sounded in her head as if Franco had only just said it.

'Go away and leave me alone,' she'd told him, and turned her back to him.

He hadn't gone away. They say that misery loves company, and it had certainly been true for the two of them that long and miserable night, when he'd pulled up an armchair and sat in it, a grimly silent figure in the darkness, watching over her.

Sliding back into the present, Lexi was surprised to discover that the room had slowly darkened while she'd been sitting there, lost in her memories. Franco still had not moved so much as a glossy black eyelash as far as she could tell.

What was it they had been arguing about? She couldn't remember, though it was likely she'd been the one who started it—she usually had. When love turned to hate it was a cold, bitter kind of hatred, she'd discovered. The target for your hatred could not do or say anything right.

Good time to make your silent exit, Lexi, she told herself—not wanting to feel like the person she had turned into back then. Stooping down to pick up her bag from where she'd placed it on the floor, she rose to her feet and turned towards the door.

'Where are you going?' Franco murmured.

Surprise stung down her spinal cord. 'I thought I'd go now and let you sleep.'

'If I promise to fall into a deep coma will you stay?'

Lexi swung back round. 'That wasn't even remotely funny, Francesco!'

Through the gloom she saw his mouth stretch into a mocking kind of grimace, 'You sound like a really snappy wife.'

'And that was even less funny, considering my track record in that particular role.' She sighed heavily.

'And I was the selfish husband from hell.'

Yes, well, she had no argument with either assessment. Neither of them had been any good at being married. Great at being lovers—warm and carefree, fabulously imaginative and gloriously passionate lovers—but as for the rest...

'Listen... ' She heaved a deep, fortifying breath. 'I hope you get better soon. And I am truly sorry about—about Marco.' She had to say it, even though the nurse had indicated that Franco wasn't ready to talk about his best friend. 'But you must know as well as I do that I don't belong here.'

'I want you here,' he stated grimly.

Lexi shook her head. 'You're going to be OK. In a couple of days you'll be wondering why you wanted me to come here at all.'

'I know exactly why I want you here.'

Ignoring that, 'I'm going back to London,' she said.

'Go through that door and I will pull out these tubes and come right after you, Lexi,' Franco warned her flatly.

She uttered yet another sigh. 'Why would you want to do something as stupid as that?'

'I told you.' The line of his mouth was severely compressed now, 'We need to talk.'

'We can talk through our lawyers.' Lexi continued determinedly towards the door.

'You will have this particular talk to my face, *cara*, because I don't want a divorce.'

She swung round yet again. 'Until today we haven't so much as spoken a word or set eyes on each other for three and a half years!' Lexi reminded him. 'Of course you want a divorce. I want a divorce.'

That said, she turned and reached for the door handle, heard a sound from behind her that sent a cold chill racing down her spine, and spun right back to discover that Franco was sitting up and attempting to pluck out the shunt from his hand. But his coordination was obviously wrecked by the drugs.

'What do you think you are you doing?' Shrieking alarm sent Lexi darting back to the bed to cover his hand and the shunt with her both of her own hands in an effort to stop him, but he just changed tack and threw back the covering sheet instead. Even as she tried to grab it the cage went flying onto the floor. The next shock wave hit her when she saw for the first time what the cage and sheet had been covering up. More bandaging strapped one powerfully structured thigh, but it wasn't that that shocked. Even in the gloom she could see the sickening extent of his bruising, which spread right the way down his left side.

'Oh, my God,' she choked, fighting to wrest the sheet from him at the same time as she tried to block him from getting up off the bed. The beeps and alarms started sounding like crazy. Reacting as if programmed to do it without thinking, Lexi reached out and took Franco's face between her palms, made him look at her.

'Please stop it,' she begged, then, because he looked so totally hurt and stubborn, she bent her head and crushed her trembling lips against his.

She kissed him without understanding why she kissed him. And she continued to kiss him even after Franco stopped fighting and went perfectly, perfectly still. It was like her own moment of madness: she didn't even stop when bright lights were suddenly blazing and the nurse was letting out a sharp gasp of shock. The alarms played a riotous symphony in harmony with the stirring mud of long subdued pleasures that split open huge fissures across her aching heart.

When she did eventually pull away she was breathing fast. She felt his fast breath feather her face and looked into eyes turned to stunning black-onyx. Tears gathered—hot tears, pained tears—and she was trembling.

'I'll stay,' she shook out thickly and brokenly. 'I will do anything so long as you lie down again. Please, Franco. Please, I will stay...'

CHAPTER THREE

LEXI sat in one of the chairs in the anteroom beside Franco's room and clutched the hot cup of coffee the nurse had just pressed on her, while a white coated man who had introduced himself as Dr Cavelli sat beside her, waiting for her violent shivers to stop.

She was in shock. She still couldn't take on board what she had done. Her lips burned and felt swollen. Tears smarted her eyes; she was still feeling the buzzing effects of the fear and panic she'd felt when she'd seen Franco trying to get up off the bed. If she had not witnessed it for herself she would never have believed that he could behave in such an irrational way. For a man basically made up of one big bruise, he'd displayed shockingly phenomenal brute strength.

'You have to understand, Signora Tolle—' Dr Cavelli spoke gently '—your husband does not require twenty-four hour nursing surveillance because his physical injuries require such intensive monitoring. It is his mental state which concerns us the most.'

Lifting her head up, Lexi repeated, 'His mental state?' with a strangled breath of disbelief.

'Overall, your husband is exceptionally strong and healthy—as he has just demonstrated.' The glimmer of a rueful smile touched Dr Cavelli's lips. 'His physical injuries are many, but already they are beginning to heal. However, he has recently lost his closest friend in violent circumstances, and his feelings of shock and grief are great.'

'Franco and Marco were like twin brothers.' Lexi nodded in bleak understanding. 'Of course he's feeling Marco's loss very deeply.'

'It is the way he is dealing with that loss that concerns us. As I believe you have already witnessed, if Signor Clemente's name is mentioned your husband either ignores the subject or becomes—agitated.'

'Of course he becomes agitated.' Lexi fired up in Franco's defence. 'How would you prefer him to react? Fall into a fit of weeping? He's a man. He's in shock and he's injured. He must be suffering terrible feelings of guilt because he survived when Marco did not, and—'

'*Signora*, that is the point I am trying to make,' Dr Cavelli intruded. 'Men and women react to extreme stress differently. A woman generally vents her distress in some way.'

Recalling the way she'd just kissed Franco, Lexi dipped her eyes from the watchful doctor's as a heated blush surged through her face.

'A typical male's response, however, is to protect himself by detaching himself from the tragedy. He blocks it out.'

'He just needs time to—recover a little.' Lexi leapt once again to Franco's defence. 'The accident only happened this morning, but already you're telling me he's on some kind of suicide watch!'

Franco suicidal? Were they all mad?

'I don't think I used quite such dramatic language,' the doctor protested distractedly.

Glowering at him—because what he'd said had been very dramatic to *her* way of thinking—Lexi was disconcerted to find that he was studying her from beneath a seriously puzzled frown, and there was an extra throb in the tension surrounding them that made her glance at the nurse, who was back at her station. She saw that she was staring oddly at her too.

'What?' she demanded sharply. 'What have I said to make you look at me like that?' Prickling with alarm all over again, Lexi set down the coffee before she spilled it. 'He hasn't attempted to—?'

Dr Cavelli gave a quick shake of his head to dispense with that fear. '*Signora*...the accident took place three days ago.'

Lexi blinked. What was he talking about? 'But I saw it on the news today,' she insisted, 'It said...' But she couldn't remember if it had given an actual time or a date. 'And Franco's father only called me this morning—'

'Your husband has been drifting in and out of consciousness for two days and only regained full consciousness this morning.'

Lexi continued to stare at him, feeling a bit like an owl perched on a branch that she was in danger of tumbling off. Twitter. She'd heard Suzy talking about Twitter. Her inner vision glanced back at the fifty-inch flat screen and recalled for the first time that they must have been watching one of those news review channels—the kind that loved reporting gory crashes and...

Laying her fingers across her mouth, she started to shake again. Franco had been lying there injured for three days and she'd known nothing about it. She—

'His agitation erupted almost as soon as he woke up,' the doctor continued. 'He refused to let us speak of Signor Clemente once his father had broken the news of his friend's death. He had his room cleared of the flowers and cards he had received from family and friends. He banned those same people from entering this hospital to visit him.'

For the first time since she'd arrived there Lexi glanced around the quiet anteroom and took in the distinct lack of friends and family she should have expected to see crowded in there.

'Wh—Where is Franco's father?' she whispered.

'Signor Salvatore Tolle is on your husband's banned list, Signora,' the doctor informed her.

Eyes rounding like saucers, Lexi gasped. 'Are you kidding me?'

Dr Cavelli shook his head. 'Your husband is very angry with the world right now. It is not unusual for such tragic circumstances to make people angry,' he assured her. 'However, when he demanded to see you and his father explained that you had not been contacted he—reacted badly. He attempted to get out of his bed, insisting he was going to London to see you. The depth of his agitation concerned us enough to suggest to his father that he contact you and bring you here as quickly as he could. Once your husband knew you were on your way here he calmed down a little.'

But when she'd tried to leave again he'd pulled the same mad stunt!

'What we believe has happened is, to help him to block out his natural grief and guilt with regard to Signor Clemente's death, he has transferred his full focus to you and the—forgive me—the state of your marriage.'

The divorce papers. Lexi closed her eyes tightly as her heart sank and the clamouring sickness she felt began to churn up her stomach. Franco had crashed his boat because he'd been thinking of those papers instead of concentrating on—

No. Pushing trembling, tense fingers through her hair, Lexi gave a fierce shake of her head, refusing to believe that the arrival of divorce papers had had the power to tip Franco over the edge.

'Our marriage has been over for three and a half years,' she mumbled, more to herself than to anyone else. She just couldn't bring herself to consider that he would react so badly to something he must have been expecting—or even been thinking of putting into motion himself!

What Franco had seemingly done was to transfer his focus onto the divorce papers *after* the accident, Lexi decided. Though she couldn't work out why he should want to use that particular thing to focus on.

'I'll go and talk to him,' she said, getting to her feet. 'He can't possibly have meant to ban his own father from his bedside. I'll go and find out why he's behaving like this and—'

'He is sleeping, *signora*,' the doctor reminded her as she turned towards Franco's door. 'Perhaps it would be wiser for you to sleep on what we have discussed before you talk to him again.'

It had not been a suggestion but a carefully worded command, and it spun Lexi about. Her eyes flashed out vivid blue warnings—she knew because she could feel them doing it. 'He isn't at death's door,' she stated bluntly. 'Neither is he a child to be cosseted and protected from the truth. And the truth is it's just not fair of him to take his feelings out on his father.'

'Perhaps by tomorrow you will have calmed down a little and thought better of...challenging him right now.'

'What kind of doctor are you?' she demanded, suddenly suspicious.

'The kind that deals with a patient's mental health,' he provided, with a small, tellingly dry smile. 'Your husband's injuries are many, *signora*. In no way would I like to think I had given you the impression that we undervalue his physical trauma, because we do not. His heart stopped beating twice at the scene of the accident. The trauma team had to fight to bring him back. His concussion was and still is very concerning—he has clouded vision and continued dizziness...'

Lexi blinked as she recalled the way Franco's hand had kept on missing its target when it tried to pull out the shunt.

'The wound in his thigh was deep and required several hours of careful surgery to reconnect vital nerves and muscles.' As Lexi went pale, Dr Cavelli spread out his hands in an expression of apology for being so graphic. 'Extensive internal bleeding required us to insert a drain in his chest cavity—I should imagine you saw the resulting spread of bruising,' he gauged. 'The loss of blood was significant enough to require several urgent transfusions, and we feared for a time—unnecessarily, we now know—that he had damaged his spinal cord as well. I tell you all of this because I believe facing him with questions about the way he is dealing with his current situation might goad him into doing something more drastic than attempting to get out of bed—like walking out of here altogether.'

'Does he have the strength to do that?' Lexi questioned dubiously.

'He has the determination and will power to give him the strength,' the doctor assessed, and, thinking about it, Lexi conceded that he was probably right. 'Your husband has made you the linchpin which is holding him together right now. Therefore I must beg you most seriously to consider the responsibility this places on you to help him through this very difficult time...'

'You lied to me about the extent of your injuries,' Lexi said the moment Franco opened his eyes.

It was very late, and she'd ignored the doctor's advice and come back here to sit with Franco while he slept.

'And you can't banish your father from your bedside unless you want to break his heart,' she tagged on. 'Why would Salvatore think of calling me and bringing me over here? It isn't as if you and I are friends, is it?'

The moment she saw the grey cast settle over his face Lexi recognised her mistake. Mentioning friends had reminded him of Marco, and, as the doctor had described, Franco had blocked her words out.

She heaved out a tense little breath. 'OK.' She tried a different tack. 'You can't keep trying to get out of this bed either. Not until they say that you can.'

'Are you staying?'

Remembering that kiss, and her subsequent promise, Lexi shifted tensely. 'I told you I was staying.'

'Tell me again so I can be sure, and this time make it a promise.'

'Franco,' she sighed out wearily, 'this is all so...'

At was as if something or someone had switched her off. Franco watched her frown and catch her bottom lip with her teeth. He took in the loss of colour in her cheeks and the signs of strain and exhaustion bruising the circles around her eyes. The slight quiver in the lip she was biting told him she was upset, and the way she had to think before she spoke told him she had been gagged by the doctor from saying what she really wanted to say to him.

Lexi was stubborn. She was not the emotional pushover everyone liked to think she was. She had a hot, impulsive temper and right now he could tell she was having a fight to keep that temper in check, because he had, in effect, chained her to this bed with him.

Did he feel bad about that? No, he felt bloody elated about that. They'd gagged her and he'd chained her to his bed. All he wanted right now was for her to confirm that.

'OK.' She heaved in a fresh lungful of air. 'I promise to stay around.'

'Then I will not try to get out of this bed until they say that I can,' he parried, and turned his hand over on the white sheet, watching as she looked down at it, knowing that she understood what the gesture meant. After a short hesitation she lifted her own hand and placed it against his.

Deal sealed, he thought as he folded his fingers around her fingers, then released a sigh of contentment and closed his eyes. 'What time is it?' he asked.

'Ten o'clock,' Lexi answered. 'You slept through dinner—'

'I'm not hungry.'

'—so I ate it,' she concluded.

That brought his eyes back open, and placed a lazy smile on his lips. He turned his head to look at her and his eyes had softened. That awful blank glaze had gone to reveal deep brown irises like velvet threaded with gold that warmed her all the way through even though she did not want it to.

'What was it?' he questioned curiously.

'*Pomodori con riso* supplied by Zeta,' she told him. 'Your father has arranged for her to—'

'Did she send a dessert?'

He'd done it again—blocked her from mentioning his father. 'A couple of truly delicious Maritozzi buns. Franco, about your father—'

He withdrew his hands from hers. 'Since when have you been Salvatore's biggest fan?' he demanded impatiently. 'He treated you like a lowlife when we were together.'

'I'm not his adored son.'

Flattening out his lips, he shut his eyes again.

In bubbling frustration Lexi sat back in her seat, then instantly sat forward again: no matter what the doctor had advised, or what Franco himself preferred, she found she still could not let the subject rest.

She reached out to retrieve his hand. 'Francesco, please just listen—'

'Franco,' he interrupted. 'I know you are mad with me when you call me Francesco.'

Lowering her gaze to his hand, Lexi watched her own fingers drawing patterns on his palm the way she'd used to do when they talked. Quite suddenly she wanted to break down and weep. They'd been together for six months. For two of those months they had been inseparable. For the other four they'd hated each other's guts.

'And when you extend that to Francesco Tolle,' he continued, giving a good mimic of her cut-crystal English accent, 'I know I am in really deep trouble.'

'You stopped calling me Lexi altogether,' Lexi recalled dully. 'I became Alexia—and if you think *my* accent was cold, yours was made of ice picks.'

'I was angry.'

'I know you were.'

'I was wildly in love with you but we—'

She stood up so fast Franco had no chance to react. By the time he'd dragged his heavy eyelids open it was like looking at a stranger—an achingly beautiful but distant stranger.

'I'd better be going. I need to find somewhere to stay.'

'Pietro will have reserved a suite for you at a hotel close to the hospital.' Aware that he was slurring his words now, as the drugs they'd fed into him began to drag him back down, Franco decided to let her escape. 'He will be waiting to drive you there.'

'I'll see you tomorrow,' she mumbled, and was gone before he could say anything else.

Releasing a sigh, Franco let his eyelids droop again and saw the other Lexi. The younger one, sitting cross-legged on the bulkhead of his sailing yacht, *Miranda*, relaying some convoluted story to him about an incident that had happened on the film set of the movie she'd come to Cannes to promote. She hadn't had a clue that she was blocking his view of the open sea in front of them. She hadn't cared that a stiff warm breeze was tangling her hair into spiralling knots, or that the tiny red bikini she'd been wearing was revealing more than it should.

And her innocence had shone out of her like a tantalising aura. She'd had no clue that what shone in him was deep, hot and very physical.

She'd liked him.

Franco threw an arm up to cover his eyes and for once wished they'd stung him with more sedatives, because he

did not want to look any harder at the sexual predator he'd
been then. The cabin beneath her, where he'd lived during
that long summer, had already been set up ready for her seduction, and he'd been burning with anticipation while she
talked.

A seduction that had taken them from Cannes to Nice, Cap
Ferrat, Monte Carlo, then San Remo—

San Remo...

Franco shifted onto his side and didn't care that it hurt
him like hell. Reaching for the bell, he waited for the nurse
to come to him. 'I want this cage removed and these tubes
taken out. I want a couple of pillows and I want my mobile
phone,' he reeled off with grim intent.

'But, *signor*—'

'Or I will get up and get them for myself.'

He did not get his first two requests, but he was reluctantly
handed his mobile phone. *'Grazie,'* he murmured, allowing
the nurse to fuss around him, placing the pillows beneath his
shoulders, mainly because he felt too damn weak to do the
job for himself.

Lexi slept like a log. She had not expected to sleep at all,
but the moment her head had come to rest on the pillow exhaustion had taken her out like a light, and she'd awoken this
morning feeling so invigorated, but baffled as to why she
should feel like that.

Or maybe she did not want to look too deeply into why,
she mused with a frown, picking up the phone and ordering
some breakfast, before quickly showering while she waited
for it to arrive. She was starving. Despite telling Franco that
she'd eaten his dinner, she'd been too stressed to do more than
pick at Zeta's delicious dishes. Now her stomach was growling as she walked across the elegant sitting room of the vast
suite Pietro had reserved for her and went to take a quick look

out of the window to check the weather before deciding what she was going to wear.

Not that her choices were many. Her weekend bag revealed a frustrating lack of common sense when she'd packed it so hastily back in London. Nothing in it was appropriate for hot and sunny Livorno in September; and she discovered she had not even packed any shoes.

A knock sounded on the suite door as she walked out of the bedroom wearing a long-sleeved stripy tunic top and a pair of black leggings tucked into black ankle boots. Assuming Room Service was delivering her breakfast, she opened the door—only to fall back two steps in shock.

There was no mistaking that Franco had been forged in his father's image. Dressed impeccably as always in a dark business suit, and in his mid-fifties, Salvatore Tolle was still a very attractive if dauntingly austere man.

'*Buongiorno*, Alexia,' he greeted her soberly.

'*B-buongiorno, signor,*' she returned in a voice made breathless by surprise.

'May I come in?'

Without saying another word Lexi stepped to one side in silent invitation for him to enter the suite. Nerves made her stay by the door once she'd closed it again. As she watched him take up a stance in the middle of the room she tried to anticipate what his visit could be about.

He took a few moments to glance around her accommodation. 'You are comfortable here?'

She pleated her hands together at her front. 'Yes, of course…thank you.'

He nodded his silver-threaded dark head. 'I have spoken to Francesco,' he announced abruptly. 'He called me last night from his bed.'

'Oh!' Lexi instantly cheered up. 'I'm so glad he did that. I was upset when I heard he had—'

'Your concern on my behalf is touching, but I would prefer

it if you resisted the urge to express it,' Salvatore interrupted in a cool voice.

It felt like having a door slammed shut in her face.

She should be used to it, Lexi told herself. The few conversations she'd ever had with Salvatore had always felt like that.

'Though I *do* thank you, Alexia,' he then surprised her by adding, 'for urging my son to—soften his attitude towards me.'

'N-no problem.' Having been stopped from saying what she would have liked to say to him, Lexi left her response at that.

Another knock sounded on the door, and this time it was her breakfast. Glad of the diversion, because Salvatore had always scared the life out of her, Lexi allowed the waiter entry and watched mutely as he crossed the room to place the tray down on a small table set by the window.

'Can—can I offer you a cup of tea?' she enquired politely, once the waiter had left them again.

'*Grazie*, no,' Salvatore responded. 'However, please—sit down and enjoy your breakfast, ' he insisted.

Lexi sat down at the small table, but the thought of eating or drinking anything in front of him just closed up her throat.

'Please tell me why you're here,' she urged, hearing the strain in her own voice. 'It's not Franco, is it? He hasn't—?'

'Francesco is fine,' came the quick assurance. 'If *fine* accurately describes the injuries he endured,' he added bleakly. 'I have come here directly from visiting with him.'

'Oh, that's…' *Good*, Lexi had been about to say, but held it back by biting down on her tense lower lip.

'Francesco does not know I am here, you understand?' he informed her then. 'He has forbidden me from approaching you, so my relationship with my son is in your hands once again, Alexia.' The rueful smile he offered her almost melted her wariness. 'However, there is a matter I need to discuss with you.'

'Will you at least sit down first?' Feeling pretty uncomfortable sitting there, while he stood tall and straight several metres away, Lexi indicated the vacant chair placed at the table.

He really looked as if he was actually going to take her up on her offer, too; but then he glanced at his wristwatch, frowned, and shook his head. 'I have to leave in a few minutes to catch my flight to New York. We are very close to procuring a large contract there, which will keep our New York shipyard busy for the next four years. Francesco was dealing with the details. Of course now that he cannot I must go in his place...'

Lexi pressed her lips together and nodded her head in understanding. She found she needed something to do with her restless fingers and picked up a glass of juice.

'I must, therefore, ask you to do me another favour,' Salvatore went on. 'Leaving my son without my support at this time is unacceptable. I will be back in time to attend Marco's funeral next week of course,' he assured her quickly, having no idea that she did not already know when Marco's funeral would be. 'However, I will have to return to New York almost immediately afterwards. The thing is, Alexia, all being well, Francesco will be released from hospital in the next few days. Since he has decided to place his complete trust in you, I must ask if you would continue to support him in my place through the coming few weeks.'

Unable to sit still any longer, Lexi got to her feet, feeling very tense now, because she wasn't sure how much of Franco's close company she was going to be able to take without—

'How long are we talking about? I have a job in London, you see, and—and other commitments.'

'I feel that a month's compassionate leave is not too much to ask of your employer.'

He felt that because he didn't know Bruce, thought Lexi, not at all looking forward to *that* conversation.

'Since Francesco is still refusing to allow anyone else to come near him, I am hoping that you will be able to convince him to bypass his apartment here in Livorno and go directly to Monfalcone, where Pietro and Zeta will be on hand to help you with his convalescence.'

He was referring to the private estate just outside Livorno, where she'd stayed during her mess of a brief marriage. Monfalcone was a beautiful *castello* built of golden stone that had mellowed over centuries. It was also the place where she and Franco had been married. A day she would much rather not think back on, because her welcome from the rest of the Tolle family had been so disapproving. In a cold fury Franco had whipped them away from there before the first waltz had been announced and taken her to his apartment in the city for a week. Continuing hostilities between the two of them had prompted a return to Monfalcone, because the *castello* was big enough for the two of them to avoid each other for most of the time.

'He will not go to Monfalcone without you,' Salvatore imparted flatly. 'He is determined to follow you to London if you decide not to stay here. I do not pretend to understand this fixation he has developed about your marriage, but I do know that it is paramount in his thoughts.'

Guilt, Lexi wanted to say—but didn't. She'd been thinking about it since she'd left the hospital, and she'd decided that his guilt over Marco's death had stirred up guilty feelings over the way he'd behaved during their short time together as a married couple—though she was not so self-pitying as to think that she had treated him any better than he had treated her.

Every time she'd looked at him she'd seen the lazily complacent smile on his handsome tanned face when he'd accepted his winnings from that rotten bet. Every time he'd made an attempt to mend fences between them, she'd struck out at him like a whip. When he stalked out of the *castello* and hadn't come back for two whole weeks she'd been heartily glad to see the back of him. She'd worn her disillusionment and bitterness like a suit of armour that contained the aching throb of raw, broken-hearted hurt, and she'd hugged it to her for long, lonely months until…

'Am I asking too much of you?'

Without knowing she'd sat down again, Lexi blinked her eyes and realised she been lost in her own thoughts for too long. Looking up at her father-in-law, she saw an expression she never would have expected to see score Salvatore's coldly impassive features. It hinted strongly at despair.

He didn't know what he was going to do if she refused to stay with Franco. Salvatore had a large multinational ship building company to run, whether or not he wanted to go and do it right now.

'I will stay,' she said, and smiled a crooked smile when she counted how many times she'd used those words recently.

CHAPTER FOUR

LEXI pulled to a stop in the doorway. The monitors had gone, and plump snowy-white pillows now lay stacked on the bed, but there was no Franco resting against them. Swivelling around, she found him seated in a comfortable chair by the window, with a rolling table lowered so it skimmed across his legs, a laptop computer standing open on its top.

'Oh, you're out of bed!' Lexi exclaimed brightly. 'That's great.'

'I am not a kid. Don't talk to me as if I am,' Franco responded, with enough sizzling antagonism to put Lexi on her guard as she stepped further into the room so she could close the door behind her. 'You are late. Where have you been?'

'Sorry, I had some stuff to do.' Dumping her collection of bags down against the wall, she walked over to him. 'When did they let you get up?'

'They didn't *let* me do anything. I got up.'

'Was that wise?'

'I'm still breathing.'

Lexi almost responded with something very sarcastic, then thought better of it and removed her jacket instead. Moving to drape it over a chair, she looked at him again. He was wearing a white bathrobe and nothing else as far she could tell. His hair wore a damp sheen to it, and yesterday's rakish five o'clock shadow had disappeared. So, thankfully, had the sickly pallor from his face. His eyes were veiled, because he was concentrating on the computer screen, and his lips were flattened tight. For Lexi, his manner was a good reminder of what it felt like when Franco turned on his cold side. Words became lethal weapons.

'Well, at least you smell nice anyway,' she murmured idly, determined not to rise to his provoking bait.

A hint of a flash speared out from behind his eyelashes. With the use of only one hand—the strapping around his right shoulder impeded the other—he continued to tap away on the keyboard with a five fingered efficiency that was impressive.

'You left the hotel by taxi at nine o'clock this morning. That was three hours ago. Have you forgotten how to wear a skirt?'

Blinking her eyes at that blunt-ended bombardment, Lexi glanced down at her legs, still encased in stretchy black fabric, and her ankle boots—which were making her feet ache because she'd done too much walking in them and it was too hot outside for boots.

'What kind of skirt would you like me to wear?' she questioned innocently. 'Short and tight? Flared and flirty? Long and floaty?' Strolling back to her bags, she picked them up and hauled them over to the window to dump them down beside his chair, then dropped down into a squat. 'I've bought all three, just in case you have a preference, plus a couple of dresses—mainly because I fell in love with them. Two nighties, some underwear...' As she listed her purchases Lexi scooped the items out of their bags and dropped them on top of his laptop without a single care as to whether she was messing up his five fingered prose. 'It really shocked me what I'd thrown in my case in London because I was in a hurry. I mean, what can a girl *do* with one pair of jeans, no spare tops, no fresh underwear and no shoes?'

He caught the shoes before they landed, his long fingers closing around the pair of strappy flats.

'Oh, and these.' Dipping into a bag, she came out with a clutch of cosmetics and a hairbrush.

'Don't,' he warned softly, when she went to drop them onto his laptop too.

'OK, so you're not impressed with girly necessities. How about this, then…?' Her next dip produced a stuffed pearl-grey floppy-eared rabbit, which she ever so gently laid against his chest. 'Present for you,' she told him sweetly.

Still squatting there, she watched his lean, hard and handsome face as he stared down at the furry rabbit. A tingling sensation caught hold of her solar plexus as she watched the tension relax from his lips so they could shift into a reluctant smile, and at last he looked at her. What she saw glinting in his eyes made her so glad she'd taken the flippancy route.

'I thought you'd done another runner,' he admitted.

It took Lexi a second or two to work out why he'd said *another* runner—until she remembered how she'd run back to England three years ago. No note, not even a spitting I hate you note. She'd just walked out of this very hospital, climbed into a taxi, and left.

'Nope.' Still she kept it light. 'I went shopping.' She waved a hand at the rabbit. 'Well, at least say hello to him.'

Silently he passed her back the shoes, then picked the rabbit off his chest and looked at it. 'He's wearing a pink bow round his neck.'

'They didn't have a blue one.'

'Does he have a name?'

'Yes. William,' she announced decisively. 'William Wabbit—because the young man that served me couldn't sound his "r" and his wabbit sounded kind of cute.'

'Rabbit in Italian is *coniglio*.'

'Ah, yes, but the guy was trying out his best English to impress me,' Lexi explained.

'Flirting with you?'

'Of course.' She put the shoes back in the bag. 'He was Italian.'

Instead of plucking all her other purchases off his lap, Franco caught hold of her hand. Even as she glanced up and saw the darkening look in his eyes she sort of knew what was coming next and tried to pull against it. But by then he'd already set her moving forward, her soft gasp the barest protest before her lips made contact with his. Warmth flooded her senses, and the feel of their mouths fused together was so natural already that she almost sank more deeply into the kiss—until she realised what she was doing and pulled back.

'Grazie,' he husked. 'For the wabbit.'

Dragging her gaze down to where the rabbit rested against his chest, she murmured, 'You're welcome,' a bit too huskily for her liking, and quickly returned her attention to jumbling her purchases back into the bags.

'How did you know what time I left the hotel?' she asked curiously, fighting to keep her tone light.

This kissing thing had to stop, she was telling herself. OK, so she'd started it. And the kiss just now had only been a typical Italian thank you kiss… But it still had to stop.

She was unaware that Franco was watching her narrowly.

'Pietro arrived to collect you five minutes after you left.'

It was only when he picked it up that she saw his Blackberry had been lying next to the laptop. He handed it to her. 'Put your number in it.'

'So you can keep tabs on me?'

'It's a communication tool not a tracker.'

Pulling a face, she took the phone from him and did as he asked without further comment. While spending the last three hours shopping, she had also been contemplating the current situation she had committed herself to with Franco, and decided that, his having lost the closest friend a man could ever have, she would try her best to fill a small part of the gap Marco had left in Franco's life until he was ready to face up to his loss.

A friend—but not a kissing friend, she determined with a frown as she handed the phone back, aware that her lips still wore the warm impression of his against them.

As he took back the phone, Franco wished he knew what was going on inside her head. Her frown was pensive, the complacent way she had been treating him told him she'd come to some decisions over the night about how she was going to treat being back in his life. The rabbit spoke volumes. The summer they were together she used to produce all kinds of cheap and wacky gifts for him, like the tiny plastic camel on a plinth that gyrated when you pressed the bottom, which she'd insisted looked just like him when he danced. And the set of three little yellow ducks she'd dropped into his bathwater then laughed herself double when they started paddling towards a certain part of his body with a speed that made him stand up fast. Then there was the whole row of frogs in all different sizes and materials, she'd lined up on the shelf above their bed and insisted on kissing each one every night because, she told him, she was convinced at least one of them was going to turn into her handsome Prince.

He had never met anyone like her. She'd been part child and part extraordinarily passionate and deeply sensual woman. And she'd trusted him so totally she did not hold anything back. She'd pinched his clothes, used his toothbrush, and thrown his friends off the *Miranda* when she'd had enough of their company without bothering to ask him if it was OK. If they went out clubbing she would ignore him to dance the night away in the middle of the heaving crush of bodies, laughing, flirting, completely uninhibited, but when she tired of dancing she would locate him like a homing pigeon and drag him away from whatever he was doing, whoever he was with, without apology or even a scant goodnight.

It had never occurred to her that he might tire of her. She'd refused to listen to sly comments about his staying power in a relationship. She'd simply loved him, and believed without question that he was in love with her, so when it had all gone sour she'd been left floundering in a sea of hurt disillusionment that had turned so cold and bitter she'd become a tragically lost stranger to him almost overnight.

He picked up the rabbit and looked at it, grimacing, because he did not doubt that this was Lexi's way of turning back the clock—but only in as far as she was attempting to ease his pain over Marco by reminding him of the time they had spent together without Marco around, he discerned. That kiss, that brief coming together of their mouths, was still burning on his lips; but all he'd seen on Lexi's lips was their faint downturn, and her face showed withdrawal—as if she'd been embarrassed but was valiantly determined to keep the atmosphere light.

Not so for last night's kiss, though, Franco reminded himself grimly. Last night's kiss had been the other Lexi bursting out from behind this one—urgent, passionate and compassionate. *That* was the woman he was determined to get back again.

Glancing up from the rabbit when she stood with her bags and moved over to his bed, he watched as she proceeded to tip everything back out again so she could refold them. Franco slid his eyes down the length of her slender legs and wondered why he'd complained about what she was wearing when the moulding of the black leggings sparked a groin heating flashback to how it felt when those long slender legs were wrapped tightly around his waist. The striped top hugged her slender curves, and she'd tied back her hair this morning, twisting its shiny length into a casual knot that rested low, just above her creamy nape. It would take him one second flat to loosen that hair again, bring it floating down through his waiting fingers. Give him another few seconds and he would—

A phone started ringing. He glanced down at his phone,

only realising it wasn't ringing when Lexi made a dive across his bed to grab her handbag. Plucking out her mobile, she frowned down at the screen for a couple of seconds. He watched her lips crush into a brooding pout.

'Sorry, but I have to take this,' she mumbled, and walked quickly out of the room.

Franco heard her murmur, 'Hi, Bruce,' as the door swung shut behind her, and just like that his mellowing mood turned stark.

Rolling the table away from his legs, he let the steely grip of cold hard anger give him the strength to rise to his feet, wincing when everything hurt, then cursing because it did. Outside the window Livorno was shimmering in the noonday heat. Below him he could see his father's black limo standing in the car park, with Pietro leaning against the bonnet chatting to one of the security men his father had put in place to keep out the intrusive press. Beyond the hospital perimeter he could see a small clutch of camera toting paparazzi, loitering like lazy lizards by the gates. Lexi hadn't mentioned them. He wondered if she'd been hassled by them when she'd arrived today. He knew they were curious—the internet was full of stories about the crash and Marco's tragic death. They'd gone hunting for older stories and dragged out his and Lexi's hasty marriage and even hastier break-up.

There had even been a comment from Bruce Dayton and a photo of him, looking smooth and slick as always, standing outside his agency. 'Lexi Hamilton is naturally devastated by Marco Clemente's death. Of course she is supporting her husband at this tragic time. That is all I am going to say.'

There was no quote from Lexi knocking about on the internet. She had not felt compelled to speak to the press. When Dayton had done so he'd made sure he was standing beside the name of his agency. Nothing like a bit of free publicity if you could get it, the calculating bastard.

And her last name was Tolle—no matter how much Dayton

ignored that fact. Why was he calling her? Did he fear he was about to lose control of her once again? Bruce Dayton was a dangerous control freak where Lexi was concerned. His silvery eyes had used to glint with possessiveness every time he looked at her. When she'd run away from here she'd gone directly to Dayton, who must have been celebrating beneath the caring concern he would have shown her. That Dayton had managed to achieve his goal and get her into his bed with him burned like poison in Franco's blood. Were they still lovers? Was Dayton laying on the pressure right now to bring Lexi back to heel?

Franco picked up his mobile. From the window he watched Pietro accepting his call. Five minutes later he was limping painfully over to the clothes closet and opening the door.

Lexi, meanwhile, was pacing the quiet corridor well away from listening ears. 'Please, listen to me, Bruce—'

'You don't plan to come back here to work, do you?' he challenged harshly.

Lexi winced at his icily accusing tone. 'I haven't said that,' she denied. 'But I do think it's time that you and I took a step back from each other,' she admitted, as gently as she could. 'You said yourself that I need to take a good look at where my life is heading.'

'Right now Lexi, I can see you heading for another big fall.'

'You and I…we were becoming too close for the wrong reasons.'

'Explain that,' Bruce clipped out. 'Are you saying you don't feel anything for me?'

'I care for you deeply, but—'

'You're still in love with that Italian swine,' he said. 'Has it occurred to you that he's plucking on your heartstrings because he's ill and probably looks endearingly pathetic?'

'This conversation has nothing to do with Franco,' she contended.

'Of *course* it's about Franco,' Bruce sliced back. 'He crooks his finger and you go running—'

'No, this is about you opening my eyes to the kind of relationship that has been developing between *us*, and I think I've always known deep down that it's not going to work.' Lexi pressed home, even though she knew it was going to hurt. 'You recognised that too, Bruce,' she reminded him gently. 'I saw it in your expression and heard it in your voice. You've been the most wonderful friend to me—the very best. But somewhere along the line our feelings for each other became confused.'

'Thanks, Lexi, for telling me that you think I'm such a limp-brained fool.'

She gripped the phone more tightly. 'I didn't mean that—'

'Good. Because I am not the one who's confused about my feelings. I can accept that you might need more time to make up your mind about us, but what I can't take is you doing it while hanging around *him*. He's like poison to you, Lexi. He always was and always will be. I will give you until after Clemente's funeral, then you had better be back here pronto or I'm coming to get you—because I am not giving up on us!'

He cut her off. Lexi leant back against the wall and closed her eyes. She should have dealt with this. She should have dealt with it months ago. Now she felt he had every right to be angry with her. The problem was she didn't like hurting people. She knew what it felt like, having been so badly hurt herself. And the worst part was Bruce was not her enemy. Franco was her enemy. If only because of the way he could still make her feel.

Re-entering Franco's room, she found he wasn't there. A glance at the closed bathroom door and she pulled in a deep breath and went back to sorting out the things she'd piled on his bed, glad of the few minutes' respite while she tried to put her conversation with Bruce to one side.

The door to the bathroom opened. Turning around, Lexi almost dropped down onto the bed when a fully dressed Franco stepped out—a Franco she never had grown used to seeing like this. It felt as if someone had stuck a live wire in between her ribs, and the electric sensation tingled all the way down to her toes.

He was wearing a dark pinstriped suit of such amazing quality it seemed to glide over his long, lean physique like a living, moving thing.

'You can't get dressed,' she breathed out in trembling objection. 'Why have you got dressed?'

Managing to drag her gaze away from its mesmerised stare at the neat red tie knotted against the pristine white shirt collar that showed off the deep golden skin beneath his chin, she felt it clash with a set of rock-hard handsome features that bore little resemblance to the man she'd been looking at ten minutes before—the man she remembered as the Franco she'd used to know.

Not this one, though. This one was the married version— the one she'd learnt was a horribly cold, distant stranger who could look at her through the impassive dark eyes of a ruthless decision maker, as he was doing right now. She wrapped her arms around herself, shivering in response to the look.

'We are leaving,' he said. No embroidery to that declaration. He simply stepped over to the table with barely a limp on show and closed down his laptop, then picked up his phone.

'I—I don't understand.' Flicking a glance at the bell push dangling over the pillows on the bed, she wondered anxiously if this was another one of his agitated moments and if she needed to bring someone in here fast, before he did himself some damage.

'It is pretty simple. I have been unplugged, I am off all medication, and now I want to get away from this place.'

'You mean they've signed you off?'

Glittering eyes set between narrowed eyelashes sent her a grimly mocking look. 'Who are *they*, precisely?'

'The...' She waved a hand. 'The doctors and—whoever. You can't just walk out because you feel like it, Franco. There might be something really wrong with—'

'You did.'

Cut off midsentence, Lexi blinked at him. 'Excuse me?' she breathed.

'You walked out of here without being "signed off," as you descriptively put it.' Putting the phone in his pocket, he gathered up the fluffy rabbit next and carried it over to where she stood by the bed. 'Actually, you ran.'

Having glued her attention to his legs, looking for a pronounced limp or something to indicate whether it hurt him to walk, Lexi jerked up her head. As if her surprised little world had just gone topsy-turvy, she found herself having to look up—and up—to reach the hard contours of his face. A clattering mass reaction stopped her breathing. It was so long since they'd stood toe to toe like this. Seeing him lying in bed or even sitting in a chair had *not* jolted her memory banks into reminding her of just how tall Franco was.

And it wasn't just the extra inches of height he had over her—it was the sheer breadth of him and the illicit vibration of dangerously exciting power idling beneath the suit. He towered over her and her mouth dried up. She blinked and was suddenly assailed with an image of him, all golden tan and ridged muscles, standing over her just like this, wearing only a pair of white boxer shorts. A shockingly terrible tingle attacked the tips of her breasts, then shot like a flaming arrow to the vulnerable place between her legs. Liquid heat poured into the same place, making her squeeze in a sharp, choky little breath, and her skin broke out in a hot-cold sweat.

'And I'm not even touching you,' Franco chided softly, reading the choky gasp because he remembered it so well. *'Yet,'* he added with silken purpose, just to see what would happen to her next.

A tide of interesting colour washed up her slender white

throat and the black of her pupils dilated until they'd almost completely obliterated the ocean-blue of her irises.

'This potent effect we have on each other is one hell of an aphrodisiac, *cara*,' he murmured delicately. 'Do you want to know what you are doing to me?'

Lexi slowly lowered her eyes in an effort to break free from his scintillating spell. She felt dizzy, and tiny muscles all over her were contracting so tightly they pulsed.

'Y-you have no reason to run.' Valiantly, she locked the single brain cell she seemed to have left on what he'd said before.

'But you did?'

Pinning her lips together, and realising that they felt plumped up and tingly, Lexi nodded her head, finding she had to part her lips again so that she could speak. 'And I will do it again if you don't turn off the sexual pressure.'

His mouth broke into a wolfishly amused grin. 'Good to know I've still got it, *amore*.'

'You and how many others?' Lexi derided his insufferable self-belief, at the same time deriding all the other good-looking men with truckloads of sexual charisma she met on a day-to-day basis—not one of whom came anywhere near making her feel what Franco made her feel.

That he'd completely misunderstood her meaning hit her as she watched his eyes cool. Even his cheeks suddenly looked carved, as if someone had scooped any hint of softness out of them. Lexi felt the sudden need to redistribute her weight equally between her two booted feet, and she unfolded her arms to drop them down to her sides, her fingers curling into fists.

'You mis—'

'Spare me the numbers.'

Turning abruptly away from her, he pushed the stuffed rabbit into one of her bags. The moment she lost his attention Lexi reached out and snatched up the bell press; gave it a long and urgent push. He caught the movement and swung back. Lexi dropped the bell push as if it was hot. As his eyes narrowed on her like stinging lasers she pushed her chin up and fed him back a wide-eyed look of sparking defiance.

To her total astonishment Franco threw back his dark head and laughed. 'So even you think I've gone crazy!'

There was no 'even you' about it. Lexi had considered him crazy ever since she'd arrived here. He might be reading her every thought and feeling, but she found she couldn't keep up with his thought patterns or the fast changes in his mood.

'You're not leaving here without someone's say-so.' She struck a stubborn pose.

'Pietro will be here in five minutes,' was all he commented, as if that was enough to relay his intentions. 'I sent him to your hotel to settle the bill and collect your things.'

The door swung open before Lexi could respond to that piece of smooth forward planning. Dr Cavelli walked in, then stopped when he saw his patient was dressed and standing.

As cool and casual as a long drink of water, Franco turned and strode across the room, a smile on his face and his hand outstretched. 'Thank you,' he murmured in smooth as balm Italian, 'for the wonderful care and attention I have received from you and your staff. However, it is time for me leave.'

The doctor had been staring at the limp free way Franco had been moving, but he jerked his eyes up to the outstretched hand, then even further, staring dubiously at Franco's beautifully polite mask of a face. 'I am not sure…'

'I am drug free and feeling much better,' Franco pointed out in a dulcet tone, then waited as if he had the patience of a saint while the doctor glanced questioningly at Lexi and she sent a helplessly bewildered shrug in return.

'There is no medical reason why you cannot be discharged, *signor*,' Dr Cavelli murmured cautiously. 'However, you will need to keep a watchful eye on your bruising for the next week or two. The risk of blood clots has not diminished, and you will need the dressings changed on your thigh wound.'

'Alexia and I will promise to keep a watchful eye out for blood clots,' Franco assured him, refusing to look at Lexi even though he was holding his breath in case she told him she was not prepared to do anything of the kind. 'And I am capable of changing my own dressings.'

The doctor looked at Lexi again as though he was waiting for her to confirm that she would be there to take care of his patient. Parting her lips with the intention of refusing to have any part in Franco's plans to walk out of there, she happened to glance at him—saw the evidence of strain showing in his proud profile and the grim tension in his elegant stance. She remembered Marco, experienced a swooping sensation deep down inside that felt as if something was twisting her organs together painfully, and she closed her mouth again, then gave a silent nod of her head.

The tension holding Franco together sprang free, almost toppling him from his increasingly painful stance. Whatever Dayton had said to her on the phone, he had not yanked on her chains hard enough—but Franco had. Sheer grim satisfaction helped to keep him upright through the ordeal of receiving the doctor's detailed advice on maintaining his present rate of recovery. By then Pietro had arrived and, ignoring the older man's shocked consternation when he realised what was going on, Franco quietly instructed him to collect his bag from the adjoining bathroom.

He almost collapsed into the rear of his father's limo. He was that exhausted by keeping up the appearance that he was magically returned to robust health.

Lexi sat beside him, flitting from concern to annoyance and back again as she studied the way he was sitting there, deathly pale with his eyes closed, one long-fingered hand pressed against his chest inside his jacket, the other lying limp on the seat between them. She could see the punch holes from the shunt on the back of his hand and the bruising circling them. But what really bothered her was the shallowness of his breathing.

'It would serve you right if you had a relapse now, Franco, what with your wicked, lying stupidity!' she launched at him, anxiety feeding her hot temper.

'I left that particularly drastic kind of wicked, lying stupidity to Marco,' Franco relayed flatly in response.

CHAPTER FIVE

LEXI swivelled around to stare at him. 'M-Marco?' she prompted, watching warily for a sign of that awful grey pallor to sink down across Franco's face. The trouble was that he was already that greyish colour.

'Pietro, the paparazzi—are they following us?'

He did it yet again. Blocked out the subject of his best friend.

'*Si,*' the older man responded. 'They sit on our tail like reckless fools. You want me to lose them?'

'You think that you can do it?'

'Ah, *si*, of course I can do it.'

'What paparazzi?' As Lexi twisted around to take a look through the back window an eager Pietro threw the car into an acute left turn.

Trying not to wince as the swerving action lanced through him like a knife, Franco told her dryly, 'They have been on your tail since you arrived in Livorno.'

'Oh.' She twisted back in her seat. 'I've stopped bothering to look for them since I gave up acting.'

'Why did you give up acting?' Turning his head against the seat-back, he looked at her. 'You were supposed to have a glittering Hollywood career waiting for you when you left me.'

Ignoring his last remark, even though he'd made it sound

as if she'd walked away from him because of her glittering career prospects, Lexi said with a shrug, 'Acting was never my dream. It was my mother's dream.' Poor Grace, who'd so wanted to be a famous Hollywood movie star all her life. 'I fell into the movie thing by accident when I was fooling around with a script off set during one of my mother's auditions. Someone heard me, dragged me onto the set, then made me read the same bit again. I did. I got the part.' As she looked at Franco she caught a faintly unsettling glint in his narrowed eyes.

'You never told me that before.'

'You probably never asked before. Why the sinister glint?' she demanded suspiciously.

'It is not sinister. So, what was *your* dream?'

Looking foreward again, Lexi didn't answer him. Her dream had been way too basic for a man like Franco to understand. A house with a garden, lots of kids, and a husband who worked a nine-to-five job then came home to his family each evening.

Growing up in a city apartment with a single mum who'd worked the oddest hours possible meant that she'd more or less brought herself up. Her garden—her playground—had been the set of one small movie or another, or the cloistered walls of her mother's dressing room backstage.

No, her childhood dreams had found no romance in the acting world.

'*My* mother dreamed of me becoming a great concert pianist,' he said, lifting up his hands and spreading out his long fingers to study them with a rueful grimace. 'All I wanted to do was to mess around with boats and engines.'

But he still played the piano like nobody else Lexi had ever heard. He could bring the whole of Monfalcone to a breathless listening standstill with a hauntingly beautiful piece of classical music played on the grand piano in the main salon, or he could ratchet up a flagging party by belting out a wild medley of pop, hot jazz and heavy rock.

With those same long blunt fingers that took apart a boat engine with such dedicated care and knowledge.

'She was beautiful—your mother,' Lexi murmured, recalling the painting that hung in the same salon that contained the grand piano.

'As was yours.' Lowering his hands, he looked at her and an ache that came very close to mutual understanding tugged like a gentle weight on her heart. 'I'm sorry I never got to meet her.'

So was Lexi. Grace would have fallen in love with Franco—the tall, dark Italian with oodles of bone-melting charm. She didn't think that his mother would have fallen in love with her, though. Isabella Tolle had been hewn from a different breed entirely from Lexi—and Grace, come to that. Grace had been an eternal dreamer, whereas Isabella Tolle had been born with all of her dreams already mapped out and secured for her.

And the last thing she would have wanted for her only son would have been a hasty marriage to a one-hit movie star who'd set out to trap him... No. Lexi stopped that thought in its tracks. She had not *set out* to trap him. She just *had* trapped him, and learned to hate herself for doing it.

'Do we go to the apartment or Monfalcone?'

Franco's casual question intruded, making Lexi blink a couple of times before she could focus her attention back on him. Remembering what his father had said to her that morning, she said, 'Monfalcone,' though with the thoughts now rattling around in her head—all to do with her time spent living there—she wished she hadn't agreed to that part of her bargain with Salvatore.

'We go home, Pietro,' he relayed to the driver.

'Ah, *si, si*.' Pietro smiled in approval. 'That is good *signor*. That is very good indeed...'

'At least one person approves of us, *bella mia*,' Franco drawled softly.

Lexi shifted restlessly on the seat. She wasn't sure that she liked the lazily veiled look Franco was levelling at her from his corner of the car. It made the hairs on the back of her neck tingle as if she was missing something important here that she should be working out.

'We are not an "us."' It needed saying—just in case Franco was having amorous ideas about the two of them.

'What are we, then?'

She opened her mouth to answer, then closed it again. She did not have an answer to what they were. Estranged husband and wife? A bit more than that, since she was returning to Monfalcone with him like a wife. Friends, then? No. Once upon a time Franco had been the closest thing to a friend she'd ever known—until she'd discovered he was only in the relationship for the fun of the sex, and of course, the bet. The only other reason had to be Marco. She was here with him because he'd lost his closest friend. But she was not allowed to mention that.

Frowning, she shook her head and turned her face to the window, leaving the question to hang in the air. Franco studied her taut profile and felt an ache deep down inside, like a battering ram trying to bridge the gap between them so he could answer the question for her the physical way.

Great strategy, Francesco, he mocked himself grimly. The doctors had gagged her, he had chained her to his side, and his father had used subtle manipulation to bring Lexi back to Monfalcone with Franco. Now you want to ruin it all with a smash-and-grab approach you are not physically capable of carrying out.

And then there was that other unknown element stirring around in the soup of their fragile relationship. 'What did Dayton call to say to you?' he prompted coolly.

The way he'd used Bruce's last name spoke volumes to

Lexi. Franco had always disliked Bruce as much as Bruce disliked him. 'I work for him.'

'I know you do.'

He did? That surprised her. She'd thought he'd shut her right out of his life, much as he was doing with Marco right now. Another bad thing obliterated from Franco's world.

'Well, then—you are an employer, so you know how it works. Don't ask stupid questions.' Lexi reacted stiffly, turning away again. She refused to discuss Bruce with him, because... Well, because she was loyal to the people that she loved, and right now she loved Bruce more than she loved...

Back-pedalling desperately, determined not to face what she had been about to think, Lexi moved in the seat as if she was trying to push something truly frightening away from her. And maybe she was, she admitted, aware of why she had severed that last too disturbing thought before it could round itself off.

I don't even have the excuse of a tragic accident to make me block out that which I don't want to face, she recognised grimly.

The journey continued with silence thickening the car's confines. The silent smoothness of the drive was a testament to the quality of luxury engineering and design.

Lexi slowly sank back in her seat and watched the view pass by them beyond the glass, tinted against the fierce rays of the sun. This part of Italy had to be one of the most beautiful places on earth, she observed hazily. The afternoon sunlight coloured everything such a warm golden colour, and the sheer stately elegance of tall tapering cypress trees dotted miles and miles of undulating landscape. Even the occasional silvery spread of an ancient olive tree rising up on its sturdy twisting trunk made an impact, as if one of the great Italian masters had placed them there with the gifted touch of his paintbrush. Familiar scents teased her nostrils and heightened her senses. Warm like the place, sweet and exotic.

Turning to look at Franco, she discovered that he'd fallen asleep. An achy little pang twisted inside her: even in sleep he did not look comfortable. Tension clung to the perfect symmetry of his face, pulling his sensual mouth down at the corners. He had slipped his hand back inside his jacket to cover the area around his cracked ribs, while the other hand seemed be lightly gripping his injured thigh. Perhaps they should have gone to his apartment and not added the extra half-hour drive to Monfalcone, she considered worriedly. Perhaps she should have put up a much fiercer fight against his leaving the hospital in the first place.

'Not much longer now, *signora*.'

The quietness of Pietro's voice brought Lexi's anxious gaze into contact with the driver's mirror, where Pietro's dark eyes reflected the same concern that she was feeling over Franco, for he had noticed his discomfort too.

She sent Pietro a small nod to acknowledge his reassurance. 'The press?' she whispered.

'They gave up once they realised where we are going.'

To a house surrounded by acres of private land they would not dare to encroach upon, Lexi thought as she slid her gaze back to the window. Another mile or so and they would turn off the main highway to head towards the hill she could see rising up in the near distance. Once over the crest of that hill they would drop into a spectacularly beautiful valley, with rolling pastures and meadows gently dipping down towards the river that meandered its way the length of the valley on its way to the sea. Once they had crossed the ancient narrow stone bridge that forged the river they would be on Monfalcone land.

Great, she thought as they crested the hill, and unhappy memories began to surface of the long, lonely weeks she'd spent trying to make herself as invisible as possible in this breathtakingly beautiful but inhospitable place. She'd been her own worst enemy—so totally off the scale of hormonal upheaval that even small problems became huge mountainous things she just didn't know how to deal with.

As if by sheer homing instinct Franco stirred and opened his eyes as they slowed down to negotiate the narrow bridge over the river. Lexi saw him wince as he tried to change the position he'd been sleeping in.

'All right?' she questioned huskily.

'*Si,*' he said, but he wasn't, and the brief, tense, wry smile he turned on her pricked at that ache she'd been feeling. It was not going to go away any time soon.

From the bridge they drove onto a long and narrow undulating ribbon of tarmac flanked by two rows of elegant cypress trees that made a grand statement about the house they were heading towards even before it came into view. As the car sped them down the lane the sunlight blinked in and out between each evenly spaced tree trunk with perfect regularity. Lexi knew from experience the effect could be dangerously hypnotic if you didn't concentrate all your attention on the road ahead.

She knew because she'd fallen prey to it once, driving away from the house in floods of tears that had only helped to amplify the phenomenon, and she'd ended up crashing the car into one of the shallow drain ditches situated on the other side of the trees. How she'd missed making solid impact with a tree she would never know. She'd just been lucky, she supposed. Not that Francesco had seen her relatively soft landing nose-down in the ditch as fortunate. He'd been furious. He'd called her 'bloody reckless and stupid' as he'd hauled her body out of the crunched car in a rage.

'Were you hoping to kill yourself, or just the baby?'

Lexi shivered as the angry echo of his voice broke over her. She'd sobbed her heart out right there in the middle of the road, and he'd taken her in his arms and let her cry herself silent. As silent as Franco had been throughout the whole wretched weeping jag, while her little car had shone silver in the ditch and his flashy red one had simmered a couple of yards away, with its driver's door hanging open and the engine still running.

'I did not know what to say to you.'

The quietly deep, slightly constrained timbre of his voice brought her eyes round to look at him. He was staring out of the other window, but as she turned her head so did he, and she was snared in the sombre darkness of his eyes. Through the flickering play of sunlight across his face Lexi saw the bleakness of the same painful recollection.

'I was out of control.' She made the confession with husky thickness, because it was the first time she'd ever accepted that. 'I set out to make your life miserable and I succeeded.'

'You say that as if I behaved like a saint.' A grim smile clipped the corners of his mouth. 'You had too much to deal with at one time. You were carrying our baby. You had just lost your mother…'

And she'd known deep down that she should have lost him too, but she'd hung onto him—clung to him even while she'd hated him by then. Staring down at her hands where they lay pleated together on her lap, Lexi felt a tremor cross her lips. Yes, she'd been out of control, both emotionally and hormonally, long before she'd crashed her car into that ditch.

They'd come here from England after burying her mother. Franco had seen to everything, even though Bruce had insisted that *he* should do it. It was into the middle of that angry argument between the two men that she'd dropped the news that she was pregnant. Bruce had reacted by thumping Franco. Strangely, Franco had taken the punch without retaliating at all. He'd been too stunned by her announcement, she'd realised later, but at the time…

'I took the high-handed noble route and rushed you into marriage when what you really needed to do was to curl up somewhere on your own and grieve for your *mamma*…'

Poor Grace, who'd spent her life dreaming of fame, but whose death had made barely a ripple on the surface of the news media—while her daughter's hasty marriage to Francesco Tolle had earned headlines across two countries. He was right. She had been given no time to grieve before she'd been plunged into wedding arrangements right here at Monfalcone. No one here had met or even heard of Grace Hamilton. They had been strangers to Lexi—coldly polite strangers who disapproved of her because they believed she'd ruined Franco's life. They'd grieved for *him* while she'd just felt isolated, caged in by her own private grief she did not feel she could express. And the worst thing of all was that she'd known Franco had already started to cool their relationship before all the rest had happened.

San Remo… The place that had brought an end to their summer madness and begun their long winter of hell.

The car slowed down again, the cypress trees having given way to a high, neatly clipped box hedge that helped to hide the house from view. Two intricately designed iron gates bearing the Monfalcone crest in gold swung open in a gap in the hedge as they approached, and from there the full glory of a classical Italian garden opened up in front of them like some breath-takingly beautiful film set, complete with dancing fountains and lichen-stained statues surrounded by strictly regimented pathways edged by more low, clipped box hedge.

In the background stood Monfalcone, its deep gold stone walls basking in the afternoon sun. Once upon a time there had been a moat, complete with drawbridge to pull up across the coach entrance that led into the inner courtyard when feuding neighbours came to call. The moat had been filled in long ago. Now neat lawns formed a skirt around the outer walls, and the drawbridge had been replaced by another set of iron gates that Lexi had never seen closed.

As they plunged into the ink darkness of the deep stone

arch the sultry warm air developed such a distinct chill that Lexi shivered and goosebumps rose on her flesh. Then they were out again, and driving into a huge sunny courtyard where deep, gracefully arching upper and lower terraces flanked each wing of the house. When she'd first come here Lexi had been in awe of the sheer classical splendour of her surroundings. The interior was just as elegant as the exterior—a place of pale cool marble and richly polished wood and the kind of furniture collected through many centuries that somehow lived comfortably side by side.

On one level she'd loved this place for its surprisingly warm and relaxed form of living. On another level she'd hated it because she'd been so unhappy here. She wasn't sure how she was going to feel this time around—it probably depended on the memories evoked by coming back here.

Franco obviously did not have the same uncertainty, for he opened his door the moment the car came to a stop at the front entrance. The long hiss he made at his first attempt to get out of the car dragged Lexi's attention to him. As she'd feared, his bruised body had stiffened up during the journey, making it painful for him to move.

'Wait, I'll come round and help you,' she said quickly, and scrambled out of the car as Pietro did the same thing.

Gravel crunched beneath the soles of her boots as she shot around the back of the limo, only to find that Franco had already hauled himself upright and was standing in a ray of sunlight, his face turned up to it as if he was paying homage to its golden warmth.

Lexi pulled to a jerky standstill, her breath trapped in her throat. He looked so much taller and younger, strikingly handsome, and yet so very vulnerable standing there like that. She knew instinctively what he was doing. Not once in the last twenty-four hours had it occurred to her that he might have believed he would not live to see his home again, that coming back here had been the powerful force driving him today. Suddenly all the strange things Franco had been meting out since his accident were afforded a painful kind of sense in this moment of silent homage.

Then the two long glass-fronted doors swept open and Zeta appeared—a short round woman with silver hair swept back from her plump, anxious face. Her eyes barely grazed across Lexi before they swept to Franco.

'Just look at you,' she scolded him. 'You are not fit to be walking, never mind leaving the safety of the hospital. Are you crazy or something?'

'*Buongiorno*, Zeta,' Franco responded dryly. 'It is good to see you too.'

Zeta huffed out a breath, then threw up her hands as if in despair. 'If your *papà* had any wits left after you robbed him of them he would—'

'Do you think I could cross the threshold into my home before I am henpecked?' Franco cut in.

Quivering with wounded pride and emotion, the housekeeper stepped to one side of the doorway. Both Lexi and Pietro leapt to offer Franco support.

'I can do this by myself,' he ground out, making them all freeze, including Zeta, and watch as he pushed his long body into movement and managed to walk past the housekeeper without revealing so much as a hint of pain.

Once he'd made it into the house all three rushed to stand in the doorway, tense, like three runners standing on the starting line, ready to move with the sound of the gun.

Lexi wanted to yell at him that displays of macho pride and stubbornness did nothing for her! But he was already negotiating the stairs by then, and she swallowed the words whole in case she encouraged him to make a sudden movement that would cause him to lose his balance.

He did it. Mr Macho and Stubborn made it all the way up

those polished wood stairs to the galleried landing above. The moment he was safely there, Lexi released her pent-up tension with, 'I hope you feel very pleased with yourself for achieving that—because I don't!'

He turned his head to look down on her. 'Very pleased,' he admitted, and then one of his really charismatic rakish smiles appeared, to soften the strain from his features. 'Now you can come up and help me out of this uncomfortable suit.'

Arrogant too, she thought, and responded accordingly. She tossed up her chin and turned to Pietro. 'Either you go up there and help him, or I go up there and kill him,' she said, her eyes alight with simmering defiance.

Too late, she sensed Zeta's shock. Too late, she regretted her impulsive reaction. For the housekeeper was now recalling months of spitting rows and seething atmospheres.

Pietro just pressed a reassuring kiss to his wife's cheek, then bent to collect their bags, which he'd dropped to the floor ready to race to Franco's rescue if he'd started to sway.

'I will put your bags in your old room, *signora*,' he told Lexi, and headed off up the stairs.

Leaving Lexi facing a definitely disapproving house-keeper.

She could see that Zeta was envisaging a return to the hostilities of three years ago. Back then Lexi would have an-swered her look with burning defiance. This time she heaved out a wavering sigh instead. 'He knew he was pushing his luck too far when he said that,' she said in defence of her sharpness. 'And he frightened me… Hello, Zeta,' she con-cluded, and stuck out her hand in the hope that the Tolles' loyal housekeeper would see it as a proffered olive branch meant to try and put their past tense relationship aside.

After a few seconds of silent study Zeta nodded her head and took Lexi's hand. They were not quite up to hugging and kissing each other, but at least it was a start.

A start for what? The question pulled Lexi's breath up

short. She just had to work out what she was doing here, because—well, because it was beginning to feel permanent, and that was dangerous...

'What is she doing?' Franco asked as Pietro helped him out of his jacket.

'I believe I heard her threatening to kill you,' the older man responded evenly, and was rewarded with a crooked half smile, which quickly disappeared into a frown.

'We make her welcome here this time, Pietro,' he instructed grimly. 'It is important to me.'

'I know, sir.' Laying the jacket aside, Pietro turned to help Franco unbutton his shirt, but his hands were impatiently waved away.

Franco was aching all over, and all he wanted to do was fall onto his bed. Even heeling off his shoes was agony, and he wondered how the hell he'd managed to put the shoes on in the first place.

Bloody-minded willpower and a grim determination to be in control of what was happening around him and to him.

'I will do the rest.' He turned away from Pietro's hovering need to help. 'Find out if my wife—'

My wife... The possessive title sounded so alien on his tongue it stopped his thoughts stone dead. He had rarely called Lexi that even when they were together—he'd rarely thought about her in those terms.

Then he remembered the last time he'd used the possessive term—to Marco—and experienced a different type of pain.

'Check if she has eaten lunch today,' he said, frowning again. He knew he'd deliberately missed out the *my wife* part because he did not feel he had the right to use it—not yet, anyway.

'Have *you* eaten?' Pietro was still hovering like a man who needed to do something helpful, but all Franco could think of was lying down on that bed.

'Si,' he said, though it was not the truth—but it saved him having to deal with further questions over choices of food. Or—worse—Zeta turning her kitchen upside down and making him his all his favourite foods to tempt his appetite, like she'd used to do when he was a boy and sick with some childhood ailment. 'If you would tell Lexi—' No. He changed that, smiling crookedly again. 'If you would *ask* Lexi to come and see me after she has settled in?'

A silent nod and Pietro reluctantly departed. The moment the door closed behind him Franco gave up trying to remove his shirt and just rolled down carefully onto the bed. He would lie there for a couple of minutes to get his breath back, then...

The lingering effects of the drugs still moving around his system and exhaustion from the journey claimed him like a heavy blanket, and Franco knew nothing else.

He certainly did not know that Lexi had taken time for a shower and to change out of her dark city clothes, which were sticking to her overheated skin, into one of her new dresses that were more in keeping with a late summer in Italy. Then Zeta had arrived with a tray of tea and light pastries, which she'd discovered she was hungry enough to sit down and enjoy.

Over an hour later she let herself out of the suite she had been allocated all those years ago—two whole wings of the house away from Franco's suite. Once deeply intimate lovers turned into married strangers, she mused as she walked the long corridors. What had the separate bedrooms said about their chance of making anything of their fated marriage? About as much chance as they'd both allowed it—which was basically none.

A grimace worked its way across her lips as she arrived at Franco's door. About to lay a soft knock on it, she stalled her knuckles half an inch from their target when she heard a muffled noise that sounded very like a broken sob. A jolt of alarm had her bypassing the polite knock, and she just grabbed the handle and pushed the door open—only to freeze in dismay at the scene that met her unsuspecting gaze.

Franco was sitting on the side of his bed and he was not alone. Claudia Clemente, Marco's beautiful sister, was kneeling at his feet between his spread thighs, her red-tipped fingers clutching at his head while she sobbed into his chest.

Almost anyone else walking in on this moving scene would have felt their heart rend in aching sympathy for both Franco and Claudia, but to Lexi it felt as if someone had reached into her chest and yanked her heart out. She would not have been surprised if she'd turned to stone where she stood. For Claudia was the woman who'd sent proof of that bet to her mobile phone years ago. She was also the woman Franco had spent the night with while Lexi had lost their baby and grieved alone.

CHAPTER SIX

THROBBING with the need to just turn around, walk out of there and never come back again, Lexi felt nailed to the spot by the rush of emotions that flooded inside her. She was hurting. She was hurting so badly she might as well have been standing there like this three and a half years ago, witnessing their betrayal. They even had a bed there as a gut jerking prop.

A barely controllable desire to go over there and yank the dainty, black clad figure away from Franco and then punch him on his red lipstick stained mouth almost got the better of her. At that precise moment she did not care that Claudia was Marco's kid sister, or that the two of them had every excuse to be indulging in a moment of shared agony.

How had Claudia got in here anyway? Had Zeta let her in? Pietro? One of the maids? Did Claudia have such a free run of this house that she could stroll into Franco's bedroom without needing permission from anyone?

As if she'd been dropped behind a haze of misty red, she watched as Franco glanced up and noticed her standing here.

'Lexi,' he murmured, and sounded so thick and strained that the swinging punch scenario replayed itself in her head. He was either really turned on or close to tears, and the latter she refused to accept—mainly because it just didn't suit the unforgiving frame of mind she was in.

It clearly didn't suit him either, because she saw two streaks of colour shoot high across his cheeks.

Guilty and with an eye witness, she noted.

She hated him.

Claudia lifted her face up off his chest and turned her beautiful dark head. She was two years older than Lexi. Once upon a time those two years had felt more like a decade to Lexi, in smooth sophistication and worldly experience. Now the age-gap felt like nothing at all, and Claudia's amazing sloe-shaped bottomless black eyes were still the most exotically beautiful eyes she had ever seen. She looked nothing like her light-haired, blue-eyed brother. She certainly did not have Marco's sunny temperament. Claudia was devious, calculating and jealously possessive of both her brother and of Franco.

'Lexi,' Marco's beautiful sister whispered as she climbed slowly to her feet. 'I did not expect to see you here.'

Lexi believed it. Claudia was so visibly shocked to see her standing there she could not contain the horror from sounding in her voice.

Lexi did not spare Franco another glance. Her insides had gone into meltdown and were churning up with the ugliest kind of bitterness. It took all of her control to keep breathing in and out. She kept her eyes focused on Claudia, who was wearing the silver wash of tears glistening on the tips of her long black eyelashes.

Crocodile tears? No, that was just too mean for her even to think it.

Claudia had just lost her beloved brother, after all. Of course she would want to come here and commiserate with Franco over their mutual loss. She had the right.

But it was still difficult for Lexi to part her bloodless lips and murmur, 'Hello, Claudia,' peeling her tense fingers off the door handle and still feeling the tension in them when she dropped them to her sides.

Deep breath, Lexi. Walk forward, she instructed her legs, which tingled because they did not want her to go anywhere near Claudia Clemente. 'I'm so very sorry about Marco.'

At least that was a genuine response. She offered commiserating kisses to the other woman's cheeks and felt Claudia's floral perfume dry her throat. From the corner of her eye she caught the way Franco's facial muscles clenched when she said Marco's name.

Well, too late for that, she thought, with a cold feeling that sat like a lump where her understanding and sympathy should be. With Claudia here there was no way he could avoid talking about Marco. With Claudia here there was no way he could continue pretending the accident had not happened, or that Lexi was the only person he could bear to have close.

'Oh, please don't say his name,' Claudia begged, and her fabulous eyes filled up with fresh tears. 'I think I am going to die from my grief.'

As a sob broke free from her throat Lexi felt a pang of guilt for suspecting the quality of her grief. Whatever else Claudia was that she despised, she could not take away from her that she'd adored her older brother. Pushing her own stony feelings aside, Lexi plucked a box of tissues from the bedside table and quietly encouraged Claudia to dry her tears.

'I had to come,' Claudia explained once she'd regained control again. 'I knew that Franco would be tormenting himself. I needed to tell him that we do not hold him to blame.'

Well, that was truly thoughtful and caring of her, but while Claudia was busy dabbing her eyes Franco had closed his eyes and was turning that sickly shade of grey.

'And M-Mamma and Papa needed to know if he would be well enough to attend M-Marco's funeral next Tuesday.'

'We will be there.' The man himself spoke at last. Then he fell into deep, dark, husky Italian, spoken too fast for Lexi to follow; but that sent Claudia to her knees again, her arms locking tightly around his neck.

Lexi removed herself over to the window and stayed there until Claudia made her final farewells and eventually left. The ensuing silence hung like a woodchopper's axe, hesitating over the downward slice that would split them clean in two.

Three and a half years was a long time to hang onto such a poisonous grudge, she tried hard to tell herself. She'd grown up an awful lot in those years, so it was logical that Claudia had done the same thing.

Deep down, though, she didn't believe that Marco's sister *had* changed. She'd seen something in the possessive trail of the other woman's fingers as they'd let go of Franco, and in the way she hadn't been able to resist bruising his lips with a final kiss before she'd dragged herself away from him.

The atmosphere she'd left behind pulsated with Lexi's continued silence.

What am I doing here?

Once again she asked herself that question. Franco needed people like Claudia around him—friends, family, lovers who would gently ease his grief out into the open.

'What's wrong, Lexi?' he murmured quietly.

'How did she get in here?' she asked.

'She arrived a few minutes ago. I could not deny her need to see me.'

She twisted around to look at him. 'In your bedroom?'

'I was asleep.' Raking slightly unsteady fingers through his hair, he explained, 'Zeta woke me to tell me that Claudia was here. Apparently she had driven here directly from the hospital after discovering I—we had left.'

Lexi nodded her head. It was weird how she was feeling—kind of closed off and iced over. 'You talked with her about Marco?'

Rubbing his hands over his face, Franco nodded. 'What time is it?' He frowned down at his watch. He was still using the same blocking tactics against her where Marco was concerned, Lexi noted. 'I could do with a drink. My mouth is parched. Do you want one?' He was reaching for the house phone beside the bed.

'If you like I can call Claudia back in here and let her share a drink with us,' Lexi suggested coolly.

'What is this?' He frowned. 'So you walked in here and found Claudia in my bedroom? It isn't as if I am in a fit state to seduce the poor woman. You always were a jealous cat about her.'

'Marco said—'

'Marco is not here any longer to say anything!' Driving himself to his feet, he groaned and struggled to gain his balance.

His shirt was hanging open, Lexi saw. His trousers resting low on his waist. He was no longer strapped up there, she noticed, and the extent of his bruising was horribly dark. Unable to stop her eyes from following the shock of dark hair that ran down his front, she imagined a pair of red tipped fingers stroking over him and felt her insides grow hard.

'Marco once warned me that you would probably end up marrying Claudia,' she persisted despite his attempt to head her off. 'He believed the two of you were made for each other—that bringing your two volatile temperaments together would be like capturing forked lightning.'

'Explosive?' Franco said dryly. 'I am not volatile. You are the volatile one in this relationship.'

But they did not have a relationship—that was the whole point! They had a marriage certificate, a load of miserable memories to share, and that was *all* they had!

'I'm going out for a walk.' Lexi made the decision on impulse; but once she had made it she discovered that she couldn't get out of there fast enough.

On a growl of pure frustration, Franco raked out, 'What the hell has got into you?'

Lexi whipped out through the door before he could say

anything else. Inside she was a shaking mess of pain and—oh, God—fear. Fear because she knew she was already emotionally involved again. Attached, attracted, needy and jealous and—

'You go out, *signora?*' One of the maids she remembered from the last time she was here was crossing the hall as Lexi walked quickly towards the rear of the house.

Biting into the inner tissue of her tense lips Lexi nodded her head. 'I need some fresh air,' she mumbled, making a hasty exit.

Once outside, she crossed the terracotta floor of the shady loggia that ran the length of the back of the house, then walked down the steps into the gardens—that spread out in front of her without the rigid formality so carefully nurtured at the front. Several gravel pathways wound their lazy way through informal flowerbeds down towards a small lake she could see glinting a short distance away, beyond the assortment of fruit trees that dappled the paths with leafy shade from the heat of the sun.

She did not know where she was going, though the lake seemed to lure her. Inside she felt as if she'd been switched off like a light.

Upstairs, standing in the window, Franco watched her make her bid for escape with a grating sense of déjà-vu. Cursing softly, because every movement was such damn agony, he looked around for his mobile phone, accessed Lexi's number, and rang it.

She did not have her phone with her, he realised a minute later. Frustration biting at his temper, he walked across the room and headed out onto the landing, then strode the corridors to Lexi's wing of the house. This was something that was about to change around here, he decided grimly as he let himself into her room, then stood for a few seconds, needing to catch his laboured breathing before he went to hunt down her bag and pluck her mobile phone from its capacious depths.

Back in his own room, he used the house phone to relay instructions to Zeta about where his wife would be sleeping tonight, then instructed the housekeeper to send one of the maids to him.

Lexi had located the old wooden bench she'd remembered stood by the lake shore, and was sitting there with her eyes narrowed against the water's sunny glint, waiting for the scrambling clutch of emotions she was suffering to calm down so that she could try to think.

About what? she asked herself tartly. About why you are here? About what you want to do next? You keep refusing to examine why you are here, and you don't have a clue what you want to do next.

A maid appeared beside the bench, arriving panting, as if she'd come down here at a run. 'Signor Francesco ask me to bring you this, *signora*,' she explained breathlessly, and handed Lexi her mobile phone.

It rang the instant the maid had turned and disappeared back up the path towards the house.

'You sent someone to my room to rummage through my bag for my phone,' she fired at him before he had a chance to speak.

'I went and got it for myself,' Franco informed her. 'And *don't*,' he warned, 'start lecturing me on whether striding around the house in my present condition is good for my health, because I know that it isn't. What the hell has got into you, Lexi? Why the sudden icy exit?'

Lexi wanted to tell him. In fact she wondered why she had never told him before—three and a half years ago, when it would perhaps have meant something—but she'd run away from facing him with his unfaithfulness that time too.

'The past is catching up with me,' she mumbled, and wished she had not heard the thickness of tears threatening her voice. 'And you won't let me talk about it.'

'Don't start crying, *cara*,' he warned huskily. 'I will be

forced to come down there to you if you do. I know we have to talk about the past.'

Rolling her lips together to try and stop them from trembling, she asked, 'Can I talk about Marco too?'

'No,' he rasped.

'Your relationship with Claudia, then?'

'Claudia and I do not have a relationship,' he denied impatiently. 'Not the kind you are implying anyway.'

Lexi watched the pair of resident white swans move across the glass smooth surface of the lake, leaving triangular ripples in their wake. Swans mated with the same partner for life, she recalled, for some reason only the convoluted inner workings of her own mind could follow. It took a lot of care and trust to be so steadfast and loyal to one person.

Something that she and Franco had never had.

'I hate you,' she whispered, which seemed to tie in somehow with the thoughts preceding it.

'No, you don't. You hate yourself for still caring about me when you don't want to care. Come back up here to me and we will talk about that if you want,' he encouraged.

Lexi gave a slow mute shake of her head.

'I saw that,' he sighed.

'From where?' Jumping to her feet, Lexi spun round, expecting to find him walking down the path towards her, but she saw nothing but garden and leafy tree branches.

'From my bedroom window.'

Looking up, Lexi tracked her eyes along the upper terrace until she found his window. Her breathing pulled to a stop. She could just make out his tall figure against the long pane of glass.

'You should be lying down or something.'

'Then have some pity on me,' he said wearily. 'I ache all over, and I can do without the dramatic trip down memory lane right now, where you storm out and I have to work out what the hell I have done to cause it this time.'

But Lexi gave another shake of her head. 'You're bad for me, Franco,' she told him sadly. 'I know I shouldn't even be here with you, and…and I don't want to become attached to you again.'

'Madre de Dio,' he growled, then added a torrent of angry Italian that he did not know if she could follow. Switching to English, he said fiercely, 'I want you to become attached to me again! Why do you think I asked you to come back to me in the first place?'

'I don't know…'

'But you came anyway.'

Yes, she'd come anyway. 'Did you crash your boat because I'd sent you those divorce papers?'

Another set of angry curses was followed by an explosive, *'No.'*

'Then how did it happen?'

A band of pain across Franco's chest tightened, catching at his breath. He didn't want to think about that yet—not now. Perhaps later, when— 'Come back up here or I will come down there to you,' he warned again. 'In fact I am already walking towards the door—'

Watching him disappear from the window, Lexi cut the connection and started running—fast. She knew she'd been bluffed the moment she arrived in his room, to find him sprawled in the chair by the window, looking pathetically weak and endearingly bad-tempered as he waged an uneven battle with the cufflinks still anchoring his shirt cuffs to his wrists.

'Help me with these,' he ground out in frustration, cutting short whatever she'd been about to say to him as he slumped back in the chair and closed his eyes as if the small task had exhausted him.

Crossing the room to his side, she squatted down. 'Is your vision still bad?' she queried, taking hold of his wrist so she could work the first gold link free.

'No,' he grunted, annoyed that she could be so damn perceptive. 'What made you just walk out?'

'I don't like the rules you've set up around here.' Having freed that cufflink, she made him wince when she reached across him to lift up his other wrist—the one on his injured side. 'If you can allow a visit from Claudia then I don't see why you can't let in the rest of your friends and family as well.'

'Claudia is a special case—*ouch*,' he complained.

'Sorry,' Lexi said. 'I accept that she has to be a special case, but...' Her hair was getting in her way as she bent over the task in hand, and she paused to loop the long tresses back behind her ear, meeting Franco's fingers as they arrived to do the same thing. Like an idiot, she glanced up and caught the full power of his glowing dark gaze as the back of his fingers stroked against her warm cheek. Sensation erupted with a swirling coil of sensual heat low down in her belly.

'But what?' he prompted distractedly.

Lexi struggled to remember what she had been going to say. In fact she was struggling to think of anything other than that look in his eyes that she knew so well. 'Your rules are irrationally selective,' she managed to finish. 'Or is it just me you don't want to discuss the accident and Marco with?'

'I need a shower. Care to join me?' he invited softly, gently stroking her hair back behind her ear so that she quivered.

More blocking tactics, she thought, and decided to ignore him for a change. Frowning, she dragged her attention back to releasing the second cufflink, then she sighed, sitting back on her heels and thereby removing herself from his easy reach.

In a way it was a mistake: it gave him leave to run his eyes over the green print summer dress she had changed into, its short swirly skirt leaving a lot of naked leg on show.

That coil of heat tightened its grip on her. 'Stop looking at me like that.' Getting up, she turned away from him.

'Like what?'

'Like you have the strength to do what you're thinking.'

'You believe I'm too feeble to at least try?'

Walking across the room to lay the cufflinks down on top of a glossy wooden chest of drawers, Lexi turned and leant back against it, folding her arms. 'Tell me why you brought me to Italy,' she demanded up front.

At first she thought he was not going to answer. His silence stretched along with the steady way he was looking at her. Then he eased out a controlled sigh and heaved himself to his feet so he could slip off the shirt. The moment he did so Lexi began to feel vulnerable, as if she was suddenly being placed under threat. Yet what could he do to her? He might like to believe he was physically able to take on the seduction of a protesting woman, but she could see he was already swaying on his feet.

He was like a man of two halves, she found herself thinking. One half darkly, painfully battered and bruised; the other half pure, golden male, glowing with robust health. Even the dark bruising did not detract from what she could see was all attractively smooth and tight. He'd bulked out in the years since she'd last seen him like this, she observed, running her gaze over his wide shoulders, then his bulging pectoral muscles and the beautifully ridged stomach, unaware that her breathing had shortened or that her fingers were clenching and unclenching where she held them tucked away beneath her arms.

'I had an epiphany.'

Blinking rapidly in an attempt to clear her head, Lexi dragged her eyes back up to his face, saw he'd been watching her look at him, and felt guilty heat pour into her face.

'Excuse me?' she murmured.

His dark eyes narrowed, glinting knowingly, 'An epiphany,' he repeated. 'About my life and what I wanted to do with it.'

An epiphany… Rolling the tip of her tongue over her lips,

Lexi straightened up and dropped her arms to her sides—though she wasn't sure why she needed to do it. 'And this epiphany told you what?'

'That it was time to win my wife back,' he enlightened her. 'Time to put aside the bad stuff and get our marriage back on track.'

'It was never on track—'

'To place our marriage on a good solid track, then.' The flick of a hand tossed semantics to one side.

'Stay where you are,' Lexi told him jerkily when he started crossing the space separating them. 'When—when did you have this epiphany?'

'Does it matter?' He didn't stop walking.

'Yes.' Lexi knew why she'd straightened up now. Even battered and bruised Franco could be incredibly intimidating—if only because her senses liked it when he came over all domineering and broodingly macho.

'When I finally accepted how miserable I was without you.'

'Y-you were even more miserable with me,' she reminded him, feeling one of the rounded brass knobs on the chest of drawers dig into her back as she backed off more the closer he came.

'I know. That is why I called it an epiphany.' He came to a stop six inches away. 'Like a sudden leap of intuitive understanding that told me I was miserable with you but more miserable without you.' He added a small descriptive shrug. 'It is as simple and as crazy as that.'

'You said it.' Wishing she could stop looking at his half bruised, hair roughened torso, she asked tartly, 'Were you suffering from another epiphany when you had Claudia clasped to your wounded chest?'

'That was sympathy.'

'Show *me* some, then, and take a long step back.'

'So you can escape?'

'Yes,' Lexi nodded. 'You know I won't physically make you do it when you're all bruised like that.'

'Ah—you are attempting to appeal to my sense of fair play?'

Lexi pressed her lips together and nodded her head again. If there was one thing she knew for absolute certain about Franco it was his sporting sense of fair play.

'Look at me, then—up here where my eyes are.' He indicated with the movement of one of his hands. 'Just one brief eye to eye contact, *cara*, and I promise I will step back.'

Thinking it was a bit like asking her to strip naked—because making eye contact with Franco had much the same effect on her already edgy senses—Lexi pushed out a short sigh then lifted up her chin.

He dared to smile, with his lips and his eyes—a tender kind of gentle humour that struck like a flaming arrow directly at her heart. 'I wish you weren't so handsome,' she told him wistfully. 'Why couldn't you have a bigger nose, or something? Or a fat, ugly mouth?'

'You know…' Reaching out to run his hands around her slender waist, he carefully drew her closer. 'Your open honesty will shame the devil one day.'

'Are you the devil in question?' She didn't even try to stop her progress towards him.

Franco grimaced. 'Probably… I suppose—yes…' he admitted. 'Because I am about to break my promise to you, and…' He did not bother to finish the sentence; he just closed the gap between their mouths.

It was like taking flight without wings to help her control her take-off, and the worst thing was she didn't even try to put up a fight. She was just a pathetic pushover, she told herself, moving closer until she felt the tips of her breasts catch hold of the heat emanating from his chest, parting her lips and sighing a helpless little sigh he caught with the sensual dip of his tongue. He kissed her until she melted against him, until she was mimicking his tongue with her own and feeling the rise of desire, tasting it like some rare, delicious fruit you could only obtain from this one source. As she let her hands drift upwards to stroke the firm muscles and smooth skin covering his arms she felt a fine tremor run through him.

Dangerous, she tried to tell herself. This—him—us.

And then she tasted the lipstick. Claudia's lipstick. It had to be Claudia's because she wasn't wearing any. And that, she thought as she pulled her head back, was the reason why being anywhere near Franco was dangerous. He could warm her right through and contrarily chill her to her bone at the same time.

His eyes narrowed at her sudden withdrawal. Lexi feathered down her own eyelashes so he could not pierce into her thoughts.

'May I go now?' she requested coolly.

Tension was suddenly flashing between them, like microwaves probing deep into her flesh, and she almost wilted with relief when he recovered his sense of fair play, dropping his arms from her and taking the promised step back.

Mouth dry, heart just an aching squeeze in her chest, without saying another word Lexi stepped around him and walked out of the room.

Watching her depart, Franco was still puzzling over what had turned her off like that when he raised a set of fingers to his kiss warmed mouth. Something made him glance down. He saw the red lipstick he'd forgotten to wipe away after Claudia's kisses—and let loose a string of soft curses aimed exclusively at himself for being such a thoughtless, insensitive swine.

For the next twenty-four hours Lexi avoided him. She didn't even go to his room to protest that he'd had her moved to the suite next door to his. Zeta took him meals to tempt his appetite, only to bring them back again barely touched, and she informed Lexi she was worried because he was too exhausted to eat. The housekeeper complained that he was working up there on his laptop and refusing to lie down to rest on his bed. She conveyed her displeasure to Lexi, who spent the evening curled up on a sofa watching television and didn't seem to care what he was doing.

Lexi was training herself not to care.

When it was time for bed she went to her new room without bothering to go in and check how he was. She just pulled on one of her new silk nighties and slipped between the cool linen sheets, switched off the lights and willed herself to sleep. The next morning she walked several circuits of the lake after breakfast, stopping to coax the resident swans with some bread she'd stolen from the breakfast table. She knew that Franco was standing on the upper terrace watching her; though she didn't once glimpse his tall figure standing there the couple of times she allowed herself to glance up.

She had her mobile phone tucked into one of the pockets of the flowery dress she'd put on with its fashionably fitted bodice and full skirt.

But he didn't call her.

It was like a war of attrition. The problem was that Lexi knew she was waging this particular war all by herself. She wanted to avoid him but she wanted him to call her. Where was the sense in that?

She thought he might come down for lunch, but he didn't. She hoped he would arrive when Zeta served her afternoon tea on the lower terrace overlooking the lake, but was informed by the satisfied housekeeper that at last he was sleeping on his bed and the laptop was shut.

By dinner time Lexi was losing the battle—the part that was supposed to be training her to stop caring about him, anyway—and she knew, just *knew*, she was about to give in. It came over her like one of those uncontrollable rushes of weakness that made you do nonsensical things. She'd gone up to her room to wash and change before dinner, but found herself hovering outside his door instead.

Zeta had told her he was still sleeping. Taking a quick peek at him while he slept wasn't the same as going in there cold, so to speak, having to face him with her own weakness, she convinced herself.

But it was just the same, and Lexi knew it even as she twisted the handle and pushed open the door. She knew it as she stepped inside and closed the door behind her, leaning against it and breathing fast, as if she was a naughty child up to mischief. Dusk had fallen and the twin lamps beside the bed cast gentle light across the room. The long windows stood open to the soft evening breeze coming in from the garden, and as she breathed in she caught the clean scent of his soap in her nostrils before she allowed herself to look towards the bed.

He wasn't there. Her heart started to pump that bit faster. His bathroom door stood open, so she could see that he wasn't in there. Aware that her limbs had acquired a spongy sensation, making her feel nervously strung out, she pushed away from the door and walked across the room to the only other place she could think he might be.

Stepping outside onto the terrace, she found him sitting on one of the chairs out there with his long legs stretched out in front of him, his feet resting on another chair. He was dressed in pale chinos and a soft pale blue cambric shirt. No socks inside the casual slip-ons he wore on his golden brown feet. On the table beside him stood an uncorked bottle of red wine and two long-stemmed glasses. As he heard her step and turned his dark head to look at her Lexi knew by his steady regard that it was game over.

He knew that she knew she was giving up the fight—with herself.

CHAPTER SEVEN

HE RAISED his hand and held it out to her. That was all it took to draw her to him. Lexi walked the few metres and placed her hand in his. His fingers closed around her fingers, warm, slightly callused, strong.

'Glass of wine?' he asked her.

'Please,' she said, but it was barely a whisper that scraped over her dry throat.

Dropping his feet to the floor he stood up. She noticed straight away that his movements were smooth and lithe—pain free. As if he'd planned everything down to the smallest detail he drew her closer to his side, slid her captured hand around his waist then let go of it so he could pour out the wine without them losing physical contact.

He handed her a glass, which she took with her other hand. 'To us,' he said, and chinked their glasses together, then waited like some powerful dark force for her to raise her glass to her lips.

'To us—or now.' Lexi found she had just enough fight left in her to extend the toast before she raised the glass and sipped from it.

It took him a moment or two to accept what she'd said before he lifted his own glass and drank.

In some dark place inside her Lexi knew she wanted to weep. Maybe he could sense it. Maybe he was aware that no matter how much she wanted him she did not want *this*. Because he released a small sigh, placed his glass back on the table and took her glass to do the same thing with it, then turned to take her fully into his arms.

'One small step at a time, hmm?' he murmured, alongside the kiss he pressed to the top of her silky head.

Lexi lifted her face to look at him, the swirling blue-green in her eyes mocking him for saying such a thing when they both knew that what was going to happen next was not going to be anything like a small step. And, anyway, she had already taken a huge step just by coming here to him, so thinking small did not come close to where she wanted to go with this.

'Of course if small is all you can manage right now...' she posed, in an attempt to make light of things.

Franco laughed—not a throw-back-his-head kind of laugh, but a low down, deep-into-his-chest kind of sexy, dark and very masculine laugh. 'I don't know what I'm up for,' he confessed with rueful honesty, 'though we could make it interesting finding out...'

Lexi turned to release a small, slightly shaky laugh. Franco felt some of the tension ease out of her slender frame. He felt the same easing out of himself. He'd achieved something here he hadn't dared expect to achieve. He'd brought down her defences without needing to touch on all the ugly stuff still waiting in the background for its moment to shatter them both.

Whether that was being fair to her or not he did not want to consider right now. She was here. She was acknowledging that she wanted—no, *needed* to be here with him. He turned with her still pressed against him and walked them both inside.

In the soft light of the room he drew her round in front of him and, as if it was the most natural thing for them to do, their lips came together to embrace. She stepped in that bit closer, lifted her slender arms and slid them around his neck. As he buried his fingers in the loose silken flow of her hair he caught her soft whisper just before she took the initiative and deepened the kiss to an open-mouthed probe of hungry passion that unfurled her longing for him like an exquisite flowering that made her ache.

Her cheeks were flushed when eventually he eased back from her; a terrible shyness Lexi had not experienced even the first time she'd been with him kept her eyes fixed on the open collar of his shirt, and the feelings dancing around inside her made her feel quivery and weak. 'I suppose we should go down and eat dinner f-first,' she heard herself mumble.

'Bailing out on me already?' he quizzed.

Not so you would notice, Lexi thought as he trailed his fingers down the length of her back. It was enough to make her body arch into closer contact with him.

'Zeta will come looking for me if I don't go down.'

His answer to that problem was to step back from her and stride across the room to pick up the house phone. The husky lowness of his voice as he spoke to the housekeeper fired up the heat in Lexi's face.

'Now she knows what we're doing,' she protested as he walked back to her.

'We are man and wife. Holding back dinner while we make love is not a hanging offence.'

'Yes, but—'

He stopped walking. 'You want to eat first?'

Oh, for goodness' sake, Lexi thought hectically. She didn't know what she wanted! 'I want to be with you but I don't want to be with you!' The confession arrived as a cry from the heart.

'I know that,' he answered gently.

'I w-want to go home to London and forget all about you but I can't make myself do it!'

'I know that too.'

'And—and asking me if I want to eat first like we're making a date for sex isn't helping me here!'

'Then I will rephrase the question. Do you want to eat, make love or fight?'

None of them—all of them! Throwing up her hands in an agitated gesture of confused defeat, she let her blue-green eyes flicker over him. He stood about three feet away, exuding the grave patience of a saint. Her man. Her lover. Her only lover! Married to him. His ring circled her finger. His name had become her name almost four years ago; yet she couldn't recall a single time that she'd used it outside Italy.

'We were so young,' she breathed, for some reason she couldn't follow right now. 'Nineteen and twenty-four when we met, Franco. It should have been the great holiday romance of a lifetime and ended at that.'

'But it didn't.'

'No.' Folding her arms, Lexi hugged herself tightly. 'We got pregnant.'

A pained look passed across his face and he lifted up that hand again. 'Lexi—'

'We are still young,' she whispered with a shake of her head. 'I should be out clubbing every night and—and trying out different men for the hell of it. And you should be out there sowing wild oats all over the place and—and crashing your super-macho boats.'

That made him laugh. Lexi didn't blame him, she almost laughed herself, but... 'This—epiphany you had about us,' she posed unsteadily. 'It could collapse into rubble once you've got over the accident and sorted out your emotions about Marco.'

'What was your epiphany?'

Lexi blinked at him. 'I didn't have one. You did.'

'Then why are you here with me right now, *cara*. What drove you back here into my life?'

Hearing just one tiny four-letter word whisper its powerful song in her head sent the tip of her tongue in an anxious flurry across her trembling upper lip. 'You were hurt—'

'I am healing. You are still here.' Heaving out a sigh, he started moving again, closing the gap between them so he could take hold of her defensively folded arms and prise them apart. 'I have made a decision. We go downstairs and eat dinner like a respectable old married couple without an ounce of gloriously impulsive passion left.'

'You're angry with me?'

'No,' he denied, trailing her out onto the landing. 'I am trying my best to give you what you feel you need right now.'

'Aggro and frustration?'

'If the label fits, Lexi.'

Lexi tried to tug to a standstill outside her bedroom door. 'I need to change and…'

'You look amazing as you are,' Franco informed her. 'All sun-kissed and healthy after the amount of exercise you have been expending beside the lake, trying to stop yourself from coming to me.'

'So you *were* watching me.' She sighed as he drew her with him down the stairs.

'Each wistful sigh, each stubborn shake of your beautiful head, each furtive glance to check if I was standing there.'

'I didn't see you.'

'I hid like a spy on secret surveillance.'

They entered the small dining room to be greeted by the flickering light from candles and the sight of the table already set for two.

Lexi pulled to a stop. 'You were coming down for dinner?'

'Mmm,' he murmured, 'but you came to visit me and spoiled my surprise.'

She'd given in too soon. That was what he was saying. If

she'd hung out just a little bit longer she could have saved herself a soul crunching loss of pride.

Zeta arrived then, coming to a halt in surprise when she saw the two of them. 'I thought you said—'

'We changed our minds,' Franco cut in ruefully. 'Apparently, at the age of twenty-eight, I am too old for impulsive bursts of lusty passion.'

Lexi flushed up to the roots of her shining hair and sent him a glowering glance. He just laughed huskily as he politely held out one of the chairs for her, then brushed a kiss across her hot cheek before he took the other chair.

Watching the way he moved, Lexi was becoming more aware of the difference a short twenty-four hours had made in him. His colour was good—fabulous, actually, she amended, watching the candlelight catch the lean golden contours of his face.

They ate their food and indulged in minor light dinner table talk, which was fine so long as she kept her vision slightly out of focus when she looked at him. However, there was nothing light about what was prowling around them, like a hungry tiger waiting for its moment to pounce on them both.

'Tell me about these dozens of men you've been testing out while clubbing,' he invited suddenly.

Now, there was an exaggeration if ever there was one, Lexi mused grimacingly, 'It's bad taste to kiss and tell,' she deflected smoothly.

'Dayton must disapprove.'

Lexi watched the candlelight flicker across the long stemmed, crystal glass she was fingering and felt a twinge of guilt over Bruce. 'Bruce has just gone on the banned list,' she stated flatly.

'But he is such a major part of your life—'

'Are you ready to talk about Marco?' She shot the challenge from the hip and watched his expression shut down like a door slamming shut across his face.

'No.'

'Why not?'

'Tell me about your childhood.'

Lexi pulled a face as that imaginary door slammed a second time. 'Not much to tell.' Reaching out, she spooned up a portion of Zeta's homemade crème caramel and placed it in a dish. 'I lived the first ten years of my life with my grandmother—'

'Where was your mother?' Franco frowned.

'Working,' Lexi said. 'It's the nature of the acting beast. She was in touring rep a lot then, and living out of a suitcase, so my grandmother brought me up. When she died, Grace had to take over caring for me, which basically meant leaving me in the care of a succession of friends in different cities while she had to work.'

'That sounds much like the succession of nannies who had the pleasure of bringing me up after my mother died,' Franco murmured.

'Oh, poor little rich boy,' Lexi teased him. 'Your father thinks the absolute world of you and you know it.'

'He was busy. He adored me when he had the time. If I wasn't rattling around this huge place on my own, I was living in at a boarding school for rich kids.'

'Is that where you met Marco?' Lexi dared.

It didn't gain her anything but the sight of his lips snapping together, before he parted them again and said, 'We were talking about *your* childhood.'

'Well, I didn't make many friends.' She grimaced. 'It's kind of difficult to form lasting friendships when you're forever on the move like a travelling circus. Here—try some of this...' Spooning up a portion of the dessert, she placed the dish in front of him. 'It's the most delicious thing I've tasted in years.'

'So which did you prefer? The travelling circus or living with your grandmother?' he probed, lifting up his spoon.

'Oh, my grandmother,' Lexi responded instantly. 'She was a bit strict—scared, I think, that I might turn out to be what she called "frivolous" like Grace, but overall we got on well together.'

'And your father? Did he have no part to play in your life back then?'

A part to play? She would have had to know who he was for him to have done that. 'Why are you asking me all these questions about my past?' she asked him, frowning as she sat back in her chair. 'You were never interested about where I came from before.'

'That is why I am asking now.'

'Well, don't.' Sitting forward again, she spooned up some of the crème caramel but couldn't quite make herself lift it to her mouth. So she laid it back in the dish, glanced up, saw the way he was studying her. The shimmering glint going on between those sooty eyelashes made her feel more prickly the longer his scrutiny went on.

'What?' she snapped when she could stand it no longer, defiant and defensive at the same time.

'I think I have inadvertently hit a tender nerve,' he drawled slowly.

'No. I just don't understand your sudden interest.'

'You are my wife—'

'Estranged wife.' Why did that sound so wrong right now? Reaching out to pick up her wine glass, Lexi sat glaring into its contents. So they were sitting here, eating a meal together like husband and wife. So they were intending to go from here to the same bed and—well—do what married couples usually did and sleep together—in every sense. Half an hour ago they'd almost missed dinner and headed straight for the bed. But none of the above made them a married couple, and definitely did not make him a husband and her a wife.

It never had the last time she'd lived here as his wife. She'd been plonked in a suite two wings away from him like some bad germ it was best to keep as far away from him as possible. And he hadn't complained. He hadn't kicked up a fuss or had her moved to the suite next door to him like he'd done this time. He'd visited her like a reluctant but rigidly polite host, with polite knocks on her door and polite enquiries as to her health, every single morning before he'd left for work, she recalled; and she felt the same bleak emptiness fill her now that had used to fill her up back then.

He'd looked so tall and breathtakingly handsome, wearing a business suit that had made him look oddly younger—when it should have been the other way round. Because the guy who'd lived in shorts and a T-shirt all through the summer should have looked the younger one.

'Lexi…' he prompted softly.

'I don't have a father,' she announced.

'Everyone has a father, *cara*,' he drawled.

'Well, I don't. Now, change the subject.'

He was lounging back in his chair now, which placed his face out of the flickering light from the candles so she couldn't read his expression. But she could feel the cogs in his brain turning over, feel him pondering whether to push her a bit more into opening up for him.

Then he took in a short breath. 'If it upsets you this much then I offer you my apologies,' he said smoothly. 'I agree. Let's change the subject.'

But now he was willing to do that Lexi found herself changing her mind too. 'No. Let's finish what you've already started and get it over with. So what do you want to know. My full family tree? OK.' She sat back again, tense as a skittish cat and defiant with it. She tossed her hair back from her face. 'Mother—Grace Hamilton. Actress but not famous.' She lifted her hand up to place Grace like an imaginary branch in the air in front of her, her fingers trembling as she did. 'Father—unknown. Because Grace was very vague about things she did not want to face and there was no name on my birth certificate.' She placed him in the air next to Grace. 'Oh, and I forgot to put my grandmother up there. Anyone else?' She pretended to ponder that, with her eyes flashing all kinds of aggression, while Franco just reclined back in his chair and listened with an infuriatingly impassive silence. 'A hamster called Racket,' she remembered. 'I wanted a dog, but I wasn't allowed one because we moved around too much. Then there is Bruce, of course.' As she spoke Bruce's name she dared Franco with the sparkle in her eyes to say a single thing. 'Bruce is the only person who has ever been and remained a constant part of my life…I wonder where I should place him on my tree?'

'Father figure?' Franco suggested, with a silken stealth that raised Lexi's hackles so much she thought for a second she was going to leap up and hit him.

'You need to wash your mouth out with soap.' She made do with sending him a withering glance. 'At least he's always cared what happened to me.'

'And lusted after you like a seething old lecher.'

'How dare you say that?' Lexi gasped out.

'I dare because he is twelve years older than you, yet he could never look at you without stripping your clothes off.'

Stung by that shocking observation, she hit right back. 'Well, better a sleazy old lecher than a two-timing young one.'

Franco's dark head went back. 'Are you calling me a lecher?'

'What do you call a guy who pursues a stupid, innocent girl with the sole intention of bedding her for a bet?'

'The bet was—unfortunate,' he growled, with an impatient movement of his hand that Lexi read as downright haunted guilt. 'It had nothing to do with what you and I were really about.'

'Tell that to your golden friends.' Lexi laughed, and it

wasn't a nice laugh. 'And let us not gloss over the fact that you collected your winnings,' she added for good measure.

'There was a reason why I did that,' he said tightly.

'I'm all ears,' encouraged Lexi.

'We were discussing Bruce Dayton's unhealthy obsession with you,' he muttered, losing all that super cool sophistication he'd brought to the dinner table.

'Bruce has been good to me.'

'The perfect father figure.'

'Stop calling him that. He's not old enough to be my father!'

'Uncle then,' Franco amended. 'Whatever—it was sick.'

Her cheeks gone pale now, Lexi thrust her chin up. 'The way *you* treated me was sick, Franco.'

He surprised her by backing right off from that accusation. Getting up from the table, he strode across the room towards the drinks cabinet, and Lexi could feel him inwardly cursing the fact that he was limping again. 'If I tell you I am deeply ashamed that I allowed that bet to stand, will you just let it go now?'

Well, *could* she let it go?

He'd turned around and was watching her with the intent expression of a man who genuinely meant what he'd just said. It some ways Lexi knew that this was a big moment in the strange up-and-down relationship they'd been having since she'd come back into his life—though it wasn't the biggest, most crucial moment.

'Seeing you accept that bet broke my heart,' she told him bleakly.

'I'm sorry,' he said heavily, then sighed because he knew that sounded inadequate after what she'd just confessed. 'Claudia was a jealous cat, and she aimed to hurt you deeply when she sent that video clip to your phone.'

She'd known that. Even back then she'd understood

Claudia's motives, though understanding them had not softened the pain she'd suffered.

'She too was deeply ashamed of the part she'd played in hurting you,' Franco went on soberly. 'Especially so when you lost your mother not long afterwards and—'

'The rest of my world came tumbling down,' Lexi completed for him. Then she heaved in a breath, let it out again, and stood up. 'I forgive you both for the bet, OK?' she announced stiffly. 'I will even forgive you for turning so cold on me the week before the bet came to light, and for hating being married to me. After all—' she released a jerky laugh '—I hated you just as much by then. But what I refuse to forgive,' she added, a flush of anger rising to her cheeks, 'is you enjoying yourself with Claudia in our bed in our apartment while I was in hospital miscarrying our baby. And now I think I will go alone to bed.'

'Just hold on a minute.' As if she'd just shot a stray bullet at him, Franco tensed. 'That last part did not happen!'

'Telephones with cameras are the bastards of intrusion,' Lexi mocked as she crossed the room at speed to the door. 'And trust me, Franco,' she couldn't resist launching at him once she'd got there, 'whatever people like to say to the contrary, cameras don't tell lies!'

'Lexi—come back here!' he raked out as she flung herself out of the room at full pelt, because she'd caught the warning spark of blistering fury lighting up the gold in his eyes.

She was halfway up the stairs when she heard the crash, then a string of angry curses. 'I hope that was you falling on your lying face!' she stopped to yell down at him. 'And so much for getting to know each other, Francesco! Great trip down memory lane—thanks!'

She didn't even see Zeta standing in the hall, staring after her in appalled dismay as she raced up the rest of the stairs. Franco saw the housekeeper, though, when she appeared in the open doorway to a string of vicious curses as he got up from the floor, rubbing his thigh. One of the dining chairs lay on its side because he'd tripped over it, and the bottle of wine he'd been holding in his hand was lying next to it, dripping its red contents onto the polished oak floor.

'Don't say a damn word,' he growled at the housekeeper when she opened her mouth to speak.

'But—did she do this to you?'

'My wife can do anything she wants to me,' he responded harshly, gripping his shoulder because he'd wrenched it trying to break his fall. 'She can put a loaded gun to my head and pull the trigger if she feels like it. It is her right, her prerogative...damn!' he cursed when he tried to put his weight on his injured leg and almost collapsed again.

Zeta came hurrying forward, but he waved her back. 'I'm OK,' he muttered less forcefully. 'Just get out of here, Zeta. This is private between me and Lexi, and we don't need witnesses while we make fools of ourselves.'

Lexi didn't feel foolish; she felt like a bubbling mass of boiling fury.

What was she doing here?'

It was all out now. The door in her head was standing wide open and everything was spilling out right in front of her: the hurt, the betrayal, all as fresh and raw as if it was only just happening. She wanted to curl up in a corner and cry her eyes out, but she also wanted to run back down there and spit out some more accusations at the man she hated so much right now it physically hurt!

Wife...what a miserable joke, she thought painfully, looking around the suite that was so similar to the suite she'd used to have—if she didn't count the several corridors in between. Different colour coordination, different view from the window, but right now it felt just like the same luxury prison cell that had doubled as her only place of sanctuary from the cold comfort offered to her!

Grimly she stripped her clothes off, dragged her nightie

on over her head, crawled beneath the cool linen sheets and then curled up in a tight ball. She was trembling—all over. Shivering and shaking with a huge lump of tears growing in her throat like an inflating balloon. To think she'd almost gone to bed with him. To think she'd convinced herself she was ready to let the past go.

Her bedroom door flew open. She knew it was Franco. 'If you've come to ask politely after my health, then don't bother!' she launched at him from the depths of the sheet she'd pulled over her head.

His disconcerted stillness sizzled across the darkened room.

'And you forgot to knock!'

'What the hell are you talking about now?' he fired back.

'Tell me...' Fighting with the sheet so she could sit up, Lexi yanked her hair back from where it had tumbled across her hot face. He was standing there, lit by the light on the landing, a huge great dark silhouette that still managed to look disgustingly gorgeous. 'Were you sent by your father to check on me each morning?'

'Sent to check on you?' Naturally he didn't know what she was talking about, since he had not been privy to her thoughts.

'The last time I lived here,' she enlightened him. 'I had this—' she gave a flick with her hand '—this image of your father, ordering you upstairs to my room to check on my health every morning before you both left for Livorno. You used to knock so politely, then stand there in the doorway—just like you're doing now—and look at me like you wished I wasn't there...'

Franco stiffened as if she'd leapt up and slapped his face. 'I was not ordered upstairs and I never wished you were not here!' he denied harshly.

'Man and wife with bedrooms five miles apart?' Lexi muttered in a thick voice that shook. 'You didn't bother to have me moved then, did you? You liked having three quarters of this stupid house between us.'

She heard his sigh as he walked towards the bed, and knew he'd caught the tremor of hurt in her voice.

'I was out of my comfort zone,' he confessed heavily. 'You did not say anything about where you were sleeping, and I didn't know how to broach the subject without sounding like an oversexed monster eager to have you close enough to jump on when I felt like it, so I left it alone.'

'You didn't want to jump on me.'

He said nothing.

'And I would have needed nerves of steel to complain about my accommodation when I knew how much you hated me.'

'You hated me too, Lexi…'

She sighed at that comeback, because it was only the truth, and he sighed too, then lowered himself down to sit on the edge of her bed. Lexi saw him wince, saw him lay a hand on his injured thigh, wished she didn't love and hate him at the same time. Then she almost choked on the sob she had to fight back when it hit her that she did—still love him. Oh, what a pig!

'What do you want me to say? That I made a mess of the whole thing? OK, I made a mess of the whole thing,' he admitted. 'I believed…' He stopped, causing a sting of a rift to open up while Lexi sat waiting for him to finish. When he did continue she got the feeling he'd carefully rethought what he wanted to say. 'I let…other people dictate to me how I should be thinking and feeling about you. But I never wished you gone—ever.'

The tagged on *ever* rang like a low-sounding bass bell, striking out dark, intense sincerity.

'I used to cry into my pillow each morning after you'd left.' She wasn't looking at him now, but down at her fingers where they crushed the sheet. 'I wanted so badly for my mother to walk into that bedroom and sweep me up in her arms and carry me away from here.'

'Lexi…' he growled unsteadily.

But Lexi just shook her head against whatever that unsteady 'Lexi' was meant to relay. 'You'd turned cold on me before we married. Before Grace died, before I learnt about that stupid bet. Knowing that, I should not have married you.'

Grinding out a soft curse, he reached to grasp her twisting fingers. 'Look, I'm really sorry about the bet. I mean it. I'm sorry. I was an arrogant fool. I believed something someone told me about you and I—I wanted to hit back at you, so I… collected my—my winnings, knowing that Claudia was recording the moment and that she was likely to send it to you.'

'You believed something someone told you about me?' Lifting up her head Lexi looked at him. 'What something?'

But he just frowned and shook his head, 'Let's talk about convenient cameras and sex romps that did not happen.'

Being reminded of that, Lexi tugged her fingers free and threw herself back down on the pillows. 'No. Go away,' she muttered, and pulled the sheet over her head.

Without any warning whatsoever that it was going to happen, Franco lost his temper. The next thing she knew she lying pinned beneath his weight, because he'd stretched out on top of her like a wrestler, pinning her to the bed.

'Talk,' he rasped, tugging the sheet down so he could glower at her. 'Because I did not sleep with Claudia. I have never slept with Claudia! I want to know why you ever believed that I did!'

If she hadn't seen the proof for herself Lexi would have started to believe him. He looked so offended. Bright golden flames of denial were leaping in his eyes.

'Where were you the night they took me to hospital?' she challenged icily.

'Blind drunk in a bar in town somewhere,' he answered

instantly. 'Too sloshed to know what I was doing and too miserable about us to care.'

'I called you—four times!' Accusing sparks flew from her eyes now. 'You didn't even bother to answer me—not once!'

Franco tried to recall what else he'd been doing while he'd drunk himself into a forgetful stupor that night. 'Marco found me and took me home,' he recounted. 'I could barely walk in a straight line. He put me to bed. I don't remember any phone calls. I don't remember anything much about that night.'

'So Claudia hid in a cupboard, waiting to jump out once you were naked and comatose on the bed, then jumped on you?'

He looked stunned. 'You saw that?'

'Of course I saw that!' Lexi tried to wriggle out from beneath him.

'Stay still,' he muttered. 'I'm hurting all over as it is.'

To her annoyance, she went perfectly still beneath him. 'Do you think I enjoy making up fantasies where my so-called husband gets passionate with another woman in our bed while I'm—?'

'Whose phone?' he cut in, and she could feel all the muscles in him tensing.

'Claudia's phone. Though how she managed to take pictures of what you were both up to while—what?' Lexi said as his face drained of colour, his eyes turning that horrible black onyx.

He didn't answer. Something about the way he suddenly rolled away from her to land on his feet by the bed and then just stood there stone still, staring at nothing, made Lexi sit up again, with a funny feeling of alarm crawling around in her chest.

'Franco?' she prompted uncertainly.

Franco didn't even hear her. A red mist had risen across his eyes, in the centre of which was an image Marco had planted there of him twined in the throes of passion with Lexi. But the twined couple he was seeing right now was himself with Claudia, as described by Lexi, who had been sent that image by—

As if he was drunk out of his head for the first time since the night Lexi had lost their baby Franco moved across the room and out of it without saying another single word.

CHAPTER EIGHT

LEXI sat hugging her knees and stared after him, aware that something terribly dramatic had happened here—only she just didn't know what it was.

He'd looked—shattered.

Was that her fault? A guilty squirm struck down the curve of her backbone. She was supposed to be here to take care of him, not to get into fights with him every five minutes. She was supposed to be sensitive to his fragile mental state.

Marco... He'd actually talked about Marco just before he—

Scrambling out of the bed, she ran after him. The guilty feeling worsened when she found him sitting on the edge of his own bed with his face buried in his hands.

'Franco?' She went to drop down in front of him. 'Are you all right?'

For a few seconds he didn't move or say anything. Feeling that clutch of concern growing inside her, Lexi reached up and gently threaded her fingers between the spread of his own fingers, then tugged them away from his face.

'I'm OK,' he husked.

Well, he didn't look OK. The grey cast was back, strain carving out each feature, as if he was labouring under some terrible shock. And the most disturbing thing of all was that she thought she could see the burn of tears lurking behind the awful haunted look in his eyes. As if he knew what she was seeing, he lowered his heavy black lustrous eyelashes and swallowed, following it up by clearing his throat. She still held his hands, so she could feel a slight tremor running through them.

Was he finally giving in to his grief for Marco?

'I'm sorry if I went too far fighting with you,' she whispered contritely. 'I keep forgetting you're—'

'Off my head?' he offered, when she hesitated over saying something similar.

'Unwell,' Lexi substituted, making a half smile tilt the corners of his tensely held mouth.

'Sick, crazy, stupid, blind...' he offered as other alternatives.

'Is your eyesight still not good?' she asked sharply. 'Is that why you had a fight with the furniture downstairs?'

It seemed to Franco to be as good an excuse as any to leave her with. Better that than the truth anyway. 'I think I might have done some damage to the wound in my thigh,' he admitted.

She looked down at his legs, her dusky eyelashes trembling as she lifted up their clasped hands so she could scan his pale chinos for evidence of blood—but there was none. All he'd probably done was bruise it—just another one to add to the many he already had, he thought grimly.

Lexi heaved in a breath. 'Right, then, we had better take a look.' Glad to have something practical to think about other than the strange, thickly intense emotions swirling around the two of them right now, she reclaimed her hands and stood up. 'You—you'll have to take your trousers off.'

'You're intending to play nurse—dressed like that?' Franco drawled, grazing a mocking glance over her short pink nightie.

'One thing I will never be is a nurse,' Lexi returned, determined to keep this light from now on, even if it killed her, because she didn't ever want to send Franco back into that terrible dark place he'd just emerged from. 'And you've seen me wearing less, so stop complaining.'

'I was not complaining, merely making an observation.'

'Well…' The next deep breath she took felt dreadfully cluttered up. 'If you can stand up, lose the trousers, then we'll be even.'

He wasn't joking about the wound she saw once the chinos lay discarded on the bed. There was a thin trail of blood seeping through the dressing.

She chewed on her bottom lip for a second. 'So, what do we do now?'

'I remove the dressing and take a look while you fetch me a fresh one.' Sitting down again, he began to pick at the sealed edges of the white strip. 'In the bathroom, by the washbasin,' he instructed.

Lexi moved off obediently. She had a feeling he was deliberately playing things light too, because he didn't want things to kick off between them again.

How had they done that? Got so far they'd almost ended up screaming at each other?

She had screamed at him, she remembered, as she took a minute to wash her hands thoroughly before picking up the sealed sterile dressing packet and taking it back into the bedroom along with a clean towel.

'Squeamish?' he asked when she went still half a metre away.

'I don't know. I've never seen an open wound before.'

'It isn't open.'

He peeled the last of the old dressing away and she saw that he was telling the truth. A four-inch purple line was all that was left to show for the surgery, except for a tiny gape in the middle, which must be where he'd knocked it.

'That healed quickly.' Walking forward again, she sat down beside him on the bed. 'Does it hurt?'

'Not much. If you open that packet you will find a small plastic tube in there, filled with clear liquid.'

Franco took the tube from her, snapped its seal and applied the liquid to the wound. 'What does it do?' she asked curiously as she watched.

'Accelerates the healing process... You ask a lot of questions for a reluctant nurse.'

'I'm not the one doing the nursing. It's not bleeding any more...'

'There should be a clean, dry pad in the packet,' Franco prompted, and she found it and offered it to him, then watched again while he used it to soak up the excess liquid. When he was done she took it from him and silently handed him the fresh dressing strip, which he proceeded to smooth into place.

'Lexi, I'm sorry,' he murmured suddenly. 'About everything we put you through.'

The 'we' sounded odd, but she didn't pick him up on it. She was more concerned with the tension knot she could feel inside her tummy, because there was something in the way he'd made that apology that she didn't quite like.

'I was an easy target.' It was amazing, she thought, how a big row followed by a fright could bring on concessions. 'I was hateful to you most of the time.'

'With reason.'

'Yes, well...' Needing something to do, she gathered up the discarded items and stood up. 'I'll put these in the bathroom wastebin.'

'Then go back to bed.'

She stilled halfway to the bathroom, oddly wounded by the flat way he'd said that. 'Thanks for the permission,' she whispered.

'And tomorrow, if you want, you can go back to London.'

Now she knew what it felt like to be stabbed in the back. She swung round, her face paled to parchment. He was sitting there, still smoothing his long fingers over the white dressing as if he expected it to fall off if he stopped. His head was dipped. In fact she realised he hadn't looked at her properly once since she'd seen that horrible strained, haunted look when she'd pulled his hands away from his face.

'Y-you want me to leave?' Even she heard the hurt choking up her voice.

'You and I both know I'm not about to do anything stupid, Lexi,' he said grimly. 'I should not have… I used emotional blackmail to get you here, then to keep you here. Now it is time for me to start playing fair again. So I am letting you know that you can go home—no regrets.'

She hadn't expected this. After all the things they'd been throwing at each other over the last few days she just had not expected him to—to… 'S-so all that stuff about—about us trying again was what? You using me as a diversion so you didn't have to think about M-Marco?'

He rose to his feet, a frowning black scowl on his face now. 'I am just trying to play fair.'

'I don't want you to play fair!' Tears were gathering. She could feel them building in her throat. 'I want you to be honest with me and just tell me—have I been a diversion so you did not have to face your guilt and grief about Marco?'

'No!' he rasped.

'Then what?' she persisted.

Like a man driven to commit murder he strode towards her, took her by her trembling shoulders and heaved her up against his chest. 'You just don't know when it is safer to say nothing, do you?' he raked down at her angrily. 'You were like this four years ago—a yappy little temptress who never knew when to shut up!'

'Y-you said you liked me yappy back then.'

'I like you yappy now. That is the whole damn point!' He sighed when he saw her soft mouth was trembling. Her eyes looked huge and hurt and— *'Santa cielo,'* he groaned in exasperation. 'I am trying to do the honourable thing by giving you a choice here, you aggravating female. Go because you want to go or stay because you want to stay—no extra coercive strings attached, your damn choice!'

'Stay,' Lexi whispered.

He frowned again, as if she'd given the wrong answer. 'Why?' he charged. 'When I have given you nothing but aggravation, hassle and hurt?'

'I was just getting used to the idea of—of us trying to be married and...' She attempted a helpless little shrug within the firm grip of his hands. 'I still have feelings for you, OK?'

Defensive and tense, she waited for him to say something. He was still frowning down at her, but a searching glint was happening behind the frown, and at least that horrible blackness had left his eyes so she could see the golden bits again. The silence stretched. Lexi wished she knew what he was thinking. Like a stork, she swapped her weight from one leg to the other, then, because she couldn't stop it, she let out a soft, slightly husky, nervy little laugh.

'And I love your legs. You always did have great legs...'

'My legs?' Franco repeated.

Lexi nodded, biting down on the quiver moving across her lips. 'Kind of long, tough and tanned. Sexy—even with all the scars you've accumulated over—'

He shut her up with a hot, bruising kiss. She dropped the things she was holding because she needed to grab hold of his arms to steady herself. Somewhere in the back of her mind she knew they hadn't finished with the Claudia thing but did not want to think about that right now.

This was what mattered: the heat of his mouth claiming hers with the same burning hunger it used to, the remembered dark groan of pure pleasure when he felt her melting response. Franco had taught her everything she knew about the power of her own deep flowing rivers of passion and he plundered deep, savouring the eager heat with which she responded to him.

No drawing back this time. Lexi knew it as surely as she knew that Franco knew it. He meshed one of his hands into her hair, the other cupping the silk covered shape of her bottom to bring her close up against him so she could feel the power of his desire for her. Thick potent heat swam through her veins and pooled low between her thighs in an erotic swirl of excitement. Her hands moved, anxiously scoring over the soft cambric of his shirt and feeling the powerful set of his biceps, his shoulders, the alluring heat of him. Her bare legs made brushing contact with his, increasing the bright sting of need growing inside her as the hair-roughened quality of his skin rasped against her smooth softness. It was like being wired up to an electric grid and she quivered, her restless fingers clutching at him so tightly she felt him shudder, then flinch.

'Oh…' she choked, remembering, and drew her head back a little. Her heart was racing and she was breathing too fast. She clashed with the simmering darkness of his eyes. No gold in evidence—just dark, dark caverns of hunger she wanted to drown in. 'I hurt you,' she groaned.

'No,' he denied, and tried to recapture her lips, but Lexi held them away from him.

'I did,' she insisted. 'You're one big bruise, and I don't know how we are going to do this without putting you through torture.'

Franco released a short mocking laugh and moved his fingers against her bottom, sliding them sensually against silk as he eased her into greater contact with him. 'You think this isn't already torture?'

It was pure instinct that made Lexi move against his potent hardness, and he groaned and shuddered, his other hand shifting from her hair to her back, then sliding with a compulsive movement to her waist to press her even closer as he captured her mouth again and this time gave her no chance to think. Passion flared between them in a fevered hunger.

Liquid heat was pooling in just about every erogenous zone she possessed.

'I want you, *tesoro*, so badly it is eating away at me.' The heat of his lips moving across her cheek as he husked the words made her shiver as he tasted the sensitive flesh below her ear.

Lexi tilted her upper body back a little so she could begin unbuttoning his shirt. Her fingers trembled so badly she struggled over the simple task, and it didn't help that Franco was tasting her neck now, whispering words in low, sexy Italian while his hands dealt with the removal of her nightie in one smooth, deft move that sent the scrap of silk pooling to her feet.

Naked in front of him for the first time in years, she froze for a few seconds and he did the same thing, even taking a step back so he could look at her, the simmering flame of his study lashing her skin with hot stings which tightened the swelling tips of her breasts so her nipples bloomed like crowns of dusky pink. Reaching out, he cupped a hand around one breast—gently, as if he was reacquainting himself with its size and its weight. Seeing the power of his fierce concentration, Lexi stood perfectly still and watched him as he stretched out the other hand and curved it around the gentle swell of her hip.

The air around them throbbed with sexual tension. His shirt was hanging open, the wedge of dark hair trailing over his front to the waistband of his undershorts a virile contrast to the deep bronze sheen of his skin. Her tongue moistened in her mouth with a desire to lean in and taste him, her fingers twitching by her sides in an anxious need to move away the shirt. She could see the jutting evidence of his manhood pressing against his undershorts, traced its powerful length with her eyes. Memories of what it was like to feel him deep inside her awoke with an excitement that held her gripped in its thrall.

As if he could tell what she was thinking he moved his hand to her stomach, then stroked downwards—and she shivered out a gasp of expectancy just before his fingertips sank into the triangular cloud of dusky curls. As he made that first fingertip dip it was as if he was laying claim to something he believed was totally his. She was hot and she was damp and her body welcomed his touch by clenching the muscles there, which he felt with a brief, tense smile of acknowledgement.

By mutual need they came together again—urgent, maybe even a little desperate, their lips fusing while she dealt with the shirt, then moved to hook her fingers into the waist of his shorts. Pushing them down his lean, smooth, tautly muscled flanks, she felt his tremor and then his gasp as she stroked her fingers along his length, then closed them around him. His fingers became buried in her hair again, so he could tilt back her head. Her lips were already parted and ready to receive the driving force of his kiss that carried them all the way down onto the bed. Lexi found herself stretched out on the cool sheet and losing contact with him as Franco rid himself of his shorts.

When he stretched out beside her and then rolled onto her she saw his bruising. 'We should take this carefully,' she whispered worriedly.

'To hell with being careful,' he growled, then dipped his dark head and claimed a protruding nipple with the burning heat of his mouth. He grazed her with his lips, his teeth, the fiery heat of his breath as he slowly moved across the swollen mound of that breast to the other breast and captured the rosy peak with a searing hunger that dragged a keening cry from her lips.

'You taste like heaven,' he told her.

Her anxious fingers speared into the glossy thickness of his hair. 'Francesco...' was all she could manage to say in response.

'*Si, amore,* it is I.' He sounded amused, yet oddly sombre

at the same time. 'You remember this? How good we are together? How it took so little to drive us out of our minds?'

Each dark question was punctuated by a different caress of his hands or his mouth. Lexi lay boneless and trembling with the need for him to keep on touching her, writhing with rising anxiety as he tracked kisses down her slender shape to her waist then sank a deep-tongued caress into her navel, where she'd always been way too sensitive to bear it without turning into a wild thing.

He lifted his head to look at her, triumph pounding through him at how thoroughly she'd lost control. He released a low laugh and bent to issue the same torment again. Lexi caught hold of the bulging muscles in his shoulders and sank her nails in, squirming beneath him in an effort to get free from such an overload of excruciating pleasure that was threatening to send her wild.

Then he wasn't laughing at anything. He was snaking back up to claim her mouth in a deep, probing kiss. At the same moment his fingers timed a controlled glide into the hot, silken folds of her body. Lexi heard her heartbeat thundering in her ears and knew already she was careering close to the edge of a climax the likes of which promised to knock her off the planet with its intensity. Somewhere in the dim background she could hear Franco trying to soothe her down from the brink, but it wasn't going to happen. For more than three years she had lived with all this passion crushed down inside, so she would not have to feel its powerful pull ever again. She'd let no other man get this close to her. She'd never wanted to feel like this again—so helplessly out of control— yet with this one particular man choice was lost to her.

She forgot about his injuries, his bruises, his wounded thigh—everything, scoring his back and his chest with her fingernails and moving her legs in quick, anxious need up and down the corded muscles in his calves. She felt hot, breathless—totally governed by what she was feeling. 'Please,

Franco, please...' she heard herself begging, feverishly kissing his mouth, his jaw, his neck, dragging her hands down his body so she could close them once again around the velvet steel of his proud erection.

'Lexi...' he whispered unsteadily. 'Slow down, *amore*.'

But she didn't want to slow down. 'Please...' she gasped again. 'I missed you so much... Please, Franco, please...'

As she felt the tremors breaking over his long, powerful frame he surrendered to her pleas and with a groan slipped between her parted thighs, slid his hands beneath her, then let her guide him where she most needed to feel him before he smoothly, surely drove himself deep.

Exhilaration ran through him like the most potent pleasure drug ever invented as her muscles closed around him, eager, possessive. He pulsed. She clung and fused her mouth to his again. They lost themselves in a voyage of rediscovery—no holding back anything. When she tripped the wire of an electric orgasm it was too soon; but he revelled in each quivering shock wave, held on and held on, until he could do so no longer and finally released his own shattering shock waves of fulfilment while their mouths remained fused and the pounding of their hearts beat in unison.

It was like dying within the most exquisite pleasure ever and then waking up again later to find you'd discovered your soul mate. They lay in a tangle of boneless limbs, too shattered to be able to move. He was burning hot and heavy on her, but Lexi didn't mind. In fact she rejoiced in his weight, and his lingering pulse still beat a tantalisingly potent force inside her. She didn't want to think or even breathe if it meant spoiling this special moment. His head was pressed in against the curve of her neck and her shoulder. Her fingers held it there. She smiled dreamily, because she loved the feel of his tongue tasting the warm dampness of her skin there. *I feel whole again for the first time in years*, she thought dreamily.

'Lexi...'

'Hmm?' she mumbled.

'*Accidenti, cara*, but I cannot move.'

'Your bruises!' As if she'd been stung by a sharp implement, Lexi came alive with a jolt of her limbs that made Franco release a groan in protest. 'Didn't I say we should be more careful? Which bit hurts the most?'

He managed to lift his head up so he could look at her, a wry humour in his slumbrous dark eyes. 'All of me.'

'Shall I try squeezing out from beneath you?'

'I'm too heavy.'

'I know,' she teased, and he smiled a lazy smile.

Several minutes went by after that, because they ended up kissing, and the kisses were so gentle and tender there didn't seem any rush to figure out a way to separate themselves without hurting him.

'It is good to have you back where you belong, Signora Tolle,' Franco husked, tasting the corner of her mouth. 'Perhaps it is not a bad idea for us to remain like this for the rest of our lives.' He gave a tiny nudge with his hips to highlight his meaning. 'Someone will discover us in a few thousand years, still locked together like this turned to stone, and think we were so romantic.'

'I don't think Zeta will wait a few thousand years to check on us,' Lexi responded with a soft giggle.

In the end Lexi managed to slide out from beneath him, leaving Franco to collapse onto the bed.

'And to think I always considered you a really macho hunk.' Lexi sighed as she got up and started gathering their discarded clothes.

'I *am* a macho hunk,' he insisted, watching her move around the room. 'Did I not just perform with supreme macho efficiency even with cracked ribs and bruises?'

Lexi stopped what she was doing—perform with efficiency? Did he have to make it sound so—physical?

'When I think of all those months of marriage when we did not indulge in sex at all, it feels like a hell of a waste now.'

'Well, if you must think in those terms I suppose those months must have been a waste to you. But for me...' She started picking up clothes again—snatching them up, actually, because if she didn't she might— 'Talking like that makes me feel like just another sexual affair to you.'

An uneasy silence ensued for a few seconds before he said, 'I think you had better explain that.'

She turned to look at him lying there sprawled in all his naked glory like a beautifully tooled bronze sculpture even his bruising couldn't spoil. Arrogant, she thought. Conceitedly sure of his own masculine beauty. Even the sleepy weight of his eyelids and the kiss warmed shape of his mouth made statements of lazy self-assurance about the deeply sensual man that he was.

And why not? He'd sent her wildly out of control only two seconds after their skins met. When had she not responded like that?

'We had a fabulous summer affair and a lousy winter marriage.' She looked away again. 'One steaming hot—the other freezing cold. When I left here I don't think you even noticed.'

'I noticed,' he murmured.

'In passing? On your way back to your old life? Tell me.' Clutching the clothes to her front, Lexi made herself face him again. 'How long did you wait before you consoled yourself by taking another woman to your bed?'

His eyes hooded altogether. For a brief moment she thought she saw that grey veil attempt to shutter his grim face. 'I don't think this topic of conversation is appropriate.'

'Appropriate for what?'

'We are trying to heal the past.'

Well, Lexi didn't feel healed—she felt hurt. Wounded, in fact, by that shuttered expression. She wanted denials. Hot, offended denials. Not—

'Is this yet another subject on your banned list, Franco?' she goaded. 'Are we not to talk about the newspaper reports that put the first woman in your bed at the Lisbon powerboat convention a short month after I left?' She tugged in a short breath. 'Of course that was the first woman the press got wind of—that does not automatically mean she was the first one to grace your bed. Perhaps you had enough sensitivity to be more discreet about the preceding lovers—'

'And you moved straight in with Dayton,' he countered. 'You tell me, Lexi.' Despite the obvious aches of his body he climbed off the bed and moved towards her—prowled, actually, like a sleek hunter scenting a hearty meal he relished tearing to bits. 'How long did it take him to coax you into his bed? Did he use the *Let me hold you while you grieve for your baby* excuse to get you there? Did you curl up against him and weep your broken heart out all over him while he subtly moved things onto something much more satisfying and intimate?'

CHAPTER NINE

GONE sickly pale now, she whispered, 'That's a disgusting thing to throw at me.'

'You think so?' Grim contempt scored lines across his handsome face. 'So did I when the bastard relayed those bald facts to me the day I was stupid enough to go to his apartment to see you.'

'That's a lie!' Lexi protested.

'Is it?' Reaching out, Franco yanked the clothes out of her nerveless fingers, separated his things, then stuffed her nightie back into her hands. 'Go to bed,' he snapped, and turned his back on her to head for the bathroom. 'Your own damn bed.'

But she couldn't move a single muscle. A cold, sickening chill of a tremor had frozen her where she stood. 'Bruce just would not lie like that… Why should he when it never happened?'

'That's right,' he derided. 'Trust loyal Bruce to always act in your best interests.' He stilled in the bathroom doorway. 'He showed me the evidence.'

'He what—?'

'He tried to fob me off with a verbal description first, then when I refused to accept it—' his big shoulders flexed in a ripple of tense glossy muscle '—he showed me the evidence.'

'But he can't have shown you any evidence when it didn't happen!'

The way she cried out that denial swung Franco round. His face looked as if it had been carved out of rock. 'Your things littered all over the place.' He speared a glance at the nightie she held crushed in her taut fingers. 'You always were the untidiest woman I ever met. When we lived our fantastic hot affair that summer you drove me crazy because you never picked up after yourself. On the boat. At the villa we rented in San Remo—'

San Remo…where everything had turned bad for them.

'He picked your bra up off the floor while I watched him,' he went on harshly. 'He dared…' In some distant part of her Lexi felt the emotional throb of his voice. 'He dared to send me a look, as if we were good old friends enjoying a moment of mutual understanding, as he tossed the damn bra onto a chair loaded down with your clothes.'

'This never happened.' Lexi took a step towards him, but he stiffened up so violently she pulled to a stop again.

'Don't tell me it didn't happen when I was there,' he ground out. 'I saw the damn frog sitting on your pillow!'

Lexi blinked in an effort to clear the glaze of confusion from her head. 'But—but that was m-my room.'

'With *his* stuff hanging in the wardrobes?'

'Yes!' she cried out. 'Bruce's clothes were in the wardrobes! You've seen him, Franco, you know what he's like about clothes! He—he must have a hundred Savile Row suits and two hundred shirts, and before I went to stay with him he spread them between the two bedrooms! I was only there for couple of months, so he didn't bother to clear them out!'

In the trammelling silence that followed her shrill explanation Lexi stared at Franco's angry face and took in the seething force of the vibrations still holding his naked frame so tense.

'Y-you came to see me—?' The frail shake wrapped around

that belated enquiry made him lower his eyelids over the turbulent shimmer in control of his eyes.

'A month after you left me.' He relayed that answer as if it had been dragged out of him by torture.

Lexi did not miss the significance of the month and the accusations she'd just thrown at him about his women. Clasping her arms around her body, she shivered.

'You were not there. He said you were attending several auditions in an attempt to get your stalled career back on track. He told me Hollywood beckoned,' he mocked bitterly, 'and you would be much better off if I...'

He didn't need to finish that sentence. Lexi found it too easy to finish it for herself. Bruce had tried to convince her to go straight back into acting, maintaining it would be the best way to work through her broken-hearted grief. He'd even set up auditions with a couple of famous directors that she'd refused to attend. When all attempts to make her see things his way had failed to move her, he'd offered her a job working with him at the agency instead.

And she'd accepted. Bruce had been determined to keep her close this time—no matter what it took. When she'd moved into her own flat he'd been angry for weeks...

'Oh, my God, he...' She flattened a hand against her mouth as the ugly words dried up like water droplets hitting a sand dune; but those watered grains of sand started melding together as everything about Bruce and their long relationship came together to make a sick kind of sense.

When Franco had accused Bruce of being a control freak he had not been plucking insults out of the air. He'd had hard evidence of exactly how much Bruce was trying to control her life. Then she remembered the other things Franco had called Bruce and nausea began to claw at her stomach. Unable to just stand there in the centre of the tumbling fallout happening inside her, Lexi turned in a dizzy reel to head for the bedroom door—only she couldn't make it that far, and ended up sinking weakly down on the side of the bed. For the last ten years Bruce had always been there, in the background of her life, a calm, often critical but always totally dependable figure watching over her—or waiting for her to grow up?

Then her mother had met Philippe and loosened the reins on her. Lexi had tripped off and fallen head over heels in love with her tall, dark, handsome Italian while all Bruce had been able to do was watch it happen and wait for the love affair to burn itself out—as, she supposed, everyone else had waited for it to burn out.

Still standing in the bathroom doorway, Franco was wishing he'd kept his damn mouth shut. He'd never meant to tell her any of that: now he'd brutally shattered her with it. And the way *he'd* regarded Dayton's obsession with Lexi did not necessarily mean it was as sinister as he'd made it out to be. Dayton was a good-looking guy, up there and out there, with a string of beautiful women trailing in and out of his life. The age gap between him and Lexi did not mean much in current society when, basically, if a guy still had it then he might as well go for it. His own father entertained liaisons with women with a wider age gap and no one batted a critical eye.

No, his view of Dayton was jaundiced by old-fashioned jealousy and the ten years the guy had hung on, waiting for Lexi to notice him as a prospective lover. He'd seen the desire in Dayton's face the first time he'd met him, known exactly where he was coming from, and had wanted to punch him ever since.

But none of that justified the way he'd made her face the truth about Dayton, because he'd done it to wound. Now he wanted to kick something because—damn it—how the hell was he going to tell her about Marco when he'd already wounded her enough with *this*?

Lexi didn't know he'd moved until she felt his fingers close around her wrists and she was pulled inexorably to her feet.

He wrapped her in his arms, the hairs on his chest tickling her nose as he heaved air into his lungs, then let it out again.

'I should not have said anything,' he said heavily. 'After the way we parted you had every right to try and put your life back together any way that you wanted to—'

'But wh—what you described never happened,' Lexi denied painfully.

'I know that now.' He drew her closer so her forehead rested against his chest.

Lexi tried to squeeze a hand between them so she could wipe a stray tear from her cheek. 'Why was everyone so against us, Franco?' she asked in a bewildered voice. 'What were we doing that was so terrible?'

His response rumbled against her brow in its gravity. 'They had their own agendas, Lexi. Dayton…Claudia…and…' Another sigh eased from him. 'What they wanted does not really matter to us—this matters.' Combing his fingers into her hair, he gently coaxed her to lift up her head. Their eyes met: his dark and somber, with bleak golden flashes; hers ocean pools of incomprehension and hurt. 'We are here, together, and we have not exactly hung around in making it back to this point. I call that fate giving them all a hard smack across the head for interfering in the first place.'

He wanted her to smile, to lighten the heavy weight in the atmosphere, but Lexi shook her head. 'It took a terrible accident and Marco's death to get us here,' she said sadly. 'Without the accident we would be talking through our lawyers about our divorce.'

'That's not true.' As she tried to pull away Franco tightened his arms around her. 'I told you I had already made up my mind I was coming to see you before the accident happened.'

'For what reason?' Her shrug told him she didn't understand why he should want to bother.

'Because I spent the last three years looking for a good excuse to do it.'

As she stilled in surprise at that dry confession, Franco lowered his head and kissed her soft, quivering mouth. Her lips clung—of course they did, she thought helplessly. He was just so gorgeously good at kissing.

'I missed you,' he said. 'I got on with my life, and the focus was probably good for business, but always in the background I missed you and what we had together. Can you tell me honestly that it was not the same for you?'

She couldn't deny it, but she was still too upset by what Bruce had done to do more than offer up a small shrug. Franco pulled her in close again and just held her. It was only when he felt her shiver he realised they'd been standing there stark naked while indulging in yet another argument.

'You're cold. Come on—let's go back to bed,' he decided.

'But you said—'

'I know what I said,' he interrupted. 'I have changed my mind.'

'I don't want—'

'I'm not offering.'

Taking hold of the fingers she still clutched around her nightie, he prised them open and took the scrappy garment from her, shook it out, then dropped it over her head. As the silk slid down over her body Lexi let him take her hand and lead her back to the bed. She curled up there and watched him. He dragged on his undershorts as if he was making big statements with the nightie and the shorts about what they were *not* going to do next.

Her eyes were glued to that potent part of him until it was covered up. She felt her heartbeat go haywire, that so familiar flicker of heat deep inside her flaring up.

'How are the bruises?' she asked a trifle breathlessly.

'Sore.' Reaching out to hit a switch that plunged them into

darkness, he came to lie down beside her. 'Next time show a little pity on me and do all the work.'

'You were so very good at it, though.' Lexi could not resist stroking her fingers down his chest as he dragged the sheets up over them, her senses indulging in a leap of excitement when he went still.

Supporting himself on one elbow, Franco looked down at her. Through the darkness her eyes sparkled up at him, and she was biting down into the cushion softness of her lower lip.

'You greedy minx,' he murmured accusingly.

Flushing, Lexi wriggled. 'Of course, if you're so sure you're not up to it...'

Without warning he rolled onto his back, catching hold of her to bring her to her knees beside him. Despite the sore bruises he still had more strength in his arms than Lexi gave him credit for.

'OK, *bella mia*,' he drawled. 'Take what you want. I am all yours...'

Four days later, Lexi sat dangling her feet in the swimming pool and chewed pensively on her bottom lip as she watched Franco power his way up and down the length of the pool with the sun beating down on his glossy, wet bronzed back.

Tomorrow was Marco's funeral. For the last four glorious days they had not so much as touched on any subject likely to spoil the old harmony they'd resurrected that night in his bed—but it couldn't go on. She needed to shop for something suitably respectful to wear for the funeral, but the one time she'd asked if she could borrow a car to drive into Livorno he'd blocked the request with, 'You need anything, tell Zeta. She will get it for you.' Then he'd changed the subject.

His father was due home today. She'd heard Franco discuss his arrival over the telephone, using that same clipped blocking tone he'd used against her trip to the shops. In all the days she had been here he had not answered a single tele-phone call that had arrived in the house, leaving Zeta or Pietro to deal with whoever wanted to speak to him. He had, in ef-fect, turned his home into a private sanctuary inside which the two of them lived as if the accident, or even the years they had been separated, had not taken place.

But his sanctuary was built inside a bubble that was about to burst, whether he wanted it to happen or not. He wasn't stupid, so whatever he was thinking behind the lazily relaxed mask of contentment he wore all the time Lexi knew he must be aware that he was going to have to burst this bubble soon.

'Franco...' she murmured as he swam up to the pool edge beside her legs.

'What?' he said, only to power away again. It was a very impressive demonstration of freestyle arrogance, because he'd been swimming up and down for fifteen minutes without stopping and did not look as if he was tiring yet. His bruises had already faded into the tanned lustre of his skin, and the wound on his thigh was nothing but a fine purple line to add to the others he already wore on his powerful legs. He would still wince occasionally if she accidentally put too much pres-sure on his ribcage, but other than that he was, she supposed, returned to full health—except for the blanket refusal to talk about Marco's death or his funeral.

As he powered back towards her Lexi timed the moment when she slid into the water and then stepped in front of him as he reached out to touch the pool edge. Finding the sun-kissed heat of her body obstructing him, he was quick to turn things to his advantage by taking hold of her waist and lift-ing her up as he rose like Neptune to his feet.

'Mmm, I've caught myself a real live mermaid,' he growled and tried to kiss her.

'That's corny.' Lexi frowned distractedly, tilting her head back out of his reach. 'We need to talk about—about tomorrow.'

'You like corny,' he insisted, and followed it up by capturing her mouth for a long, lazily sensual kiss. 'You like taking walks in the sultry moonlight and holding hands even when we are only walking downstairs—all corny, romantic stuff, *cara*.'

Refusing to be diverted, she insisted, 'We need to talk about tomorrow, Francesco.' She watched his expression change—tighten up—and, releasing a small sigh, cupped his damp face. 'Please listen to me,' she begged. 'You can't go on ignoring the fact that Marco will be laid to rest tomorrow, and that everyone you've been avoiding since the accident is going to be there.'

Frowning—no, scowling now, he countered very grimly, 'Yes, I can.'

'Well, I can't afford to ignore it, then.' Lexi changed tack. 'I need to buy something to wear for the funeral. I need to know how you want me to respond to questions about the two of us being together again.'

'You're not going.' Opening his arms, he dropped her back onto her feet.

'Yes, I *am*!' Lexi protested.

'You're staying here.'

He was about to dive back beneath the water again, but Lexi grabbed his arm to stop him. 'That is not your decision to make. Marco was my friend too, you know. I *liked* him!'

Shrugging her hand aside, he just turned and hit the water, then swam off! Bristling with frustration, Lexi heaved herself back out of the pool, grabbed a towel and wrapped it around her as she stalked off towards the house. Entering the back way, she headed grimly for the kitchens, found Pietro there enjoying a mid-morning snack, and asked if he would mind taking her into Livorno in half an hour.

Of course he couldn't say no to her, but she could tell by his wary expression as he agreed that he wished he could. It was the flickering way he glanced over her shoulder that made her realise why he was looking so wary. Franco stood a few feet behind her. As she spun around to look at him she caught the tail end of his frowning exchange with the other man.

Snapping her lips together, she pushed right past his obstructive frame and headed for the stairs. If he made it necessary she would call for a taxi to come and collect her, she decided stubbornly.

She'd pulled on a towelling robe and was scrambling through her small assortment of clothes looking for something to wear when she sensed Franco lounging in the bedroom doorway—the bedroom next door to the one they'd been sharing for the last four days.

'I'm not playing this game any more,' she announced without looking at him. 'I've let you get away with it for long enough.'

'I know.'

'You assured me days ago that you were not going to do something stupid, so you can quit with the blocking tactics—What do you mean, you know?'

Turning, she almost forgot how to breathe when she saw him standing there wearing nothing more than a pair of low riding swimming shorts and a towel hanging around his neck. He looked so much like the Franco from that long golden summer it came as a shock.

He shrugged a wide, still wet shoulder, the expression in his eyes shadowed by his spiky eyelashes. 'You cannot abide most of the people who will be there.'

'I am not paying my respects to *them*,' Lexi pointed out.

His small sigh accepted that. 'I predict it will be more like a circus than a funeral—the press will be crawling around all over the place, and you would have to be nice to Claudia.'

'I can do nice when I know I need to,' Lexi said stiffly, interpreting from his words that he didn't want her to go to Marco's funeral because he was afraid she would get into an unseemly cat fight with Claudia. 'I played nice with Claudia

when she was here weeping all over you. I can also appreciate that she has just lost her brother. You forget—I've been
there. I lost my mother not so long ago. I remember how bad
it feels to lose someone you love.'

'OK…' He moved, taking the towel from around his neck
to use it to rub his wet hair. 'I don't want you there.'

Hurt beyond bearing by that blunt announcement, Lexi
felt herself go pale. 'Are you ashamed of me or something?'

He should have come back with a quick, explosive *no*,
but he did not answer, and his silence was like a stiletto sliding smoothly into her chest. Lexi turned back to the clothes
closet and blindly selected something to wear with fingers
that shook so badly she dropped the skirt she'd slid from its
hanger and had to bend to pick it up.

'It is not a case of being ashamed, Lexi,' he sighed out suddenly. 'I just want to protect you from any cruel gossip that
might blow up.'

But he'd spoken too late, and his explanation did not make
any sense—unless…

'Gossip about you and your other women, by any chance?
Well, since you put that subject on the banned list, along with
just about everything and everyone else, let me inform you
that I have an imagination, Franco. I've already worked out
that more than half the women there will probably know you
as intimately as I do—including Claudia!'

'Damn it,' he said again. 'That is not what I meant!'

'Well, try speaking in straightforward sentences!' she
launched at him. 'Because all you've done since I came back
to Italy is toss out these cryptic messages to me, so how am I
supposed to know what you mean? Oh, although I *do* recall
you being very eloquent about my relationship with Bruce!'

'Don't bring *him* back into this,' Franco growled irritably.
'I have something I need to tell you, but I've been trying hard
to hang on until after the funeral. The thing is, I cannot be

sure how many other people know, so I would rather not put you in the firing line for a bloody great shock.'

'Then get it over with and tell me now.'

'No,' he muttered.

'Why?' she persisted.

'Because I want to damn well wait!' He lost his rag so spectacularly he made Lexi blink at him. *'Santa cielo,'* he rasped, throwing his hands up, 'can I not be allowed to get through the next twenty-four hours without all this aggravation from you? Why can't you just trust that I know what I am doing? Is it too much to expect plain and simple support from you for one more day?'

He was talking about Marco. It finally registered with Lexi that he'd been engaging his blocking tactics since she'd arrived here in Italy because the 'something' he was keeping from her involved his closest friend. Now the grey pallor was definitely back, she saw, and the strain was dragging on his features, almost painful to see.

'OK,' she whispered. 'I won't ask again until you're ready to tell me.'

For some reason her promise did not seem to make him any happier. 'You can come to the funeral if that's what you want to do. But I tell you this, Lexi: move one half-inch away from my side and I will do something we both regret—got that?'

Wanting to ask why he had changed his mind, Lexi gauged the sizzling tension emitting from him, pressed her lips together and just nodded her head.

He moved back to the door with the grim stride of a man glad to leave the room. An hour later a car arrived to deliver a selection of outfits suitable to wear at a funeral for Lexi to choose from.

Franco had shut himself away in his study and she did not see him again for the rest of the day. It felt as if she was being punished for standing up to him and spoiling their few days of harmony. By the time they met up again for dinner his father had arrived home, and their meal was a very stressful, sober affair, with the prospect of what was to take place the next day hanging heavily over all three of them.

The two men excused themselves from the table as soon as the meal was over. They disappeared into the study—to talk business, Lexi presumed—and in a lot of ways she was glad they'd left her alone. Franco might be talking to his father again; but throughout dinner his tone had been flat and stilted and Salvatore was either too jet-lagged to bother taking on his son in the mood he was in, or he was as aware as Lexi that Franco was treading a very fine line emotionally.

That night she slept in her own bed. She wasn't sure why she made the decision to do that, but when Franco made no effort to come and find her she assumed that he was glad she'd given him the space to be on his own.

Not that it lasted. Halfway through the long, empty night she'd spent lying wide awake, worrying about him because he'd become so distant and withdrawn, she gave in to the craving that had been eating away at her since she'd heard his bedroom door close hours ago and got up, sneaked into the darkness of his room, then slid into the bed beside him.

He was awake. It didn't surprise her.

'Shh,' she whispered before he could say anything. 'You don't need to talk. I just needed to hold you.'

And he let her. He took her advice and said not a word, but at least he curved an arm around her to draw against him. They stayed like that for what was left of the night, paying silent vigil to the ordeal to come.

CHAPTER TEN

THEY came to mourn Marco in droves. Masses of people packed the church, spilling onto the grounds and onto the street. He was well known and well liked, and the tragedy of his young age and his spectacular death made the mourning of Marco all the more poignant.

Lexi stood quietly beside Franco. His father flanked his other side. Behind them stood the full *White Streak* team, although in their sober black suits, Lexi had not recognised them until they'd lined up outside the church, waiting in turn to commiserate with Franco over Marco's loss. Each one of them had cast a curious glance at Lexi before moving respectfully away.

In front of them stood the Clemente family. Marco's mother and father, his sister Claudia and his many other relatives, all grief-stricken and bereft, but still eager to commiserate with Franco over the loss of his lifelong friend. When they'd arrived inside the church Marco's *mamma* had thrown herself against Franco's chest to sob her heart out. He'd held her close and murmured soothing words to her that had thickened his voice and driven the colour from his face. They'd all asked concernedly how Franco was doing. His stilted dismissal of his own injuries made it clear to Lexi that he found his situation in all of this almost too hard to bear.

She began to appreciate why he had locked himself away

from it all. Survivor guilt, she thought, listening to his quiet voice making sombre responses and feeling his tension like a swarm of stinging bees attaching themselves to her flesh. She knew that he did not want people's sympathy and commiserations, though he had to accept them. And as the ordeal lengthened through the Catholic Mass she could feel the stinging buzz of Franco's tension increasing, until she worried he might actually turn and make a bolt for it.

What he did do almost snapped the fine thread of her own self-control.

It was Marco's father who turned to him and gravely invited him to say a few words for their son. Franco must have been expecting it to happen, because he stepped out from their pew and onto the podium with no hint of hesitation—yet she'd felt the fine tremor rip through him a second before he'd moved. He spoke with a quiet, grave fluency about his friendship with Marco, spanning its twenty years with precious memories, causing a fresh wave of aching grief to spread through the gathered assembly. Even Salvatore became overwhelmed.

Had Franco been composing all this while he lay awake last night? Was this the reason he had shut himself away in his study for half the day?

Lexi felt a sinking twist of guilt: she had not appreciated what he must have been struggling with while she'd fought with him yesterday. He had not wanted her to come. He'd wanted to get through the day without the need to worry about her and the curiosity he knew her presence beside him would evoke. He'd tried to block out all reference to Marco since the accident—yet here he stood, having to open up his grief and loss in front of hundreds of people. She hurt for him—hurt so badly she reached out and clung to Salvatore's hand. She fought back her own rush of tears—for Marco and for Franco.

From the church they moved in sombre procession to

Marco's final resting place, and still the day did not end there. Next they drove to the Clemente estate, with its world-famous vineyards and beautiful *cascina*.

'OK?' she dared to whisper to Franco as the three of them sat in the rear of Salvatore's Mercedes.

'*Si,*' he responded, but that was all he said.

'You did well, Francesco,' Salvatore said huskily. 'I am proud of you today.'

This time Franco did not make an answer—for what could he say? This was still not over. They had a wake to attend, time to relax a little and socialise; but all he wanted to do was tell Pietro to turn the car around and take them home.

He got through the first hour by choosing to avoid those people who knew Lexi from their summer together. They were all there—the golden people, as she'd used to call them, most of them friends of his still. People who seemed, thankfully, to want to respect the politics of reverence and politeness by keeping their distance. Though he could see they were curious to see Lexi with him—and perhaps a little uncomfortable too, for none of them had treated her particularly well.

Even Claudia kept away from them, which he found coldly amusing. She must have worked out by now that Lexi would have told him the part she'd played in breaking them up. They ate delicate finger food from platters extended to them by circulating waiters, talked when they needed to, and then, quite suddenly, it all became too much for him. He was standing with Lexi by his side, talking to a lawyer friend, when it happened. From the corner of his eye he saw Claudia making her way towards them, and he knew he could not be pleasant to her—no matter how much today was about putting personal grievances aside. Abruptly excusing them, he grabbed Lexi's hand and walked her out through the French windows and along the terrace until they'd put the majority of the people at a distance.

He didn't know why it was happening but he felt so hot, and his heart was pounding. Leaning a shoulder against one the stone pillars that supported the loggia, he let go of Lexi's hand so he could loosen his tie and drag open a couple of buttons on his shirt, then he breathed in a lungful of humid air.

'Are you all right?' Looking up at his face, Lexi felt concern clutch at her stomach because he looked as if he might just pass out.

'Fine,' he said. 'Just hot and…'

Reaching up, she touched he hand to his pale cheek. 'You don't feel hot. You feel quite cool.'

'Inside hot,' he enlightened her. 'How much longer do you think we have to stay?'

He was asking *her* that question? Lexi lowered her hand and looked out across the garden to where the Clemente vines marched in regimented lines towards the horizon.

Throughout the whole long day he had barely spoken to her. He'd kind of worn her like a side arm, kept tucked in close to him and hidden almost out of sight. If it had not been for the way he'd tightened his grip if she so much as tried to move away from him she would have thought he'd forgotten she was even there. Twice she'd actually got away from him. Once to say a private farewell to Marco before they'd left his flower bedecked graveside, and the other time when they'd first arrived here and she'd made a quick visit to the cloakroom. When she'd turned away from Marco's grave Franco had been standing just a few yards away waiting for her to go to him. The next time he'd been waiting for her right outside the cloakroom door. Both times he'd said nothing, his expression as impenetrable as the self-control he'd been exerting. He'd just caught her hand and drawn her back to his side, then returned them to the throng.

It was an absolute no-brainer that he'd meant what he'd said about her not straying from his side. It was also a no-brainer that he had no intention of allowing her the chance to talk to anyone on her own.

'You're the boss,' she therefore responded, a trifle satirically. 'I'm just your mute sidekick.'

He melted her bones with a slow grin. 'You are the bossy one in this partnership,' he threw at her lazily. 'You threw my friends off my boat when you'd had enough of them. You dragged me out of clubs and restaurants without bothering to ask me if I was ready to leave. You even flirted with any man in your vicinity then told me off if I dared to complain.'

Flushing when she realised he was only telling it as it had been back in that golden summer, Lexi grimaced. 'It's no wonder your friends didn't like me much.'

'That's a joke.' He laughed. 'The guys, at least, were fascinated by you and jealous of me. They used to wish it was them you were dragging away.'

Lexi looked at the stone floor beneath her shoes. 'I didn't want *them* to myself.'

'I know,' Franco murmured.

'And if I was bossy with you, I don't recall you putting up much resistance.'

'That is because I didn't want to resist,' he told her dryly. 'I like it that you made all the decisions and trailed me around like your sidekick, *bella mia*.'

He was just teasing her when he said that, Lexi decided, and responded with a rueful smile. 'So today you're getting your own back on me?'

Said lightly as a tease-back, she did not expect all hint of humour to suddenly drain away from him. 'No, today is about respecting Marco's death and getting through this without—' He stopped, swallowed, then made a gesture with one of his hands before deciding roughly, 'Let's get out of here.'

Giving her barely a chance to register his meaning, he was grabbing hold of her hand and pulling her further along the terrace, so fast she had a struggle to keep up with him.

'But where are we going?' she demanded breathlessly.

'Around the house to the front. Pietro will take us home.'

'But we can't just leave without telling anyone! It would be rude—and what about your father? Franco!' She sighed when he just kept on going. 'Will you just stop and listen to me?'

But he didn't stop and listen. Within minutes they were in the back of his father's Mercedes and driving away from the Clemente estate, with a bewildered Pietro at the wheel.

'Pietro will come back for my father,' he said, before Lexi could repeat the question. 'We are only half an hour away.'

'But…you just walked out on Marco's wake,' she gasped, because she was still struggling to believe he had done it.

He made no comment, and if Lexi had believed he could block out everything he didn't want to talk about before this moment, she soon learned during the half-hour drive back to Monfalcone that he could put up a solid brick wall against any argument she attempted to make.

He didn't speak a single word. He just sat there beside her, pale and still, with a brooding frown strapped to his face. His mood disturbed her—it was disturbing Pietro too, because she kept seeing him taking quick frowning glances at Franco through the rearview mirror as he drove.

The car came to a stop at the front doors and then he was climbing out and coming round to open her door for her, placing a hand on her arm to help her out.

'OK, this is what's going to happen.' He spoke at last as they walked into the house to the sound of Pietro taking off back to the Clemente estate to collect Salvatore. 'You are going to pack a bag—casual things—while I find Zeta. I will see you back here in fifteen minutes.'

'But—where am I going now?' Lexi cried out as he strode off towards the kitchens.

'We are going away for a few days,' he said. 'Fifteen minutes, Lexi, or you come as you are!'

Staring after him, Lexi worried that the day been just too much for him to deal with. Had he flipped again? Was that it? Cursing herself for forgetting that only a week ago Dr Cavelli had been warning her of his concerns about Franco's mental health, she was seriously considering ringing the hospital to ask the doctor's advice when Franco came striding back, to find her still standing in the hall, as pale a ghost and as anxious as hell.

He must have known what she was thinking because he pulled to a stop, letting out a sigh. But all he said was, 'You have decided to come with me as you are?'

It was a challenge and a smoothly delivered threat at the same time. And, strangely, there was something about him—the way he looked and the way he was moving—that told her this was the real Franco, the cool, decisive one who thought on his feet and did not waste time explaining himself. He wasn't crazy—just determined.

'If I come with you, you'd better not be losing your mind again, because I won't like it!' she launched at him stressfully.

'I am not crazy,' he delivered incisively. 'Are you coming?'

'Of course I'm coming.' She made a dash for the stairs.

'Ten minutes, Lexi,' he called after her.

'Damn you, Franco,' she snapped right back.

But she still arrived back in the hall within the ten minutes, wearing jeans and sandals, her weekend bag hastily packed, to find that he had changed into similar clothes and was already waiting for her. A set of car keys jangled impatiently in his hand and a bag sat on the floor beside him along with a soft-sided cool bag. The moment Lexi arrived at his side he picked the bags up and walked outside.

She stepped outside and saw his red Ferrari glinting in the sunlight and she knew they were about to indulge in yet another spat.

'You're not allowed to drive for another week,' she said. 'It's on the "dos and don'ts" list the hospital sent home with you!'

Simmering in silence at the rebuke, he just tossed her the car keys, removed her bag from her grasp, then strode off to put the bags in the boot.

He had to be really eager to leave here, Lexi thought nervously. Trembling now—she had not expected this response from him—Lexi could only stare as he opened the passenger door and climbed into the car. His quickly changing moods were beginning to get to her, and on top of that she had never, *ever*, driven a car like this one.

Sucking in a deep breath, she got in behind the wheel.

Next he tossed a pair of sunglasses at her. They wanted to fall off her nose, because the frames were too big, but she didn't dare say anything because she knew why he had done it. He wanted her to protect her eyes from the flickering sun between the trees when she drove down the lane.

He had to instruct her as to how she moved the seat forward, and even how to start the great beast of a thing. Moving off as if she was driving an army tank, she was surprised to discover the controls were actually quite sweet. As they passed the place where she'd ditched her own car three and a half years ago anyone could have plucked tunes on the tension between them.

'Now you are back, I'm will have a hedge laid in those gaps,' he muttered. 'And the next car I buy you will be a bloody great land cruiser, not some flimsy cute baby sedan.'

She dared to glance at him and saw that he was pale. 'I didn't lose the baby because I crashed into a ditch, you know,' she told him gently.

'We will never know that for sure.'

'Yes, we do,' she insisted. 'I lost the baby because there had been a problem with the placenta. It happens, *caro*…'

The *caro* brought his face round. It was the first time she'd used the endearment, and his darkened eyes held onto hers so intensely she had to ease her foot down on the brake to slow them right down or risk another accident.

'We still get the hedge,' he husked—and it was really a very silly conversation, because right at that moment neither of them was thinking about hedges or the size of a car or even her doomed pregnancy.

Dragging her eyes free from his, she concentrated on the road ahead again, wondering if sexual tension could be bad for you—because she was feeling decidedly light-headed right now.

Lexi negotiated the narrow bridge with care, a troubled frown creasing her smooth brow. 'You keep talking about us as if we're really back together, but that's not what I agreed to,' she reminded him, pleased with herself that she hadn't scraped the car's shiny red paint.

'So I am still on trial? Is that what you're saying?'

Was she? Lexi thought about that for a minute. 'Our marriage is on trial,' she revised. It had to be—at least until she knew what that 'something' he was still holding back from telling her was.

They reached the junction that met with the main highway. 'Which way?' she asked.

'We go to Livorno.'

'To your apartment?'

'We are going to the Tolle docks,' he enlightened her.

As if he'd lit the litmus on her self-control, Lexi exploded. 'We are not going anywhere near the wreck of your bloody stupid powerboat, Francesco!'

'When did I say that I wanted to check out the *White Streak*?' he demanded in bewilderment.

That was the trouble. He didn't tell her anything, so she had to guess what he was thinking! 'Then why are we going to the Tolle docks?'

'Because,' he said, 'the *Miranda* is there.'

'You still have the *Miranda*?'

'All shipshape and ready to sail.' He nodded. 'We are taking her out. Give me a shout when you need directions,' he said, then stretched himself out in the seat and closed his eyes!

Lexi bit down on her tongue to stop herself from demanding to know who he thought he was, casually making that decision without any input from her. But then he'd been making decisions all over the place without bothering to request any input from her.

And he called *me* bossy, she thought, turning them onto the main highway. Then she tracked back, and felt a happy little fizz of excitement erupt deep down. The *Miranda*. She'd fallen in love with his boat from the very first day he'd taken her out on it. They'd spent the best times of their summer together on the *Miranda*, sailing along the French and Italian Riviera in a flotilla of sailing yachts, keeping his friends close but not so close they could intrude on what the two of them had going on.

'I thought you would have built yourself a newer, more up-to-date yacht by now,' she murmured.

'I have,' he confirmed, without opening his eyes. 'But the *Miranda* is—special.'

Because the yacht held special memories for him too?

As she drove them on towards Livorno Lexi saw herself as she'd looked the first time he'd invited her to spend the day with him on the *Miranda*. She'd worn a little red bikini with a skimpy red sarong around her waist. Franco had had on his usual shorts and a T-shirt, and she'd smiled at him but felt so shy she hadn't been able to look into his eyes. The thrill of being alone with him for the first time had charged up her senses, and she'd felt quivery on the inside, breathless and flushed.

'Thanks,' she'd mumbled, landing lightly by his side in rubber-soled flip-flops. It was the first time she'd noticed how he towered over her—big and dark and potently sexy. 'Wh—where can I stash this?'

The brightly coloured canvas bag that swung from one of her sun-kissed shoulders had contained everything she'd considered she might need for a day's sailing.

'I will do it.' Smooth as anything, he'd lifted the bag from her shoulder and carried it over to the sleek, low bulkhead that gave access to whatever was below decks. She'd tried to take a peek, but he'd blocked her view as he'd come back up on top, forcing her to take a couple of hurried steps back.

'You're skittish,' he'd said, and started frowning. 'You are not scared of me are you?'

'Of course I'm not,' she'd answered firmly.

He'd pointed towards the cream leather seating that hugged the shallow basin in which they stood. 'Then sit down and relax.'

She remembered sitting down and thinking, *Claudia Clemente is going to kill me when she finds out about this.* She'd known even then that Claudia wanted Franco all to herself, Lexi recalled, frowning as she steered the car onto the street leading down to the Tolle docks. Back then, though, she had not understood the kind of enemy she was making for herself. So she'd gone out for a day's sailing with Francesco Tolle and become his lover before they'd sailed back into Cannes.

'A fast mover,' she murmured now.

'Scuzi?' the man lazing beside her responded.

'You,' Lexi enlightened him. 'For our first date you took me out sailing for the day, but I don't remember that we did much sailing. You had me below decks and spread out on your bed before I'd managed to draw in more than a couple of breaths.'

'Two hours twenty minutes. I was counting… Pull in at the gates just ahead,' he instructed and sat up. 'I thought I was very patient.'

'With a bet on the table I suppose you *would* think like that.'

'Lexi, you know I did not make love to you because of some stupid bet,' Franco sighed out irritably.

Did she know that? Yes, she knew that. Somehow the bet was losing its importance. Lexi frowned when she made that discovery.

She pulled in at the gates as instructed, and a security guard came out of his office, touching his brow to acknowledge Franco, grinning at Lexi because she was in charge of his flashy red super car. He opened the gates.

'This place is vast,' she said, sitting forward so she could look curiously around her. She had never been here before, and she kept twisting her neck to the left and the right in an effort to take in the huge buildings on either side of them as she drove. 'Do you ever get lost in here?'

'Never,' drawled the man, with insufferable self-confidence. 'Take the next left. It leads to my private marina.'

His 'private marina'? It made Lexi pull a face. 'Where are your offices?'

There was a pause before he answered, and when he did speak his voice was as dry as dust. 'Three miles in the other direction, *cara*. You don't have a clue what kind of family you married into, do you?'

'You build big ships,' Lexi informed him.

'Ah, *si*.' Franco mocked that simplistic response. 'We even build little ones occasionally—and there she is…'

And there she truly was…

Staring through the windscreen at the sleek white-painted yacht glistening in the sunshine, Lexi felt a lump of helpless tears grow thick in her throat. There were other boats moored in the marina, a couple of them very impressive-looking; but Lexi only had eyes for the *Miranda*.

'She still looks so pretty,' she whispered softly. Not too big, not too small, but just—perfect.

It was like bumping in to a long lost friend when you least

expected it, and she laughed as she brought the car to a stop beside the aft deck and climbed out. She didn't think twice about stepping from the quay onto the *Miranda*, and then just stand looking around her.

In the process of collecting their things from the boot of the car, Franco viewed the smile that had softened her face. So she still had good memories about the *Miranda*, he thought—and hoped he was not about to ruin them.

'Here,' he said, swinging their bags one by one towards her so she could catch them and place them on the deck before he joined her. He handed her the cool bag. 'You stash this stuff in the galley while I see to these.'

He strode ahead with the other bags, leaving Lexi to follow him down the narrow steps that led below. Nothing had changed down here. The same wood still covered most surfaces, and the same smell of fresh varnish caught her nose. A table that doubled as a bed when needed took up most of the cramped space next to the tiny galley kitchen, and the same nautical maps still decorated the walls. As Franco strode towards the other end of the boat Lexi lifted the cool bag onto the narrow work surface in the galley, then bent to open the fridge door.

'I'll go and start the engine,' Franco said as he passed by her again. 'Join me on deck when you've finished down here.'

He disappeared, leaving her staring into the small fridge, surprised to find it was already chilled and that someone had stocked it with basic provisions. He must have planned this trip before they'd even left the house this morning, she realised, frowning as she added the plastic cartons of meals prepared by Zeta into the crowded fridge.

The engine fired and she rushed to finish what she was doing, then clambered back on deck. Franco was standing by the wheel, his head tilted to one side, listening with expert ears to the engine's quiet purr.

'Someone's been in and stocked the fridge,' she relayed. 'How long have you been planning this trip?'

'Come and take the wheel while I cast off.'

Once again he walked away without answering her question. Irritation snapping at her, Lexi took hold of the cool aluminium wheel and watched him pull in the ropes, using a foot to shove them off from the quay. She felt the *Miranda*'s smooth gliding movement and tightened her grip on the wheel.

'OK, ease out the throttle,' Franco instructed.

'No,' she refused. 'You come back here and do it. I haven't been near a boat since the last time I was on this one. I've forgotten what to do!'

'No, you have not.' He came to stand right behind her. 'Just look straight ahead and go easy on the throttle... Your "dos and don'ts" rulebook says I am not allowed to do it, Lexi,' he informed her coolly.

'Oh...' Crestfallen by the unwelcome reminder, she asked, 'Does the same rule count on the sea?'

'No idea.' He didn't sound as if he cared, either. 'However, since you brought up the rule thing you now have to deal with it. So take us out of here so we can catch some breeze and put up the sail.'

There was no arguing with that kind of logic. Lexi felt hoist by her own petard. Crushing her bottom lip between her teeth, she clutched at the wheel with one hand and reached out to clasp the throttle stick with the other. A tiny fizz of alarm churned her insides as the engine took hold and the yacht powered forward.

Tossing back her hair to send it streaming over her shoulders, Lexi concentrated so hard on steering them towards the gap between the two breakwaters that her eyes began to sting; but she didn't care. She'd forgotten how long the *Miranda* was, how sensitive she was to the smallest movement of the wheel.

'Don't you dare move away from me,' she warned tensely.

'I'm right here.' He rested his hand on her waist in reassurance. 'Take us out onto the open sea, *cara*. Enjoy yourself,' he encouraged softly.

Franco was glad she could not see the bleakness on his face right now. For this was it. He had kept his silence for long enough, and as soon as he found a place they could safely anchor, where she couldn't jump ship, he was going to tell her everything he had been holding back. He'd held true to the Italian belief that you did not speak ill of the dead before they had been laid to rest. He'd done it in respect for his long friendship with Marco, and because he'd needed the extra time with Lexi to bring her to the point where she was beginning to believe in them again.

'We're coming up to the breakwaters,' she whispered, as if this was the beginning of a fabulous adventure.

Detecting her small tremor of excitement, Franco eased closer to the warmth of her body. 'Steady as she goes, *cara*,' he intoned gently. 'Be ready to feel the difference between the calm water inside the marina and the first tug of the ocean swell.'

'Which way when we get there?'

'I don't have a clue.'

He sounded as if he didn't care. 'So we're just sailing off into the sunset? Running away like we ran away from Marco's funeral?'

'Concentrate on what you are doing,' was all he said.

'Why are you constantly stonewalling me when I ask you something?' Lexi snapped out in frustration. 'You never used to be like this. You used to be a really open guy I could talk to!'

'I am still quite desperately in love with you. Is that open enough for you?'

Lexi almost swerved them into the solid mass of the breakwater, forcing Franco to place his hands over hers on the wheel to guide the *Miranda* back onto a safe course, while she just stood with his smooth declaration playing in her head and rolling her emotions up in a ball that stuck hard in her throat.

Franco sensed the clamour inside her. He felt the tremor of her hands beneath the steadying grip of his on the wheel. The swell hit them portside. He took control of the throttle with Lexi trapped between him and the wheel, a useless player, while his sailing head took over and he guided them onto a smoother course. The wind caught her hair and blew it back across his shoulders. He glanced down and caught a glimpse of her face turned pearlescent pale.

'No comment?' he drawled in wry observation. 'The lady has finally stopped talking.'

'Your timing is useless.' Lexi burst into shrill trembling speech. 'I could have killed us just then!'

'I am good at driving people to kill.'

That flat comment hit her like a punch in the stomach. Lexi groaned and spun around to look up at him. 'You didn't kill Marco,' she told him painfully.

'You think not?' Still in control of the *Miranda*, he flicked her a brief cynical glance. 'You were not there. You don't know what happened.'

'It was an accident,' Lexi insisted. 'You hit turbulence and…'

'Time to put up the sails.'

'Stop doing that!' Sheer frustration made her hit out at him, her clenched fist making contact with his rock-solid chest. He winced. She quivered in remorse when she realised where she'd hit him. 'Sorry.' She smoothed the flat of her hand over the area she'd just punched. 'But you have just got to stop shutting me out!'

'I know,' he sighed after a minute. 'I just want you to know where I'm coming from before I stop shutting you out.'

Standing taut within the circle of his arms, she asked, 'What is it that you're finding so hard to tell me, Franco, that can be worse than what we've already said to each other?'

He looked down, his eyes narrowed against the glint of the sun on the water. She felt his chest heave up and down beneath her resting palms. He parted his lips to let the air out, then looked back at the shimmering horizon ahead of them with the stunning Italian coastline sliding by them on one side.

'I think Marco meant to kill himself,' he said, then swallowed thickly and brought his teeth together in a tense clench.

Too shocked to respond, Lexi froze for a few seconds, then, 'No,' she said thickly. 'Please don't say things like that.'

'Or maybe he meant to kill me and made a damn mess of it—' This time a tense laugh raked the back of his throat.

'For goodness' sake, Franco—why would you suspect something like that?' she demanded painfully. 'He was your friend!'

'No, he wasn't. Look…' he sighed again. 'Can we finish this later? I need to find a place we can anchor or risk sending us the same way that Marco went…'

This time he wasn't trying to block her out, Lexi realised; she could hear the difference in his voice. And his face wasn't wearing that awful grey cast, nor his eyes that black blank look. He was genuinely struggling to concentrate.

'Do you want me to put the sail up?' she offered, earning herself a tense twitch of a smile.

'What I want is for you to be gloriously impulsive like you used to be and grab me and kiss me then tell me how much you love me. But I don't suppose—'

'All right. I love you, OK?' Lexi complied swiftly. 'Just stop th—thinking such horrible thoughts.'

'You're going to take that back later,' he predicted.

'No, I won't—not unless I'm the crazy one around here,' she responded candidly. 'Because I can't think of one other reason for letting you put me through this last week. I must still love you.'

'Gagged by the doctor, chained to my bed, beautifully manipulated by my father to make you stay with me.' Franco listed the measures he had taken to keep her with him. 'Now I have trapped you on the *Miranda* in the middle of the ocean so you can't run away.'

'Thanks for the excuses,' Lexi murmured tautly. 'Shall I do the sail now?'

Franco shook his head. 'We don't need it. I've spotted somewhere to anchor.'

As he turned the boat towards land Lexi spun in the circle of his arms and saw the heat misted cliffs soaring up in front of them: a spectacular sight. The colour of the ocean darkened to deep green as they sailed into a tiny cove cut out from the rockface. Franco cut the engine, then instructed her to take the wheel while he headed aft to let down the anchor.

Silence suddenly engulfed everything. The *Miranda* swayed gently beneath her feet. She watched Franco walk towards her, then come to a stop, and even with the sun beating hotly down on her Lexi felt a chill cover her flesh when she looked into his face.

'OK, here it is.' He was not going to hang around with this now. 'Marco stopped being my friend in San Remo, when he told me he'd slept with you the night I had to leave you alone to deal with some business for my father in Milan.'

CHAPTER ELEVEN

FRANCO watched Lexi's face and saw exactly what he had expected to see. First came the confused frown, then the dawning shock of utter disbelief. Then came the question—he was waiting for the question.

'You believed him?'

'*Si,*' he confirmed.

'But—why?' she breathed in bewilderment.

'He was very convincing.'

'And the closest thing you had to a brother,' Lexi offered thickly. 'While I was just your summer distraction who stupidly got pregnant?'

'He told me this before you found out you were pregnant.'

Lexi dipped her head and closed her eyes, reliving the way Franco had gone cold towards her. She felt the pangs of her own hurt all over again, because she'd believed that he'd become bored with her as his friends had told her he would. Then Claudia had sent her proof of the bet and within twenty-four hours her mother had died, sending her life into freefall. Quite pathetically, she recognised now, she'd turned to Franco for support and he'd let her. He'd supported her right through the coming weeks while she buried her mother and learned that Philippe had spent her money. Then to top it all off she'd realised she was—

She pulled in a deep, painful breath. 'You thought the baby was Marco's.'

Franco ran a set of tense fingers through his hair. 'I thought it could be possible,' he admitted. 'I'd always been so careful with you, so it made sense.'

'Did you tell him what you suspected?'

'No,' he answered.

'Why not?' Lexi demanded. 'If you believed I'd been to bed with him, was carrying his child, why didn't you tell him? Why take responsibility for me onto yourself?'

'You needed me, not him—'

'Oh, well, thanks for being so noble, Franco! Thanks for marrying me and turning the next four months into the worst days of my life!'

He couldn't argue with that. He *had* married her and made her a life a misery. He'd made his own life a misery. He hadn't wanted to be near her but he hadn't wanted any other man near her either—especially not Marco.

'I was in love with you.'

'Oh, don't feed me that old chestnut,' Lexi condemned in trembling disgust. 'I was the bet you all wanted to win that summer—the jolly joke you all had at my expense!'

'It started out like that.' He finally admitted it. 'But that lasted only as long as it took me to get to know you.'

'Bed me, you mean.'

'No,' he denied.

'Yes!' Lexi insisted, throwing herself past the wheel and down into the galley because she had a horrible fear she was going to be sick. She heard Franco follow her down there. 'I don't know how you managed to live with yourself afterwards,' she tossed at him angrily as she bent to grab a bottle of water out from the fridge. And she was trembling, white as a sheet and hating him—hating him all over again.

'I didn't live with myself,' he said.

Flinging round to face him, she hated it too that he was

standing there looking and sounding so damn calm while she was falling apart! 'How is it that I got all the punishment while Marco remained your very best buddy?' she lanced at him. 'It did take two of us to cheat on you, after all!'

'I told you. He stopped being my friend.'

'So the story about him taking you home and putting you to bed the night I lost my baby was a lie, was it?'

'Now that was quick, considering the state you are in.' He dared to commend her with a brief smile. Then he lifted up a hand. 'Lexi—'

'Don't you *dare* say my name like you want to apologise to me,' she breathed shakily,

'We met up by accident in the bar I was in. I did not arrange to meet him there.' Grimly determined to get out the whole story, Franco ignored the way Lexi turned her back on him and continued doggedly on. 'When I saw him, I went to hit him but I was too drunk so I missed my target, fell on the floor, and basically passed out. Marco picked me up and took me back to my apartment. I don't remember anything after I crashed out on the bed.'

'Poor Claudia got her dearest wish to sleep with you and didn't care that you were comatose.' She swung round again. 'Is that the way you mean to tell it?'

'It was the only way it was going to happen, because I never felt a thing for her...not sexually anyway. Tell me,' he said then. 'Was I undressed?'

Mouth flattening tight, Lexi slumped back against the galley wall, frowned at her feet and gave no answer.

'I ask because I woke up the next morning with a thick head, still wearing my jeans,' Franco went on patiently.

'No T-shirt, though,' she whispered. All she'd seen in that cruel video was his top half, broad and bronzed against the sheet, with— 'Claudia was wearing a bra and pants.'

'Then use your head, *cara*, and think this through—'

'Stay back,' she threatened as he took a step her way.

'They planned it, Lexi,' he persisted, going still again. 'They wanted you out of my life. The video of me accepting the bet was just damn spitefulness on Claudia's side, but the other one was a coordinated plot between Marco and his sister to make you leave me. And he was ruthless about it. Who do you think it was who recorded the moment?'

Marco. Lexi tugged in a painful breath of air. 'Why, though?' She had to ask the question even though it hurt. 'He was your closest friend, and I thought he liked m-me.'

'I have come to realise that Marco only liked Marco,' he answered grimly. 'I've known him for over twenty years and turned a blind eye to most of his shortcomings. He was my friend and I—I cared about him. Until I believed he had slept with you.' Bleak cynicism cast a shadow across his face. 'What kind of friend betrays you by doing that?'

'What kind of lover betrays you by believing *I* could do that?'

'Fair point. No answer.' He held his hands out. 'I was young and arrogant and full of myself. I did not see why he should lie to me about something so important. He blamed you, and I was too willing to listen when he advised me to look at all the men you flirted with—the way you turned them on without seemingly knowing you were doing it.'

'I didn't do that!' Lexi gasped in hot denial, though she was already starting to blush. Back then she hadn't given much thought to what her happy go lucky flirtations were actually doing to the men she flirted with.

'Did you catch me coming onto other women?' Franco lanced at her.

'No.' Lexi dipped her head again, then felt forced to add, 'I used to drag you away when they came onto you.'

'Well, it was a very simple step for me to believe you could have taken your flirtation with Marco the next level.'

Had she flirted with Marco too? Yes, she'd flirted with Marco, Lexi accepted uncomfortably. He'd been the laid-back, sunny one of their crowd. Franco's best friend, whom she'd trusted and who'd always laughed and teased her about her practising her new found feminine wiles on him.

'He was in love you too, of course.'

Lexi blinked. 'I beg your pardon?'

'Marco,' he explained. 'When two friends fall out over a woman it usually means they are both in love with the same one... None of that is any kind of defence for the way I behaved during the months after we married. There *is* no defence,' he stated abruptly. 'But today, if you're willing, we can start again and try to do better this time.'

'Is that why we are here on the *Miranda*? To start again? Same venue, different odds?'

'The odds are up to you, Lexi.' He sounded so grim now, distant. 'I want us to work. The thing you need to ask yourself is do *you* want us to work? I need to check some things out on deck,' he added abruptly, and turned to disappear up the steps and out of sight.

Well, she thought once she was alone, *did* she want their marriage to work?

Of course she wanted it to work. She wasn't such a self-pitying klutz that she couldn't accept some of the responsibility for what had happened. After all, she hadn't exactly been the sweet, bewildered bride a man with Franco's proud personality could look at and find her melting his cold stance.

A long sigh broke free from her chest. So what was she going to do about it?

She noticed the uncapped bottle of water in her hand. She didn't really want it, so she turned to put it back in the fridge, wondering who it was who'd stocked the fridge for them, because most of the room was taken up with bottles of Franco's favourite beer.

Struck by a sudden idea, she took two bottles out and placed them on the galley top, then walked down the boat to push open a door at the far end that led into what was grandly described as a stateroom, though it was only big enough to take a double bed and set of drawers squeezed beside a cupboard.

Their two bags sat on the floor, and she'd bent to haul hers up on the bed with the intention of changing out of her sticky jeans when she saw them—the half dozen green frogs made of all kinds of shapes and materials, lined up in a row on the narrow shelf that ran the length of the bed. It was silly to feel weak tears sting her throat when she saw them sitting there, exactly where she'd left them, as if they'd been waiting patiently for her to return. It was even sillier to let a soft sob escape when she saw the grey rabbit sitting right in the middle of the row, as if he was making some kind of defiant statement to the frogs. Franco must have brought the rabbit with him and put it there. It had to have been the first thing he'd done when they'd arrived.

A sound made her turn, and she found him lounging in the narrow doorway, watching her through dark half-hooded eyes.

'You kept them,' she whispered.

'You expected me to throw them away?' His voice throbbed with dry challenge. 'They are yours, Lexi. They belong to you. They hold your dreams of a handsome prince and ideal love, which I obviously never lived up to.'

'Is that why you stuck the rabbit up there? To m-muscle in on my dreams?'

He looked at the rabbit, sitting there three times the size of its companions, and gave a crooked smile—because the rabbit *did* look as if he was muscling in on the frogs. 'No. He is there to represent me. My dreams. With a bit of luck on my side you will kiss the rabbit as you move along the row. Think of me, waiting for my turn.'

'I always thought of you when I kissed the frogs.'

'Your handsome prince?' He turned the crooked smile on her. 'I don't think so, *cara*. I let you down so badly I made a better villain in your fantasy world...' He straightened up and pulled in a deep breath. 'I came down to tell you I have to move the boat. There are rocks close to the surface. I cannot risk the *Miranda* swinging into one and damaging her hull. I've decided to use the sails. We will move much faster while there is a stiff breeze up. I need to find a safer place to anchor before it grows dark.'

'OK.' Lexi nodded her head, but he'd already turned away by then. 'I'll come and help. I...I just want to change out of these jeans and...' Her voice sounded so strained she was surprised when it trailed away to nothing. It took an effort to make it work again. She tried again. 'And you—you're still the only man I've been with...the only man I've wanted to be with... Can—can we talk about that instead of princes and villains and frogs?'

She could tell by the severe set of his shoulders that he would much rather escape right now. Franco had done a lot of opening up in the last hour, after spending too long holding it all in. Oh, they'd fought over many things during the last week, Lexi recognised—fought over other people's interference in their lives. But they hadn't touched base on what they were feeling—not really—not if she didn't count the time he'd told her he still loved her as they left the marina, and even that had become lost in the storm of shock she'd had straight afterwards.

'I do truly still love you too, Francesco,' she whispered shakily.

'Madre di Dio!' he swore, reeling back against the doorframe and spearing with her a burning glance. 'I have to move the damn boat, Lexi! And you throw this at me *now*?'

Her lips trembled as she parted them. 'I didn't throw it at you, I just—just told you s-so you would know.'

He closed his eyes. 'This is payback because I shocked you with such a declaration earlier.'

'Well, if you want to take it that way then go and play with your ropes and sails!' Lexi threw at him hotly. 'Because I am not repeating it!'

She spun away, and yelped when she was spun right back again. Two powerful arms hauled her up against his chest.

'That wasn't fair,' he growled.

'I know,' she admitted. 'I just got all h-heated up—'

A pair of eyes the colour of tiger's-eye quartz flamed down on her. He yanked her closer and fused their lips in a burning kiss. 'Now, *that's* heating you up, *amante mia*,' he taunted softly, then let go of her and disappeared through the door while Lexi stood, still burning.

The sails were up and they were running with the wind by the time Lexi came up on deck. Standing at the wheel, Franco watched her pause and raise her chin, letting the warmth of the wind blow her hair away from her face. She'd changed into the white bikini she'd been wearing by the pool for the last few days. A white sarong printed with flowers was draped around her hips, and she looked long and sleek and so much his kind of woman he smiled at himself for thinking it.

She was carrying two bottles of beer with the caps already removed.

'*Grazie,*' he said, when she handed him one of the bottles.

'Do you want me to do anything?'

'No, just come and stand here where I can see you.' He did not give her an option, just hooked an arm around her and drew her to stand in front of him.

As she settled against him Lexi saw he was in his element. With the sun on his face, the wind in the sails and the skimming hiss of water against the sides of the boat the only sound in a beautiful silence. This, she thought, was Franco's world.

'Do you have any idea where we are going?' she questioned curiously.

'*Si*, there is a pretty cove with a small beach and a restaurant within reach before the sun goes down.'

'Oh,' Lexi pouted. She didn't really want to leave the boat to eat in a restaurant. 'I didn't bring anything to wear suitable for eating out.'

He looked down at her, not fooled by her regretful tone in the slightest. 'I was not intending for us to eat there,' he drawled. 'I was merely describing the place we are heading for. I have other plans for dinner.'

'Zeta's pasta?' Lexi suggested.

Since she was glued to his front she knew exactly what he had planned for dinner. When he raised an eyebrow in that arrogant way he had she just laughed, kissed his chin, then turned around so she could lean back against him.

'Like the old times,' she murmured softly after a few minutes. 'I like this starting again.'

'No more questions? No more doubts?'

He spoke lightly, but Lexi knew there was a serious enquiry behind the question. They both knew they still had a lot of things to trawl out and work through, and they still had not talked about what had really happened when the *White Streak* crashed, but—

'I meant it before, when I said I wanted to talk about us— our feelings, not everyone else's feelings. They've messed up our lives enough as it is, but right now I just feel—scared.'

'Scared of what?'

She felt him grow tense behind her. 'That we're trying to recapture something here that shouldn't be recaptured. '

'You don't believe I still love you,' he declared after a second.

'I don't believe we've been back together long enough to know for sure *what* we are feeling,' she confided unhappily.

She watched his fingers tightening on the wheel. 'So I'm still on trial here?'

'I didn't say that—'

'You might as well have said that,' he countered.

'You should've told me what Marco said about me.'

'I know.' Lowering his head, he pressed a contrite kiss to the top of her head.

'I had a right to defend myself,' Lexi murmured.

'*Si,*' he agreed.

'And I had a right to have you trust me more than you did.'

'I know that too,' he accepted heavily. 'Marco knew all my weaknesses and he played on them. He was the only person I'd confided in that you were the one. I told him I was going to marry you, and do you know what he did?' Putting his bottle on the bulkhead freed him up to draw her even closer. 'He laughed like a drain. Then he asked if I would still want to marry you if I knew you had slept with him while I was away. I beat him up and threw him in the pool. When he climbed out he was still laughing. He wanted to know where the hell I got off, thinking I had exclusive rights on you. A bet was a bet.'

'But he must have known by then that you'd already won the bet!' Lexi protested. 'We hadn't exactly hidden the fact that we were lovers.'

'I wasn't thinking straight. I wanted to kill you. I wanted to kill him. Instead I turned myself into the ice man and brought the group together so I could claim my prize. I knew Claudia was recording the moment on her mobile, and I knew she would not be able to resist sending it to you. It was the salve for my wounded pride. The worst punishment I could come up with. I was saying, *Look how little you mean to me, Lexi Hamilton.*'

'It worked.' Lexi sniffed back a sob. 'I was devastated.'

'Then all the other stuff happened,' Franco continued bleakly. 'Your mother and Philippe Reynard were killed. I had distanced myself from you by then but you looked so lost I couldn't get back in there quick enough to give you support.'

'Then I discovered I was pregnant.'

'And I behaved like a spoilt, heartless brat. I loved you, but it scared me to love you. I couldn't marry you fast enough, but

I made you feel like you had ruined my life. When you left me I beat myself up for driving you away, but my bruised pride would not let me go chasing after you. When I did eventually pluck up the nerve to come and see you I got to see Dayton instead.'

'Let's not go there,' Lexi said quickly. 'I've spoken to him. He knows I know what he did, and he knows our friendship is over for good.'

'As Claudia knows,' Franco concluded. 'As Marco knew when we argued before the race.' He took in a deep breath, then told her what had happened. 'I knew he was going to do something crazy when he said goodbye to me,' he said thickly. 'I never meant to drive him to the point of—'

'It wasn't your fault.' Lexi turned to put her arms around him and looked at him anxiously. 'You have got to stop thinking that it was. You spoke so beautifully about him today, Franco,' she reminded him softly. 'Remember Marco as that person—the one you loved as a brother.'

They arrived at their destination then, and the boat demanded their attention. Perhaps it was a good thing, because it gave them time to detach themselves from the ugliness of the past—to throw it all away for good. They worked well together, in unison, like they'd used to do—as Franco had taught her all those years ago. Then they cooked Zeta's pasta and took it up on deck to eat beneath the stars, drinking beer out of the bottles like they'd used to.

It was pretty much an exact replay of that perfect summer, Lexi thought as she sat cross-legged on the deck beside Franco's outstretched strong golden legs and watched the restaurant lights beyond the tiny cove shine softly in the distance.

Yet there was still one small question that begged an answer. 'What made you decide that Marco had been lying about me?' she murmured softly.

He didn't say anything for such a long time Lexi felt all

the tension start to creep back. Then he heaved in a deep breath and reached for her, lifting her up to bring her down so she straddled his warm thighs. His eyes were dark in the soft light from the single lantern they'd lit. He looked sombre and thoughtful as he gently combed a lock of her hair away from her cheek.

'Let me tell, instead, what loving you meant to me,' he murmured deeply. 'Loving you, *anima mia*, meant losing the ability to focus for long on anything without thinking about you. It meant checking the phone a hundred times a day in case you'd called. It meant walking into a room and searching it in case you might be there, and waking in the middle of the night with your name on my lips and your perfume in my nose and the taste—*Dio*,' he husked, 'the taste of you on my tongue. It meant I was lonely in a crowd of people. It was the joke I laughed at while I was crying inside, and the nagging ache that constantly dogged me low down in my gut, always there, driving me insane—yet the hell of it was I never wanted it to go away.'

Close to tears, Lexi pressed her fingers against his lips. 'Please don't say any more,' she whispered. 'You're breaking my heart.'

'My heart was broken,' he said, reaching up to remove her fingers, kissing them, then keeping hold of them. 'Don't cry. When you cry it tears me apart. Loving you was wishing, and hating myself for wishing, and wanting you so badly. I used to conjure up the image Marco had put in my head of you with him, but the image always faded to show me just you. *This* Lexi,' he described softly. 'The one with the toffee-gold hair and the ocean-green eyes—loving *me*. Loving me, Lexi. And you never stopped, did you? After everything I did to murder your feelings for me, you could not stop loving me either. I saw it from the moment I looked into your beautiful face.'

'Are you saying that you *didn't* bring me back to Italy because you realised that Marco had been lying to you?'

Reaching up, he ran the tip of a finger along the trembling line of her mouth. 'I did tell you several times that I'd already been planning to see you before the crash happened,' he reminded her. 'I just wanted you back. Your divorce papers gave me one hell of a jolt. They made me realise it was time to stop fighting myself, put the thing with Marco behind me and fight to get you back. Then, as I flew through the air that day and wondered if I was going to survive, it came to me in a blinding flash that Marco had lied to me. He had implied as much before the race, but...'

'It doesn't matter,' Lexi put in quickly. She did not want to think of him flying through the air, believing he was going to die. 'I love you, Franco,' she murmured urgently. 'In every single way you just described about me, but I don't want—'

Whatever it was Lexi did not want became lost when Franco captured her mouth in a hungry, hot, passionate kiss. Before she knew it she'd lost her bikini top and they were lying flat on the deck, making love in the velvet darkness— the way they'd used to do.

Later they went to the stateroom, holding hands all the way even though it made moving through the narrow doorways almost impossible.

'You forgot to kiss the frogs,' Franco said as they came together beneath the sheets.

'To hell with the frogs,' Lexi responded irreverently. 'It's you I want to kiss.'

* * * * *

THE MORETTI ARRANGEMENT

KATHERINE GARBERA

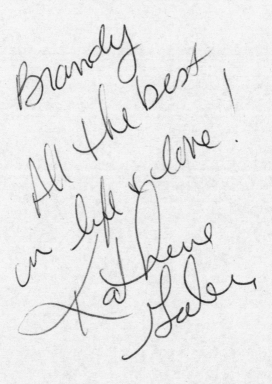

Brandy
All the best
in life & love!
Katherine
Garbera

USA TODAY bestselling author **Katherine Garbera** is a two-time Maggie winner who has written more than sixty books. A Florida native who grew up to travel the globe, Katherine now makes her home in the Midlands of the UK with her husband, two children and a very spoiled miniature dachshund. Visit her on the web at katherinegarbera.com, connect with her on Facebook and follow her on Twitter @katheringarbera.

One

"Signore Moretti, is everything okay?" his secretary, Angelina De Luca, asked as he returned to his office.

Dominic didn't know what he'd do without her. She was even more of a godsend now that they had a leak in the Moretti organization.

"No, Angelina, I'm not okay. I need to see Antonio in my office immediately."

"*Sì*, Signore Moretti."

"Angelina?"

"*Sì?*"

"I've given you leave to call me Dominic."

"Yes, you have, but when you come into the office looking as angry as you do today…I think it's best that I observe all rules of propriety and lie low."

"Have I ever treated you unfairly?" Dominic asked.

"Not at all," Angelina said with a smile.

Dominic smiled back at her. He'd be interested in his pretty secretary, if it weren't for his family's curse.

A curse that promised that each generation of Morettis would be either lucky in love or lucky in business, but never in both.

Lorenzo Moretti, Dominic's grandfather, had been very lucky in business but had died a bitter old man. Dominic's father Giovanni had been and still was very lucky in love. He and Dominic's mother shared a love that was deep and abiding.

And now his brothers were screwing things up for their generation despite the blood vow they'd all taken in their teens. They had promised each other they would be the generation of Morettis to take back the proud name that had once been revered on both the Grand Prix track and in the world of luxury sports cars.

He lived in Milan but traveled the world entertaining guests at Team Moretti's VIP rooms at all of the Formula 1 Grand Prix races. As the CEO of Moretti Motors he was currently overseeing the launch of a revamped model of their 1970s classic Vallerio Roadster.

The car had been named for one of the fastest F1 drivers ever. Lorenzo Moretti's best friend, Pierre-Henri Vallerio.

"Is there anything I can do?" Angelina asked.

"Just keep doing your job," Dominic said. He'd been relying more and more on his assistant to make sure that things were running smoothly. Last year he had realized someone was stealing Moretti secrets. It had started with partial engine design and modifications showing up in cars made by their chief competitor, ESP Motors. Before long, Dominic, Antonio and Marco had realized that the spy was someone working for their organization.

They had traced the leak back to the corporate offices here in Milan. But they had been unable to uncover anything further.

Marco was busy as Team Moretti's F1 driver. He didn't have the time to delve into what was happening in the corporate offices of Moretti Motors.

Antonio was busy dealing with the Vallerio family. He had to continuously ensure that the use of the Vallerio name on the new Moretti Motors Vallerio Roadster was well within the rights of the contract Pierre-Henri had signed years ago.

So that had left Dominic with the task of making sure the spy was caught. And he would take great pride in prosecuting the thief. He desperately wanted retribution.

"I'll get Antonio down here as soon as possible," his secretary said. "Also you had a call from Ian Stark. I put him through to your voice mail."

"Thank you, Angelina."

Dominic left his assistant's desk and entered his office, which had been occupied by every CEO of Moretti Motors since his grandfather had purchased this building in 1964. No expense had been spared when Lorenzo had designed this office. He said that he wanted everyone who entered this room to know that the man who sat at the desk was one of power.

A man who could make things happen, Dominic thought. He walked over to the wall where his *nono*'s portrait hung. In it, Lorenzo stood next to his first F1 car—the first Moretti Motors car that he had designed and driven in the Grand Prix.

He looked up at his grandfather and was reminded of the promises he, Antonio and Marco had made to each other. He was so aware that their dream of rebuilding Moretti Motors had in his brothers' eyes been accomplished. But Dominic wanted more.

He wanted the legacy his grandfather had left to them to continue. He wanted Moretti Motors to become synonymous with luxury, speed and greatness. And he couldn't do that while someone was selling the secrets they'd spent the last three years developing.

Angelina called Antonio and greeted him politely when he came down to see Dominic. Once the two men were in Dominic's office, the smile faded from her face. She loved her job at Moretti Motors—not that she thought she'd have it for much longer.

She was in a bad place. It didn't help that she'd allowed herself to be manipulated. At the end of the day she was responsible for her actions.

And she knew that any kind of explanation she came up with as to why she'd done what she had…well, that wasn't going to get her any sympathy from Dominic Moretti.

She was half in love with the man. Really, what wasn't to love? He was tall, muscular…a fine-looking man with an earthy sexiness.

He had dark eyes that seemed to stare into the very heart of her. But she knew he had no mystical powers—he couldn't really see the lies she kept carefully hidden away.

"Angelina?" Dominic's voice came from the intercom.

"Sì?"

"Please make a reservation for myself and my parents for Friday at Cracco-Peck."

"Will nine be a good time?"

"Sì," Dominic said.

She made the reservation and then sent an e-mail to Dominic and his parents with the confirmation information. She was privy to every detail of Dominic's life…well, just the business ones, but Dominic Moretti was a man who lived for his company. He wasn't just the CEO of Moretti Motors, he *was* Moretti Motors. His brothers also shared responsibility for the company, but it was Dominic who lived and breathed it.

And she was slowly stealing the secrets that he

had worked so hard to develop. In fact, just two days ago she'd gone to London to meet with Barty Eastburn of ESP Motors to give him the company's latest plans.

Her mobile phone rang and she glanced at the caller ID. Her brother. "Renaldo, I can't talk now."

"We have to, Ange. I need something else. Eastburn isn't satisfied with what you've given him."

"Renni, I really can't. Everyone here is being watched. I—"

"They are going to kill me, Ange. I know it's not fair to ask you to save me again, but I have no one else."

She wanted to cry. Her brother was the only family she had and yet she'd never been able to rely on Renni. He was younger than she was by a mere fifteen months, but she felt years older.

"I'll see what I can do. What does he want?"

"You'll have to come to London. He's booked a ticket in your name."

Angelina didn't know if she could keep doing this. She didn't want her brother to die and she knew he wasn't being melodramatic. He'd gambled and lost big time to exactly the kind of men that she had warned him to avoid. And now it seemed the only way to pay off his debts was for her to keep betraying her boss.

"I'll…I can't decide right now," she said. "I don't like doing this, Renni."

There was silence on the line, but in the background she heard the noises of the dock. How had her brother gotten so lost?

"I understand, Ange. You've done more than a sister should have to."

She heard that note in his voice. The one that always scared her because it signaled that Renni was about to do something really stupid and dangerous. And as much as she wanted him to take responsibility for his life, she didn't want to have to visit her brother in the hospital again.

"I'll be there," she found herself saying.

"Thanks, Ange."

"This has to be the last time, Renni. If I do this you come back to Milan with me. No more gambling."

"I'll do it. All of it. I promise."

She hung up the phone and rubbed her temples, knowing better than to believe Renni's promises. She knew that he meant the words that at this moment Renni wanted to stop. But wanting and doing were two different things.

The door to Dominic's office opened and he and Antonio came out. The men were still talking and for a moment she wanted to just say that she quit and run away.

But instead she eavesdropped on their conversation and heard Antonio mention that they had finished the design of the Vallerio Roadster and that the new engine design was on his desk.

"Angelina, can I see you in my office?" Dominic asked after Antonio had departed.

"Yes. Do I need to bring a notepad?"

"No."

She stood and preceded Dominic into his office. Once there she went to a guest chair and sat down. He closed the door and just stared at her for a long minute and she realized that the ruse was up.

Somehow Dominic must have discovered she had been stealing secrets for ESP Motors' Barty Eastburn. And as sad as she was to be losing her freedom, she also felt relief. She wasn't cut out for the kind of subterfuge she'd had to engage in over the past year.

"I've asked you in here because I need your help setting a trap."

She actually felt the blood drain from her face. Oh, God, what was she going to do? "A trap?"

"I had two sets of plans made for the new engine configuration. I want you to send one to Emmanuel and one to Stephan."

"Wouldn't it be better to just bring both men in and question them?" she asked. She didn't want Dominic to suspect either of the two company executives. They were good men with families, she thought.

Dominic shook his head. "I've hired an outside investigations firm and they have advised me that the spy has to be caught red-handed. Otherwise there's something called plausible deniability and I'm not about to let the man who stole from me get away with it."

Angelina nodded. She felt a sense of doom as she realized that this really was the end for her. There was no way that Dominic's firm wasn't going to figure out that she was the leak.

The following afternoon found Dominic satisfied that he'd set everything in motion that he possibly could to catch the spy. He'd hired Ian Stark of Stark Security. He and Ian had gone to college together. After graduation they'd both gone into their families' businesses.

Stark Security had been in the business of protecting the rich and famous for over a hundred years, not as a bodyguard service but as an intellectual properties security firm. Ian protected the secrets of the famous. And he did a damn fine job of it.

Now he was going to catch Dominic's corporate spy. In fact he was already en route now. Which was cause for celebration, Dom thought.

However, his brothers were all occupied right, and though he was having dinner later this evening with his parents, he wanted to celebrate now.

Or was he just looking for an excuse to ask his lovely secretary out for a drink?

Yes, he was.

He walked out of his office and found her desk empty. He was just sitting down in her chair to write her a note when she came back in.

"Ah, there you are," he said.

"Yes, here I am. Did you need something?"

"Yes. Get your coat, we are going out for a drink to celebrate."

She smiled at him. That shy sweet smile that had played a part in a number of fantasies for him lately.

"What are we celebrating?"

"Success," he said.

"I'll drink to that," she said.

He stood and realized how small his assistant was and how very feminine. The dress she wore today was cut close to her body and had a plunging neckline. The skirt flounced around her legs as she stepped closer to him.

Her curly hair reached almost to her jaw, and swung around her creamy skin whenever she moved her head. She had stepped close to get to her desk, but he didn't move away.

He took a good look at her kissable lips. How the lower lip was fuller than the top one. He started leaning down toward her before he realized what he was doing.

"Dominic?"

"Hmm?"

"What are you thinking about?" she asked. She seemed nervous and licked her lower lip as she watched him.

God, he wanted her mouth under his. He wanted to know exactly what she tasted like, what she felt like in his arms. And now that he was taking care of the problems at Moretti Motors, he could move his focus elsewhere.

An affair was exactly what he needed, and

Angelina was the woman he wanted. "I'm thinking about you."

"In what way?" she asked.

She seemed almost nervous. Normally he preferred a more sophisticated woman—a woman who knew the score and didn't become attached. And in the last two years working with Angelina he knew she wasn't that type of girl.

Maybe he should walk away, but he couldn't. He'd tried to ignore Angelina since she'd started working for him. At first it had been relatively easy since they'd still been struggling to bring the company back up to speed, but for the last year or so he'd started seeing Angelina more and more as an attractive woman and not just his secretary.

"I'm thinking about kissing you," he told her.

Her hand covered her lips. "Why?"

"Why shouldn't I?" he asked.

"We work together, Dom," she said.

"Is that a problem?"

She tipped her head to the side, one inky curl felling across her face, and he tucked it back behind her ear before she could. Her skin was soft, but then he'd expected it to be. He *hadn't* expected her to turn her head to the side and rub her cheek against his finger for a brief moment.

"I think it is a problem," she said. "I like my job too much to compromise it."

He dropped his hand and stepped away from her. He could respect that. "You are a top-rate assistant and you would be hard to replace."

"So you'd fire me?" she asked.

"No. Just transfer you to another department. I wouldn't want you to feel pressured to date me…it's just that lately I can't seem to stop thinking of you in terms that aren't exactly suited to the office."

"I've had a few thoughts about you, too," she said.

He arched one eyebrow at her. "Have you? Want to tell me what those thoughts were?"

She shook her head. "I don't think that's a good idea. But I will join you for the celebratory drink. What are you celebrating?"

"Stark Security found our leak. As of tomorrow morning that person will be in police custody and we will be back on track."

She flushed. "Did they give you the name?"

"No, not yet. Ian doesn't like to deliver that type of news over the phone."

"How did he figure it out?"

"I'll tell you while we are having our drink."

She glanced down at her calendar. "Oh, I can't go. I forgot it was Wednesday."

"What do you have on Wednesdays?" he asked.

"I meet my book club. This week I'm hosting, so I can't be late. I'm sorry, Dominic. But congratulations to you on finding the leak."

She gathered her purse and coat and walked out the door. Dominic rested his hip against the edge of her desk and watched her leave. He had a feeling of what might have been but let it go. Having Angelina at his side was important to the future success of Moretti Motors.

Two

Angelina didn't think twice about the call she was going to make. She couldn't do it anymore—work for Dominic and continue to sell his secrets to ESP Motors. She was still worried about her brother. Renaldo's safety had been her only motivator.

But it had gone on long enough. Tonight she'd had to put her own happiness on hold to take care of her younger brother…stop it, she thought. There was no excuse she could give even to herself that would justify what she'd done.

Instead of going home when she'd left the offices, she'd wandered through the streets of

Milan, ending up at the Piazza del Duomo. Now she sat at a small café nursing a glass of wine and watching the evening crowds.

Their lives seemed so simple, so uncomplicated compared to hers. How had her life gotten so messed up? How long before her freedom was taken from her and she ended up in prison?

She knew Dominic was going to prosecute her. And she couldn't blame him. *Dios,* she wished she'd made a different choice when Renaldo had first come to her.

But after she'd said no and the men he'd owed the money to had beat him…well, visiting her brother in the hospital and seeing him so close to death had changed her mind.

No matter that she'd been half in love with Dominic Moretti, Renaldo was her brother and she couldn't allow him to be killed when she had the means to save him.

Somehow she doubted that explanation was going to make any difference to Dominic.

"Angelina?"

She glanced up to see Marta Kingsley, another secretary from Moretti Motors, standing by her table. "*Ciao,* Marta."

"Can I join you?"

"Of course. Are you alone?"

"I'm meeting a guy that I met online," Marta said.

"Online dating? I can't believe you do that."

"It's a lot of fun actually. And I don't think I'm going to meet Mr. Right this way but hey, I'm an American in Milan and it gets me out of my apartment."

Angelina laughed for the first time since she realized that Dominic had found his corporate spy. "It does get you out."

Marta smiled. She was very pretty and her life seemed uncomplicated. Angelina knew that Marta went out at least three times a week.

"You should try it."

"I don't think so," Angelina said. "My life is pretty complicated right now."

"I get that. Dominic is one demanding boss."

"Yes, he is." And he was also a very enchanting man. Her mind kept replaying his asking her out for a drink. God, she'd wanted to say yes. But she'd known if Dominic found out she was his spy, he'd be doubly angry that she'd led him on.

"Do you like working for him? The one time I filled in for you, I was scared the entire time of doing something wrong."

"He's not that bad. He seems gruff, but he's not really. And if you do your job to the best of your ability…well, that's all he asks."

"I'm just glad that he's not my boss," Marta said. She stared at a man standing on the corner, looking about. "Ah, I think that's my date."

"Which one?"

"The one in the cranberry-colored T-shirt. Um…he looks different than his online profile photo."

"Don't they all?" Angelina asked. "I tried online dating for a while, but never found a man who matched what he said in his profile."

"That's true enough, but then I don't exactly match my profile, either."

"You lied about yourself?" Angelina asked.

"Just fudged a few details. Like I found that being an American drew the wrong sort of men, so I dropped my nationality off the page and I said I was twentysomething instead of thirty."

"Oh, why? Do you want to start a relationship with lies between you?" Angelina asked.

"Not really, but I think everyone lies about something."

Angelina wanted to argue, but found she couldn't. Thanks to her own actions she'd become one of the people she used to loathe. "I guess you're right."

"Don't sound so disappointed," Marta said. "The world we live in is one based on half-truths." Her mobile rang and she glanced at the caller ID. "That's my date. He must not recognize me. I'll see you at work tomorrow."

"*Ciao,* Marta."

Her friend left and Angelina felt a sense of…melancholy. She was sad that she'd let Renaldo change her. But then she'd always known he would. From the day their parents had died in a car crash when she was eighteen, she'd known her life would change.

Renaldo had been sixteen, an age at which some men, men like Dominic would have been mature enough to handle responsibility, but Renni wasn't cut from the same cloth as Dominic Moretti.

Heck, not many were, she thought. She swallowed the last of her wine. She had to stop thinking of Dominic as some sort of romantic leading man. He wasn't. No matter that he'd asked her out for a drink tonight. No matter that he'd almost kissed her.

He wasn't for her. He'd never been the man for

her. Even if she hadn't sold his secrets to save her brother, Dominic was never going to be her man. He was out of her league.

She got to her feet deciding it was time to head home. She wondered what tomorrow would bring. Would the police be waiting at the office and arrest her?

Marta caught her eye as she walked past the open-air patio and waved at her. Angelina waved back, trying to pretend she was like the others in the Piazza. But deep inside she knew she would never be like everyone else again.

Dominic had a nice evening with his brothers and parents, then returned home to wait for Ian to drop by.

Looking about his empty house, he realized there was something missing from his workaholic life. He could never settle down to love one woman, would never leave himself open to that kind of betrayal again. But he could see himself in a long-term affair.

The doorbell rang and Dom went to answer it. He greeted his friend, then groaned as he glanced at the car parked in front of his house. "A Porsche?"

"I like the car. It's the first one I bought with my own money," he responded.

"Still, they are a major competitor of mine. Show some respect."

"Ah, Dom, you know that I have two Moretti Motors cars in my garage at home."

"You couldn't drive one here?"

"Nope. It'll drive Tony nuts to see that Porsche outside," Ian said with a quick grin.

Dom thought of what his brother's reaction would be and smiled at his friend. "Yes, it will. So, what do you have for me?" he asked as they seated themselves in the living room.

"I think I should wait for your brothers to get here."

"Marco can't make it."

"Racing business?" Ian asked.

"No, his new wife."

"I thought you guys were cursed. No marriages for any of you."

"Marco's wife, Virginia, is the granddaughter of the woman who cursed *Nono*. She thinks her marriage to Marco broke the curse."

"Could it be that simple?" Ian asked.

Dominic had no idea; he shrugged. "They seem happy."

"I guess that's all that matters when it comes to relationships."

"Happiness?" Dominic asked.

"That's been my experience," Ian said. "If a woman is happy, then everything is good."

Dominic had no such experience; his affairs were usually brief. He'd always believed if a relationship was structured like a business deal he'd have a better chance at making it work.

"Dom, you've got a big piece of trash in front of your house," Antonio said as he came through the door.

"Most people don't consider a Porsche trash, Tony."

"I can't speak to others' ignorance," Antonio said.

Ian laughed and stood to shake his hand. "Good to see you."

"You as well. So, did you find our leak?" Antonio asked.

"I did. I think it's going to shock you both."

Dom had seen it all in his time as CEO of Moretti Motors. They'd encountered corporate spying before and had implemented internal security measures but it looked as though their prior loss-prevention techniques had failed. "Nothing would shock me."

Ian looked straight at Dom. "Not even the fact that the leak is your secretary, Angelina De Luca?"

"What? Are you sure?" Dom asked. He crossed to the bar on one wall, poured two fingers of whiskey into a highball glass and swallowed in one long draw. Filled with rage, he wanted to smash something. He couldn't believe that he'd entertained the thought of starting an affair with her while she had been betraying him. He'd relied on her....

"Positive. She's been feeding information to ESP Motors. I saw the last drop myself."

"How the hell is that possible?" Dom asked.

Antonio spoke up. "She's had free rein of our corporate offices. She knows everything."

"I know that," Dom said.

"What do you want to do next?" Ian asked. "I have enough evidence to go to the police and press charges. We can have her arrested."

"Do you have enough to prove ESP was behind it? Did you catch them in the act?"

ESP was the company founded by Nigel Eastburn, Lorenzo Moretti's biggest rival on and off the racetrack. Both men had started their own car companies after retiring. The launch of the

Vallerio model had pushed Lorenzo ahead of Nigel. In the 1980s, when Moretti Motors had started to fail, ESP Motors—named after Nigel and his two partners, Geoffrey Saxby and Emmitt Pearson—had moved ahead. That was why Moretti Motors wanted their new Vallerio Roadster to be a success—to take back the pride that they'd lost when ESP had become the name synonymous with roadsters.

"I'm sure I can get irrefutable proof that ESP is behind the espionage if you give me another week or so. I need to make sure the person contacting Angelina isn't working independently," Ian said.

"Who is it?" Dominic asked.

"Barty Eastburn."

"Nigel's grandson? That is big. Well, I'd rather take him down than just Angelina." Dominic hoped he appeared nonchalant, that the rage he felt toward his secretary was well hidden.

"Angelina can't get off without punishment," Antonio said.

"She won't," Dom said. The fierceness of his tone seemed to startle Antonio.

"Don't do anything rash, Dom," his brother said.

"*I* will handle it. Ian, please let me know as soon as you are ready to spring the trap on Barty."

"Do you think Angelina will help us with it?" Ian asked.

"Yes, she will."

"How can you be certain?" Ian asked.

"Because I'm not going to give her a choice."

Ian and Antonio left shortly after ten and Dominic paced broodingly through his home. He had dialed Angelina's mobile number several times but hung up before the call connected. He was so angry right now that he knew talking to her was the wrong thing to do.

But as he paced around his home office he knew he couldn't wait until morning to confront her. He needed a plan of action. He needed something to occupy his mind.

He stopped under the portrait of his *nono,* Lorenzo Moretti. The man who had the vision to make Moretti Motors what it was today. And Dominic shook his head.

His brothers and he had tried very hard to make sure that *Nono*'s problems weren't theirs.

But being cursed with women…well, that was something that Dom seemed to share with his grandfather. Angelina's betrayal cut deeper than he'd expected.

He walked to the bar and poured himself another drink. He tipped his head back and drained the glass. What was he going to do about Angelina?

He realized that he held all the cards. He could do whatever he wanted with Angelina. And he wanted *her*. He wanted her completely.

But what he really wanted, he realized, was to make her *pay*.

Revenge wasn't a noble trait, but she had stolen from him. All the while he'd been attracted to her and so trusting of her, and she'd been plotting with his enemy. The question was why?

He couldn't stand to be alone with his thoughts anymore. He put his glass down, looked up Angelina's address on his BlackBerry and called a cab. He'd had too much to drink to drive safely.

He had the cab take him to Angelina's apartment building. She lived in a decent place and there was nothing about her lifestyle that indicated she needed more money. Certainly not the kind of money she'd earn by selling him out.

What did she need the money for?

He paid the driver and walked toward her

building. It was chilly on this spring evening but not cold. He stood on the street looking up at the windows for a minute. He had no plan and that was odd for him. He was acting on an impulse and he had no idea how it would play out.

But he didn't turn around. He went into her building. There was no doorman and he went to the elevator and pushed the button for her floor, pleased Ian had supplied him with so much of Angelina's personal information.

The apartment building was less attractive from the inside than it had been from the street. The floors were dirty and showed signs of age. The building itself smelled faintly of onions and dust.

Was this it? Was living in this dismal place what had motivated her to try to get some extra cash?

He shook his head. He wasn't going to sympathize with Angelina. She'd taken from him and she'd have to pay.

He rapped on her door. It was so late, he wondered if she'd even answer. He heard no sounds from inside her apartment and knocked again. This time he heard footsteps.

"Who is it?"

"Dominic."

He heard the snick of the lock being disengaged and then the door opened inward. She leaned forward and glanced up and down the hall. "Are you alone?"

"*Sì*. May I come inside?"

She stepped back and let him in. Pivoting on her heel, she walked into her apartment. Dominic followed close on her heels right into the living room.

"Do you want to sit down?" she asked.

After he'd taken a seat in a large leather arm chair his anger got the better of him. He couldn't stop himself from blurting out, "Why?"

Angelina didn't appear the least surprised that she'd been found out.

"It's complicated," she told him. "I'm not sure that I can explain it."

"You're a smart woman. Try."

She took a deep breath and he thought he saw sadness in her eyes, but he refused to feel sympathy for her.

"I have a brother—"

"What does he have to do with you stealing from me?" Dominic asked.

"Everything," she said. "He's the reason why I got involved with ESP Motors."

"Does he work for them?" Dominic asked, pushing to his feet.

"Not exactly. He's a bit of a gambler," Angelina said. She wrapped her arms around her waist. "Renni doesn't have a sense of responsibility like you do."

"What do you mean by that?"

"My brother is a weak man. He gambles, a lot. And when he gets into trouble he comes to me for help. He's my little brother, so I do what I can."

"Because your parents are gone?"

"Yes, we only have each other."

"What kind of trouble is he in?"

"He gambles in illegal places because he really doesn't have the funds for high-stakes poker in casinos."

"So he owes criminals money?"

She nodded. "Yes. But this time I couldn't cover his debts and he met a man in a London pub who offered him money in exchange for Moretti Motors' secrets."

"A man who works for ESP?" Dominic asked.

"He not only works for ESP, he's an executive there. Renni got really drunk and ended up talking about me to this man."

"Who is this man?"

"Barty Eastburn. Renni told him I was your assistant and Barty offered to help him out if I gave him information from your office."

Dominic was torn by her revelations. He tried to tell himself he was motivated by the fact that she could give him Barty Eastburn to prosecute, but he knew deep inside that he wanted Angelina and this was a way to have her.

"I'm going to make you an offer, Angelina. And it is not negotiable. If you accept it I will keep you and your brother out of jail. If you do not, then you will be arrested tomorrow morning." He wanted Angelina and knew he couldn't let her go to prison. His desires in this moment were torn between Moretti Motors and a woman. Perhaps he had his grandfather's curse. Dominic refused to make Lorenzo's mistakes, though. Angelina wouldn't be his downfall the way the women in Lorenzo's life had been his.

By the look on her face he knew he had her exactly where he wanted her.

Three

Angelina had no idea what Dominic would offer her in exchange for staying out of jail, but she'd take it. Anything would be better than incarceration. *Anything.*

She hated the thought that she had no options, but she realized she'd given away her choices when she'd allowed Renni to manipulate her. She'd always believe that if she was going to make a stupid decision, then she couldn't complain about the consequences.

"What do you have in mind?" she asked. Her voice sounded wispy to her own ears. Obviously she wasn't going to do a good job at hiding her nervousness.

Dominic stood and walked over to where she sat on the couch. Sitting down next to her, he touched her face with one finger as he had earlier today in the office. His touch was warm, exciting all of her nerve endings.

"I'm so glad you know the truth," she said, the words coming out without her intention.

"Are you?" he asked, stroking her face.

She shivered with awareness her fear of jail time melting away under his touch. In fact, she thought of nothing but Dominic and how he felt next to her. "Yes. I hated lying and sneaking around. It was horrible."

Dominic stared at her. "Then why did you do it?"

"He's my brother, Dominic. I had to help him if I could," she said. "Wouldn't you do the same thing for Antonio or Marco?"

"You know I would. But I can't just forgive this, Angelina."

"I know. Moretti Motors is your life."

"That doesn't mean I'm an automaton."

"No, you're not," she said, turning her head into his touch. He cupped her cheek, his fingers tunneling into her hair. She opened her eyes and looked up at him. Attraction sprang to life between them.

She kissed his hand while watching his eyes. Saying no to him earlier had been hard. Harder than she'd thought it would be, but she shouldn't have been surprised. She'd been attracted to Dominic from the first moment she'd met him.

"What do you have in mind?" she asked.

"Something very intimate."

That made her pulse race. She shouldn't be excited by his deep voice, but she was. "Like what?"

"Like an agreement between you and me."

She felt a twinge of nervousness but quickly quelled it. This was Dominic. Being in his bed was a much better alternative than being in prison. "I'm listening."

"I want you to become my mistress, Angelina."

Hearing the words out loud was surprising though she'd known he was attracted to her. "Um…I'm not sure I'd really like that."

"You'd prefer prison?"

"Of course not. Are there any other options?"

"No. You gave them up when you started stealing from me."

"What choice did I have? They were going to kill my brother!"

Dominic looked at her. "Am I such a monster that you couldn't come to me?"

"No," she said. There was no way she was going to tell Dominic Moretti that her pride had kept her from opening up about Renni and his problems. She couldn't stand the thought of the man who needed no one knowing that she couldn't handle her own problems. One of the things he said he liked about her was her independence.

"Then what was it?"

She stood and walked around her very common little living space. There were two things she valued in the room: a picture of her parents in front of the Trevi Fountain on their honeymoon and a vase that her brother had painted for her when she'd left for college. The vase was silly and clearly amateurish, but he'd made it for her and it meant the world to her.

"You aren't going to be able to understand," she said, realizing that a man who lived in a house like Dominic's wasn't going to get why she'd sell secrets to save her brother. To a man who had more money than Midas, even if it was only recently, he wouldn't get that sometimes if you were poor circumstances were out of her control.

He walked over to her, making the room seem smaller by his sheer physical presence. "That doesn't really matter. We can't go into the past and change it. We can only move forward."

"There is one thing we can change. I am supposed to make another drop at the end of the week."

"What information?"

"I don't know. Um…Barty is going to call me tomorrow to confirm the details."

"Haven't you paid off your brother's debts yet?"

More times than Dominic would appreciate hearing about. But as long as Renni stayed in London he was tempted into heavy play and she ended up bailing him out again. She knew she needed to be firmer with him, but hadn't been able to. "No, not yet."

He took her jaw in his hand, surprising her with his quick move. "Don't lie to me anymore."

He wasn't hurting her at all, but the firmness of his grip kept her in place. "What do you want to hear?"

"The truth would be nice," he said.

If only it were that simple. She had always wondered if she'd taken the action she had because she'd wanted to get Dominic's attention. Had her desire to have him see her as more than just an ultraefficient secretary led to this?

He loosened his grip on her jaw, slid his hand down her neck to her shoulder. "Tell me what's going on, Angelina."

She swallowed hard. "I've paid off his original debt, but Barty keeps getting him into games that he can't handle and when he loses…I have to get more information so Barty will keep paying off Renni's debts."

"So now you are stuck between me and your loyalty to your brother."

"I don't see that at all. I'm stuck between you and jail."

"Either way you have a choice to make."

"Yes, I do," she said, quietly. "Why are you offering me this deal?"

Dominic didn't say anything for a long minute. She felt the seconds ticking by slowly as she waited.

"Because I want you," he said. "And I always get what I want."

"Why do you want *me?*"

"You're an attractive woman," he said.

"Damned by faint praise."

He liked her attitude and the fact that she wasn't behaving like a victim. It was that spunkiness that had long drawn him to her in the first place.

"There's a spark between us," he added.

She tipped her head to the side. "Yes, there is."

"I want you as my mistress for six months."

"And at the end of that time will I still have a job?"

"If I feel I can trust you," Dominic said.

"That's fair enough. You're being more than generous," she said. "Um…what does your mistress do?"

"She denies me nothing. I will make love to you wherever I desire. You will live in an apartment that I have for you."

"Why?"

He shrugged. Telling her that keeping a separate apartment would make the ending of their relationship easier wasn't going to go over well. He knew that from experience.

But he didn't want to use either of their homes—that would make the relationship seem paramount.

"Dominic?"

"I like having a residence that will just be for our affair. And, your place is not in a convenient location."

"So if I accept this…"

"Arrangement," he supplied.

"Arrangement, then. If I accept it, you will not press charges against me or my brother?"

"Has your brother passed on information to ESP himself?"

"No, he hasn't. Other than getting money from Barty, I don't think he has any specific knowledge of what's gone on."

Dominic didn't like her brother at all. The other man was taking terrible advantage of Angelina and she was letting him. A part of him knew it was that same trait in her that was going to allow her to accept his offer.

"Very well, but your brother must return to Milan. And if he has any further dealings with Eastburn, his immunity will be revoked."

Angelina bit down hard on her lower lip. "I don't know if he can do that, Dominic. He will promise you anything, but in the end he always breaks his word."

"That won't be your concern."

"How do you figure?"

"You have bailed him out enough. It's time to let him stand on his own."

Dominic knew he wouldn't back down on this point. Angelina's days of selling her soul for her brother were over.

"If I don't agree to this?"

"Then the both of you will be prosecuted and sent to jail."

"I guess I always knew you would find me out and my whole life would change."

Dominic looked around her apartment. It was small and cozy and from the arrangement of the furniture and the prints on the wall he could tell she'd done her best to make this place her home. "You are right. Your life is about to change. You can let it happen around you or you can take control."

"How do you figure?"

"Well, now you can stop lying. And stop keeping all your fears bottled inside you."

"What's in this for you?" she asked. "I know I'm not an unattractive woman, but I'm hardly the type of woman who inspires these kinds of gestures in men."

Dominic thought about her question. "I can't

speak to their actions, but you are the woman I want. It's turned into an obsession, Angelina. And I know that I don't want to let you have that kind of control over me."

She frowned at him. "That sounded like a compliment at first, but then not so much. Are you saying I'm some kind of devil you are trying to exorcise?"

He laughed and for the first time since he'd heard her name from Ian he felt an end to the relentless emotion of anger that had been blanketing him. "My attraction to you is powerful, but I don't want to exorcise you from my life."

"You don't?"

"No, Angelina. I don't. I want to take you to my bed and let the attraction between us run its course. I wanted you before I found out you were selling my secrets," he said. "That hasn't changed. Making you my mistress will give us both a chance to enjoy the physical attraction between us."

"What if what we have turns out to be nothing but a spark and it dies out quickly?"

"Do you honestly think it will?" he asked, pulling her into his arms and kissing her.

Having Dominic's arms around her was both everything she'd ever wanted and everything she'd feared. She didn't have the experience to handle a man like Dominic yet at the same time this felt right.

The intensity in his eyes awakened something deep inside her that she'd always been afraid of. She knew she was weak-willed, witness the current idiocy with her brother, but there was something ephemeral about Dominic. He touched parts of her that she'd always ignored. Parts that she didn't want to have to acknowledge.

She was over her head, but then that was nothing new and for once she wanted to just let go of her fears and worries. And in Dominic's arms she could do so.

His lips rubbed over hers, making her stop thinking and just experience him. His tongue teased her lips but didn't enter her mouth and his hands moved over her neck and shoulders, up to her face.

She liked the feel of his hands against her face. He made her feel cherished and beautiful. Two things she could safely say she'd never experienced before. But that didn't mean she knew how to handle it or him. Or that she even wanted to.

"I think that answers the question of attraction," he said, ending their kiss.

She blinked up at him, realizing how silly it had been to think that the attraction between them wasn't real.

"You're staring at my mouth."

"It's so perfectly formed," she said. "It looks hard but your lips were soft against mine."

"Were they?"

He quirked one eyebrow at her, stroking his finger down the side of her neck. She shivered as he rubbed the pad of his finger over her pulse. She felt it increase and fought to keep her expression serene. To somehow keep him from guessing that he had any affect on her. But she knew that he was used to being around much more sophisticated women.

"Yes," she said. "You're a very attractive man."

"Thanks," he said.

Startled, she had to laugh. "You are too much."

There was an innate charm that imbued everything he did. She wondered if it stemmed from his childhood. Or maybe his birth order. Something about being the oldest Moretti and knowing that he'd take the lead in anything he and his brothers did had made him very aggressive.

He was watching her carefully and she felt as if he were seeing all the way to her soul.

She shrugged and tried to pull away from him.

But he slid his fingers around the back of her neck and held her still.

"Don't. I won't allow you to back down from me, Angelina. Your passion is mine."

"Is it?"

He nodded. He was so sure of himself. So confident that she wanted to just let him take control of this situation. More than he already had. She wanted to make love to him and then fall asleep in his arms, but that was dangerous thinking. Dominic was the one man she knew who could really dominate her life.

"I don't know if I can do this," she said at last. "I want to, but giving myself to you, Dominic, is scary."

"Scary? Why?"

"I'm excited and nervous and turned on all at once. That's a very heady mix of emotions."

"You're a heady woman, Angelina."

"Am I?"

"Yes, every curve of your body entrances me and makes me want to caress you. I have to hold you in my arms, feel you pressed against me."

The fear she felt abated at his words. She knew that if she let herself go to him and became his mistress she'd never be the same.

Enough, she thought. She couldn't keep dilly-dallying in her mind. She knew what she had to say to him. What she had to do.

She wanted an affair with him and she wanted to make up for the skullduggery of the last several months. She wanted a chance to get to know Dominic Moretti.

He cupped the back of her head and drew her closer to him. She leaned forward and found herself within an inch of him.

Her lips suddenly felt dry and she licked them. He touched his tongue to her lips, following the trail of her tongue. He tasted good, like scotch and a taste that she knew was uniquely Dominic.

The worries she'd carried for so long faded to the back of her mind. "Okay."

"Okay?"

"I'll be your mistress."

"Six months. For six months you will be mine completely and then we will move on."

"Agreed," she said.

He brushed his lips over hers, angled his head and thrust his tongue deep into her mouth, claiming her and she knew she'd never be the same again.

He tunneled his fingers into her hair and held

her head back while he plundered her mouth. She slipped her arms up around his neck, moving up on her tiptoes so she could be closer to him.

His hands slid down her shoulders to her back. She felt his hands skimming over her spine and then they came to rest at her hips. He lifted her off her feet and into his arms as he turned and sat down on the sofa.

Her legs fell on either side of his hips and she found herself straddling him. She lifted her head and looked down into his midnight eyes.

She saw passion in the lines of his Roman features. His hands as they moved over her incited further desire in her. And for the first time in her life she realized she was doing something that was just for her. She wasn't motivated by anything other than the desire to be with Dominic.

Four

Dominic forgot about revenge and corporate espionage when he took Angelina in his arms. He twisted his hands in her thick short hair and held her head as he plundered her mouth. He needed to make sure she knew that she was his. As of this moment she belonged to him.

He didn't analyze the intelligence of his actions, the way he usually did. Angelina De Luca wasn't like other women, and that had never been more clear to him than right now.

Her lips were full and soft under his. Her tongue met his with small darts and she held on to him with surprising strength. She moaned deep in her throat as he slid his hands up her hips to her waist.

The pants she wore frustrated him because he couldn't easily touch her skin. "From now on you will wear only skirts."

"I will?"

"Yes. As my mistress…you will be mine, Angelina. You will do what I ask, when I ask it."

"I'm not really the type of woman—"

He put his fingers over her lips. "Forget who you were before this moment, Angelina. From now on you are mine."

"Forever?"

"For the next six months."

That should give him enough time to have his fill of her body. Should. But would it? He only knew that this moment was one that he'd waited for and he wasn't about to let Angelina De Luca mean more to him than an other mistress would.

"Okay," she said. Putting her hands on either side of his face. "Six months. What else?"

"Later," he said, pulling her head back to his. "Tomorrow morning I'll have my lawyer draw up the agreement."

She started to pull back, but he held her close.

Bringing his mouth to hers, he pushed her doubts aside with the force of his will.

He drew his hands over her body, enjoying the feel of her. He'd worked late with her many nights, wishing they were spending the hours in a much different way. Now she was here in his arms.

He slipped his hands between their bodies and lifted up the hem of her blouse. The skin at her waist was smooth and cool to his touch. She shifted back on his thighs and looked down at him as he touched her.

"You have very pretty skin, *mia* Angelina."

"*Grazie,* Dominic," she said. She cupped his jaw and ran her fingers over his face. "I love the feel of the stubble on your jaw."

"I have a heavy beard," he said, but his mind wasn't on this conversation. It was on the flesh he was slowly revealing as he drew the fabric of her blouse up her body.

The blouse was pretty and feminine and he found a zipper in the side of the garment and undid it. She stilled in his arms. Just hovering over him.

He slipped his hand into the gap made by the unfastened zipper. He felt the edge of her bra.

The fabric felt lacy as he caressed the fullness of her breast.

He pulled his hand out from under the blouse and caressed her through the fabric of her shirt. She shifted her shoulders, drawing his eyes to her hardened nipples. Placing his palm over the center of her breasts, he rotated his hands against her.

Her head fell back, revealing her long, pretty neck and he was transfixed by the sensual nature of this woman. He wanted her, but he felt a deep stab of lust that went beyond anything he'd experienced before.

"Dominic," she said. Just his name, spoken so deep and husky and so damned entrancing made him realize that any illusion of power he had was just that—an illusion. She was in charge. She was in control of him and his passion. And he wanted to wrest it back from her.

He leaned forward and kissed her neck. Nibbled his way from the base where her pulse pounded strongly. The scent of her perfume blended with a more natural essence of woman. He licked at her skin and felt her shiver in his arms.

"Dominic…"

"*Sì?*"

"I need more of you."

"How much more?" he asked. He wrapped his arms around her and spoke directly into her ear.

She shivered again. He felt her nipples tightened against the center of his palms. He moved them over her and she squirmed closer to him.

He bit lightly on the lobe of her ear, waiting for her reply. "Angelina?"

"*Sì*, Dominic?"

"How much more do you need?" he asked, tracing the shell of her ear with his tongue.

"All of you," she said.

She shifted on his lap, finding his erection with her center, and rocked her hips over him. He was tight and full and needed to feel her naked in his arms.

But he took his time, needing to wrest back control. And no matter how much he thought he might explode from the very thought of her hot core sliding over him, he was going to take his time.

He would seduce her in increments until she was a writhing mass and had no doubts who owned her body and soul.

He drew her blouse up over her arms and tossed it onto the floor. Her bra was pale blue lace with a pretty beige accent, but her breasts were all he wanted to see. Reaching behind her, he unhooked the bra, pulling the straps down her arms until she was finally naked from the waist up.

Angelina couldn't think as Dominic held her in his arms. No longer sad as she had been in the piazza earlier, she realized that Dominic was giving her a chance at something she'd always wanted.

Him.

She had been so afraid to take him. Afraid to believe he could be hers. And though he was only offering her six months, she knew that six months could change a person's life. And if she played her cards right…maybe, she and Dominic could have so much more. And even if they didn't, she knew she'd still cherish this time with him.

And since her parents' death, she'd had so little time in her life where she could just relax and enjoy a relationship. Dominic's caresses and his attention made her feel as if she were really alive. She reached up and touched his face, felt the shadow stubble on his jaw.

"What?"

She shook her head. How could she say that he made her want to start dreaming of a future again?

Made her want to believe in the dreams she'd abandoned to save her brother? "I'm just so glad to be here with you right now."

God, he was making her hot. His hands on her breasts were magic. He knew how to touch her so that she received the most pleasure from each caress. It had been a long time since she'd been in a man's arms. And Dominic had long been her fantasy man.

He nibbled on her neck and shoulders, holding her at his mercy. It didn't surprise her that Dominic would be so dominate. She dug her nails into his shoulders and leaned down, brushing against his chest. He felt so good. Her nipples were hard points when he pulled away from her.

"Do you like that, *mia?*"

"*Sì,* very much."

She closed her eyes and held her breath as he fondled her, running his finger over her nipple. She saw the absorption on his face as he brushed his finger back and forth until she bit her lower lip and shifted in his arms.

She moaned a sweet sound that he leaned down to capture. She tipped her head to the side so that she could open her mouth wider and let him all the way inside. She held his shoulders and moved on him, rubbing her core over his erection.

She needed to touch him, to feel his body against hers instead of the starched cotton of his Savile Row shirt. But he still held her wrists at the small of her back. Her breasts were thrust toward him, and watching the way he looked at her made her very proud of her less-than-perfect body.

Because she saw blatant desire in his eyes.

"Let me touch you," she said.

"Not yet."

He traced a path from her neck down her chest with his tongue. Circling the full globes of her breasts, narrowing the circle to come closer to her nipple but never touching it.

"Dominic…"

"*Sì*, Angelina?"

"Kiss me."

"Where?"

"There," she said, gesturing with her chin to her chest.

"Here?" he asked, sucking on the white fleshy part of her breast.

"No, Dominic."

"Here?" he asked, his breath moistening one nipple.

"Yes. Yes. Kiss me there."

He complied and she shook to her core as his

lips closed around her nipple. He suckled strongly on her and she shifted against him as she went completely liquid between her legs. She craved this man. Craved more of his touch.

She struggled to free her arms so she could pull him closer to her. "Let me go."

"Not…yet," he said.

He moved his mouth from one breast to the other, taking his time and nibbling against her skin. She felt overly sensitized by the warmth of his mouth against her.

She shifted on his lap, frustrated by her pants and his. Frustrated at the lack of control she had in this moment as Dominic continued to drive her slowly toward an orgasm. Her entire body felt so susceptible and she was out of control.

"Dominic, stop."

"Not yet, *mia* Angelina. I want to see you come for me."

"Not like this. You aren't even undressed."

"I don't have to be," he said.

She felt his free hand moving between their bodies, undoing the button of her pants and drawing down the zipper. His hand slipped inside and she shifted on her knees, lifting her body so that his fingers could reach to the very core of her.

"This doesn't feel like no," he said.

"It's not," she admitted. "I want you, Dominic."

"You are going to have me," he said. "But not until I've heard you scream with pleasure."

God, he hadn't been this hot since—never. This was more than just sex and it was important to him that he bring pleasure to Angelina. He wouldn't be satisfied with an orgasm until he knew he'd wrung out every ounce he could from her. He rubbed her nipple and she shivered in his arms. He pushed her back a little so he could see her. Her breasts were bare, nipples distended and begging for his mouth. He lowered his head and suckled.

He still held both of her wrists in one of his hands at the small of her back. The action kept her breasts thrust up toward him.

Her eyes were closed, her hips moving subtly against his hand, which he'd cupped around her body. He teased her with his finger through her panties. The humid warmth of her body branded him as he continued to stroke her. He blew on her nipple and watched as gooseflesh spread down her body.

He loved the way she reacted to his mouth on her breast. Her nipples were so sensitive he was pretty sure he could bring her to an orgasm just from touching her there.

"When you come for me, Angelina, that will seal our deal. There will be no backing down. You will be mine."

He bit carefully at the creamy skin of her chest. "Do you agree?"

"*Sì*, Dominic."

"Say it," he said.

"I'll be yours."

He groaned at the sound of her agreeing that she belonged to him.

He kept kissing and rubbing, suckling her nipples, trying to quench his thirst, until she rocked her hips harder against his hand. He was straining inside his trousers. He had her hot wetness against his palm, and his hot erection against the other side of his hand.

It was one of the most sensual things he'd ever felt. He pulled his hand free of her pants and then lifted his hips. He so wanted to feel her on him. He wanted to do away with the layers of clothing between them. He needed to feel her long sexy legs wrapped around him until they were truly one person.

He bit carefully on her tender, aroused nipple.

She moaned and shifted against him, her hips rocking over him.

"I need more."

"More of what?"

"Your hand, Dominic," she said.

"Beg me," he said.

She opened her eyes and looked up at him. She was completely at his mercy. "Please touch me again."

"Like this?" he asked, slipping his hand back into her pants, rubbing her again through the crotch of her panties.

"No." She shook her head.

He stopped caressing her. "You don't like that?"

She rocked her hips over his hand. "More. Please, Dominic, give me more."

He pulled the crotch of her panties to one side and slid one finger against the warmth of her core. She moaned.

"Is that what you wanted?"

"Oh yes."

He traced the opening of her body with his finger and then slipped the tip into her. She tightened around him, rearing up on her knees and then sinking back down.

"Oh, Dominic."

He liked the sound of his name on her lips when passion overcame her. He added a second finger and she rubbed herself against him again.

This time he pressed his thumb to her and rubbed up and down, sending her soaring. He felt the climax rip through her body as she screamed and convulsed in his arms.

He brought his mouth down on hers and drank the sounds of her passion. Wrapping himself in her ardor as she came.

He rocked her until her orgasm faded. Letting go of her wrists, he stroked her back and kept kissing her. Holding her close, her bare breasts brushed against his chest. Now he was ready to take her. He was so hard he thought he'd die if he didn't get inside her.

He glanced down at her and saw she was watching him. The fire in her eyes made his entire body tight with anticipation. He gently pushed her back so that she stood before him. Getting to her own feet, he stripped her pants off.

"Are you on the pill?" he asked.

"No," she said.

"Damn."

"I'm sorry."

"Don't be," he said, framing her face and kissing her. "I think I have a condom with me."

He took the condom from his pocket and then removed his pants before sitting back down. "Come here."

She climbed on his lap once again. Unbuttoning his shirt, she pushed it off his shoulders. "You are very sexy, Dominic."

She traced his muscles and her touch was almost too much. He quickly put on the condom.

"Are you ready for me now?" she asked teasingly, her hand going to his erection. She caressed him and then moved her hand up his abdomen. Her hands were small and infinitely exciting. He wanted to let her touch him all night, but he was too near the edge and he wanted to be inside her when he went over.

"Ah, Angelina," he said. "You are so tempting."

"Am I?" she asked. He noticed a slight hesitation in her voice.

"You have no idea," he said.

"I'm glad. You tempt me, too. Make love to me, Dominic. I want to experience every bit of passion you have."

He shifted his hands, gripping her thighs so that he could enter her. Her hands fluttered between them and their eyes met.

He held her hips steady and entered her slowly, thrusting deeply. Her eyes widened with each inch he gave her. She clutched at his shoulders as he started thrusting harder. Her eyes were half closed and she was biting her lower lip.

He caught one of her nipples in his teeth, scraping very gently, and felt her start to tighten around him. Her hips moved faster, demanding more, but he kept the pace slow and steady. Wanting her to come again before he did.

He suckled her nipple and rotated his hips to catch her pleasure point with each thrust. Soon he felt her hands clench his hair as she threw her head back, her climax ripping through her.

He varied his thrusts to find a rhythm that would draw out the tension at the base of his spine. Leaning back against the couch, he tipped her hips to give him deeper access. Then she scraped her nails down his chest. Blood roared in his ears and he called her name as he came.

Wrapping his arms around her, he held her close. He'd gotten more than he expected. He had wanted revenge, but now there was so much more between them.

"Dominic?"

"Hmm?"

"Thank you."

"For what?" he asked.

"For everything."

Her thanks made him feel very uncomfortable. He knew his lovemaking had nothing to do with vengeance but hearing her sincere gratitude made him feel…

Well, made him *feel*. He'd been careful to never let a woman evoke any emotions in him since… No, he wouldn't go there.

He lifted Angelina to her feet. "I've got to clean up. Where's the bathroom?"

"Through there," she said, gesturing toward the darkened doorway to the left.

Walking down the hall, he glanced back to see her standing in the middle of the room, naked and vulnerable. He could not allow himself to fall under her spell—he had to maintain emotional distance. She was now his mistress—that was all she could ever be.

He like pushing her to her limits and each time she hesitated he knew he was finding another place where she was afraid to let him go. In this case it was that fragility that she revealed in her nudity.

He never would have guessed that Angelina

had any issues with her body given the confidence with which she carried herself. He'd realized when Ian told him Angelina was the one selling company secrets that he didn't know everything about her—but he'd never understood how complicated she really was.

"You're staring at me," she said.

"I am."

He drew one finger down the center of her body. Her curves were full and tempting. So soft compared to the hardness of his own frame.

"What are you thinking?" he asked.

"That I wished we had come together because of our mutual attraction and not because of my misdeeds."

"I asked you out tonight before I knew the truth. You declined," he pointed out.

"Yes, you did. But I knew you were going to find out about me and I couldn't go out with you with that lie between us. Whatever else you might think about me, please believe I never wanted to hurt you."

"Then why *did* you lie?"

"I felt trapped," she said.

"Tell me more about your brother," he said, moving to sit at the head of the bed.

Five

Angelina stood in her living room for about a minute before she heard the water come on in the bathroom. Realizing she didn't want to be standing here naked when Dominic came back into the room she reached for her clothes but heard Dominic's footsteps behind her before she had put anything on. She glanced over at him. He was naked and very male. She couldn't help but notice the way he filled the small living room with his presence.

Oh, man, she had it bad. She wanted nothing more than to cross the room and wrap her arms around his waist and feel his arms around her.

She wanted to take comfort from his body and offer him the comfort of hers. And she had no idea if that was something he was interested in.

Dominic looked down at his watch and then back at her, giving her her answer. He was leaving. And somehow tomorrow morning she'd have to figure out how to face him and how to make this relationship…this arrangement…work for both of them.

"I need to get my robe if we're going to talk," she said.

"Of course."

She walked past him, and maintaining her cool was the hardest thing she had ever done. Because she wasn't cool. She couldn't be nonchalant.

Hold it together, she told herself. Get used to it. This was going to be her life—for the next six months at least.

She fumbled for her robe and pulled it on. The ivory-colored, silk-lined robe was too heavy for this spring evening, but it was the only one she had and it had been a gift from her grandmother. And when she pulled the sides closed and tied the sash at her waist she felt as if her grandmother were giving her a hug.

She closed her eyes and drew strength from the

woman who was long gone, but had always been Angelina's ally.

"Angelina?"

"*Sì*, Dominic," she said, turning to see him standing in her doorway.

He'd put on his pants but left his shirt off. "Do you want me to leave?"

"Don't you want to go?" she asked.

His eyes narrowed and he crossed his arms over his chest then leaned against the doorjamb.

"No," he said.

"Then stay."

She could say no more than that. She knew she had to keep her emotional distance. Falling for Dominic, letting him know that was a possibility was pure foolishness.

"Can I ask you something?"

"Yes."

"Why would you settle for this kind of relationship with me when you could have something real with another woman?"

"This feels real to me," he said, walking into the room.

He sat down on the edge of her bed and then snagged her wrist, drawing her close to him. "Doesn't this feel real to you?"

She swallowed hard. She wasn't explaining this the right way. She wanted…she wanted him to say that there was more between them than an arrangement, but there was no way that was going to happen. She knew that wasn't possible—not yet. Maybe never. She'd used him, and now it was his turn to use her.

"I guess so."

He pulled her even closer, wrapped his arms around her waist and rested his head on her shoulder. The move was unexpected and she didn't know what it meant. But she realized that thinking and analyzing this wasn't going to bring her the answers she sought. Not tonight.

She wrapped her arms around him and held him close for a few minutes. "I'm sorry for betraying you."

"I know you are."

"What are you going to do next?"

"I'm going to trap Barty Eastburn and make sure that bastard never steals from anyone again."

She nodded. "You'll need my help."

"Yes. Ian is going to come up with a plan and we will be discussing it tomorrow."

Dominic let go of her and stood. He pulled back the duvet on her bed and motioned for her to get in. She climbed onto the bed, though she knew her robe was going to be too hot to sleep in.

He took off his pants and she had a chance to just stare at his almost naked body. The boxer briefs he wore clung to his buttocks and thighs as he turned away from her. When he turned back she stared at his body. He was toned and muscled and she wanted nothing more than to explore his form.

"Like what you see?" he asked.

She gave him an embarrassed grin. But Dominic was at home in his skin and held his hands out to his sides. "Look all you want."

"I want to touch you, too," she said.

"If you're good, that might be arranged." He sat down on the bed next to her.

"What constitutes good?"

"Lose that robe and I'll tell you."

She loosened the sash and had the robe halfway off before she remembered she wasn't drop-dead gorgeous like Dominic Moretti. But by the time the thought entered her head it was too late. Dominic had taken the robe and tossed it on the floor.

She sat there in a pool of light from her bedside lamp, naked and vulnerable, and for the first time in her life, that didn't bother her.

Dominic knew spending the night with Angelina was a mistake, but he'd be unable to walk away when he'd seen those wounded chocolate-colored eyes of hers.

She was easily the sexiest woman he'd seen in years. And a part of that sexiness came from the total unawareness she had of her own attractiveness. There was a guileless way about her that drew him.

A part of him feared that it was all a lie—she had been a spy. But tonight—just for tonight—that didn't matter. He wanted to enjoy every second he could with her until the sun came up and they were forced to move on to the role of mistress and master.

"That's very good, Angelina. Now lie back against the pillows."

She curled on her side, drawing the sheet up to her breasts and wrapping one arm around his waist. He put his arm around her shoulder. This quiet moment of holding one another had nothing to do with revenge or any kind of arrangement. Was she his Achilles' heel? Was this how Lorenzo had found himself cursed—falling for some of this quiet comfort in a woman's arms?

Dominic had no answers. He only knew that he

needed this tonight. That making love to Angelina had taken the edge off his anger.

"What do you want to know about Renni?" she asked, running her fingers over his chest.

"If I offered him a job…would he take it?"

She sat up, her hand square in the middle of his chest. "Would you do that?"

"I'm thinking about it."

She kissed him, taking her time. And when she lifted her head from his, he felt like a different man.

This relationship with Angelina was going to be a double-edged sword. She was going to always feel grateful to him and he was going to…he was going to stop acting like a sap and remember that what they had was nothing more than a six-month affair.

Once his brother wrapped up the Vallerio problem and got the rights to that name back, there'd be nothing standing in the way of Moretti Motors making a full comeback. Over the last few years they'd surpassed what *Nono* had done during his storied run as CEO, and now Dominic had his eye on setting a new standard of excellence.

"What are you thinking?" Angelina asked. "You looked so fierce just now."

"I was thinking about Moretti Motors and how close I came to letting all the success I worked so hard for slip through my fingers."

"And that you'll never do it again?" she asked.

"Damned straight."

Ian was already in the office when Dominic arrived the next morning. He'd left Angelina's apartment early, before she was fully awake. He had a list of things that he needed to get finished before he could start thinking about setting Angelina up as his mistress.

"I need ten minutes before we start," Dominic said to Ian.

"Not a problem. I'll go give Tony a hard time about cars."

"Thanks."

Ian left and Dominic sat down in the leather chair that had been his grandfather's. He took a minute to jot down the arrangement he'd offered Angelina and then clarified some points before contacting his solicitor. He knew the man would make sure Dominic was covered in all regards to this relationship.

He typed a quick e-mail to Bruno Marcelli, his solicitor, and then sat back in his chair. He wanted some formal guidelines set up for his relationship with Angelina, to protect him because he was in danger of forgetting that she wasn't more than a mistress. He also needed to find a place for her to live.

He rang Antonio's office and Ian returned to his office a few minutes later.

"Have you had a thought about how we can get enough on Barty Eastburn to have him arrested?" Dominic asked as Ian took a seat in the guest chair.

"Yes, but first I wanted to talk to you about this idea you have of not prosecuting Angelina De Luca."

"I've made my mind up, Ian." Dominic had called Ian first thing.

Ian shook his head. "I don't think you're being smart about this."

"Duly noted. Now talk to me about Eastburn."

"Dominic—"

"I'm not going to change my mind, Ian. I've taken care of the problem with Angelina and it won't be an issue."

"How?"

"How what?"

"How have you taken care of it?"

"By offering her an alternate arrangement. She will even help us trap Barty if need be."

"Okay, fine. Near as I can tell, Eastburn is hoping to muck up Moretti Motors' reacquisition of the Vallerio name for the new roadster. My guy inside ESP said they want to bump back the release date of the car, giving ESP Motors the chance to get their roadster to market before you."

"Like hell. I'll sue him if he tries to use the engine we developed."

"Bruno Marcelli has a team already on it. Antonio is working with the legal team to make sure that ESP is stopped from releasing any cars until we can ascertain that they haven't been made using Moretti Motors' proprietary information."

"Good. I will talk to Antonio when you and I are done here," Dominic said. "What do we need to do now?"

"We have to get Eastburn on record asking for someone to bring corporate documents from your office. Will De Luca do it?"

"Yes, she will," Dominic said. Angelina would do whatever he asked. That was one of the things he'd discussed with her last night and that he'd had Bruno put into their agreement.

"Great. Then all we need is to find out how he

usually contacts her. When will she be in the office this morning?"

"She should be here now. She wouldn't have disturbed me since the door is closed."

Ian nodded. "If you're ready to bring her in, I recommend we do that now."

Dominic nodded. He lifted the handset on his phone and hit the intercom button.

"*Sì*, Dominic?" Her voice came through the line.

"I need you in here, Angelina."

"I'll be right in."

When he hung up, Ian was watching him. "Are you involved with her?" his friend asked.

"That's not pertinent to this investigation," he replied.

"I'm asking as your friend, Dom. I have never known you to get involved with anyone you work with."

"This is different. We have an arrangement."

Ian started to say something else, but the door opened and Angelina walked in. It was impossible to look at her curvy frame clad in a slim-fitting shirtdress without remembering what she'd looked like this morning, naked in bed.

His erection stirred and he knew now why he'd

always resisted getting involved with a woman he worked with. This was going to be damned uncomfortable until he got through the intense period of wanting her.

What if that never happened?

"You asked to see me?"

"Yes, please have a seat," Dominic said. "Ian has a few questions for you about how you passed information to Barty Eastburn."

She flushed a little. "I usually got a call from Renni."

"Who is Renni?" Ian asked.

"My brother. He had some gambling debts that Barty took care of. So Renni calls me when he has had to borrow more money from Barty."

"Does Barty ever call you directly?"

"Sometimes. Or he has me call him."

"Would you be willing to tape your phone calls with him?"

"Of course she will," Dominic said.

"We need her consent, Dom. Without it, the courts will say she was coerced."

"I will do it, Signore Stark."

Angelina looked up at Dominic before she added, "I will do whatever it takes to make this right."

Six

"Signore Stark, I am supposed to go to London next week to meet with Barty. I was going to tell him I'm through passing him information," Angelina said.

She was trying to concentrate on the meeting, but instead she was swamped with images of her and Dominic from the night before. It was hard to look at Dominic and not want to be back in his arms.

Of course the way he was looking at her, totally impersonal, made it a bit easier. But that also made her nervous. What did he expect from her?

"That's good. When are you supposed to meet him?"

"Next Wednesday. Dominic is scheduled to go to the F1 race in Catalonia, Spain."

"Good. So we can set up this meeting with Barty. I will follow you to London," Ian said.

"I don't like it, I should be there," Dominic said.

"You can't be, Dom. If you aren't where you are supposed to be, Eastburn will suspect you're on to him."

"I agree with Signore Stark," Angelina said. "Barty isn't a very trusting man. He always has me followed when I leave a meeting with him."

"How do you know?" Dominic asked.

"I saw his man," Angelina said. She'd never admit it to these men, but it had scared her at first. She didn't know what Barty's man would do to her. And for all that she was confident of herself and her abilities to take care of herself, the man was so tall and broad, she knew she wouldn't stand a chance if he attacked her.

"Are you sure he was following you?"

"Yes, and it's the same man everytime. The one time Renni was with me, the first time, he said that the man—Patrick, he called him— worked for Barty."

"So the man's name is Patrick?" Dominic asked.

"*Sì.*"

"Is this the man you call Patrick?" Ian asked, pulling a photo from a manila folder.

She looked at a photo of herself and Barty. Ian tapped the man sitting at a table behind them.

"Yes, that's him," Angelina said. "How did you discover it was me?"

"I followed the trail of paperwork," Ian said. "Dom was very good at limiting who had the information, and the two men we thought were suspects never left Milan and never delivered information anywhere."

She noted that Dominic's eyes narrowed as Ian spoke about her betraying him. She wondered if being his mistress was really going to be recompense enough. She suspected it wasn't and that really upset her.

"Well, I don't know who Patrick is to Eastburn, but he seems to have his fingers in a lot of pies," Angelina said.

"I suspected as much. I'm going to run him through a few of my databases. If he's involved in organized crime…well, I have another client who will be interested in that."

"What will we do next week?" she asked Ian.

She didn't care about anything but making things up to Dominic.

"You will do what you've always done with Barty. I will follow and record the meeting. Does he search you when you arrive?"

"No. At least he never has."

"He must be very confident that you won't betray him," Dominic said, a tinge of anger in his voice.

"I think it is more that he knows he holds all the cards."

"Not anymore," Dominic said. "What's the plan, Ian?"

"I want Angelina to wear a wire so we can record the conversation. I have a very sophisticated one that I can embed in a brooch."

"I can do that. What do I say to him?"

"Just let him do the talking. Have you ever suggested information you can give him?"

"No. He's always known exactly what he wants and asks me for it."

"Good. That's all I really need. Together with the photos we should have enough proof."

Angelina nodded. "I told my brother he had to come back to Milan this time. I really was trying to find a way to stop having to give Barty information."

"Why didn't you go to the police or to Dominic?" Ian asked.

She looked at both men. "I didn't know what to say to the police. Renni has a criminal record. I couldn't chance getting him in trouble, maybe have him go back to jail. I didn't want that. He's all the family I have."

"That's understandable," Dominic said. "But why not talk to me?"

"Everyone looks to you to solve their problems and I didn't want to be just one more person in a long line," she said.

"That's a lame excuse," Dominic said.

"Yes, it is. The truth is I'm used to fixing my own problems. It never occurred to me to turn to you."

"I guess stealing from me seemed different to you," he said with a bitter edge to his voice.

She felt a sting of tears at his words. "I never thought of it that way, but I can see that you're right. Stealing from you wasn't the right thing to do. But, unlike the great Dominic Moretti, I'm only human and infinitely fallible."

"The important thing is that we're moving on now. You're making reparations to Dominic and making amends by helping us trap Barty," Ian said.

She could tell by Dominic's lack of reaction that he didn't think there was anything good about this situation. She realized that she'd given herself to a man who didn't want anything from her beyond what their agreement stated.

Suddenly she was very unsure that she could turn this negative into a positive. That she could find a way to make Dominic Moretti forgive her for her crimes. Because she saw the seeds of a man she could really like.

After Ian and Angelina left, Dominic thought back to his earlier reaction. Perhaps he'd been too harsh with her, but hearing Angelina talk about meeting with his enemy had been more than he could take. And he *was* human, despite what she seemed to think.

He needed to be alone. He was going to take one of his Moretti coupes to the track outside the city and drive it as fast as he could. Anything to get away from this mess and clear his head.

He knew he was making mistakes with Angelina, which was one thing he couldn't abide.

There was a knock on his door. "Enter."

Angelina stood there with her notepad in one

hand and a very hesitant look on her face. "Do you want to go over your schedule for the day?"

No, what he wanted was to reaffirm that she was his mistress. That her loyalty was owed only to him.

"Close the door and lock it, Angelina, and then come over here."

She swallowed and tipped her head to one side. "What do you have in mind?"

"Whatever I want, remember? That is our arrangement."

Angelina locked the door and then leaned back against it. "I know I said…anything you wanted, but I never expected you to ask me for anything personal here at the office."

"Neither did I. But I want you and you are my mistress, aren't you, Angelina?"

"Yes, I am," she said, straightening from the wall. "Do you want me, Dominic?"

"More than I should," he said, giving her the truth. She was a courageous woman and he realized part of why he needed to make love to her now was the fact that she had placed herself in danger. The men who were after her brother wouldn't hesitate to hurt her.

"Come to me," he said.

She moved slowly toward him with sensual grace, the ruffled hem of her dress bouncing lightly around her thighs. He stood and crossed the small space between them in two long strides. Sweeping her up in his arms, he carried her to his desk.

Her mouth opened under his and he told himself to take it slow. That if he was going to retain any objectivity where she was concerned, he really needed to keep his cool, but that simply wasn't possible. She was pure feminine temptation. He slid his hands down her back, down to the end of her dress, and slipped his hand underneath. He felt the silk of her hose and then just bare skin.

He set her on her feet next to the wide mahogany desk. He wanted, needed, to keep things light between them. To make the sex between them something of a game so that he didn't forget to keep his objectivity and so that she didn't forget that this was temporary. That they were lovers only until the six months was up.

"Do you like it when I tell you what to do?" he asked, coming up behind her. He wrapped his arms around her waist and drew her back against his body.

She turned her head to the side, resting it on his shoulder, and he felt a curious emotion inside him. An emotion that had nothing to do with lust. For a moment he tightened his arms around her, wanting to bury his face in her thick hair.

He wanted to pretend that her betrayal didn't matter. That it didn't matter that she'd spent time with his bitter rival Barty Eastburn. That it didn't matter if he fell for her because he was no longer a man cursed by past generations.

But all of that did matter. "Angelina?"

"*Sì,* Dominic?"

"Do you like it when I tell you what to do?" he asked again.

She glanced up at him, a slight blush coloring her face. "I do. There is a certain freedom and being able to act without..."

She trailed off and he realized what she was going to say. "Without taking responsibility?"

"Yes. I'm sorry, that's not fair to you."

"In this case it's perfectly fair. You have agreed to give your body to me whenever I ask. And I have agreed to give you pleasure until you forget your name."

"Wow, that's what you agreed to?" she asked, a teasing note in her voice.

"*Sì.*"

She smiled at him, making him very aware that

she hadn't smiled at all in the meeting with Ian. In fact, this was the first time today he'd seen genuine happiness on her face. And he was the one who caused it. He'd made her happy.

It shouldn't matter to him; she was only his mistress. But it did matter. He stopped thinking and started to feel.

"Bend forward, place your hands on the desk," he said.

She did as he said, bracing her hands awkwardly on the smooth surface. "Like this?"

"Just like that. Wait, are you wearing panties?"

She flushed. "Yes! Or course."

He bit the inside of his mouth to keep from smiling. "Take them off."

She straightened and turned to face him. She lifted her skirt to her waist revealing thigh-high sheer hose and a tiny pair of race-car-red panties. Slowly she took the sides of her panties and drew them down her legs.

When she reached her knees she pushed them to the floor and delicately stepped out of the undergarment. She started to lower her skirt, but he stopped her.

"Leave your skirt up and turn back around."

She hesitated and he saw the vulnerability in

her eyes. He kissed her. He didn't draw her into his arms but took her mouth with his and reassured her the only way he could. If she didn't like this, he would stop and just make love to her on the leather guest chair.

She grasped his shoulders and pulled herself closer to him. Her head tilted to give them both deeper access to each other's mouths. And once again he was struck by the fact that where this woman was concerned he had no discipline. She'd undermined him again. Right now all he wanted to do was free his erection and take her.

He took her hips in his hands. Her butt was firm and smooth and he caressed the furrow between her cheeks.

She swiveled her hips against his touch, and he slipped his touch deeper until he caressed that slit between her legs. She was wet and hot with her desire. He stroked the edge of her femininity, circling the edge of her body with his finger. She said his name on a long sigh.

"Yes?"

"You make me so hot," she said. "No other has ever taken over my body the way you do."

"Good. Unbutton your blouse," he said. "I want to see your breasts."

He kept his hand between her legs as she slowly undid the buttons. The blouse fell open down her shoulders, over her arms.

Her bra matched the red panties at his feet. It was a demi-bra with cups that only covered the bottom half of her breasts. They looked delicate and tempting. The lace detail was black and a contrast to her creamy skin.

"Turn around again," he said, his own voice husky and deep.

She did as he said and leaned on the desk, thrusting her butt back toward him. He leaned over her, his big body completely blanketing hers. He bent his legs so his erection rubbed at her core. Through the fabric of his pants he felt her heat.

The top of her blouse almost fell off of her body. And from his angle looking over her shoulder, he could only see the tops of her breasts, and the barest hint of the rosy flesh of her nipples. He reached up one hand and drew the lace down away from her nipple, completely exposing it.

He ran the tip of one fingertip around her aroused flesh. She trembled in his arms. He undid the front clasp of her bra and brushed the cups away. He took one of her nipples between his fingers and pinched her lightly. She shifted against him. Her hips thrust back against him and she shifted until her core rubbed over the ridge of his hardness.

She tried to turn in his arms, but he held her in place. "Dominic…"

"Yes?"

"I want to touch you."

He wanted that, too. But he knew if he felt her fingers on his chest or on his erection, he would be inside her and this moment would end. And he wasn't ready for that yet.

"No," he said, growling deep in his throat. He leaned forward to nibble at the elegant length of her neck. He ran his tongue down the side of it until she shivered with pleasure. He reached between her legs to find her nether lips. Stroking her, he kept his touch light until she went up on her tiptoes and thrust her hips back into him.

Then he lightly traced her. She screamed his name as she tried to turn in his arms. But he held her still, his hands on her body.

He felt her heart beating frantically in her chest. Her hips moved urgently trying to find the pinnacle of her release. He drove her relentlessly toward it but stopped before she climaxed, holding her at the edge of sensation so that she would enjoy it more later.

"Do you like that?"

"Yes. Yes, I do, Dominic, but I need more."

"More of this?" he asked, scraping his finger over her nipple.

She shook her head. He took his hand from her breast and unzipped his pants, freeing his erection.

"More of this?" he asked, leaning forward to speak directly into her ear as he pushed one finger into her body. She tightened on him and he felt the tiny contractions as she began to orgasm. He quickly pulled his finger back out and she moaned at the loss.

"Yes. That."

He pulled her to him and lifted her slightly so that her buttocks were nestled against his abdomen. He leaned over her, bracing his hands on the desk next to hers, and let her feel his chest against her back. Blood roared in his ear. He was so hard, so full right now.

He caressed her creamy thighs. *Dios,* she was soft, something he hadn't forgotten from the first time he'd had her. She moaned as he neared her center and then sighed when he brushed his fingertips against her humid warmth.

He turned his head to watch her as he tested her

readiness, this time with the tip of himself. Her eyes were heavy lidded. She bit down on her lower lip and he felt the minute movements of her hips as she tried to take him deeper, to make him enter her. But he held his hips steady and waited, prolonging the moment until he couldn't take it anymore.

He needed her *now*. Their naked loins pressed together and he shook under the impact. Naked loins…dammit, he needed a condom.

He reached into his pocket and pulled out the packet he'd put there earlier. He donned it quickly and then came back to her. She'd stood there waiting for him. Her hips lifted slightly and he knew that she was as hot for him as he was for her.

He had to have her. *Now.* He cupped both of her breasts in his hands, plucking at her aroused nipples. He adjusted his stance, bending his knees and positioning himself, and then entered her with one long, hard stroke.

She moaned his name and her head fell forward leaving the curve of her neck open and vulnerable to him. He bit softly at her neck and felt the reaction all the way to his toes when she squirmed in his arms and thrust her hips back toward him.

A tingling started in the base of his spine and

he knew his climax was close. But he wasn't going without Angelina. He wanted her with him. He caressed her stomach and her breasts. Whispered erotic words of praise and longing in her ears.

She moved more frantically in his arms and he thrust deeper with each stroke. Breathing out through his mouth, he tried to hold back the inevitable. He slid one hand down her abdomen, through the slick folds of her sex. Finding her center, he stroked the aroused flesh with an up-and-down movement. She continued to writhe in his arms no closer to her climax than before.

He circled that aroused bit of flesh between her legs with his forefinger, then scraped it very carefully. She screamed his name and tightened around him. Penetrating her as deeply as he could, he bit down on the back of her neck and came long and hard, emptying himself into her body.

He wasn't cold or alone anymore, he acknowledged, and that scared him more than he wanted to admit. More than he would ever admit. Because Moretti's legacy was built for a solitary man and he wasn't about to give up his heritage for Angelina. No matter how right she felt in his arms.

Seven

She was damp between her legs and her entire body was still trembling from the incredible orgasm she'd just had in his arms when Dominic pulled away and gave her such an odd look it felt like he was a stranger.

"You may use my washroom if you need to," he said.

She nodded and bent to pick up her panties. She pulled her clothes on and walked away from him on shaking legs.

The intimacy of what had just transpired between them had forced them further apart rather than bringing them closer together. She closed the door and avoided looking at herself in the mirror.

She'd thought that starting this affair with Dominic was a way to stay. The obvious one of staying out of jail. And, perhaps she hoped to get a little closer.

And she wondered if the bad luck she'd always had with men was going to dominate this relationship, too. She longed to have a man fall for her and treat her like a princess.

Being treated like a sexy lady was fine, too, but as she wrapped her arms around her waist she realized it also left her feeling hollow.

She heard the outer door of Dominic's office open and she wondered if he'd left. She hastily cleaned up and refastened her clothing. A glance in the mirror told her what she already sensed. She looked as though she was about to cry.

She refused to shed one tear. She'd made the choice that had led to this and she really needed to own up to her actions. And she had enjoyed the lovemaking with Dominic at his desk. His desk.

Oh my God, she thought.

She was entering an entirely new phase in her life…she had to let go of the past and of dreams that she'd clung to like a girl. She was a woman—with a woman's mistakes and experiences behind her. And if she had a chance at ever getting Dominic to see her as something more than a mistress, she had to start taking more control in their relationship.

She'd let Renni use her because she loved him and she had the bad feeling that if she wasn't careful she would let Dominic do the same thing.

She exited the washroom to find Dominic and Ian both in his office.

"Are you okay?" Dominic asked.

She nodded. "Yes. I'll go back to my desk now unless you need me?"

"That's fine. Ian wants to go over the arrangements for you both to head to London. He will be out in a few minutes."

She walked out of his office, feeling as if she'd never get back to her desk, but then she was there. She sat down on her chair and really had to fight to keep her equilibrium.

The phone rang and she answered it, glad for the distraction. "Signore Moretti's office, this is Angelina."

"*Ciao,* Angelina. This is Bruno Marcelli, Dominic's solicitor."

"He's in a meeting right now, can I take a message?"

"Yes, please tell him that the arrangement he asked me to draw up is ready for his review. I'm going to fax it over now," Bruno said.

"Is it for the Vallerio agreement?" she asked.

"No, it's a personal matter. In fact, it involves you, Ms. De Luca. The fax I'm sending is for you," he said.

"Is this regarding my personal arrangement with Dominic?" she asked.

"Indeed. Signore Moretti has authorized me to offer you the services of one of our solicitors and my associate Signore Lunestri will be contacting you later today to discuss it. There will be no charge to you for this service."

"*Grazie,* Signore Marcelli."

"You're welcome. *Ciao.*"

She hung up the phone and a minute later heard the ring of the fax machine. She stood and went over to the machine, wanting to remove the papers from the tray before anyone else came into the office. It was a private machine, but being Dominic's mistress and having others know it wasn't what she wanted.

This wasn't turning out the way she wanted it

to. And she remembered the vow she'd just made to herself in Dominic's washroom. The promise that she'd take control of this. She pulled the papers off the machine and read them over carefully.

In her mind she started to change the entire way she'd been viewing her affair with Dominic. She had felt guilty for her actions in the entire corporate espionage thing, but she realized she had to let go of her guilt.

Dominic wasn't going to forget it and she never would, either, but it could no longer be the focus of her every action around him.

She took a pen and started making notes on the document, which was very generous. She was sure that Dominic didn't expect her to turn down his offer of a new wardrobe or an apartment, or the many other things he could give her, but she knew, deep inside, that she didn't want *things*.

She wanted Dominic Moretti, and the only way to win him was to make him realize she wasn't like every other woman he'd known.

The new penthouse apartment that Dominic had selected for her was large with an entire wall of windows overlooking the city of Milan. It was quiet and felt empty despite the fact that it was filled with sleek ultramodern furniture. In the two weeks since she'd signed the agreement to become Dominic's mistress, she'd realized that living with him was going to be a challenge.

She'd gone to London to meet Barty wearing the brooch and bringing the false information with her. Ian had been in place, and they had been ready to entrap him, but instead Patrick had shown up to retrieve the information.

So she'd had to leave Renni in London to continue his gambling in case Barty was onto the trap they were trying to set. Ian had worked out the details and Angelina had simply gone along with them. Deciding to let herself be a pawn. It was what she'd been in this mess from the beginning.

She'd made a concerted effort to try to make him see her as more than a mistress.

Like when she'd made them a picnic lunch and convinced him to leave the office for an hour. They'd driven out of the city and had a quiet meal. They'd talked about books and travel, and she'd realized they had a lot in common on a very basic level. She'd mentioned that she loved finding out the history of old buildings. And Dominic had confessed he did the same, but with cars.

The next day he'd given her a book on architecture in Milan, and then he'd taken her that evening to one of his favorite old buildings. They'd explored the old stone facades and talked. Just talked. Angelina hadn't realized how long it had been since someone had listened to her and shared an interest with her that wasn't related to work or money.

Though there were times when she felt she'd succeeded, when she looked around this ultramodern place that he'd outfitted for them, she felt as though they were nothing but sex partners. He had to know that this place wasn't…wasn't the kind of place she could picture herself living in.

Was she giving him too much credit by suspecting that he had done it for her? She knew he must have some clue that she was falling for him. It was hard not to tell him how much she cared about him in the middle of the night when he made love to her. Their evenings together weren't like the obviously sexual games he played at the office or in the showroom or even in the new Moretti Motors Vallerio Roadster.

"Do you like it?" he asked, coming to stand behind her.

"Do you?" she asked. She'd been very careful

to keep things between them stress free. She wanted Dominic to realize that they could have a longer relationship and to be honest she was trying to be exactly what he wanted. She was adventurous in the bedroom and tried to be sweet out of it.

"I've just seen it."

She shook her head. "Dominic, didn't you approve the furniture in here?"

"No."

"Why not? You told me you were buying this place, not renting it."

"It will only be my home for the next five months or so. The furnishings don't matter too much to me—except the bedroom. I did ask for a king-size bed so we will both have enough room."

"Do you do this for all your mistresses?" she asked.

"You are different," he said.

She smiled at him as she felt tears sting the back of her eyes. "Thank you."

"You are very welcome. Now let's explore the place. Check out the bed."

She followed him into the kitchen, thinking that he always made her feel like the sexiest woman alive even though she was nothing close to it.

There was something about having a man want her the way Dominic did that took her breath away. Her mobile rang when they entered the kitchen area. "Do you mind if I get that?"

"Who is it?"

She glanced at the caller ID. "I'm not sure. It's an out-of-country code."

"Don't forget to use the recording button that Ian installed on your phone."

"I will," she said.

She hit the button to answer the call and record it. "*Ciao,* this is Angelina."

"*Ciao,* Ange."

"Renni, how are you?"

"Good. I'm calling you because I need a favor."

"What do you need?"

"Do you remember Jillian Stiles? I dated her two years ago?"

"Not really," she said. Her brother went through women very quickly. "Why?"

"She's going to be in Milan next month, and since you aren't going to be living in your place I thought maybe she could use it," he said.

She'd let Renni know when they'd planned for

him to come to Milan—before Barty's behavior had changed their plans.

"I don't know. Let me think about it and I'll call you back."

"She needs to know soon," Renni said.

"Why can't she stay with you?" Angelina asked.

"She'll be coming with me from London, and I've got a new job now," he said, referring to the job that Dominic had gotten him in the Moretti Motors plant. "And if she stays with me I will not go to work. I'll stay home and play with her. I don't want to let you down, Ang."

How was she supposed to say no to that? "Oh—"

"What does your brother want?" Dominic asked, putting his hand over the mouthpiece of the phone.

"To let his ex-girlfriend stay at my place next month."

"Why?"

"So she can save money," Angelina said.

"Are you going to do it?" Dominic asked.

"Probably. Renni doesn't want to take a chance on messing up at his new job. I think he took your warning to heart."

"I'm glad to hear it. If you let her stay there, will your stuff be safe?" Dominic asked.

"I don't know."

Dominic looked at her for a minute. "We'll move your stuff here before she comes. That way you know she won't go through anything."

"I...okay."

"Finish up so we can go and check out the king-size bed."

He removed his hand from the mouthpiece and she told Renni that his friend could use her place. Dominic had gone into the living room and she stood in the doorway of the kitchen area watching him. And thinking that there was a lot more to him than he wanted the world to see.

Dominic wanted Angelina all to himself, which had been one of the reasons he'd offered her brother a job. Now she'd have freedom from having to worry over the boy. And despite the fact that Renni was only two years younger than Angelina, he was still a boy.

"I'm sorry about that."

"It's nothing. I'm glad that he is taking his job seriously," Dominic said.

"Me, too. I was afraid that he'd do something

to jeopardize this and you'd be forced to terminate him."

Dominic had the same fear. Angelina was the only authority the boy had known for many years and he was used to answering to no one, not even the law.

But that had changed when Dominic had talked to Renni. Dominic had made it very clear that if Renni wanted to stay out of jail, he had to support himself and not involve his sister in any more nefarious activities.

And so far…for two weeks, Renni had kept his word. And for Angelina's sake, Dominic hoped that would continue. He'd learned that Angelina had a very soft heart where her brother was concerned.

And a jealous part of him wanted her to care and worry over him the same way. And he knew she'd never be able to do that if he sent her brother to jail.

He had found that he liked spending as much time with Angelina as he could. Living in two separate places had been difficult and he'd moved as quickly as he could to get them under one roof. This place was very upscale and sophisticated, befitting a man of his stature. But to be honest he didn't care about that. He had just wanted to give something to Angelina that she couldn't have gotten for herself.

"I understand about brothers," Dominic said. He'd tried to keep things light between the two of them, but he was a bit on edge waiting to see if Ian could find another connection to Barty Eastburn. Barty hadn't shown up for the meeting with Angelina, so that meant they had to find evidence against Eastburn another way. They suspected Barty knew Angelina had given herself up to Dominic.

"What are you thinking?"

"About work."

"What about it? I finished sending the final plans for the new Vallerio motor to the design group today. I know everyone is ecstatic over the fact that you are now officially going forward with the revamped Vallerio Roadster."

"Yes, they are," he said. The one nice thing about having an affair with Angelina was the freedom to talk about his work with her. But there were times, like now, when he wanted to remind her that the information she was discussing was still meant to be kept under wraps. "You know that this needs to be kept quiet."

"I do. I wouldn't have said anything except that I thought it might be on your mind," she said. Before they'd become lovers Angelina had been spunky and always standing up to him, but now she backed down quickly if she thought she'd upset him.

"Why do you always do that?"

"What?"

"Back down and apologize for everything."

"I'm just trying to be nice."

"Nice?"

She nodded.

"Don't be. You should know me well enough to realize that I don't like yes men."

She tipped her head to the side and gave him a very shrewd look. "But you do like accommodating women."

"True enough, but I know how to get you to be more biddable."

"You do?"

"Indeed. Come here and I'll prove it."

She shook her head. "You come here."

"That's not what I asked. You want to be nice to me, don't you, Angelina?"

She hesitated and he had no idea what she was thinking but the emotions that moved across her face were easy to identify. Fear, hope and something that looked a lot like caring.

"I'm always nice to you. I got your breakfast without complaining," she said.

This morning he'd had an important meeting with both of his brothers and there simply hadn't been time to order in as they usually did, so he'd had Angelina run out and get them breakfast. Normally he wouldn't have asked her to do that kind of thing since she was his assistant, but he had to admit he'd wanted her out of the office while Antonio brought them up to date on what was going on with Vallerio Inc.

"I made that up to you," he said. He'd taken her to lunch in the piazza and bought her the pretty gold charm bracelet, which now graced her slim wrist.

"Yes, you did. Did I thank you properly for that?"

He nodded. "Are you going to come over here or not?"

"That depends."

"On what?"

"If you are going to use your body to distract me."

"You don't like that?" he asked.

"I love it," she said. "I had no idea how sexy you could be, Dominic."

He arched one eyebrow at her. "You didn't find me attractive before our affair started?"

"I did. I just didn't allow myself to think about you in…carnal terms."

He laughed. There was something about Angelina when she let her hair down that made him relax and forget that he always had to be on his guard. Always keep his eye on the prize as his grandfather had told him on his deathbed.

"You mean you didn't lust after me?"

She shook her head. "I had plenty of lust, I just didn't think that you'd ever want me. Or that I'd ever be here with you like this."

"And now that you are?"

"I'm afraid that it's going to end all too soon."

Eight

Angelina had been surprised by Dominic's invitation for her to attend Moretti Motors' reception debuting their new roadster. But she'd happily agreed.

The entire Vallerio Inc. board had flown in from France to attend. Angelina suspected they were also here to celebrate Nathalie's engagement to Antonio.

She liked Nathalie a lot. They had become friends over the long weeks that Nathalie had spent in Milan negotiating with Antonio.

She knew that both Moretti Motors and

Vallerio Inc. were in talks to release the coupe version of the car next year as well.

"*Bonjour,* Nathalie. Congratulations on your engagement," Angelina said, moving to where the woman stood near a tall cocktail table.

"Thank you," Nathalie said. "I still can't believe I'm going to marry a Moretti. My grandfather is either laughing with delight that I caught a Moretti or spinning in anger that once again a Moretti caught a Vallerio."

"Wasn't your grandfather good friends with Lorenzo Moretti?"

"Yes, until Lorenzo broke my *tante* Anna's heart. Very tragic…I'm making light but it was sad. It seems like Lorenzo Moretti was doomed when it came to women."

"Cursed," Dominic said, coming up behind the two women. He held a champagne flute in each hand. He looked dashing in his tux as he handed one of the glasses to her.

She took it, lifting it toward him in a salute. "To Moretti Motors continued success."

He clinked his glass to hers and they both took a drink.

"You don't believe there is still a curse, do

you?" Nathalie asked. "I thought that Marco and Virginia broke it when Enzo was born."

Angelina had only heard rumors about the Moretti curse. The gossip was that the Moretti men could either be lucky in business or lucky in love, but never in both. Lorenzo Moretti, the founder of Moretti Motors, had been lucky in business turning the small company he started into one of the world's top luxury automakers. His son Giovanni had been lucky in business until he'd fallen in love with Philomena at which time Moretti Motors started to fail. Dominic, Antonio and Marco had decided that they would be the generation to be lucky in business again.

"How could the curse be broken?" Angelina asked.

"Virginia is the granddaughter of Cassia Festa, the woman who cursed my *nono*. And she had access to the original language that Cassia had used to cast that curse. She read over the words and figured out the meaning behind the curse and then deemed that if Moretti and Festa blood were mingled the curse would be broken," Dominic said.

"So now there's no more curse?" Angelina asked.

Dominic shrugged. "Who worries about curses when they are as successful as I am?"

She smiled because she knew he'd meant her to. But she wasn't feeling it. Instead she was worried that Dominic didn't seem to care that his family's curse meant that the men were destined for either fortune or love.

Though to be fair, Marco and Virginia seemed very happy. Marco's fortune hadn't changed and he was still winning F1 races. Antonio and Nathalie hadn't been together that long, but Angelina didn't see any signs that either Moretti Motors or Vallerio Inc. was going to face financial hardship.

"Dominic, you are never going to convince a woman to stick around with that kind of attitude," Nathalie said.

"I have other attributes you might not be as aware of."

"She better not be," Antonio said, coming up behind his fiancée. He hugged her close and dropped a quick kiss on Nathalie's lips.

"*Buona sera*, Angelina."

"Good evening, Antonio." She wasn't too certain what Antonio thought of her. She knew that all of the Moretti brothers were aware she had been spying on the company and that made her feel as though she didn't deserve the happiness she had found with Dominic. Maybe she was starting her own bad luck.

"I don't mean to hurry everyone away, but we need to mingle. Marco and the rest of Team Moretti should be arriving any minute and many of the guests will want to talk to him and Keke," Dominic said.

Keke had been a Team Moretti F1 driver who had been injured in a car accident; actually he'd almost died. And Angelina remembered how upset the Morettis had been about it. They treated everyone who worked for the company like family.

Like a real family, she realized. Not at all the way she and Renni had been because it was just the two of them. But a big extended group of people that she could rely on. It was a different kind of feeling and she liked it.

"Angelina?"

"Hmm?"

"I need you to entertain the press group," Dominic said.

"Certainly. What do you want me to do?" Angelina asked.

"Just the tour of the factory like we discussed earlier," Dominic said.

Everyone at the reception would be taken on a factory tour in small groups. Angelina was happy to be included as one of the Moretti Motors representatives. She knew it wasn't so much due to her being Dominic's mistress but more because he was starting to trust her again.

Angelina was tired a bit after the long day at work. Dominic was out of town for an F1 race all of the Morettis traditionally attended. She felt very much his mistress when he left her behind in Milan, which made her feel foolish besides.

Dominic hadn't promised her any more than he'd given her. He treated her well. She unlocked the door to the apartment he'd insisted they live in. The welcoming scent of orange blossoms greeted her as she put her keys on the hall table and walked into the living area. There was a crisp breeze blowing in from the balcony.

"*Sì*, Angelina. I'm sorry I didn't call. I got an earlier flight back."

"I'm so glad," she said. "I missed you."

"Good."

"You can be very arrogant at times."

"You're right I can. Did you miss me in bed?"

he asked, crossing the room and taking her in his arms.

"Yes," she said. She had missed his arms around her during the night and the comfort she took from knowing he was there next to her.

"Me, too. I didn't expect to miss you," he said, his confession coming quietly from him.

"Me either," she said. He led the way to the couch and sat down, pulling her down on his lap.

He kissed her passionately and she pulled back. "Can we pause for a bit?"

"Why?" he asked.

"It's…it's been a long day," she said, holding herself stiffly. "I think I'd be happy to have your arms around me."

She knew she was being needy, and a part of her wanted to push hard to see exactly what she meant to Dominic. If he pushed her away, then she would simply try to stop caring for him. Try to keep herself from falling for him.

"I'd love to hold you. Go change into something comfortable and get into bed. Have you eaten?"

She shook her head. "But I'm not hungry."

"I will join you in a minute."

Angelina left Dominic in the living room to go

and get changed. She took her time washing her face, and tried not to read too much into Dominic's actions. He was a kind man—she shouldn't be surprised that he'd take care of her when she didn't feel well.

But what did surprise her was that he'd do something so unselfish for her. There was nothing for him in his comforting her. Nothing at all. And she knew she hadn't been able to get any further information from Barty or ESP Motors, but tonight it didn't seem to matter.

Tonight it felt to her as if Dominic cared about her simply because she was his woman.

She changed into the silk pajamas she kept on a hook on the back of the bathroom door and came out to find the covers turned back on the bed. Dominic had stripped down to his boxers and a T-shirt.

He held his hand out to her and she went to him. She climbed into the bed on his side and then slid over. He got in after her and pulled covers over her before drawing her close to his side. She rested her head on his shoulder and closed her eyes, relaxing for the first time…since her mother had died. No one had held her like this since her parents had died.

She sniffed, trying not to cry thinking about the hugs that she missed.

"What's the matter?"

"Nothing. I was just thinking of the past," she said.

"What about it?"

"My parents. I didn't realize until this moment how much I missed the simple things they did for me."

He hugged her closer, dropping a kiss on the top of her head.

"You lost someone to share your life with," he said.

"Yes, and my dreams."

"What are you dreams, *cara mia?* Share them with me," he said, stroking his hand down her back.

She shifted in his arms until his hand was rubbing right where she ached. "I don't know what my dreams are anymore. I think I've always wanted to live in the countryside, have a family of my own."

"Would you stay at home with the children?" he asked her.

"Yes, I'd like that very much. I know that might not be possible, but I'd be willing to sacrifice material things if I had to. What about you?" she asked, meeting his dark gaze with her own.

"I think I'd like my wife to stay home with the kids. My mother was there for my brothers and me after school. She had her own life during the day, but we knew she was there...I think that's very important for children."

"I agree," she said. She tipped her head down and closed her eyes. She didn't like to think of Dominic married and having children, because she had started thinking of him as her man and now she knew that he probably wouldn't be.

Dominic fielded questions from the international television media as he led his group through the factory. So far all of the comments and questions he'd received had been very promising. They'd had a request from BBC's Top Gear to test out the Vallerio Roadster, which pleased him.

It was the kind of press they could use. Nathalie was charming a group of investors from France and Antonio was scowling each time Nathalie laughed at something one of the men in her group said. Dominic thought it was funny that his brother, who had never been tempted by any one woman, was now so tied in knots over his fiery redhead.

He escorted the last group through the factory and noticed that Renaldo De Luca was still in the work area. He should have been at the reception and not back here. Renaldo smiled at Dominic when he saw him and waved, then gestured to the pretty girl with him.

Dominic took out his mobile phone and sent a quick text message to Angelina asking her to get her brother and his date out of the factory. This wasn't the place for romance—especially tonight.

She immediately responded that she would take care of it. Dominic wondered if she would ever really be able to get her wayward brother under control. He doubted it, because for some reason Renni cared only about himself.

"That concludes our tour. Tomorrow starting at ten a.m. we will be offering test rides in the Roadster out at our track. You can sign up for a ride at the desk near the far side of the room. I hope you enjoy the rest of the evening."

As his group dissipated, Dominic saw Ian moving toward him. The other man looked as though there was something important on his mind.

"Got a minute?" Ian asked as soon as he was close enough to be heard.

"Yes. Here or in my office?"

"Office would be better," Ian said.

"Should I get Marco and Antonio?"

"I think you might want to hear this first."

Dominic didn't like the feeling generating in the pit of his stomach. He glanced around the reception area and didn't see Angelina. "Give me a minute."

"No problem."

Dominic left the reception area to go back to the factory. The last of the tours had moved through and the factory was eerily empty.

He heard the sound of voices and wasn't surprised to find that Renaldo and Angelina were the source. "I told you not to mess this up."

"I didn't, Ange. I just wanted to be alone with Penni. I'm sorry, it was stupid to come in here."

"It was stupid to bring her in here. Everything in this room is still under wraps."

"I said I'm sorry. What more do you want?"

She shook her head. "I want you to be a man, Renni."

"I have been since Dad died."

She shook her head. "No, you haven't. You say that, but not one time have you stepped up and taken care of something for me. Or taken care of me, your only sister—that's what men do."

"I can't live up to the standards set by your precious Dominic."

She shook her head. "I'm not asking you to. I want you to be your own man. To think before you act and for once handle something on your own."

"I am trying, Ange. I really am. I will find Dominic and tell him I'm sorry about being in here."

She took a deep breath. "Okay, you do that. But he might not want you to keep working for him."

"Then that's the price I'll have to pay."

Dominic heard something in Renaldo's voice he'd never heard before, and it sounded like responsibility. He didn't expect anyone to be perfect, and Renaldo's actions tonight were harmless.

"There you two are," he said, stepping out of the shadows.

Both of them turned to face him. Angelina took a step forward, but Renaldo stopped her with his hand on her shoulder.

"I'm sorry, Signore Moretti. I didn't think tonight when I brought Penni back here."

"No, you didn't think. Apology accepted."

"It won't happen again," Renaldo said.

"I know it won't," Dominic said. He believed

that Renaldo was starting to grow up. Maybe it had been his sister's tears or the fact that she'd almost had to go to jail for him, but something had woken Renaldo De Luca up.

"Go and enjoy the rest of the party," Dominic said.

"Yes, sir."

Renaldo left and Angelina still didn't look at him. She was beautiful tonight in her formal dress. It was black—as most of her clothing was—and formfitting. Her shoulders and neck were bare and as she kept staring at the floor he couldn't help but notice how vulnerable she looked.

"What are you thinking?" he asked.

She lifted her head and he saw the glitter of tears in her eyes. "Thank you for going easy on him."

"No need to thank me. I know that mistakes happen, and owning up to them like he did shows me the kind of man he's becoming."

She nodded. "I…I've been so worried about him."

"Why?"

"Because I haven't let him fight any of his own battles. He was devastated when Mom and Dad died…you can't imagine what it was like that first year."

Dominic crossed the space between them and drew her into his arms. He wished he'd been there for Angelina then. Wait a minute. What was he thinking? If he'd been there for her, he probably wouldn't have any of the things that he called his own today.

Angelina was a distraction to him, and though he'd never lose his business focus, if he'd met her before he'd gotten involved in the day-to-day running of Moretti Motors, he'd easily have been content to let himself fall in love with her. Damn, was that what he was doing?

That couldn't be right. And if it was, it meant she was too much of a distraction. If he let her take over any part of his life, Moretti Motors would fall back into the hands of outsiders. One thing that Dominic promised himself he'd never let happen.

Would he, though? He'd had a chance at love and had blown it. In college he'd fallen hard for a pretty American named Kate, and they'd become engaged after one semester. Dominic had thought that Kate was his world and expected her to feel the same about him. But she'd returned home to Texas for the summer while he worked in Moretti Motors as a management trainee. When it was time to return to school, Kate had called him and said she wasn't coming back. She missed the States and her home there too much. Dominic had thought about leaving Moretti Motors and going to her, but she'd discouraged him from doing so.

Why then did his heart feel as though Angelina was the missing piece?

After that night at the reception Angelina noticed a change in their relationship. Dominic stopped treating her like a mistress and more like a girlfriend. More like a woman he was going to continue seeing. But it had been almost six months now and she lived on pins and needles, so afraid that Dominic would stick to the letter of the agreement they'd signed.

"Want to go out for a drink after work?" Marta asked while they were at lunch.

"I can't."

"Do you have a date?" Marta asked.

"Yes," she said.

"Well, me, too, but not until later," Marta said.

"Still computer dating?"

"Yes. I know my Mr. Right is out there."

"What do you mean your Mr. Right?"

"The one guy meant for me. Do you believe in that?" Marta asked.

Angelina shrugged. "I've never really thought about it. I've never dated a lot. But, with Renni relying on me I couldn't."

"But that's not a problem anymore, is it? I meant to tell you your brother is one hot guy. I'd think about asking him out, except I know all his dirt from you."

Angelina laughed at her friend. Marta didn't know the half of what Renni had done and she never would. As far as Angelina was concerned, Renni's troubles in London were a different lifetime. They'd both moved on and were in a much better place now.

"So who's your date with, some hottie?"

"Yes, he's a hottie."

"And a mystery man? Is it someone from work?" Marta asked, glancing around the cafeteria. She leaned across the table. "I won't tell a soul."

For the first time Angelina was tempted to tell Marta her personal business. But she couldn't break a lifetime of habits and she was used to keeping her own counsel. She'd never been a woman to share secrets with girlfiends even when she'd been younger.

"Yes, someone from work. But I don't want to talk too much about it."

"Is the relationship serious?" Marta asked.

Angelina glanced down at the salad she was eating. She had no idea. She looked at the charm bracelet Dominic had bought her back at the beginning of their relationship. It was laden with charms he'd given her over the last six months. He'd given her other jewelry, more expensive pieces that she suspected he'd given to his other mistresses as well. But this was the one piece that meant the most to her.

"Oh, no," Marta said.

"What?"

"Your silence tells me two things."

Angelina looked up, waiting to hear what her friend was going to say.

"Either he's married—"

"He's not. I wouldn't get involved with a man who was married."

Marta shrugged. "I wouldn't judge you. Falling in love is something that happens when you least expect it. It's the Mr. Right thing. Sometimes he's already in a doomed relationship."

She didn't know that she agreed with Marta, but she did know that Dominic was hers. She shook her head. Was that really it? Of course it was. She loved Dominic. She wouldn't have agreed to be the mistress of any other man.

Only Dominic Moretti because he was the only man who made her feel alive and…complete.

"What else do you think my silence means?" Angelina asked.

"That you care more for him than he does for you," Marta said.

Angelina could only stare at her American friend.

"Why are you looking at me like that?" Marta asked.

"Because you saw something that I was afraid to admit."

"It's not because I'm wise or anything—it's just that I've been there before. Why do you think I came to Milan?"

"Why?"

"To escape. I was tired of seeing him every day and not being able to be with him. Even after I moved out of the neighborhood where we'd once lived and changed jobs…he haunted me."

Angelina reached across the table and took Marta's hand, squeezing it to offer some comfort for the pain she saw in the other woman's eyes. But then Marta shook her head. "But that is all in the past. He wasn't my Mr. Right, and moving on was the only sensible thing to do. So what about your guy?"

Angelina wasn't sure she bought in to Marta's little pep talk, but it was clear that her friend was trying to cheer her up. "What about him?"

"Is he a lost cause or do you think he will fall for you?"

Angelina thought about the way Dominic held her in bed every night. How he'd pull her close to his side and hold her until he drifted off. That felt like more than lust.

And he really did take care of her—and not just sexually or even financially. He was willing to hold her when PMS made her weepy or to listen to her talk about her dreams of living in a little house in the countryside instead of in the city center of Milan.

"There are times when I think… Well, yes, he is my man."

Marta glanced at her watch. "I have to get back to work. I hope for your sake that he is the man you think he is."

Angelina shared that hope. In fact, she was risking her heart on that hope. And tonight she was going to take a big risk and ask Dominic to continue their relationship after their agreement ended.

Nine

"Where is Angelina?" Antonio asked as he walked into Dominic's office.

Dominic glanced at his TAG Heuer watch before responding. "At home getting ready for our date tonight."

"Date? Are you sure you know what you are doing with her? I didn't say anything when you completely ignored the fact that she was stealing from us and moved in with her, but are you really using your best judgment?"

"I am not doing anything that would put the company in jeopardy. You and I both know it wasn't her choice to pass that information to ESP. They are the ones we want to catch, not her. Trust me."

"I do. If it wasn't for you I don't know where we would all be today. It was your vision to bring Moretti Motors back to the glory it experienced during *Nono*'s heyday."

"What's your point?"

"I don't want to see you get hurt with this woman, Dom. You know she's betrayed us once."

"I do know that. But she was doing it to protect her brother."

"What makes you so certain she won't have to protect him again?"

"Because Renaldo is now owning up to his life," Dominic said. He didn't want to discuss his personal life with his brother. Antonio had done his own thing, gone against Dominic's wishes and fallen in love with Nathalie Vallerio. A move that had almost cost them the rights to the Vallerio name.

"You weren't exactly thinking with your brain when you fell for Nathalie."

"My point exactly. That's why I'm talking to you now."

"What do you want from me?" Dominic asked.

"Just be careful, Dom. We don't know if Angelina is completely trustworthy."

"There hasn't been a leak in over six months and Ian has been working closely to make sure that Barty Eastburn hasn't recruited anyone else from our company."

"Fair enough. I wanted to talk to you about the press release we are sending out for tomorrow. I know that you approved it, but we need to change the wording on the Vallerio Incorporated section."

They discussed what needed to be changed. Press releases were normally handled through the publicity department. But because this was the big launch of a new type of engine that Moretti Motors had won exclusive rights to use from Vallerio Inc. both Dominic and Antonio had decided to vet the release.

By the time the meeting ended he realized he was going to be late for his date with Angelina. Antonio was almost out the door when Dominic stopped him.

"Do you think the curse is broken?" he asked.

"Yes. The way I feel about Nathalie has shown me that I can have it all. It didn't make me not want Moretti Motors to succeed anymore. In fact, because of our joint ventures with Vallerio In-

corporated, I'm even more determined to see that
we continue to grow our business."

Dominic nodded. "I wondered if *Nono* cursed
himself because he gave up the woman he loved."

"He might have. For him it was Moretti Motors
or nothing. He would never have been able to
make a relationship work while running this
company," Antonio said.

"I agree. It was in *Nono*'s nature never to put
anyone before Moretti Motors," Dominic said.
"Though Dad is the opposite."

"Yes, he is. Are you serious about Angelina?"

Dominic shrugged. "I think I am. We had an
agreement…but I'm thinking of asking her to
make it permanent."

"Permanent as in marriage?"

"Not marriage but a long-term affair." Dominic
had thought of little else for the last two months.
He couldn't say for sure what it was that had made
him start thinking of a future with Angelina, but
something had. He only knew that when he'd
started thinking about living without her, he'd felt
hollow inside.

"Am I being a fool?" he asked his brother.

"Love is a tricky thing…"

"I'm not in love. She just makes my life comfortable away from work. She gives me companionship."

Antonio watched him with those shrewd eyes of his. "I don't know what to tell you, bro. Nathalie added something to my life that I didn't realize was missing until she was there. Is that how you feel about Angelina?"

Dominic shrugged. He shouldn't have started this conversation. Whenever he discussed anything but Moretti Motors he felt as though he was out of his league. He loved his family, but women had always been a bit of a mystery to him. "I don't know. I only feel that I want her by my side."

"Then go for it. You know we focus a lot on being *Nono*'s grandsons, but we are also Papa's sons. And that man is a romantic. A man who knows that passion for a woman is the greatest joy one can find."

"*Grazie,* Tony."

Antonio wraggled his eyebrows at Dominic, a goofy thing his brother had done since they were boys. "Don't mention it. Everyone knows I'm the smooth lover in the family."

Dominic punched his brother in the shoulder. "Everyone knows you are the goof-off."

"Very true," Antonio said. "It's because I'm happy. Everything with Moretti Motors is going as we planned. I have a woman I love in my life… Who could ask for anything more?"

Dominic walked out of the building with his brother, realizing for the first time that he wanted what Antonio and Marco had found with their women. And that life was finally within his grasp with Angelina.

Angelina loved driving with Dominic. It was easy to tell he was the grandson of a legendary F1 driver and the brother of another. His skills behind the wheel were superb and he put her at ease as he wove through the evening traffic in Milan as they headed out of the city.

"Where are we going?" she asked as he fiddled with the radio, putting on a CD of her favorite artist. Angelina rested her head against the back of the seat trying not to read more into this moment, this night, than she should.

Because of the nature of their relationship they'd spent a lot of time going to private places for dates or just staying at the penthouse apartment.

"Lake Como. Is that okay?"

She nodded. "I love it there. When I was a child we used to go for holidays."

"My family had a house there, as well. When we were boys we spent a lot of time on the lake."

"What was it like growing up with two brothers?" Angelina asked. "I love Renni, but I would have liked a sister."

"My brothers are the best friends that I have. From the time I was very young I was aware of our family's legacy from Grandfather—"

"The curse?"

"*Sì*. And as I got older I realized that I didn't want to take a chance on letting Moretti Motors slip further away from our family. It was important to me that Tony and Marco both realized what a gift our grandfather had left us," Dominic said.

"I can see that. You did a good job of rebuilding the company. That was one of the things that drew me to Moretti Motors when I was job hunting."

"It was?"

"*Sì*. I wanted to work for a company with corporate integrity and wasn't just about money. Your organization has a sense of pride in everything that Moretti Motors does be it the retail luxury car market or your F1 team."

Dominic glanced over at her. "Reputation is really all we have that we can call our own. Fortunes can be won or lost."

She reached over and squeezed his thigh.

"What was that for?"

She rubbed her finger in a little circle pattern on his leg. "I'm sorry I almost ruined your reputation by stealing information."

He put his hand over hers. His big fingers engulfed her smaller ones and he lifted her hand to his lips, brushing them against the center of her palm.

"We are past that now, aren't we?" Dominic asked.

"I still feel…shame, I guess, about what I did." It was more than that. She hated that the reason he'd noticed her as a woman and not just his assistant was tied to that act of betrayal. And no matter how much she tried to tell herself that it didn't matter, a big part of her knew it did.

"You have to let it go. I did."

"Did you?" she asked, trying not to be distracted by the movement of his thigh muscles under her hand.

"Yes. Though it was hard for me because your actions felt like disloyalty. And I'm also a bit jealous that you would go to another man," he said. There was a bit of vehemence in his voice that suggested he might not be as forgiving as he'd said.

"I never had a loyalty to anyone but you and to my family."

"And that is why I am letting it go. That and the fact that we can never have any kind of relationship if I didn't."

She caught her breath. "Relationship? Do you mean something beyond the six months we agreed to?"

He glanced over at her. "I do mean that, Angelina, but we will talk when we get to my villa."

She felt a flutter in the pit of her stomach, and for the first time since her parents died that scared, lonely part of her relaxed. The feelings she had for Dominic were strong, and knowing that he wanted to continue the relationship with her made her realize that Marta had a point to something she'd said earlier.

There was a Mr. Right for each woman, and Dominic was hers.

"Tell me about your holidays at Lake Como," he said.

"My grandparents brought us one summer. Only that once. Renni and I were eight and ten and *Nono* rented a boat and we spent all day on the lake. I pretended I was a princess and Renni was a pirate."

He glanced over at her and smiled. "Sounds like it was fun."

It had been. "It was. I haven't thought of that time in years."

"That's natural. You're not someone who looks back all the time."

"True. Life is lived in the now, isn't it? I learned that from working with you. When someone makes a mistake you don't brush it aside, but you learn from it as you move on. I had never seen anyone do that before."

"Given the nature of my family, it's either learn and move on or wither and die talking about the glory days. And talking isn't productive."

"Isn't it?"

"Not unless there's a purpose to it."

He continued talking to her about his life philosophy, and she listened, soaking up the sound of his voice and the feel of his leg under her hand. She liked the connection she felt to Dominic and realized that no matter what happened later in their relationship, he'd given her something that no one else had.

He'd given her the belief in herself that she was more than worthy of being his woman.

Their drive continued. The moon was full and the late-summer sky bright. She couldn't wait for the start of autumn.

"Tell me about your holidays on Lake Como," she said.

He thought back to those long days when he'd been a young boy. "When I was eight or so, I didn't realize we were the poor relations. My grandfather had let us move into his compound in Milan since my mother worked nearby, and he had servants to help during the day with raising us."

"What changed?" she asked.

He was a man who'd built his life on pride. He admitted that and knew that how the world perceived him was important to him. "It was that summer. Tony and I used to gang up on Marco... What can I say—he was an annoying little brother."

"Aren't they all?" she said with a hint of laughter in her voice.

"Indeed. Well, we dared Marco to jump out of the tree house my father had built for us. And his friend Gui was visiting with us, as well. So Marco and Gui go up in the tree house and jump from the platform. It was about three meters high, and when Marco landed he twisted his knee and broke his leg. Gui was right alongside him and only twisted his ankle."

"You must have been upset that he got hurt, but how did that change your perception of money?"

"Gui's family was very angry and threatened to sue my parents for negligence. It was a bigger deal than we imagined, and my grandfather pulled us aside and told us to stop being so…ridiculous—that's the term he used. He said that one generation of Morettis had squandered their money and not to let our generation continue the pattern."

Angelina reached over and squeezed his thigh. "You were just a boy."

"I was old enough to know that what I'd done was wrong. My mother was upset because we might have to sell the Lake Como house. It had been a wedding gift from her parents."

"I am so sorry. So one act of brotherly teasing changed the direction of your life?" she asked.

He shrugged. "I probably would still be who I am today, but that incident made me stop being so irresponsible."

His cell phone rang and he let go of her hand to answer it.

"It's Stark. We need to talk."

"Tonight, Ian?"

"Yes. I have some important information on the investigation… Dammit. A cop just pulled me over," Ian said.

"What for?"

"Driving and talking on my cell phone. It's illegal in London."

"Call me back," Dominic said.

"I will."

Dominic disconnected the call.

"What did Ian want on the phone?" she asked.

"He's had a break in the ESP Motors investigation," he answered at length.

"Good," she said. "I'll be very happy when that entire mess is behind us."

"Will you?"

"Yes, I regret ever doing anything to make you feel like you were betrayed."

He nodded. Her words cemented in his mind that asking her to continue their relationship was the right choice. She had made a mistake and she had changed. He'd seen the evidence himself over the past six months. And he knew he didn't want to go back to the way life had been before he'd blackmailed her into his bed.

Ten

Dominic had arranged to have dinner set up on his Lake Como villa's veranda. His parents' house was a few miles up the road and Antonio and Marco both had their own places here as well. Lake Como was where they all called home.

Lake Como was a beautiful area frequented by the jet-set crowd. Millionaire businessmen, heads of state and Hollywood celebrities all owned property here, but that wasn't what had drawn him here. It had been the tranquility of the area and the fact that this was the one place where his parents had always managed to keep a home.

Because his mom's family had gifted the property to them, it had been a matter of pride that his father had never sold that house.

When his father had lost the chairmanship of Moretti Motors, their immediate family fortune had changed. They'd been forced to sell their house in San Giuliano Milanese and had to live with distant relatives until his mother started making decent money as a teacher at a local university.

"I love this place," Angelina said as she walked out of the living room area onto the veranda.

"Me, too. I'm sorry we haven't had time to come out here before this."

"It's been a busy summer," she said. "Next year will be calmer once we get the Vallerio launched."

"Indeed it will be," he said. Next summer he'd spend more time at the lake with Angelina and his brothers. Marco was thinking of retiring from F1 racing and he would take over managing Team Moretti when he did. That would give Dominic one less responsibility at work. And he could spend the extra time with Angelina.

"I have something important to talk to you about."

"You mentioned our relationship in the car."

He walked to the balustrade's railing and leaned against it. Angelina looked exquisite in the mood lighting. Her hair curled around her pretty face and her dress clung to her curves. Her nipples were visible under the bodice of her dress and he still had her panties in his jacket pocket.

She was completely bare under that dress and he wondered if conversation was really what he wanted right now. He knew it wasn't. He was still aroused from her hand on him in the car and he wanted to say the hell with talking and just lift her skirt and take her.

But lust wasn't the problem between them. Communication was. And he needed things to be settled between them. He needed to know that she was his for the foreseeable future. He needed…her.

"You're staring at me." Angelina's voice interrupted his thoughts.

"Am I?"

"Yes, you are. What are you thinking, Dominic?"

"I'm wondering what you feel for me," he said.

She took a deep breath and walked toward him, her hips swaying gently with each step. She stopped when she was at his side and leaned forward, resting her arms against the banister as she stared at the horizon. "Why do you want to know?"

He turned to face the same direction as she was and moved to stand behind her. He placed his hands on either side of her body and leaned over her.

"Because I care for you, Angelina," he said, speaking directly into her ear. "And I have no idea if your feelings for me have changed."

She turned her head to the side, brushing her lips over his jaw. "I care for you so much, Dominic."

"How much?"

She shook her head, her silky curls rubbing against his face. "I'm afraid to tell you."

"Why?"

She took a deep breath and then looked at him. Met his gaze head-on and he felt the impact of her emotions. "Because if you don't feel the same way about me, I'm going to feel very vulnerable."

"I will protect you, Angelina. Even your feelings. Haven't I done that very thing from the beginning?"

"Yes, you have," she said. "Even when it

wasn't in your best interest to look out for me, you did. Why did you do that?"

He definitely wasn't going to tell her that he'd done it for one reason and one reason alone. He could only guess that he'd started loving her a long time ago.

He wrapped his arm around her middle and pulled her back against the curve of his body. Damn, she was a weakness he hadn't anticipated. A weakness that he knew could be his downfall.

Women and Moretti Motors didn't mix. Yet he didn't want to let her go. "Tell me how you feel," he said. He put his mouth to her neck and nibbled at her skin.

She shifted in his arms, turning to face him. She went up on tiptoe and kissed him deeply. Her tongue slid over his and he was struck again by how right she felt in his arms.

He took control of the kiss and she twisted against him sinuously. He lifted her, setting her on the banister.

He pulled up her skirt and then lowered his zipper. He didn't take the time for a condom, needing to be inside her. He kept his erection poised to enter her body and felt the damp wetness of her welcome him.

"Tell me," he said, swiveling his hips to tease her.

She put her hands on his shoulders and leaned down to bite his earlobe.

"*Ti amo,* Dominic Moretti. I love you."

"Very good," he said, entering her with one long stroke. He took them both quickly to the pinnacle of release and they climaxed together. Dominic had the answers he hadn't realized he'd been seeking and it surprised him that they were right here in his arms. That this one woman was the thing that he hadn't been able to find on his own or in his success at Moretti Motors.

Angelina sat across the table from Dominic enjoying the dinner his staff had prepared and trying very hard not to dwell on the fact that she'd told him she loved him and he hadn't said it back.

She felt incredibly exposed at this moment. She'd never been more nervous of the outcome of a meal. What if she was like poor Marta, haunted by Dominic until she had to leave not only Milan but Italy? What if…

"Do you like the veal?" Dominic asked.

He was relaxed and in a very good mood. Something she'd noticed early on in their relationship that sex did for him. It relaxed her, too, and normally she loved seeing his face so calm and his easy smile.

But a knot had formed in the pit of her stomach and she knew that until he told her how he felt, it wasn't going to go away.

"It's very good," she said, putting her fork down and reaching across the table for her wineglass. She took one deep swallow and then another.

"Are you okay?"

"I need to ask you something," she said.

"Okay." He, too, put his fork his down and leaned back in his chair.

A gentle breeze blew up from the lake, stirring the hair at the back of her neck. She closed her eyes for a minute and let go of the sense of panic she felt. What did it matter how Dominic felt toward her? Her love for him wasn't going to change.

But she knew that if he didn't love her she'd end up being the one to carry the burden of their relationship and it would never be balanced. That was something she'd learned the hard way with Renni. And it was only Dominic who'd shown her that she couldn't always be the one to rescue Renni; he had to do it for himself.

"Angelina?"

"I'm sorry. It's just this is harder to say than I thought it would be."

"What is this about? Have you been in contact with Eastburn again?"

She shook her head. "No. Why would you think that? I told you that I wasn't going to steal anything else from Moretti Motors."

Dominic took a swallow of his wine. "You are clearly nervous and can't find the words to tell me whatever is on your mind."

She twisted her fingers together, tried not to let his accusation stand between them, but it did. And before she could ask him about his feelings, they needed to clear the air about their past.

"You said you'd forgiven me for what I'd done, but I think I need more than that."

"Okay, what do you want from me?"

"I guess some kind of acknowledgment that you know I'm not a thief. I had never taken anything before this incident and I haven't done anything since. If you can't see beyond the circumstances that caused me to make that bad decision, then I guess we don't have anything else to say to each other."

"I can. I understand that your brother is your weakness. He's the only man you care about."

She shook her head. "He's not the only man I care about, Dominic. I also care deeply for you. I told you I loved you. Did you think I was lying?"

"I never thought you lied about your feelings. I just don't know anything else that would make you this nervous. The last time you were this way, I had a meeting with Ian and learned that you were the spy. Can you understand my reaction?"

"Yes. I'm sorry about my part in this. I was just trying to find the words to ask you about your feelings for me. But now I feel stupid that I made it into something else."

Angelina felt small and more exposed than ever.

"Angelina, *mia bella*, don't apologize. I jumped to conclusions."

"Why?" she asked.

"I am nervous, too," he said.

She laughed.

"That wasn't very nice."

"I'm sorry but Dominic Moretti is never nervous. You are the one who strikes fear into your competitors."

He reached over and stroked her face, something she noticed he liked to do. "That is very true. But you aren't a competitor, Angelina."

"No, I'm not. I'm just the woman who loves you," she said. Having confessed her feelings, she was finding that she liked expressing them.

"I like hearing you say that," he said.

"I like saying it. I can't believe how my life has changed," she said. "To go from the constant fear that I'd be arrested to having you…it's more than I dreamed possible. Sometimes I almost don't believe that this is real. That you are my lover and that the life we've been living is mine."

"I don't want you to fear anymore. I brought you here tonight to ask you to keep living with me," he said.

"Another arrangement?"

He shook his head. "I think we are beyond that. I don't want you to be my mistress any longer. I don't want to hide our relationship from our friends."

"Oh, Dominic," she said. "That is what I want, too."

"Good," he said. "Then it's settled."

"Not yet."

"What else is there?"

"I want to know how you feel about me," she said.

"I care about you very much, Angelina."

"Just care?"

"No, it's more than—"

"Signore Moretti," his butler, Gennaro, interrupted from the doorway. "I'm sorry to bother you but you have an urgent call from Signore Stark."

"I'll be right back," Dominic said to Angelina, and she nodded. She could wait to hear him say he loved her. It would be a bit of icing on a night that was already more perfect than she could have imagined.

Dominic stalked into his library and answered the landline that Ian had called on. "Moretti here."

"Why haven't you been answering your mobile?"

"I turned it off to enjoy the evening with Angelina. I didn't want anything to interrupt us. Which you are doing right now. What do you have for me?"

"Big news. ESP Motors is having a press conference tomorrow to announce a new engine design that they are putting into production on all of their cars."

"You called me for this? We leaked the wrong plans, you know that. All that Barty Eastburn has is a revamped version of a V-8. He's going to look like an idiot."

"No, he's not. Dominic, he has your plans. The real plans for the Vallerio Incorporated engine. The one that Emile worked so hard to design."

Dominic sank into the leather chair next to the desk. How the hell had this happened? "That's not possible. We kept the plans under lock and key. No one knows about the new plans except me and Emile Vallerio. That's it."

"One other person knows, Dominic."

"Angelina?"

"Yes, she has access to your office, *and* you've been living with her for the last six months. I consider her a prime suspect."

"Dammit. That's impossible."

"I'm sorry to be the bearer of bad news, but I called Emile's office, and he said you have the only copy of the plans. I've got enough evidence to go the local authorities. But all they will do is set an injunction against ESP Motors. Do you want me to do that?" Ian asked.

"Who did you talk to in Emile's office? Emile himself?"

"No, he was in a meeting. His assistant, Belle,

answered my questions, and then Emile called me back."

"Go to the authorities, then. Do you have evidence against Angelina?" he asked. He couldn't imagine that she'd betray him again. For one thing, he just didn't believe she could have faked being in love with him.

"Yes. The tape clearly says that De Luca is bringing the plans on the Eurostar from Paris. I met the train in St. Pancras station and Renni was on it."

"Renni's not Angelina. Are you sure she gave him the information?"

"Not a hundred percent, but he works in your factory…do you think he got it himself?"

"I have no idea. Let me talk to Angelina and I'll call you back."

What if she had betrayed him again? What if she were playing him for a fool? But he knew she wasn't. He'd had her watched. Had been careful not to leave any proprietary information in his own office. How would Renni have known where to go?

Deep inside where he'd always feared that he was like Lorenzo Moretti, he was afraid he had the confirmation he'd been looking for. His love for Angelina had brought the Moretti curse down on him.

His love had made him weak, and if not for Ian would have cost Moretti a fortune.

"Dominic?"

"Angelina, come in please. We have a lot to discuss."

"Yes, we do. I believe you were going to tell me," she said.

"Before we get to that," he said, "I need to talk to you about something very important."

"Okay," she said, moving slowly into the room.

She looked uneasy and he knew his attitude wasn't helping. But if there was a leak and it involved her brother, then that meant Renni was in trouble again. That her brother was back to making the same stupid mistakes he had in the past. And this time Angelina wasn't going to be able to bail him out, because he wasn't about to let her sacrifice herself and their happiness for Renni's.

Yet a part of him believed that she might not want to be with him if he put her brother in jail. But he couldn't continue to let De Luca steal from him.

"Are you okay, Dominic? Did Ian give you bad news?" she asked, coming farther into the room.

"I'm fine. Everything is fine. Ian finally got the break he was searching for at ESP Motors."

"Good. Did he find a way to connect Barty to the espionage?" she asked.

"*Sì*, he did. Angelina, I'm not sure how to say this, but the information came from our office."

She blanched. "Do you think I did it?"

He shook his head. How could he have thought that for even a minute? She simply wasn't the type of woman to lie that way. "No, but I think someone close to you did."

He was trying to figure out when Renni could have gone to London to deliver the plans to Barty. Dominic had been in the office for twelve to fourteen hours a day. As he ran over the past week in his mind, he remembered that Renni had driven Angelina to work last week when she'd been too sick to accompany him to the Grand Prix race in Monza in Italy.

"Does ESP Motors have more information from us?"

"They have the new Vallerio engine design."

"How did they get it? I thought Emile kept them," she said.

He had lied to her and everyone else, making sure that the plans were safe in his office. "I had the only copy locked up in my office. Though I know that Emile and his assistant knew this, I don't think the Vallerios would sell us out now."

"No, they wouldn't," she said. She crossed her arms over her stomach, and he'd come to know her well enough to realize she was upset. Really upset. He wondered if her mind had gone along the same path as his to Renni.

"Has your brother had any access to your office?" Dominic asked.

"I didn't let him into your office, Dominic," she said. "Do you think I'd do that? I didn't take those plans and give them to Barty Eastburn. I didn't even know you had them in the office."

"I know that."

"Then how would Renni know?" she asked.

Dominic closed his eyes and reran every encounter he'd had with Renni De Luca. He remembered catching him in the production facility with a woman—a woman who was French. He wondered if she worked for Emile. It made sense.

"What was the name of the woman Renni was with at our reception?"

"Um…I can't remember. Beatrix or Brigitte? Something with a *B*."

"Belle," Dominic said, realizing he'd just found

the answer to how Renni had known that the plans were in his office.

"Yes, that's it. Why?"

"I think I know how your brother knew where to find the plans."

"I…what are you going to do?" she asked.

"What I should have done the first time," Dominic said, getting to his feet. "Put him in jail."

Eleven

Angelina had to get away before she broke down crying. And she wasn't going to get out of Dominic's villa before that happened. She turned to leave, but he stopped her with a hard grip on her arm.

"Where do you think you are going?"

"To ask Gennaro to call me a cab. I can't stay here while you plan to arrest my brother. He's going to need a lawyer and my help. I don't want to listen to any more of your accusations."

"I can't let this go," Dominic said.

She saw the anguish in his eyes, and that did make her cry. "I know."

His mobile rang before she could say anything else and he answered it.

"Moretti here," he said. "Send the cops to arrest Renni. We need to call Emile. He has a leak in his office."

She listened while he talked to Antonio catching him up on everything that had happened. As he talked she tried to piece everything together. How had Renni gotten plans that were only in Dominic's office?

She leaned back against the wall, wrapping her arms around her waist. She was so tired. She really was. The men in her life wore her out.

Damn, Renni. How had he taken the plans and given them to Eastburn? The night of the reception he'd been in an unauthorized area, so she knew he would have no problems getting into any part of the Moretti Motors building. In fact, he'd visited her office a number of times...and when she'd come back from lunch the other day, her keys had been in the in-box.

Had that been it? She needed to find Renni and talk to him. If he'd taken her keys and broken in to Dominic's files, she was never going to forgive him.

Dominic had turned his back on her and she

knew that staying here wasn't going to help anything.

She walked out of the library as quietly and as quickly as she could.

She dialed Renni's number. "Hiya, Ang," he said, answering on the first ring.

"Where are you, Renni?"

"Back in London. I really missed my old life," he said.

"Angelina?" Dominic asked, coming into the hall.

"Gotta go, Ang," Renni said, hanging up.

"Who was that?" Dominic asked.

She shook her head. She couldn't do this. She was trapped between her brother and the man she loved.

"Renaldo?" he guessed.

"Yes."

"Where is he?"

She shook her head again.

"I'm sending you back to Milan," Dominic said. "After this is resolved, I'll call you."

She nodded stiffly. There was no way she could deny him, but would her love change if he had her brother arrested?

Dominic stayed with her until the cab came.

As the cab drove away, she rooted around in her purse for a tissue and blew her nose. Then she took out her mobile phone.

The plans for the new engine had just been finalized and she guessed that Renni would have taken them with him to London. She would have to book herself a flight, but she *was* going there and she *was* going to confront her brother and Eastburn.

She needed to confront her brother and this time prove her loyalty to Dominic.

It had taken Dominic until the time he'd reached Milan to realize that Angelina wasn't the sort of person who would leave confronting her brother to him.

He knew why he'd jumped to conclusions, blamed his own fears of not believing she could really love him and that they could have it all.

He had expected to be betrayed by love, and in a way it had betrayed him and more than likely cost him the only woman he'd ever loved.

He finally realized that she must have gone to London in the hope of confronting Barty. He called his private pilot and had him ready the corporate jet.

He dialed her mobile number, but she still wasn't answering his calls. He called Ian instead.

"This is Stark."

"Ian, I think Angelina is on her way to London. Where are you?"

"I am tailing Eastburn, and he just entered Renaldo De Luca's London flat."

"I'm on my way to London. I don't know where Angelina is, but if she shows up, keep her away from her brother and Eastburn. I don't want her getting hurt," he said.

At least not any more than he had hurt her already. The flight wasn't a long one, but it felt like forever. Dominic tried to work but in the end realized that without Angelina his life would be nothing—his successes were hollow. Now he realized the truth about the Moretti curse.

The truth was that his grandfather and even his brothers to some extent had all cursed themselves. They'd believed they couldn't have love and success, and so had sabotaged their own relationships so that they never had a chance at having it all.

He realized, too, that he'd never told Angelina he loved her, and he regretted that.

As soon as his plane landed he was in the car

he'd had waiting and was speeding across London. Well, that wasn't accurate. The traffic was horrific and he had to stop to buy a congestion ticket to get through London proper to Renni's flat.

When he arrived he found Ian waiting outside with two policemen. "We have a warrant for the arrest of Barty Eastburn and Renaldo De Luca."

"Good. Let's go inside and get them," Dominic said.

"Have you seen Angelina?"

"No, but I had to leave to get the warrant. Let me ask Steve," Ian said, going to check with one of his men. He returned a minute later. "She might be inside. A woman matching her description entered a few minutes ago."

"Dammit," Dominic said.

He realized he didn't care about arresting Barty or Renaldo. He just wanted to find Angelina and hold her in his arms again. He wanted to tell her he loved her and beg her to forgive him for believing she'd betray him.

They climbed the stairs and knocked on Renaldo's door. They heard voices arguing and then the door opened. Barty stood off to one side with a bloody nose and Renni was seated on the couch. Angelina was standing in front of the open door.

The police rushed in and arrested both men. Neither of them said anything as they were cuffed and led away. Ian followed them through the door.

"What about me?" Angelina asked.

"I'm not having you arrested," Dominic said.

"Why not? I thought you believed I was in on it, too."

He shook his head. "Deep inside I didn't believe it."

"Don't do this to me again, Dominic. I love you and that makes it too easy for me to believe the things you say. But now I know you can never trust me."

Dominic drew her into his arms. "I trust you, Angelina. It's myself I've never been able to trust. I've always been afraid that if I loved a woman I'd lose myself, and that was the one thing I didn't want to do."

"Are you saying you love me?" she asked.

"I do love you. More than I ever thought I could love any woman."

"Are you sure?"

"Yes, I am."

"How did you know to come here?" she asked.

"Did you have proof of my innocence before you came to London?"

"No. When you took my car and left Lake Como I realized that you were hurt and angry and then I started to calm down. Once I did I realized you'd never betray me again."

"Because I was afraid of you?" she asked.

"Because you loved me and you aren't the type of woman who would ever betray someone she loves."

"You're right about that," she said.

He kissed her and held her close to him. "I love you, Angelina."

"I love you, too, Dominic."

Dominic didn't let go of Angelina for the rest of the day even when they went to the police station to talk to her brother. Renni hadn't taken the plans out of spite, but to set up Barty so that the other man would leave both of the De Luca siblings alone.

After they got everything straightened out, Angelina and Dominic checked into the Ritz-Carlton and he made love to her in their suite. Only then did the panic in his soul cease. He held her in his arms and looked down at her face. "I do love you."

"I know you do."

"You're going to marry me and give me lots of sons."

"Am I?"

"Will you?" he asked.

"Yes," she said. "Yes, I will."

The next few weeks were long for Angelina and Dominic, but they stood together by Renni's side as he gave compelling evidence against Barty Eastburn. The prosecuting attorney was willing to let Renni off with a reduced sentence of 180 days in jail.

Dominic offered to try to get him off without any jail time, but Renni said that he wanted to take care of this problem on his own. He was tired of having other people rescue him.

"I'm impressed with your brother," Dominic said as they were on his corporate jet heading back to Milan from London.

"Impressed?"

"That he took responsibility for his action. And that he did it for you."

"I know. He wanted to prove to me that he could take care of his own problems."

"Now that your brother is taken care of, you are free of obligations," he said.

"Yes, I am. Why?"

"I have a new task for you."

"Really? What is it?"

"Planning your dream wedding."

"I don't have one. I never thought I'd marry."

"Well, you and I are getting married, and I want the day to be perfect for you."

"As long as you are by my side, it will be," she said.

Epilogue

Lake Como sparkled in the midafternoon sun and the wedding guests milled around the grounds enjoying the festive mood that filled the air. Dominic smiled at his bride across the crowded dance floor. She was currently dancing with his father.

"I can't believe you tied the knot," Antonio said.

"Me either. I think we finally broke the Moretti curse. Now we have a real legacy to leave to our children."

"Children?" Marco asked coming up behind

them. Little Enzo smiled up at Dominic from his father's arms. "Are Nathalie and Angelina expecting?"

"Angelina isn't yet, but we do have a month-long honeymoon planned," he said.

"Nathalie isn't either," Antonio said. "Where are you going? You two have been quiet about the location."

"I bought a house for Angelina in the countryside. Just thirty minutes out of Milan, but I think she'll like it. We are going to go there for the month and settle in. See if it's the kind of place that she's always dreamed of living in."

"Will you be happy there?" Antonio asked. "The commute into Moretti Motors will be long and tedious."

Dominic shrugged. He didn't mind the drive as long as Angelina was happy. She was his life now, not the car company, and with the curse broken he knew they would be happy for the rest of their days. Because he had unraveled the true power of the curse and knew that it had to lie within his own soul.

"You are staring at your bride like a lovesick fool," Marco said.

"I learned the look from you," he said.

"I happen to look very sexy when I stare at my wife," Marco replied.

"Who told you that?" Antonio asked.

"She did," Marco said.

The band switched to an old Nat King Cole song, "Stardust," and Angelina walked toward him. Dominic met her halfway. He pulled her into his arms and danced with her.

"I love you," he said, needing to tell her as often as he could. She'd made his life so complete.

"I love you, too," she said, rising on her tiptoes to kiss him. He kissed her back and then hugged her close. Over her head she saw his parents dancing, their love shining as it always had. And Dominic realized he wanted that for Angelina and himself. Some day, twenty years or so from now, he wanted to dance with her at their child's wedding and still feel as in love with her as he did today.

"What are you thinking?" she asked.

"That you broke the Moretti curse."

"I'm glad I did. I can't imagine life without you."

* * * * *

VALENTINO'S PREGNANCY BOMBSHELL

AMY ANDREWS

This book is dedicated to all those bionic
ear pioneers who strived to give deaf people
everywhere options they'd never had before.
Such achievements are totally inspiring.

Amy Andrews has always loved writing and
still can't quite believe that she gets to do it for a
living. Creating wonderful heroines and gorgeous
heroes and telling their stories is an amazing way
to pass the day. Sometimes they don't always act
as she'd like them to—but then neither do her kids,
so she's kind of used to it. Amy lives in the very
beautiful Samford Valley, with her husband and
aforementioned children, along with six brown
chooks and two black dogs. She loves to hear from
her readers. Drop her a line at www.amyandrews.
com.au.

CHAPTER ONE

PAIGE DONALD could feel Valentino Lombardi's gaze on her from across the altar. Not even the beauty of the ceremony or the happiness in her heart for her friend, Natalie, could distract her from the intensity of it.

It caressed every inch of her body, making her even more self-conscious about what she was wearing.

The bridesmaid's dress clung to non-existent curves. The hem grazed her knee and she suppressed the urge to yank it lower. This wasn't her. This frothy, clingy, femme fatale dress with shoestring straps and low back.

Very. Low. Back.

The crimson creation didn't say busy single working mother with a high-needs child who hasn't slept an entire night through in three years.

It said Sexy. Flirty. Time for pleasure. It said the playground is open, come on in. And Valentino Lombardi, possibly the sexiest man she'd ever laid eyes on, probably the sexiest man in existence, looked like he wanted to be first to ride.

But she didn't have time. Not for flirting. Or riding. Or pleasure. Or any of those trivialities. And especially not for a man who looked like he held a PhD in trivia. There were never enough hours in the day as it was.

There was just never enough time.

She had a sudden hankering for her faded grey trackpants and her favourite oversized T-shirt back in her wardrobe at home in Brisbane. Or better still her baggy blue scrubs. She didn't like being this…on display. She felt awkward.

The heat from Valentino's gaze radiated towards her and she slid him a mutinous back-off-buddy glance. It was one she'd perfected since Arnie had walked out on her and it usually stopped a man dead in his tracks. But Valentino just grinned and gave her a saucy wink.

Great! Please, God, don't let me have to dodge this Italian Neanderthal all night.

'Can I have the rings, please?'

Paige could have kissed the priest as Alessandro's best man was given a job to do other than look at her. Unfortunately, though, his actions commanded the attention of the entire female population of the church, including her, and Paige found herself drinking in the way his exquisite suit pulled across broad shoulders and how the fine wool of his trousers outlined powerful quads and one very fine backside.

Very, very fine.

He glanced at her as he stepped back into his place and his espresso eyes told her he knew exactly where hers had been. A smile touched his lips, beautiful lips that could have been carved by one of the masters. Except they were warm and vital.

Desirable. Kissable.

There was a frankness in his gaze that stopped the breath in her lungs. She searched for something more, beyond the promise of tonight. Something deeper. A connection. Something that told her he was interested in more than getting her between his sheets. But all she found was heat and sex and lust.

Totally superficial. Like the man.

Another flashy male. All sparkle, no substance.

Still, her heart skipped a beat and she sucked in a ragged breath.

Paige hit the 'send' button and placed her mobile on the table, drumming her fingers. Her gaze returned, yet again, to Valentino as he worked the room. She tried to ignore him and her steadily growing irritation as women almost swooned at his feet but the rich sound of his easy, frequent laughter made it impossible. It reached out from across the room as if he had physically caressed her, drawing her attention like a moth to flame.

Valentino Lombardi was not a man you could ignore. With his killer dimples, boyishly curly hair and Italian playboy charm, he was pure vice.

Paige's phone vibrated and she reached for it, her pulse spiking.

McKenzie fine. Sleeping well. Stop worrying.

Paige's fingers flew over the keypad. *Apnoea mat on?*

Alessandro laughed again and Paige drank the sight of him in as she pressed 'send'. He threw his head back, giving the belly laugh its full freedom, and her gaze followed the bronzed length of his exposed neck peppered with dark stubble.

Another vibration dragged her eyes back to the table. *Yes. Go and dance for crying out loud!*

Paige smiled despite the gnawing, ever-present worry.

She could almost hear her mother saying the words. But she'd never had a night away from her daughter. Frankly she didn't know what to do with herself.

Don't think I'll stay the night. If I leave after cake can be home by midnight. 'Send'.

Paige checked her watch, doing a quick calculation in her head. Yep. She could definitely make it home by then.

'Everything okay?'

Paige glanced up into the bride's face. Nat had fresh bluebells threaded into her blonde locks, which brought out the colour of her eyes and matched the crystal beading decorating the neckline of her ivory gown. Alessandro's hand rested possessively on her shoulder and Paige felt a sudden yearning she couldn't explain.

Why? She'd been where they were. Had the divorce to prove it. She certainly had no desire to do it again.

She smiled at her friend. 'Just telling Mum I might not stay the night.'

'Paige? No.' Nat grabbed her hand. 'Your parents have booked and paid for it. Including breakfast. Your mother would skin me alive if I let you leave.' Nat squeezed Paige's hand. 'It's just one night. Don't you think it's time you enjoyed a well-deserved break?'

Paige shied away from the earnestness of her friend's expression. Everyone said that to her—you need a break, Paige. But she was a mother first and foremost and McKenzie needed her. That's just the way it was. Nat would understand one day too.

The phone vibrated and Paige grabbed it, relieved to break eye contact with the bride. She opened the message and read it three times, a ghost of a smile touching her lips. She held it up to Nat.

Don't. You. Dare.

Nat grinned. 'Have I mentioned how much I like your mother?'

Paige rolled her eyes. 'Okay, okay. I'll stay.'

'Good.' Nat squeezed her hand. 'The speeches are about to start.'

A deep laugh floated towards them and Nat looked across to where Valentino was chatting with some nurses from their work. 'You should take a page out of Val's book. He's certainly having a good time.'

Paige felt her gaze drawing to him again. 'Isn't he just,' she said dryly.

Nat sighed. 'I tell you, if I wasn't utterly besotted with Alessandro and was up for a brief fling, I'd be over there too.'

'Hmm,' Paige murmured noncommittally.

'Do you know he used to date Adrianna de Luca?'

Paige gave her friend a mystified look. 'Who?'

Nat rolled her eyes. 'One of Italy's top catwalk models.'

Of course he did. 'Fancy that.'

'They were in all the magazines last year.'

Paige hadn't read a magazine in for ever. Or a book. Sunday newspapers were about her limit. 'Of course they were.' Her voice dripped with derision.

Nat regarded her friend seriously. 'Not all men are like Arnie, Paige.' She looked up as Valentino laughed again and poked her elbow into Paige's ribs. 'Come on, you have to admit, he's a bit of a spunk.'

'I hope you're talking about me, *il mio tesoro*,' Alessandro interrupted, nuzzling his new wife's neck.

'But of course.' Nat smiled, turning to Alessandro, her lips poised to meet his as he lowered his head.

Paige felt a tug at her dress and was grateful for a reason

to avoid the blissful clinch she knew was happening beside her. She looked down to see, Juliano, Alessandro's four year old son.

'Where's McKenzie?'

Paige smiled at the boy. 'Juliano, you look magnificent!' He was dressed in a mini-tux and was the spitting image of his father.

With the boyishness and dimples of his father's cousin.

Juliano stood a little higher. 'Nat says I'm handsome.'

'Nat is one hundred per cent right.'

Juliano beamed. 'Is McKenzie sick?'

Paige shook her head, saddened that it was such a natural conclusion for Juliano to jump to. 'No. She's at home with her grandparents.'

Juliano's face fell. 'I wanted to ask her to dance.'

Paige's heart just about melted and she pulled Juliano in for a big hug. 'You are so sweet. I see you have your father's charm.' She glanced at Alessandro, who winked at her. 'Another time, huh?'

Nat had wanted McKenzie to be her flower girl but Paige had declined. The truth was, crowds made Paige very nervous for her daughter. As an ex-prem with chronic lung disease and poor immunity, every single person was a potential source of infection, a silver bullet to McKenzie's weak defences. It just wasn't worth the risk.

'Okay.' Juliano nodded, squirming out of her embrace. 'See ya,' he chirped, and ducked away, heading for the dance floor.

Paige watched him, smiling even though her heart ached. What would she give for her daughter to be so able-bodied, so carefree? She returned her attention to her phone and replied to her mother's text.

Promise you'll ring if there's a problem.

It took five seconds for the reply. *I promise.*

Paige texted back. *Anything at all. No matter how trivial.* She released the message into the ether and held on fast to the phone, tension tightening her stomach muscles.

She knew people thought she was too uptight about her daughter but what did they know? It was she who lived every day with the reality of McKenzie's fragile health, not them. And one thing was for certain—being vigilant had kept McKenzie alive.

With the operation only a couple of months away now, Paige was determined to keep McKenzie healthy and avoid any more delays. It had been rescheduled three times already. No more.

The phone vibrated in her hand and Paige opened the message. *I'm switching the phone off now. Go and have fun. That's an order.*

Paige smiled. She'd obviously stretched her mother's patience enough for one night. Thank God for her parents. She would never have got through the past few years without them.

A tinkling of cutlery on glass cut through the low murmur and Paige turned to see Alessandro standing. She pushed all thoughts of the world outside the room aside, determined to follow her mother's orders, and motioned for the drinks waiter.

'So,' Valentino said, topping up Paige's half-full glass with some more champagne, 'I believe it is a custom in your country for the best man and the bridesmaid to dance the bridal waltz together.'

His voice was low and close to her ear and her body

reacted as if he had suggested something much more risqué than a customary dance in front of a room full of people. It took all her willpower not to melt into a puddle. Not to turn her head and flirt like crazy.

Except it seemed like a million years ago now that she'd last flirted and she was pretty sure she didn't have a clue how to go about it. And why she would choose to do so with a man who was all glamour and sparkle, after her experience with Arnie, was beyond her.

The bitter burn of memories was never far from reach.

'That's right,' she said, refusing to look at him, focusing instead on the bubbles meandering to the surface of her champagne.

'*Eccellente.* I'm looking forward to that.'

Well, that made one of them. The thought of them dancing, his arm around her practically bare back, their bodies close, was sending her heart into fibrillation. Sitting next to him at the table, aware of his every move, every breath, their arms occasionally brushing, his deep voice resonating through tense abdominal muscles, was bad enough. Being pressed along the magnificent tuxedoed length of him? Frankly it scared the hell out of her.

She felt gauche and unsophisticated and totally out of her depth next to his man-of-the-world, model-dating perfection.

What if she stuffed up the steps? Or trod on his foot?

What if she liked it too much?

'You are worried your boyfriend will mind that we dance, yes?'

Valentino's comment snapped her out of the vision of her clinging to him like some sort of groupie as he pressed kisses down her neck. She glanced at him, startled.

A big mistake.

Thus far she'd managed not to look at him this close up. And now she knew why. This near, he was simply dazzling. Gorgeous hair the colour of midnight waved in haphazard glory, thick and lustrous with not a hint of grey. It brushed his forehead and collar and Paige finally understood the itch some women talked about to run their fingers through a man's hair.

Jet-black eyebrows quirked at her as her gaze widened to take in his square jaw line, heavy with five-o'clock shadow. His full lips curved upward and were bracketed by dimples that should be outlawed on anyone over five. His eyes, dark like a shot of the best Italian espresso, were fringed by long black lashes and promised fun and flirting.

A buzz coursed through her veins at the fifteen different kinds of sin she could see in them.

Valentino smiled at the little frown that knitted Paige's caramel brows together and crinkled her forehead. She was a most intriguing woman. Her grey eyes were huge in her angular face dominated by prominent cheekbones and a wide mouth.

She wore no eye make-up to enhance them, she didn't need to. They drew the gaze regardless. Her strawberry-blonde hair had been severely styled into a pixie cut that feathered over her forehead and would have looked boyish on anyone else but only seemed to enhance the hugeness of her eyes and the vulnerability he saw there.

She was no beauty. She certainly wasn't his usual type. He liked them curvy. Everywhere. Not rail thin like Paige. And confident. Women who were secure in their sexuality, who smiled and flirted and enjoyed life. Women who knew the score.

And yet…

There was something about her that intrigued him. Not least of all the fact that she'd been the only female in the room who hadn't clamoured to be closer to him.

'I see you texting. All night,' he prompted when she still didn't say anything. 'I figure a beautiful woman…' He shrugged and shot her his best hey-baby grin, 'it must be a boyfriend?'

Paige shook her head to clear it as Valentino's smile muddled her senses. 'I'm a little old for a boyfriend, don't you think?'

'Paige. We are never too old for love.'

The slight reprimand in his voice didn't register. Nothing registered beyond the way he'd said her name. Paige. He had drawn it out a little at the end, giving it a very European flair, and it had stroked across every nerve ending in her pelvis.

She shut her eyes. This was madness. He was just a man. God knew, she hadn't even thought about the opposite sex since her husband had walked out on her. And, besides, she just didn't have time for a man. Especially not a model-dating, Italian playboy whose interest in her would no doubt wane the minute after he had his way with her.

Which wasn't going to happen.

Even if, deep down, in a secret, hidden part of her, she wanted it very, very badly.

I am a single-mother of a high-needs child.

I am a single mother of a high-needs child.

She turned back to her champagne and took a long deep swallow, the bubbles pricking her throat as they slid down, matching the prick at the backs of her eyes. 'I am.'

Tonight, as always, Paige felt absolutely ancient.

'Excuse me,' she murmured, rising and headed for the refuge of the bathroom.

Valentino watched his cousin dancing with his new wife, a gladness in his heart that Alessandro had finally found love after the train wreck of his first marriage.

It always humbled him when he saw two people ready to make a lifetime commitment. Sure, after an early escape he'd worked out it wasn't for him, but that didn't mean he didn't believe in it for others. His parents were, after all, still blissfully married after fifty years.

He spotted Paige making her way back to the table and he was struck anew by how not his type she was. The crimson dress outlined a figure that had more angles then curves. Her breasts were small, her body one long, lean line, and she moved with purpose rather than grace.

And yet...

He rose as she approached the table and held out his hand. 'I believe it's our turn.'

Paige's heart thundered. His gaze had tracked her from all the way across the room and her heart beat as if she'd just dashed one hundred metres in less than ten seconds. She looked up at him, caution wrangling with temptation. How easy would it just be to surrender? To forget her mangled heart and the type of man who had mangled it in the first place and succumb to the invitation in Valentino's eyes?

But Paige had never been into masochism.

She ignored his hand and headed towards the dance floor.

Valentino grinned. If she thought for a moment that he couldn't read every emotion, the battle in those large grey eyes, she was utterly deluded. He followed her to the floor, his gaze glued to the elegant length of her naked spine the dress afforded him, and wondered what it would take to convince her to let her guard down.

Paige reluctantly let him shepherd her into the circle of his arms. His big hand sat low, just above her butt and just this side of decent. It was firm and hot and she felt a lurch in areas that hadn't felt anything in a very long time.

Valentino felt resistance as he tried to pull her a little closer. 'Relax,' he murmured to her temple.

She jerked her head back slightly to forcibly remove the brush of his lips from her skin. Relax? He may as well have asked her to fly to the moon. She glared at him. 'Let's just get through this, okay?'

Valentino chuckled. Paige wasn't one for stroking egos. Another factor he was finding surprisingly appealing. He'd drifted through life never having to work for the attention of a woman—ever. From his mother to his sisters and cousins, to the girls at school and beyond, he'd always had them twisted around his finger.

He was starting to realise how boring, how predictable, his life had been.

They moved to the music and Paige automatically followed, her senses infused with Valentino's clean male scent. She sought desperately for something to say to instil distance, to break the hypnotic pull of the music and his warm breath.

Anything.

'So, Valentino, Alessandro tells me you are a cochlear implant surgeon.'

Valentino smiled at her robotic question. He looked down into grey eyes that were averted to a point beyond his shoulder. That she could see over his shoulder was a first for him too. Most women he'd dated, apart from Adrianna, had been shorter. At six feet two, he still had a few inches on her but the fact that it would just take one tantalising tilt of her chin to claim her mouth was an intriguing proposition.

'Yes, Paige. Alessandro tells me you have a daughter who needs one?'

Paige stumbled at the mention of McKenzie, grateful for a moment that Valentino's body was there to lean into, to steady herself. But then aware, too aware, of the muscles beneath his shirt, the strength in his arms, the heat of him, the power of him.

'Yes,' she said, pushing away from his chest and holding herself as erect, as far away as was possible, which was severely hampered as the dance floor filled with other couples and they were jostled closer together.

'She's scheduled for two months' time.'

Curiously Paige found herself wanting to tell him about McKenzie, about her fragile health and the long road they'd both been on, but as much as she was desperate for conversation to maintain distance, the ups and downs of her life were not for public consumption.

'Is she a patient of Harry Abbott's?'

Paige's face lightened. Now, Harry, her boss, she could talk about. She could talk about him and his genius all night long. Finally she felt on solid ground. 'Oh, yes. Only the best for my little girl. Do you know him? He's an absolute pioneer in the field.'

Valentino smiled, amazed at the difference in Paige as passion filled her eyes and she came alive, her face animated. Is this what she would look like beneath him in bed? His hand tightened against her spine, inching her un-resisting body closer.

'Of course.' He shrugged. 'Everyone knows Harry.' In fact, it had been Valentino's very great pleasure to finally meet the man a couple of months back during an interview.

Paige nodded. 'He's an absolutely magical surgeon, so clever and such a fair boss. And great with his patients. He insists everyone in the audiology department knows how to sign so the patients are at ease.'

She chatted away, finally comfortable in his arms. So comfortable, in fact, she didn't notice that the song ended and another began. Or that they were now so close their bodies rubbed deliciously against each other as they swayed to the tempo.

Valentino, on the other hand, had noticed. In fact, he could barely register anything else. Her chatter faded into the background along with the music as his body re-sponded to the subtle friction of her dress against the fabric of his trousers and the waft of frangipani and woman lit a fire in his groin.

She shifted against him as someone from behind bumped into her and he almost groaned out loud. 'Paige.'

His voice, low and throaty, snapped her out of her prattle and she was instantly aware of the chemistry between them. The ache of her taut nipples as they chafed against the fabric of her dress and his shirt. The darts of heat radiating from the fingers of his hand on her spine, shooting waves of sensation over her bottom and the backs of her thighs. The heat in her pelvis stoked by the heat in his.

Her eyes locked with his, the lust, the intent in his espresso gaze frightening. She opened her mouth again to use conversation as a weapon to repel him, to push him away.

But Valentino got in before her. 'Do you think if you talk enough you'll be able to ignore what's going on here?'

Paige's eyes widened at his insight. 'I...I don't know what you're talking about,' she denied, feeling frantic, like a mouse on a treadmill set on maximum speed.

'Paige.' Valentino ground out her name as he flattened his palm against her spine, bringing them even more intimately into contact. 'I think you do.'

For a few seconds Paige wanted nothing more than to grind herself against him. It was an urge she had to suppress with an iron fist.

The music stopped and people clapped. She used the distraction to gather every ounce of willpower and step out of his arms. 'No. I don't.'

And she spun on her heel and got as far away from Valentino Lombardi as she could.

An hour later Paige couldn't take being sociable another second. She knew it was bad form to leave the wedding before the bride and groom but she just couldn't stand being in the same room as Valentino, watching him dance and flirt, for a second longer.

She made her apologies, assuring Nat she was staying the night but pleading a headache. When the lift arrived promptly she almost pressed a kiss to its cold metallic doors. The impulse was short lived as they opened to reveal Valentino, his jacket slung over his shoulder, his bow-tie undone, leaning against the back wall.

They stared at each other for what seemed an eternity. 'Going up?' he murmured.

Damn, damn, damn. Paige entered the lift after a brief hesitation during which an errant brain cell urged her to run. But she was damned if she was going to show this man he had any power over her. She turned her back on him, keeping to the front of the spacious lift, and searched the buttons for floor twelve.

Of course, it was already lit. Great! Same floor. Next they'd have adjoining rooms! The doors shut and she clutched her bag, reaching for patience.

Valentino, afforded an unfettered view of her spine, looked his fill. He couldn't deny he wanted to see more of her back. And her front. He wanted to see her become passionate and animated again. And not about a nearly seventy-year-old surgeon who was old enough to be her grandfather. But about him. And what he was doing to her.

But she'd made it perfectly clear that any attraction was not going to be acted on. Valentino Lombardi had never had to beg in his life—he wasn't about to start.

The lift arrived at their floor and Val smiled as Paige practically sprinted from it. He followed at a more sedate pace, not really wanting to know where her room was. What if they happened to be neighbours? Would knowing she was in the next room be any good for his equilibrium? Wondering if she slept naked? Wondering if she was as sexually frustrated as he that she might help herself to ease the ache?

He shook his head. *Dio!*

Except it seemed they were to be neighbours and if her cursing and muttering was anything to go by as she rammed the keycard in her door, he was going to have to lend a neighbourly hand.

He hung his jacket over his doorknob and strolled towards her, resigned to his fate. 'Can I help with that?'

Paige slotted the card in and out several more times, wanting to scream as she twisted uselessly at the handle. She turned to him, glaring like it was all his fault. 'I hate these things.'

Val smiled. She was animated when she was angry too. Her cheeks flushed pink, her chest rising and falling enticingly, grey eyes sparkling like headlights in fog. He reached for it. 'Allow me.'

Paige didn't protest. She couldn't as his scent infused her senses. She'd done it all back at the wedding. There was no more resistance left. His fingers were sure as they slowly inserted the card into the slot and slowly pulled it out again.

Would he be that slow with her? That thorough? The light turned green and she shut her eyes as he turned the doorknob and opened her door.

'Entri.'

Paige looked into her room. Her big empty room. She flicked her gaze to Valentino's big hands with his sure fingers.

Val was surprised by her hesitation and although he couldn't see her eyes he sensed the battle from earlier had returned with gusto. 'Maybe I could join you?'

Paige felt absurdly shaky inside. She wanted to cry, burst into tears. She hadn't realised how lonely the last couple of years had been until an attractive man had propositioned her.

She looked at him instead. Saw the naked desire heat his gaze. This was crazy. 'I don't…' What? Have sex? Make love to? What could she say without sounding gauche or desperate or like a sixteen-year-old who'd never been kissed? 'Sleep with men I've just met.'

After all, it had taken her three weeks and a handful of dates to succumb to her attraction to Arnie.

'I promise you, there will be no sleeping.'

Paige swallowed hard. Both at the gravel in his voice and the sincerity in his gaze. 'I don't understand,' she said. Her throat was parched as she fought a little longer, hoping the sexual malaise invading her bones would lift. 'Any woman in that room tonight would have accompanied you here in a flash—why the hell do you want me?'

Val gave her a lazy smile as anticipation built in his gut, his loins. 'Because you're the only woman who wouldn't have.'

So she was a challenge? She supposed she should have been insulted but funnily enough they were precisely the right words for him to use. It told her she was something to be conquered and discarded, like all the others. Which, contrarily, right now, suited her just fine. She didn't have time or room in her life for the distraction of a love affair. But she did have tonight.

Obviously the only thing he was interested in.

It was win-win.

Paige pushed off the wall and without saying a word brushed past him and entered her room. She hoped it looked confident and sexy and that he couldn't hear the boom of her heart or the knocking of her knees.

She stopped in front of her bed, opened her bag, took her mobile out, checked it for messages then placed it on the bedside table before tossing the bag aside. She heard the click of the door behind her in the muted light and didn't have to turn to know that he was walking towards her. And in seconds his heat was behind her, his breath at her neck.

He said nothing as his fingers stroked up her arms. Neither did she. Nor did she say anything when his hands peeled the dress off her shoulders, baring her to her waist.

But she did cry out when his thumbs swept across her bare nipples, already hard and eager for his touch.

And when he kissed her neck.

And when he whispered her name.

Paige woke disorientated to a warm hand laid possessively low on her abdomen and a strange buzzing as a pale dawn broke through the gaps in the heavy curtains. She glanced at the clock—five-thirty. They'd been asleep for thirty minutes—Valentino had been true to his word.

The buzzing came again and movement caught her eye as her mobile vibrated and moved slightly across the surface of the bedside table. It must be a text message.

It took another couple of seconds for the import to set in. A text message.

McKenzie.

Instantly frantic, she grabbed her phone and accessed the message, her hands shaking, her heart pounding.

McKenzie woken with a slight temp. Don't worry. Everything under control.

Paige read the message three times, feeling progressively more ill. Oh, God. Her daughter was sick again and where was she? In the arms of some Italian Lothario thinking only about herself.

She leapt out of bed, ignoring the pull of internal muscles, grabbing for her clothes, furious at herself and Valentino for last night. She should have followed her instincts and gone home. Not stayed. Not let herself be seduced into a one-night stand, no matter how amazing it had been. Seduced into forgetting about the one person who meant more to her than anything else on the entire planet.

Her baby was ill. She had to get to her.

She didn't even look at Valentino as she threw her things together in record time. Or as she fled the room.

As far as she was concerned, if she ever saw him again, it would be too soon.

CHAPTER TWO

PAIGE arrived for her last day of work before her holidays at St Auburn's, with a spring in her step. She hadn't had a spring in her step for a long time but it was there today. She couldn't believe that McKenzie's operation was just three days away now. Her daughter hadn't been unwell or had a fever since the night she'd slept with…since Nat and Alessandro's wedding two months ago, and she had even put on a little weight.

Things were finally looking up. Finally going their way. All she had to do was convince Harry to let her be in the theatre to observe McKenzie's operation on Monday and life would be complete.

A butterfly flapped its wings in her stomach as she rehearsed the words again. Not that Paige really thought it would be an issue. Yes, it wasn't usual but she knew Harry well enough to feel confident that he'd overlook the rules for his right-hand woman.

Paige was actually humming as she entered the operating theatre change rooms. Dr Gloria Reinhart, the anaesthetist Harry used for his lists, was changing into her scrubs and Paige bade her a hearty good morning.

'Morning,' Gloria said, staring at Paige, an odd look on her face.

Paige frowned. 'What?'

Gloria shrugged. 'Nothing. It's just that I've never heard you hum before.'

Paige didn't need a translation. She knew she was serious. That she wasn't much fun. She came to work, ran Harry's theatre and his clinics with ruthless efficiency, not particularly caring whether she made friends or not. She didn't socialise or have time for gossip or idle chit-chat.

She was respected. Whether she was liked or not hadn't been a priority.

Paige grinned. 'Well, it's about time that changed, don't you think?'

Gloria responded with a grin of her own. 'Past time, I'd say.'

They chatted while Paige changed into her scrubs and then went in different directions—Gloria to the staffroom for a cuppa with her colleagues, Paige to Theatre four to set up for the first case.

The theatre list was sticky-taped to the door of theatre four's anaesthetic room and Paige removed it. Not that she needed it, she knew exactly which patients were being operated on today. In fact, if pushed, she could probably recite the list for the next month, even though it was next Monday's she was the most fixated on.

There were two paediatric patients on the list this morning. Children were always done first. It caused less stress for the parents, who didn't have to wait around all day worrying about their child going under general anaesthesia, and also for the children, who were often at an age where they were frightened of the clinical hospital environment and didn't understand why they couldn't eat and drink and run around.

A little thrill ran through Paige's stomach at the thought that, come Monday, McKenzie Donald would be first on this list and her spirits lifted even further. Paige couldn't remember a time when she had felt this positive. It had been a long hard three years with many a detour and road-block. It was hard to believe the path was suddenly clear.

Theatre four was frigid when she entered via the swing doors and Paige rubbed at the goose-bumps on her arms. Soon she would be gowned up and under hot lights and wistfully remembering the cold, but for now it seeped quickly into bones that had very little covering insulating them.

You're too thin.

The words Valentino had uttered that fateful night as he had lazily run his finger up her spine crept up on her un-expectedly, as they so often did, echoing loudly in her head and sounding very close in the silence of the empty theatre. So close, in fact, she looked behind her to check he hadn't actually appeared.

Nope. Just her.

She shook her head and frowned. She'd thought about the man so much in the last two months it wouldn't have surprised her to have conjured him up. She'd tried, usually quite successfully, to pigeonhole her thoughts of him to night-time only, to her dreams, but sometimes they crept up on her unawares.

She should have been insulted by his assessment of her body but one look at the heat and desire in his eyes and she'd known that he hadn't been turned off. In fact, quite the opposite—he'd wanted her badly.

It was merely a statement of fact. She was thin.

She hadn't had much of an appetite since the twins had been born prematurely. Daisy's death, Arnie's desertion and McKenzie's fragile health had robbed what little had remained. She ate only to fuel her body, with no real enjoyment when she did.

All her energy was focused on getting McKenzie to eat. McKenzie's appetite. McKenzie's nutritional needs. McKenzie's caloric requirements. Paige Donald came low down on Paige Donald's list of priorities. And, besides, things just tasted so bland.

A hoot of laugher outside in the corridor pulled Paige out of her reverie and she pushed thoughts of Valentino aside. This was daytime. Tonight she could think about him again, dream about him again. Vivid dreams that woke her in a sweat with parts of her throbbing, his name on her lips, his taste in her mouth.

She busied herself getting the theatre set up, grabbing the trolleys and positioning them correctly around the operating table, wiping them down with a solution of surgical spirits. She exited the theatre via the back door into the sterilising room. Four sterilised trays wrapped in special blue disposable cloth were waiting for her and she grabbed the nearest, along with extra drapes and gowns and two pairs of size-eight gloves for Harry and his resident.

She dumped them on the trolleys inside the theatre, ready to be opened by the scout nurse while she herself was at the sinks scrubbing up. She went back out again, selecting other bits and pieces she knew Harry would need— suture material, dressings and, of course, the actual implant device itself.

Paige turned the boxed bionic ear around in her hands.

It was hard to believe that something so innocuous could give such a precious gift. That come Monday one would be implanted into McKenzie's head. She hugged it to her chest, sending up a quick prayer into the universe.

Please let everything be okay.

She went back into the theatre, dropping the extras on the trolley. A noise from the anaesthetic room alerted her to Harry's arrival and she smiled. It was nice working for someone as dedicated as she was. Paige glanced at her watch. Now, while they were still alone, was as good a time as any to ask her boss the question.

She shoved open the swing doors with her shoulder, ready to launch into her spiel. Excited even. Except the man in the anaesthetic room wasn't Harry. He wasn't thin and a little stooped and grey-haired. He was big and broad with curls of dark hair escaping the confines of his theatre cap to brush the neckline of his scrubs. Even if she hadn't dreamt about that back every night for the last two months, the lurch low down in her pelvis would have alerted her to his identity anyway.

Valentino Lombardi looked up from the theatre list he'd been studying and turned. Neither of them said anything for a few moments as a host of memories bubbled between them.

Valentino swallowed. He'd been prepared to see her again but totally unprepared for the sucker punch to his gut as her big grey eyes, round with shock, met his.

'Paige. Bella. We meet again.'

Paige blinked. She even blushed a little as the things they'd done together made her awkward beneath his gaze. It didn't help that he filled out a pair of surgical scrubs better than any man on the planet.

She'd seen him in a tux and in the buff and now in a set

of scrubs. Was there nothing the man didn't look magnificent in? 'Valentino?'

What did he think he was he doing here? Was he here to observe? To assist? Didn't he live in Rome? Or London? Where was Harry?

Valentino saw the confusion in her gaze and shot her a lazy grin. He'd relegated their one night two months ago to a pleasant interlude and done his hardest to forget about it. But standing before him now in baggy scrubs, no make-up, her hair covered in a sexless blue theatre hat, he finally admitted he hadn't forgotten one second of their time together.

A strange unease descended on them and he couldn't bear it.

Paige's heart skipped a couple of beats and then accelerated as his low flirty voice oozed into all the places that still craved his touch. The pinkness in her cheeks deepened as she remembered where his mouth had been. Oh, God! This wouldn't do at all.

'Dr Lombardi.' Paige's voice was stern as she glared at him and regained her composure. 'What are you doing here? Where's Harry?'

Valentino laughed. So much for small talk. He regarded her for a second. What he had to tell her next would have an impact on her probably more than anyone. Harry had stressed the need to break it to Paige gently.

'I'm afraid Dr Abbott had to rush to Hobart in the early hours of this morning. His grandson was kicked in the head by a horse and is in Intensive Care.'

Paige gasped, pressing a hand to her chest. Oh, no! How awful. 'Was it Andy or Ben?' Harry's daughter and her family lived on a horse stud just outside Hobart.

They were a close-knit family despite the distance, and Paige knew this would be devastating for them all.

'Ben.'

Oh, dear, Ben was only four. One year older than McKenzie. Paige moved closer to him, needing to know more. 'How is he? Is he…has he…?'

Valentino covered the distance between them, reaching out for her, clasping her shoulders gently. 'He's critical. That's all I know.'

Paige looked at him, trying to process it. Trying to understand how fate could be so cruel to a little boy and a man who had only ever done good things. 'That's just so…awful. I can't believe it.' She shook her head to clear it, searching his espresso depths, waiting for him to tell her it was all a bad joke. 'I just can't…take it in.'

Valentino nodded. 'Yes.' What else could he say?

Paige wasn't sure how long she stood there, staring at him, trying to clear the block of confusion in her mind. But she suddenly became aware of the slow, lazy circling of his fingers against her upper arms and the clean, male smell of him. When the temptation to lay her cheek against the V of his scrub top came upon her she knew she had to step back.

Valentino released her and watched as she retreated to the nearby bench and leaned against it. 'I'll be covering Harry's patients until he's ready to return.'

It was then that the full impact of this incident hit home. McKenzie. She glanced at him sharply as her heart thudded like a rock band in her chest.

No. No, no, no.

Why? What had she done, what had McKenzie done to deserve such upheaval? The surgery had been delayed too many times already. So many things had gone wrong in her short life. The one constant had been Harry and his absolute faith that he could give McKenzie the gift of hearing that prematurity had robbed her of.

And now that was in jeopardy too. 'My daughter's surgery is on Monday.'

Valentino nodded. 'Yes. Harry mentioned that.' In fact, Harry Abbott had gone to great pains to explain to him that Paige would be understandably concerned and probably not all that happy.

Paige felt awful. She wanted to scream and rant and cry. For Harry as well as herself. Disgust built inside her too. How could she even be thinking of herself, of McKenzie, when little Ben was critically ill?

'It's okay. I'll do her surgery.'

Paige glanced at him sharply as a tense 'No' fell from her lips.

Val's jaw tightened. 'You don't think I'm a good surgeon?'

Paige had the urge to laugh hysterically. This was a truly bizarre conversation. She was having trouble keeping up. 'How do I know, Valentino? I don't know the first thing about you.'

Valentino raised an eyebrow. 'Really? I have one night that says differently.'

Paige slashed her hand through the air, rage bubbling inside that he would make an innuendo at such a time. 'You know I meant—professionally,' she snapped. 'Don't ever, ever, talk about that night again. Okay?' she demanded. 'Just don't.'

Valentino had every intention of talking about it again. In fact, standing before her, his loins stirring at the memory of them, he had every intention of doing it again. But he could see she was close to the edge and that night, for now, was better off left in the past. He put his hands up in front to calm her.

'I am a world-class cochlear surgeon. I'm head of the department in a large London hospital. I chair an international cochlear implant committee. I have performed this operation countless times on both children and adults. And...' he placed his hands on his hips '...I am a damn good surgeon.'

Paige shook her head, his arrogant stance and impressive credentials falling on deaf ears. He didn't get it. He just didn't get it. This was McKenzie.

McKenzie.

Her child. Did he think she would allow a total stranger to cut into her? Drill a hole in her head? Did he think that was an easy thing for her to consent to? Never mind allowing someone she didn't know to do it?

Still, she was torn. McKenzie needed the operation and if they delayed now, who knew how much longer it might be? Her heart broke, thinking about yet another delay for her beautiful baby girl locked into a world of silence. 'I'll wait. I'll cancel and wait for Harry to return.'

Valentino flinched inwardly, surprised that her rejection of his skills would feel so personal. He gave a stiff bow. 'Of course, that is your prerogative.'

Paige nodded. 'Yes.'

'It could be a long time,' Valentino murmured. 'Harry was talking about months, maybe a year if Ben needs extensive rehab.'

The thought of McKenzie waiting that much longer was like an ice pick to her heart. She wanted to weep and wail and beat her chest. She shrugged instead, struggling for nonchalance, the effort nearly killing her. They'd waited this long...

Valentino could see the abject disillusion written all over her face and shimmering in her big grey eyes. 'Why don't you hold off making a decision until after today? Watch me in action. Then tell me you don't want me to operate on your daughter.'

Paige couldn't believe he would think it was quite that simple. 'It's not just about that, Valentino,' she snapped. How were they supposed to have any kind of doctor/mother-of-patient relationship with their one-night-stand between them?

God, why had she been so impulsive two months ago? She was never impulsive!

Valentino regarded Paige, her implication clear. 'I will treat McKenzie like any other child who is a patient of mine.'

'And me?'

Valentino shrugged. 'Like any other mother.' Liar. He stood still, waiting for the thunderbolt.

'Oh? How many of the other mothers have you slept with?'

Valentino gave a grudging smile. 'I thought we weren't talking about that?'

Paige sighed, too weary and plain heartsick to respond properly. 'No. We're not.' She glanced at him, the epitome of cool, calm and collected, while she felt all at sea. There was still so much she couldn't wrap her head around. 'I don't understand how you're even here, now…in the country.'

'Harry interviewed me months ago. He's thinking of retiring—'

'Retiring!' Paige spluttered. 'He never mentioned retiring to me!'

'He's sixty-eight years old,' Valentino calmly pointed out.

'Yes, but…' Harry talked to her about everything. And he still had so much to give, to contribute.

'I've wanted to work in Australia for a while now,' Valentino continued, his gaze on the little frown nestled between her caramel brows. 'I think there are things I can learn here to take back home with me. I have my visa, all I need is the right job. I was attending a symposium in Melbourne—'

'"Bionic Ear in the Twenty-First Century?"' Paige enquired absently, not really caring. Harry had given a paper at it two days before.

Valentino nodded. 'Harry contacted me in the early hours of the morning and asked me to fill in. I got the five a.m. flight out of Melbourne.'

'Oh.' So they'd be working together too. This wasn't how it was supposed to pan out. None of it was. But, then, when had her life gone according to plan over the last three years? Bitterness rose like bile in her throat. Wasn't it her turn to catch a break?

Valentino pushed off the bench opposite, which he'd propped himself against, and took three paces until he was standing in front of her. 'Watch me today, Paige,' he murmured. 'Then we'll talk.'

Paige felt his husky tones wash over her, soothing the burn and the knot of worry that sat like an iron fist deep in her gut.

And before she could refute him, rebuff him again, he turned away and she watched as he exited the anaesthetic room.

So much for feeling positive. How could her day have gone to hell so early?

It took about ten minutes into the first surgery to convince Paige of Valentino's capabilities. He was, indeed, an extremely good surgeon. Efficient, steady, sure and capable. Methodical in his approach, supremely knowledgeable, unfailingly polite and, despite the mask and being covered head to toe in green, devilishly charismatic.

There wasn't one nurse he didn't flirt with, including Di Hamilton, who'd been married for thirty-five years and had twelve grandchildren. It was obvious he adored women and Paige watched as every female fell under his spell.

But he was a man's man too. From the nervous surgical resident who was assisting to the orderly adjusting the theatre light, he won them all over, talking football and Australian beers and the price of petrol.

They all loved him. Paige wished she could say the same. Between concentrating on her job, the thoughts circling in her head at a thousand miles an hour and the cataclysmic brush of his arm or fingers as she passed him an instrument, she was totally over him by the end of the day.

Every breath, every move, every chuckle or low request for something stroked along her pelvic floor and took her right back to that night. Being under him. The way he'd felt inside her. Which only agitated her even more. She had bigger things to worry about. Like poor Harry and his grandson. And McKenzie.

It was like she was in a bubble with him, just the two of them, everyone else fading into insignificance. She knew that was the way it often was between surgeon and scrub nurse, requiring a special kind of synchronicity. But it was more than that and she knew it. She'd anticipated Harry's every move in Theatre for the last two years but had never felt this more base reaction.

She just wanted out. To get as far away from St Auburn's

and Valentino Lombardi as possible. To hug McKenzie and remember what was real in her life and what was fantasy.

When the last op was finished, Paige couldn't get out of her gown quickly enough. Thankfully Valentino had left the theatre to go and do post-op checks in the wards and she was able to breathe again. To function without a pulse that kept racing and a stomach that wasn't looping the loop. To clean up. To do her job.

She was back in the audiology department thirty minutes later, making notes in patient charts, very aware that she had the next six weeks off and conscientious enough to ensure everything was up to date on today's operative cases.

'Here you are. Gloria said you'd be here.'

Paige's heart gave a jolt and she braced herself as she looked up from her chart. He was lounging in the doorway in trousers and business shirt, open at the neck and turned up at the cuffs, looking dark and tousled and incredibly sexy.

'You have hat hair,' she commented, before casting her eyes downwards again.

Valentino chuckled, ruffling his locks. 'Yes.' He guessed that was one of the advantages to her pixie cut. Not a lot of hair there to get bent out of shape.

'I thought you might like to know that Ben's condition has stabilised a little.'

'Oh!' She glanced up quickly. 'What a relief!' She'd tried to ring Harry during the break between lists but had got his message bank. 'Thank you.'

If anyone knew what it was like to watch your child

critically ill in an intensive care unit on life support, it was Paige. Her heart went out to Harry and his family. She didn't envy them the days ahead.

Valentino nodded. 'We're all going for a drink after work. Why don't you come? I can give you a lift if you like.'

Paige ignored the traitorous pull she felt at his invitation. Was he insane? 'Sorry. I can't.'

Valentino gave her a wry smile. 'Can't or won't?'

Paige shook her head. 'Can't.'

'Who takes care of McKenzie when you work?'

'My mother.'

'I bet she wouldn't mind staying on for an extra hour.'

Paige knew for a fact she wouldn't. But that wasn't the point. She wanted to see her daughter. She missed McKenzie desperately when she was at the hospital and resented the hell out of Arnie for putting her in a position where she had to work to support them both.

Paige took in the lazy grace with which he lounged in the doorway, the charming smile on his face and those dimples, which thankfully the mask had hidden all day. What did an Italian playboy know of her mundane, hand-to-mouth, practically housebound existence?

'Sorry. I can't.'

Valentino pushed out of the doorway and sauntered towards her. He placed two hands on the desk where Paige was sitting. From his height advantage he could see the ridges of her prominent collarbones. And the unlined curve of breast which told him she wasn't wearing a bra under her modest T-shirt. 'You know you want to.'

This close he looked better still. And smelled absolutely divine. She put her pen down and plastered a bored look on her face. 'I don't expect you to understand, with your carefree, different-girl-every-night lifestyle, but I'm a mother.' She said it slowly so he understood. 'At the end of the work day I go home to my child. I even look forward to it. That's what a parent does.'

Valentino gripped the desk hard. She was wrong. He did understand. There'd been a girl once, a long time ago. And, briefly, a baby.

He frowned. He hadn't thought about Daniella, about the baby that never was, in years. He pushed off the desk lest the urge to speak about it, to tell her he did know, overcame him.

He folded his arms. 'Suit yourself.'

Paige nodded. She intended to. His dimples and his lazy lounging had gone and he was all dark brooding intensity. It was equal parts sinister and sexy. 'Hadn't you better be going?' she asked pointedly as the silence between them grew.

'I was wondering if you'd had a chance to think over McKenzie's operation?'

Had a chance? She'd thought about little else all day. And she knew she didn't have it in her to postpone again over something so petty in comparison to her daughter's deafness. Not when she had the services of a world-class surgeon and a place on his Monday-morning list.

Still, her pride, all she had left these days, made the words difficult and she hoped she wouldn't choke on them. 'Yes, I have.' She nodded, dropping her gaze to the top button of his shirt. 'I'll not be cancelling.'

Valentino regarded her for a moment. He could see how hard it had been for her to say the words. He hadn't wanted that. He'd sensed from the beginning that Paige was like a tightly coiled spring, just holding it all together. It wasn't his object to break her. Not like this anyway. 'Good. I guess I'll see you Monday morning.'

And he turned away, heading for the door.

'Wait.'

He turned back. She'd risen from her seat and was looking at him with desperation in her eyes.

'I need to ask you something. A…favour.'

Valentino clenched his fists at his sides. He could tell she was uncomfortable asking something that was obviously quite personal to someone who, apart from one frenzied night two months ago, was a relative stranger. 'Okay.'

'I want to be in there. With McKenzie.'

Valentino took a moment searching for a way to soften the instant denial that had sprung to his lips at her completely unethical suggestion. No wonder she'd looked so hesitant. 'Paige.'

'Not scrubbing in or anything. Just…there. Nearby.'

He searched her big grey eyes. Saw the worry. The anguish. '*Bella*, you know I can't allow that.'

Paige shut her eyes. This was so unfair. Harry would have. She felt like she was about to burst into tears and his endearment didn't help. She would not break down in front of him. 'Don't. Don't call me *bella*.'

'You need to be a mother on Monday,' he murmured. 'McKenzie needs you to be a mother.'

'Harry would have allowed it,' she said, defiance in her gaze.

'No, Paige, I doubt very much he would have.'

Paige swallowed hard. 'Please.'

Valentino wanted to go to her. He could see her struggle,

knew this was difficult. But he could also see she wouldn't want his sympathy. He ground his feet into the carpet. 'Don't you trust me?'

Paige bit down hard on the lump in her throat. 'Of course I do.' And she did. She knew McKenzie was safe in Valentino's skilled hands. But she'd never been apart from her, had been by her daughter's side through all her ups and downs. She couldn't let her go through this momentous surgery all alone.

'Then let me do my job. And when it's over, you can do yours.'

Paige swallowed another block of emotion welling in her throat, desperate to persuade Valentino. 'Is this about the drinks?'

Valentino stilled, her implication smarting. His eyes narrowed as he tempered his words. 'Be very careful, *bella*. I don't like your insinuation.'

To her horror a tear squeezed out before she could blink it away and she was as vulnerable and as exposed to a man as she'd ever been. Not since Arnie had walked out on her after Daisy's death had she felt so completely at the mercy of a man.

What did he want? Did he want her to beg?

That she wouldn't do.

Valentino stepped towards her as the tear trekked unhindered down her cheek. 'Paige.'

She dashed it away and held out her hands to ward him off. 'Go. Just go, damn it!'

Her words pulled him up short and as much as the doctor in him urged him closer, the man knew she was only just holding it together and the last thing she'd want was to break down in front of him.

He nodded. 'See you Monday.'

Paige waited for him to leave before flopping back in the chair and bursting into tears.

CHAPTER THREE

PAIGE was finger painting with McKenzie when the doorbell chimed on Sunday afternoon.

Who on earth could that be?

She just didn't get visitors, other than her parents and they'd left a few hours ago. And if she did, she liked to have prior knowledge, screen them first. The days of people just popping in were long gone. Even Nat knew to call first before she brought Juliano around for a play.

Paige tried to control, as much as she could without making her daughter a virtual prisoner, the numbers of people she exposed McKenzie to. The more outside contacts, the greater the risk to McKenzie's less than robust immune system. Paige knew only too well that a mild illness a normal toddler could shake off in a few days usually landed McKenzie in hospital on a drip.

She knew people thought she was a control freak but she could live with that.

'Coming,' she called as she quickly washed her hands under the tap in the kitchen. It was probably somebody trying to sell her something and with the operation tomorrow weighing heavily on her mind she really didn't have the patience for it.

She yanked open the door, mentally drawing herself up to give the person on the other side the thanks-but-no-thanks-now-go-away spiel and shut the door on them as quickly as possible.

Except Valentino Lombardi smiled down at her, dimples a-dazzling, and Paige felt her chest deflate. He was wearing faded blue jeans, a white T-shirt and wicked aftershave. His hair was damp, curls clinging to the back of his neck, as if he'd not long been out of the shower.

It made her excruciatingly aware of her own rumpled state. Baggy trackpants and a tatty oversized T-shirt falling off her shoulders and streaked with paint. 'Oh.'

Valentino quirked an eyebrow. She had a smudge of dried red paint on her cheek. He liked it. 'You were expecting somebody else, yes?'

Yes. Anybody but you. She frowned. 'How do you know where I live?' Had he been following her?

Valentino grinned. 'Alessandro.'

Of course…Paige made a mental note to call Nat and ask her not to give out her address to Italian Lotharios.

Valentino noticed the tightening of her lips. 'Don't be cross with them. I told them I wanted to meet McKenzie before the surgery tomorrow.'

McKenzie chose that moment to appear, grabbing hold of Paige's leg with her paint-smeared fingers and shyly looking up, all the way up, at Valentino. Paige shifted slightly to accommodate her daughter, her hand automatically going to cup the back of McKenzie's head.

'Ah.' Valentino smiled. He crouched down so he was at eye level with the diminutive little girl. As her chart had indicated, she was thin but her eyes were bright and intelligent. 'Here she is.' He signed as he spoke. 'Hello.'

McKenzie's eyes, so like her mother's but framed by blonde ringlets, widened for a moment before she shyly signed her greeting back.

'I'm Valentino.'

Watching McKenzie's tiny fingers form all the letters that made up her name always clawed at Paige's heart and today was no different. Had she known her daughter would be deaf, she would have chosen a much shorter name.

'Hello, McKenzie,' Valentino signed back, speaking the words also. 'I'm very pleased to meet you. You have paint on your nose.'

Paige watched as McKenzie, shy by nature, actually grinned at Valentino as he gently swiped at it with his finger. She could see the same sort of recognition in her daughter's gaze that she'd seen in other females whenever he was near. An awareness of him as a man, a purely feminine response to his charisma.

For goodness' sake, she was three years old! Did the man have to charm every female he came into contact with?

Paige drew her daughter closer, her hand firm on McKenzie's shoulder. 'Do you usually make house calls?'

Valentino grinned one last time at McKenzie and rose to his full height. Paige was annoyed. But, then, when wasn't she?

'No.'

'Then why are you here? You could meet my daughter tomorrow morning on the ward.'

Because Harry had asked him to speak with her. And he had agreed, even though he knew Paige was big trouble. Her appeal to him the last time they had been together, her pride, as tears had shone in her eyes, had captivated him.

He should run a mile. He didn't do this. He didn't get involved. Yet he'd thought of little else except her all weekend. And then there was Harry.

But not yet.

'I wanted to see you were okay. After Friday.' He held up a bottle of wine and a brown paper bag. 'I brought a peace offering.'

Paige stiffened. Did he really think she could relax over a glass of wine with him? 'There was no need. I'm fine.'

Fine she may be but all Valentino could see was a woman who was starving, both physically and emotionally. Shutting herself off, denying her body the things it needed. The things every body needed. Denial was not good for anyone.

He crouched down to McKenzie again. 'What do you say, McKenzie?' he said as he signed. 'Can I come in?'

McKenzie smiled at him and nodded, holding out her multicoloured hand. He took the little girl's offering and rose, quirking an eyebrow at Paige.

Paige glared at him. 'That was low.'

He smiled and took a step forward as Paige fell back passively, like she feared his nearness. He took full advantage as McKenzie led him into the apartment. 'You need to eat,' he said, moving past her. 'Lucky for you I've found the most amazing delicatessen near where I'm staying.' He looked down at McKenzie and moved his hands as he said, 'Kitchen?'

Paige stared at him as McKenzie pointed and then happily led Valentino to where he wanted to go. How had that happened? It was a few moments before she registered the drift of Valentino's chatter coming from the other room and the fact she was still standing like a powered-down robot in the hallway, staring after them.

She sighed and shook her head as she followed. How long would it take to get him out? By the time she'd reached the kitchen Valentino had seated McKenzie on the bench beside him, poured two glasses of wine and was supervising as her daughter distributed a variety of olives into little bowls.

She leaned against the jamb. 'Making yourself at home, I see.'

Valentino looked up at an unsmiling Paige. Her shirt had fallen off a shoulder and he could see the distinctive hollow above the bony ridge of her collarbone. He also noticed the lack of bra strap. Not that he could make out anything interesting beneath the shapeless shirt.

'McKenzie is very helpful.'

It was strangely sexy to see him in her kitchen, laughing with her daughter. His broad shoulders stretched the confines of his white T-shirt as his hip rested casually against her counter. Even more sexy was the way he signed and talked without conscious thought, as if it was completely natural.

McKenzie, noticing Valentino's interest had wandered elsewhere, turned and grinned at her mother, and Paige's heart rose in her throat. Her daughter never took to anyone this quickly. Trust her to take to a guy who, like her father, was never going to stick around.

Absently she noticed that Valentino had had the good sense to wash the paint off McKenzie's hands first.

Valentino removed the still warm baguette from the bakery bag. 'Ah.' He held it to his nose and inhaled the yeasty fragrance. *'Quello sente l'odore di buon.'*

He offered it to McKenzie to smell as well, which she did mimicking him perfectly. 'You like?' he signed, and McKenzie nodded. He located a knife in a drawer near his hip and sliced the bread into thick discs before arranging them on the plate next to the olives.

'Is there somewhere we can eat this?'

Hell!

Paige, also used to signing and speaking while her daughter was around, followed his lead. 'Will the deck be good enough for your lordship?'

He looked at McKenzie and winked. 'Perfect.'

Valentino scooped McKenzie off the bench and she skipped after her mother the second her feet touched the floor. He loaded the food and wine onto a nearby tray and followed the women through the house.

They passed through an airy lounge room cluttered with children's toys and framed photographs. Valentino's gaze fell on a largish one standing on top of the television. It was Paige with an older couple. Her parents? She was younger, her figure fuller, rounder, no angles. Her hair in a caramel bob. And she was laughing, her grey eyes lit with an easy humour.

Interesting.

His gaze returned to her as she stepped out onto the deck, her back ramrod straight, very different from the relaxed woman in the picture. Although it was lost in the fold of a voluminous shirt, he still remembered how her back had looked, long and elegant, bare to the hollow, on the night of Alessandro's wedding.

Still remembered running his fingers down the naked length of it as they had danced, and the way her breath had caught, the ragged edge to her breathing.

Heat in his loins had Valentino gripping the tray a little harder and searching for something to take his mind off how well he knew every inch of her body.

Not just her back.

'Does she know about tomorrow?' he asked as Paige indicated for him to take the seat opposite her at a sturdy wooden table.

Paige glared at him as she made room for McKenzie on her chair. 'Of course.'

Valentino ignored the steel in her voice and the seating suggestion as he sat himself at the head of the table closest to her. If he had to force-feed her, she was going to have to be within arm's reach.

'Okay,' he said, plonking the tray between them and handing her a glass. 'Do you want to tell her who I am?'

Paige took the glass automatically. It was a perfectly sensible idea. She'd put off telling McKenzie that Dr Harry wouldn't be doing her surgery until bedtime. Now, particularly as McKenzie seemed quite enamoured with Valentino, seemed as good a time as any.

'McKenzie?' Paige touched her daughter's arm. 'This is Dr Lombardi.' She spelt out each letter of his name even though she knew that at three McKenzie had no concept of spelling.

McKenzie looked at him. 'Valentino,' he reiterated, signing his first name.

Paige bristled. 'Dr Valentino,' she corrected, her voice firm, her signing slashing at the air. 'Dr Harry had to go and visit his grandson who is very sick so he can't do the operation to make you hear again. Dr Valentino is going to do it instead.'

McKenzie looked from her mother to Valentino and back to her mother. 'Dr Valentino is going to make me hear?' she signed.

Valentino looked at Paige, saw the way she nodded confidently, even though her eyes were worried.

'Yes,' she said.

McKenzie turned to look at him with her big blue eyes as serious as her mother's. After a moment she transferred her gaze back to Paige. 'Okay,' she signed, and reached for a piece of bread.

Paige blinked. That had been easy. McKenzie adored Harry. Trusted him. He'd been her specialist for over three years now, since her diagnosis in the NICU, and she loved it when he came to visit her in hospital. Paige glanced at Valentino, searching for a reason. He looked up at her simultaneously with dark espresso eyes and smiled at her, dimples on high beam.

Her stomach looped the loop. Could it be that simple?

McKenzie tugged her arm and she dragged her gaze from his. 'Can I watch *The Wiggles*?' she signed.

She nodded and said, 'Sure.'

McKenzie climbed off the chair and Paige followed her inside to set up the DVD, thanking modern technology and *The Wiggles* for their special DVDs for deaf kids, complete with Auslan interpreter at the bottom of the screen. Just because her daughter was profoundly deaf, it didn't mean she didn't like to wiggle with the rest of the toddlers.

Paige smiled as McKenzie's curls bounced and she laughed at something the red Wiggle had said. But beneath her smile was profound sadness that McKenzie couldn't even hear the sound of her own laughter. Only the prospect of tomorrow, of starting a whole new chapter, dragged Paige out of her gloom.

Valentino watched an even more subdued Paige walk back towards him. She pulled up her chair, picked up her glass and absently swallowed a mouthful of the crisp Pinot Grigio he'd chosen because it came from the area near where he'd been born in the north of Italy. There was no recognition on her face of the glorious crisp, spritzy taste.

He picked up the plate of olives and brought them close to his face, inhaling deeply. 'Hmm. Don't these smell divine?'

Paige looked at the plate with disinterest. 'I'm not hungry,' she murmured.

Valentino smiled. It was going to be fun reviving her appetite. 'Who says you have to be hungry to eat?' He picked up an olive glistening with oil and stuffed with feta and sucked it into his mouth. 'Food is to be enjoyed, *bella*. Not endured.'

Paige watched as the olive disappeared from sight behind Valentino's plush lips, leaving the merest trace of oil smeared on his lips. It was a compelling sight.

'Try one,' he coaxed.

Paige, forgetting that her daughter was nearby, suddenly knew how Adam had felt when presented with the apple. She'd bet he hadn't been hungry either. 'If I do, will you just go?'

Valentino grinned. 'Soon.' He presented the plate to her and nodded encouragingly.

Paige rolled her eyes. Anything that got him and his dimples out of her house soon was worth a try. She selected the same kind he had from the array of plump specimens on the plate. She popped it into her mouth, chewed it twice and swallowed it. 'Happy?'

Valentino tsked. 'You need to savour it, *bella*. Inhale its aroma.' He picked one up and waved it under his nose, inhaling deeply. 'Roll it around your mouth.' He sucked it in with a satisfying *phft*. 'Let it sit on your tongue,' he murmured, shutting his eyes as the salty flavour fizzled on his taste buds.

His eyes fluttered open to discover her gaze firmly fixed on his mouth. Her black pupils had dilated in the grey pools of her eyes and his breath became constricted in his lungs.

He pushed the plate closer. 'Try again.'

Paige shook her head as his low murmur wrapped seductive tentacles around her pelvis. As if seducing an olive with his mouth hadn't been bad enough. 'Are you always this bossy?' she grouched.

Valentino stared into her eyes. 'You are beautiful but you need to eat more.'

Paige let her gaze drop to the array of olives, embarrassed by his empty compliment. She hadn't felt beautiful in for ever. 'I'm just not hungry any more. Not since…'

Valentino heard the catch in her voice. Understood her silence. It may have been a tiny blip a long time ago which he'd buried beneath wine, women and song, but he understood loss a little. 'Since your daughter died.'

Paige nodded slowly as her gaze drifted back to his face. 'Alessandro?'

Valentino inclined his head. 'He mentioned it.'

He seemed so empathetic, his dark eyes soft like velvet. But how could he possibly know? 'I wouldn't expect you to understand.'

'I understand some.'

He held her gaze for a moment or two and then dropped it to the plate and picked up an olive. 'Be careful of this one, it still has its pit.' He presented it to her mouth and pushed it gently against her lips, stroking it against them. 'Don't be deceived by its plainness. The buttery flavour is truly sensational. Creamy. Seductive.'

No one was more surprised than he when she sucked it

into her mouth with no protest. She started to munch and he put his finger against her lips. 'No. Don't. Stop. It's not popcorn. Let it sit in your mouth. Savour it. Roll it around. Tell me what you taste.'

Paige was as surprised by the request as she was by the fact that there was even an olive in her mouth in the first place or that his finger rested tantalising against her lips. She pulled back slightly. 'It's just food.' She shrugged. 'It tastes like food.'

Valentino sighed and shook his head. 'Shut your eyes.'

'What?' Did he think she was mad? 'No.'

Valentino almost shook her from pure frustration. 'Just shut your eyes,' he implored, bringing a hand up to gently shutter her lids.

Paige wanted to tell him to leave. To pull away. But his fingers were incredibly slick from the olive oil and wonderfully fragrant.

'Now, tell me what you taste.'

Paige knew he wasn't going to let this go so she took a moment to tune into the olive sitting in her cheek. She pushed it onto her tongue as he had suggested and mentally homed in on the taste. 'Salty. But smooth, like thick double cream.' She opened her eyes, surprised at herself.

Valentino smiled. 'That's the spirit.' Not giving her a chance to change her mind, he reached for another. A black Kalamata marinated in herbs. 'What about this one?'

Paige closed her eyes again to block out the image of him as he inched it towards her. Her nostrils flared as it slowly moved towards her. What was that herb? Rosemary? Her stomach rumbled.

Valentino pushed the olive past lips that parted slightly at the merest touch, like a flower to the first rays of the sun.

A little burst of heat fizzed to life in his loins. The oil moistened her lips and the urge to follow the path of the olive with his own mouth was an urgent thrumming in his blood.

Paige bit into the flesh, bruising it a little, and let out an almost suppressed 'Oh' as a burst of flavour exploded against her palate. Rosemary and chives and something else. Something spicier. Her lids snapped open and Valentino was so close, so sure. Maybe the spice hadn't been in the olive at all.

'Hmm.' She licked her lips and got another burst of flavour. 'That is good.'

Valentino sucked in a breath. She had no idea. Oil still smeared her mouth and he wanted nothing more than to relieve her of it. Their gazes locked as memories of their night together were suddenly thick between them.

'That's nothing,' he said, dragging his eyes away from her face that was a delightful mix of uncertainty, confusion and newly discovered pleasure. 'You have to taste this camembert. It's incredible. So rich and creamy.'

He loaded up a piece of bread with the soft cheese. 'Did you know,' he said as he presented it to her, 'that you shouldn't have cheese on crackers? It should always be eaten with bread?'

Paige eyed the loaded offering coming closer and knew from the still frantic beat of her pulse she couldn't let him feed her again. She reached out and took it from him, suddenly too hungry to deny herself but not stupid enough to invite liberties that she wasn't free to give.

Valentino watched as she took a bite. 'Remember, slowly. Let it melt against your tongue.'

He watched and waited. Waited for the cheese to hit

her taste buds and for her to realise she'd been starving for too many years. When her eyelids briefly closed, he knew he had her.

'Good, isn't it?' He smiled as he reached for one himself. 'The aroma is intoxicating, yes?'

Paige had to agree. Intoxicating. Yes. Just like him. But, seduced as she was, she knew she was treading on very dangerous ground with him. Too dangerous. She savoured the bread and cheese and washed it down with a mouthful of wine that suddenly seemed to sing in her mouth.

Valentino smiled at her and she knew she had to put a stop to it. 'What are you really doing here?'

Still he shied from the information he'd come here to impart. 'I told you. I came to meet McKenzie.'

Paige raised an eyebrow. 'Really?'

Valentino made them another cheese offering each and pushed hers towards her. 'And to, how do you say, clear the air? Set the ground rules. We're going to be working together in the coming months, whether you like it or not.'

Paige stilled. Ben? She sat up straighter. 'You've heard about Ben, haven't you?' Harry had spoken with her briefly on Friday night but she hadn't been able to get hold of him since.

Valentino nodded. 'He has a significant brain injury. They don't think it's fatal but there will be considerable…deficits. They are expecting a lengthy rehabilitation period.'

Paige searched his face for the truth of it. The horrible, horrible truth of it. That's why he'd come. 'You could have rung.'

Valentino shook his head. 'I think you are very close to Harry. I knew you were worried. I didn't want to tell you over the phone.'

Paige nodded absently, knowing it was kind, appreciating it on some level. Poor, poor Harry and little Ben. A deep well of sadness opened inside her and she was quiet for a moment, her thoughts troubled.

After a while she looked at Valentino and it suddenly sank in. For the short term, he was her new boss. They were going to be working together. And he wanted ground rules.

Well, good, she had a couple of her own.

She narrowed her eyes. 'Number one ground rule. We're never going to be…' She broke off, shying from the intimacy of the word.

'What, Paige? We're never going to be what?'

Paige glared at him. He knew exactly what. Did he think she was some shy, wilting Victorian virgin? That she couldn't say the words? Her chin rose defiantly. 'Lovers. Again.'

Valentino smiled. He had to give her points for guts. 'Agreed.' He tended to keep his relationships short and sweet and this one reeked of complicated so her rule suited him.

He made another cheese and bread combo and handed it to her, gratified to see her eat it without protest. 'So let's just be friends. I'm going to be your boss. Your daughter will be a patient of mine. It wouldn't be right to be anything other than colleagues. Friends.'

Paige stared at him. He could seriously do that? 'We can do that? You and I?'

'*Naturalmente.*'

She shot him an incredulous look. 'Do you have many female friends?'

Valentino chuckled. Already she knew him surprisingly well. 'Women love me,' he evaded with a knowing grin.

Of that she had no doubt. Paige laughed in spite of it all. In spite of having an impossibly sexy man right in front of her who she knew carnally and who had just admitted his track record with women didn't usually run to friendship.

She should have been running a mile.

But being friends would certainly make the time until Harry came back to take over McKenzie's care easier. And it would make working for him a lot smoother. She and Harry worked well together not just because she respected his abilities but because she liked him.

Except, of course, Harry had ever seen her naked...

But surely she could have the same kind of relationship with Valentino? If they worked at it. They were both professionals after all.

Paige offered her hand. 'Okay. Friends.'

Valentino looked at her hand. 'In my country we're not big on handshaking,' he teased. 'We prefer to kiss.'

Paige rolled her eyes but kept her arm fully extended. 'There's a shock. Just as well we're in my country, then.'

Valentino chuckled and enfolded her hand in his. 'Friends.'

Paige nodded as a flush of heat spread up her arm and coursed through her system. Not a very good start...

The next morning McKenzie was happily ensconced in a bed in her own private room at St Auburn's. She was comfortable here, her home away from home, unworried as she watched television that she couldn't hear but engrossed nonetheless. Paige sat by her side, her heart splitting in two, her heart palpitating wildly every time she thought about her daughter's imminent surgery.

She'd wanted this. She'd wanted it for so long. But now it was here, it seemed too much. Too much for a little girl who'd already been through enough. She was jumpy and nauseous. Her empty stomach growled at her and she ignored it. She just hadn't been able to face the usual piece of toast she forced down every morning.

'*Buongiorno.*'

Paige turned to find Valentino lounging in the doorway. He wore dark trousers and a deep green business shirt with a paisley tie. He looked relaxed and confident and was like a sudden balm to her stretched taut nerves. She shot him a strained smile.

'McKenzie?' Paige touched her daughter's arm.

McKenzie looked away from the television and her face broke into a wide smile as she waggled her fingers at an approaching Valentino.

Valentino grinned back. 'Are you ready?' He signed as he spoke.

McKenzie nodded and when he held out his hand to her, she high-fived him. Valentino dropped his gaze to Paige, who was currently shredding a tissue into a million pieces. He placed his hand gently on her shoulder and gave it a squeeze. 'How are you?'

Paige bit down on her lip hard. She would not cry. She just wouldn't. She looked up at him. 'Terrified.'

He could see that. He gave her a gentle smile. 'I'm going to take very good care of her.'

Paige nodded. Too emotional to speak. Too scared to open her mouth lest she break down.

'Here,' he said, thrusting another one of those brown paper bags at her. 'I brought you some *biscotti* from the deli. It's to die for.'

Paige frowned and took it automatically. 'I really couldn't eat a thing.'

'You have to pass the time somehow. You may as well eat really good food.' He winked at her, keeping it casual, upbeat, even though he wanted to gather her close and whisper assurances in her ear until she relaxed. But he sensed she was barely keeping herself together and he didn't want her falling apart before it had even begun.

'See you after the op,' he murmured, before swaggering out of the room.

Three hours. Three interminable hours later they pushed a sleeping McKenzie, her head swathed in bandages, back into her empty room, accompanied by a nurse. Paige, who had gnawed through half of the *biscotti* out of sheer nervousness, felt all the worry fall away like the *biscotti* crumbs as she stood. Relief coursed through her, strong and sweet. Her legs wobbled and she grabbed hold of the bedrail.

Paige's breath caught in her throat as she surveyed her daughter. For a moment, lying so still and pale against the white hospital sheets, McKenzie looked like her sister. Memories of Daisy swamped her, those last horrible days rising large in her mind as an awful feeling of dread rose in her chest.

Was McKenzie even breathing?

The nurse busied herself around the bed as Paige leaned over her and pressed kisses to her daughter's face so different without her blonde curly halo. She needed to touch her, needed to know, to be sure.

'McKenzie,' she crooned.

McKenzie stirred, her eyelids fluttering open for a second. 'Hello, baby,' Paige whispered.

She dropped her forehead onto her daughter's chest, shutting her eyes, riding the surge of release as the cold, hard grip of worry slackened its hold. McKenzie's heart-beat coursed strong and sure against her forehead and it was instantly comforting.

It was well after lunch before Valentino joined them. Paige knew there was only a morning list today and had expected to see him some time in the afternoon.

'Hi,' he whispered, approaching quietly.

Paige looked up. He was wearing the same clothes as earlier *sans* tie, showing off the golden skin of his neck. She had the strangest urge to press her face to it.

'Hi,' she whispered back, not wanting to disturb a sleeping McKenzie.

Valentino crouched down beside her. 'It all went really well. In a few weeks we should be able to switch the device on.'

Paige nodded. His voice was a low murmur and she was suddenly overwhelmed by the gift his skilled fingers had given his daughter. She'd been sitting here for hours, trying not to think about it, trying to concentrate on the here and now. But Valentino had opened the door.

A rush of emotion swamped her chest and she could feel her eyes filling with tears. 'Thank you,' she whispered.

'Hey,' Valentino crooned as tears spilled down her cheeks. Her face crumpled and he pulled her head onto his shoulder. 'It's okay.'

Paige nodded as a sob escaped. Then another. For the first time in years she actually felt as if it was really, actually okay.

And she had him to thank for it.

CHAPTER FOUR

TODAY was the big day.

It was totally surreal for Paige. She walked into St Auburn's, McKenzie in tow, pressed the lift button for the fourth floor, stepped out, turned right and walked through the open doors marked Audiology.

It wasn't any different from what she'd done three days a week for the past couple of years.

Except it was. Everything was different.

Today was the day they'd know whether the operation had been a success or not. Today was the day McKenzie would hear.

A week ago Valentino had seen McKenzie for her routine two week post-op check. He'd been pleased with her progress and they'd set this date for the activation of the device.

'Hi, Paige. Hello, McKenzie.' Greg Palmer, the team's social worker, was first to greet them. He grinned at McKenzie as he signed. 'Today's the day, huh?' he said to Paige.

Paige gave him a tight smile as McKenzie went straight to the corner of the large entrance lounge to where she knew the puzzles were kept. 'Yes.'

He squeezed her arm. 'It'll be fine.'

Paige nodded as she pressed a trembling palm against her stomach. Of course it would be okay. 'I'm a little early. Is Ellen in yet?'

Greg frowned. 'I think Valentino's going to do the honours.'

'Oh.' She hadn't counted on that. Ellen was one of the two audiologists in the department and today was her day on, so Paige had just assumed…Valentino must have made room in his schedule to be there for McKenzie.

The knot of nerves in her belly twisted even tighter.

Today, if all went according to plan, was probably going to be quite emotional. And she'd cried in front of Valentino once too many times as it was.

'I think he's already in his office.'

Paige shot a nervous look towards Harry's office. *Valentino's office.* She wanted to go in, was eager and excited on one hand but scared and nervous too. What if they got no result?

'Go,' Greg urged, squeezing her arm again. 'It'll be fine.'

Paige took a deep breath and nodded. 'Come on, McKenzie,' she said, crossing the room to her daughter and crouching down next to her. 'Let's go and see Dr Valentino,' she said as she signed.

McKenzie smiled at her and took her hand and they headed for the door behind which lay a whole new life. Paige knocked lightly and entered at Valentino's command.

Valentino looked up from a pile of charts on his desk as Paige's deer-in-headlights eyes sought his. He knew all about the squall of emotions going on inside her. Had seen it on hundreds of parents' faces as the big moment arrived.

She looked tired, dark shadows beneath her incredibly huge eyes making them appear even more stark in her face. Her clothes, as usual, were two sizes too big, skimming the bony angles of her body, hanging instead of hugging. Had she eaten any of the goodies he'd had delivered to her house every day for the last few weeks?

'Paige,' he said, standing, denying the dictates of his body urging him to go to her. He transferred his attention to McKenzie instead. 'Hello, there.' He grinned. 'Are you ready?' She nodded and he signed, 'Come in.'

Paige held fast to her daughter's hand and didn't move. 'You don't have to do this. Ellen will be in soon. You have surgery.'

She didn't know why she was so resistant to Valentino switching on the implant. A few weeks ago she wouldn't have cared less had it been a trained monkey. But this man, this sexy Italian playboy surgeon, was different. There was more than a professional connection between them, no matter how they tried to avoid it.

There was intimacy. And Paige knew from bitter experience that intimacy left you vulnerable. Something she swore she'd never be again when it came to men.

She doubted it would have mattered had she not slept with him. But she had. And while he was obviously a pro at separating himself from that, standing before him now, she knew she couldn't.

Valentino shrugged. 'I had a cancellation.'

Paige frowned as she searched her memory for this week's theatre cases. 'Who?'

'Paige.' The reproach in his voice was heavy. 'You're off duty, remember?'

'I know. It's just…' Paige didn't understand why she just

couldn't let it go. Why she was resisting. 'That's why we have two audiologists so the surgeon is free to operate.'

'And miss the pay-off? This is the best part of my job, Paige. That moment when my patient hears something for the first time. It's what makes it all worthwhile.'

Paige felt humbled by his response. And petty for equivocating. Every day since McKenzie's surgery tempting edible treats had arrived on her doorstep. From flaky pastries to scrumptious pizzas to the richest of chocolates. All from Valentino.

She'd been trying to dismiss him as a charming, love-them-and-leave-them pretty boy but how could she when confronted not only with his gifts but his heartfelt words? He was a great surgeon, good with his patients, excellent with their mothers and obviously emotionally invested in the gift he gave.

After everything he'd done for her, could she really deny him the rewards?

McKenzie spied the low kiddy table strewn with puzzles and tugged on Paige's hand, dragging her into the office. Paige let an eager McKenzie go and shut the door behind her.

'Why don't you sit down with McKenzie while I get set up?'

Paige nodded and walked on wobbly legs to the table, sitting on the child-size chair beside her daughter.

'Has she had any repetition of those earlier dizzy episodes?' Valentino asked as he tapped away at his computer.

'No.' The first few days post-op Paige had noticed McKenzie would stagger a little on standing. She hadn't been concerned, knowing it was directly attributable to the disruption of the inner ear and they'd settled quickly.

Valentino pressed one last key on the laptop and glanced at Paige. 'Okay. Ready. Let me check how the wound's doing first.'

He got up from his desk and took the seat on the other side of McKenzie. He tapped her hand and when she turned to him he signed and said, 'How is your ear, McKenzie? Can I have a look, please?'

McKenzie nodded her agreement and cocked her head to allow him access. He lifted the angelic curls that covered her right ear out of the way to expose the small shaved area where he'd operated. Two weeks ago there'd been some slight swelling over the bony area behind her ear but now it looked normal. 'It's healed beautifully,' he murmured.

He let her hair flop back over the site. 'Okay, then,' he said to Paige, but signed for McKenzie's benefit. 'Let's fit the external component.'

Paige nodded, apprehension swirling in her gut. 'Dr Valentino is going to fit your new hearing aid,' Paige signed.

Not that it was the type of hearing aid that McKenzie was used to but having worn them most of her life it was the simplest way to explain it to a three-year-old.

McKenzie kept playing as Valentino fiddled with the external component, fixing it directly over the area where he'd implanted the internal part. It was a small circular unit that consisted of a microphone, a speech processor and a transmitter. It linked magnetically to the internal mechanism, which consisted of a receiver and a stimulator.

He then retrieved his laptop from his desk, and set it up at a smaller desk directly behind where McKenzie was sitting. He fiddled some more, plugging the external component into the laptop via a long cord.

'Okay, you know the drill now,' Valentino said. 'I'm going to run the neural response telemetry first. It should take about ten minutes. She won't be able to hear this.'

Paige nodded. She knew that Valentino would pick a few of the electrodes now implanted into McKenzie's cochlear to stimulate via the computer. He would get a reading back which told him that the auditory nerves had responded.

Unlike hearing aids that magnified sound, the cochlear implant directly stimulated the auditory nerves inside the inner ear.

The minutes seemed like hours as the silence in the room built. The urge to drum her fingers on the table was like an itch and she deliberately tucked her hands in her lap.

Valentino nodded. '*Buon*. Good,' he murmured. 'The nerve is responding perfectly so we know the implant's working.'

A rush of adrenaline kicked in at Valentino's confirmation and Paige gripped the table as she gave him a tight smile. She'd been having nightmares that they'd get to this point only to find the implant was a dud.

The first hurdle had been surpassed!

Valentino saw the slight sag to her shoulders and a flicker of relief light her profile, and despite the battle raging inside over professional distance he reached out and gave her shoulder a quick squeeze before returning his hand to the keyboard.

'Okay, I'll switch it on now. Yes?'

Paige nodded. This was it. This was the moment. One or two clicks of the mouse and her daughter should be able to hear sound.

Paige looked so tense Valentino wondered how much longer she could go before she snapped in two. 'It's important not to expect miracles,' he murmured gently. 'A lot of children don't react—'

'I know that,' Paige interrupted. *Just do it!*

'I know.' He nodded. 'But I'm going to go through it anyway. It's different when it's your own child.' He waited for her to protest and when she didn't he continued. 'McKenzie may not do anything at all once it's switched on. That's common. It's hard to know with little ones what they're hearing, particularly if they're pre-verbal or have been deaf all their lives as McKenzie has. They don't even know what sound is.'

He stopped and checked that Paige was with him and then continued. 'I have it on very low so sudden noise doesn't frighten her, but she could cry. That's quite a common reaction.'

Paige nodded again, pleased suddenly that Valentino had taken the time to mentally prepare her for the range of possibilities, even though she knew them back to front. The fantasy in her head was very different from what would probably happen so it was a good reminder.

'Yep. Okay.'

'This is just the first step. It's going to need several mapping sessions as well as intensive speech therapy to train McKenzie's brain to recognise the sounds she'll hear as speech and to learn to talk herself.'

Paige nodded again. 'I know.' She was prepared for the long haul.

'Why don't you sit opposite her and then we'll start.'

Paige rose and moved to the other side of the table. McKenzie, engrossed in her puzzle, didn't even notice.

Valentino clicked the mouse a couple of times. 'It's on. Why don't you try calling her?'

For a few seconds Paige wasn't capable of speech. Of anything. She'd been looking forward to this moment for the last two years and now it was here she was totally overwhelmed. Just like that. One click and a whole new world for McKenzie. It seemed like such an anticlimax. Surely it should at least be heralded by trumpets. Or angels?

A swell of emotion rose in her throat and stuck there, her heart beat like an epileptic metronome, her lungs couldn't drag air in and out fast enough.

'It's okay, Paige,' Val murmured as he watched her emotional struggle. 'Take your time.'

Paige glanced at him. He was smiling at her encouragingly and she swallowed hard. He was obviously well used to the raw emotion of the moment.

'M-McKenzie.' Her voice shook and she cleared her throat. 'McKenzie, darling, can you hear me?'

McKenzie played on, blissfully ignorant to sound or to her mother's turmoil. Paige flicked her gaze to Valentino.

'It's okay,' he said. 'Keep on going. I'll keep adjusting it louder.'

A part of Paige was desperate to gesture to McKenzie, gain her attention. This was the biggest test of both of their lives and Paige couldn't believe how much she wanted her daughter to pass. But pre-empting the process by letting McKenzie know she was speaking to her was pointless— they were after an uncoached reaction.

'McKenzie? I love that puzzle you're doing, sweetie. It's just like that one we have at home with the koalas, isn't it?'

The silence in the room reached a screeching crescendo. She raised her eyes to Valentino, her heart beating so loudly now in the utter silence she thought it might explode out of her chest. 'Nothing.'

The air of helplessness in the word was heartbreaking and surprisingly Val felt Paige's anguish deep in his gut. When had this little girl and her mother become so personal?

He shot her his most comforting smile. 'The telemetry is telling me her nerves are being stimulated. You know sometimes it can take a few weeks for kids to recognise any useful sound.'

Paige nodded, her lips pressed tightly together. She did know. But still she felt gutted.

'I'm going to try clapping.'

'Okay.' Paige tried to keep the dejection out of her voice and failed.

Valentino gave three loud claps. Paige watched as her daughter startled and swiftly turned her head in the direction of the offending noise. She gasped as tears rushed to her eyes.

She'd heard! McKenzie had really heard.

After three years of living in a world where no noise existed, McKenzie could actually hear.

If someone had asked Paige to describe the emotion threatening to suffocate every cell in her body she wouldn't have been able to. She was totally overwhelmed. It was a miracle.

A miracle!

Valentino grinned at McKenzie. 'Hello. Did you hear that?' he signed, and clapped again. 'Clapping,' he said, and did it once more.

McKenzie swivelled her head to look at her mother. The

expression on her face was one of pure wonderment. She pointed to Valentino and clapped.

Paige laughed through her tears, dashing them away with the backs of her hands. Her daughter looked like she'd just invented clapping. Like she was the only person on earth who could hear! And Paige knew exactly how she felt.

'Well, I think that was fairly definite, yes?' Valentino smiled.

Paige nodded wildly, even though her face was threatening to crumple. Her deaf daughter could hear. It was simply the most amazing thing she'd ever witnessed. Even though she'd been present through so many activations in her two years with Harry, this time it was simply incredible.

She rose from her chair and in three paces was by McKenzie's side, picking her up, kissing her face, rocking from side to side. She wanted to spin and twirl, dance like a mad thing, but was aware of the cord attaching McKenzie to the laptop.

Still McKenzie rocked enthusiastically and giggled, holding tight to her mother's neck, enjoying the ride. Paige laughed too, giddy with joy and hope, lighter than air.

'It's amazing. Amazing, amazing, amazing!'

Valentino chuckled. 'Yes, it is.'

Paige slowed and pulled McKenzie against her for a long hard hug. Valentino was watching them with a big smile, dimples on high beam. Even sitting in his chair, he looked big and broad. His long bronzed fingers rested against the keyboard.

Fingers that had given the gift of hearing to her daughter.

'Thank you Valentino. Thank you,' she said over McKenzie's head. 'I don't know how I could possibly thank you enough. Words just seem…inadequate.'

Valentino dismissed her words with a quick wave of his hand. McKenzie's reaction, Paige's reaction, had been thanks enough. He grinned at her. 'I have a great job, don't I?'

Paige grinned back. 'Yes, you do.'

McKenzie squirmed and Paige realised she was still holding her tight. 'Sorry, darling,' she said, lowering her to the floor. McKenzie went back to her puzzle as if nothing momentous had happened and Paige laughed again.

Valentino adored the sound. It was quite melodious and he realised he hadn't heard her laugh, truly laugh with joy and abandon, until now. He guessed she hadn't had a whole lot to be happy about in the last three years. He was glad to have been instrumental in it.

'I like hearing you laugh,' he murmured.

Paige dragged her gaze away from her daughter, sobering a little. He was staring at her mouth and there was intenseness in his espresso depths. Her stomach muscles undulated as if he'd brushed seductive fingers against her belly. 'It's nice to have something to laugh about for once.'

Valentino nodded. 'Shall we continue?'

Paige drew in a suddenly husky breath. 'Please.'

That evening Paige flopped down on her couch utterly exhausted. Who'd have thought excitement could wear you out? They'd spent the rest of the day at her parents' place, watching McKenzie like a hawk, engaging her as much as possible, trying to gauge the extent of her new-found ability.

On the whole there were no major changes to indicate anything had changed. McKenzie didn't seem to respond to their voices but Paige had no doubt now that would come. Towards the end of their visit, however, McKenzie did, very obviously, hear the crash when her grandfather accidentally dropped a metal bowl on the kitchen floor, turning instantly towards the sound and running to the kitchen to check it out.

They spent a hilarious hour dropping as many non-breakables on the floor as possible and revelling in McKenzie's amazed reactions. It was like watching her discover the world for the first time and Paige seriously doubted she'd ever tire of it.

There was a long way to go. She knew that. But today had been a resounding success and as she propped her feet up on the lounge, McKenzie tucked up safely in bed, Paige could honestly say she was content.

She sighed and shut her eyes, weary beyond belief but with a smile on her face. This had been an absolutely fantastic day!

The sharp peal of the doorbell startled her. Who on earth could that be at…she checked her watch…eight o'clock? She groaned. It was only eight o'clock? It felt like three in the morning.

Paige struggled out of the chair, a feeling deep down in her gut intensifying the closer she got to the door. It couldn't be? Could it?

She eyed her standard trackpants and baggy top and briefly wished she was wearing something different. More…feminine. But a spurt of irritation overrode it. She wasn't dressing to please him. And if he was going to keep turning up on her doorstep unannounced then he could take her as he found her. At least she had showered. She yanked open the door.

Valentino smiled down at her. 'Minestrone!' he announced with a flourish.

Her irritation dissipated instantly. She couldn't be cranky with him. Not after today. And he was wearing blue jeans and a snug-fitting T-shirt, his damp hair curling on his nape. 'Are you trying to make me fat?' she grouched.

He lifted the lid off the bowl and brought it close to her face. Mouth-watering aromas wafted her way. 'Yes, *tesoro*. That's exactly what I'm trying to do.'

Paige's stomach grumbled as the smell enveloped her in a warm cocoon. Every day for the last three weeks some sumptuous dish or other had been delivered to her doorstep. It seemed tonight was to be no different.

Except for the personal delivery.

'Let me guess. Mrs Agostino at the deli?'

Valentino gasped and clutched at his chest, feigning injured pride. 'Made it myself. One of my mamma's recipes.'

A man who could cook? Arnie had been the laziest man on the planet. Charming but utterly useless. She hadn't noticed it in the beginning but then their lives had taken a dive and Arnie had not risen to the occasion.

Just when she thought he was like her ex, Valentino went and did something that surprised her. Paige opened the door wider. 'Come in, then.'

She led him to the kitchen, reaching up for two bowls. She heard the scrape of glass against marble and turned to see him pouring two glasses of red wine the colour of ripe mulberries.

He held it out to her and she almost refused. McKenzie

would no doubt wake at some stage during the night, as was her usual pattern, and be up early, as bright as a button. And she was really out of practice with drinking wine. But today he'd performed a miracle and she would have drunk out of a poisoned chalice right now if he'd offered it to her. So she took it.

Valentino smiled and lifted his glass. 'To McKenzie.'

Paige shook her head. 'To you.' And she clinked her glass against his.

They ate their bowls of soup sitting on the lounge. She only half filled hers, giving Valentino the lion's share. But when she'd finished she'd wished she'd kept a little more for herself.

Valentino had been tempting her palate so much these last few weeks she was actually noticing flavours and textures again. Her appetite was hardly normal but instead of ignoring her stomach when it grumbled she actually went looking for something to put in it. Lucky for her, with Valentino's edible gifts hanging around, there was plenty of choice.

She looked longingly at Valentino's bowl. He lifted his eyes from his food and looked at her and she quickly dropped her gaze. But then she noticed how his jeans moulded to powerful quads and she remembered how they'd felt beneath her fingers and she quickly looked away. Thank God she'd had the sense to sit on the cushion furthest away from him on the three-seater after he'd chosen the single lounge chair.

'Would you like some, *bella*?'

Startled, Paige glanced at him. The look on his face was one of pure innocence, the soup bowl thrust towards her. But his eyes and the slight lift of his mouth told her he was perfectly aware of the double meaning.

'No. I'm really full.' Her stomach growled at her loudly as if in protest and she blushed as he chuckled, placing her hand on it to calm the recalcitrant beast.

She was never hungry. Or at least hunger was so inconsequential in her life; she never paid it any heed.

She grabbed her barely touched wine and took a sip. 'So, this is your mother's recipe? What's that herb I can taste? It's so fragrant but I'm afraid I'm out of touch with all things culinary.'

'Basil.' Valentino watched her as she took another sip of wine, her lips pressed against the glass. 'Fresh basil, straight from the pot. My mother always says when in doubt add basil.'

Paige smiled. When he was sitting here like this in her lounge room she could almost forget he was a smooth, seriously sexy playboy with a girl in every port. That he'd dated a supermodel. It was like he was just an ordinary Joe, enjoying a quiet evening at home.

Oh, dear. She did not like the direction of her thoughts. Next she'd be convincing herself she could change him.

Because that had worked so well with Arnie.

'Your mother's deaf, right?'

Valentino nodded. 'Since birth. Maternal rubella.'

Paige nodded slowly. 'So you've always signed?'

'*Si.* I've been signing since before I could talk. We all can.'

'All?'

'Me, my father, my five older sisters. Even Alessandro.'

Five sisters? No wonder he knew women. She'd bet her last cent he'd charmed every one of them. 'Was that hard? Growing up with a deaf mother?'

He shrugged. 'It was the way it was. I never really

thought about it. I'm sure it was a lot harder for her, having six kids to manage.'

'So you speak two languages and sign in them as well?'

'I sign in three actually. I had to learn BSL, British sign language, when I went to London and then when I came here I had to learn Auslan, although it is very closely related to BSL so that was reasonably easy.'

Damn it, did the man have to be so perfect? She folded her arms more tightly across her stomach. 'Has your mother ever expressed a desire to have an implant? She must be a perfect candidate.'

Valentino nodded absently. Paige had pulled the fabric of her shirt taut across her chest and suddenly he could see a lot more. Like she wasn't wearing a bra. Suddenly their decision to be friends was making less sense.

'She is. And I really want her to have one but she doesn't. She doesn't see that there's anything wrong with her. She has a full life, she can communicate and is quite active in the deaf community back home.' He shrugged. 'And I respect that.'

'Does that make me an awful person, then? Do you think by going down this path with McKenzie, my daughter will think that I think something is wrong with her?' She searched his face for an answer. 'Is it wrong of me to want this for her?'

Valentino frowned. He sat forward and placed his bowl on the table. 'Of course not, Paige. My mother is a firm believer in doing what you feel is best. As am I. Implants just increase options for the deaf. She would be proud of you.'

Paige felt a trill of pleasure squirm through her belly at

the thought of Senora Lombardi's approval. 'I bet she's proud of you.'

Valentino grinned. 'But of course. Tells everyone about her son the surgeon.'

Paige laughed. 'That sounds familiar in any culture.'

Valentino regarded her for a few moments. 'There it is again,' he murmured. 'That laugh.'

She grinned. 'It might actually become a habit.'

Valentino's gaze flicked to her shirt where it had fallen off one shoulder and her nipples made two points against the fabric.

Friends, friends, friends.

He returned his eyes to hers. 'Wouldn't that be nice?'

Paige sobered. Very novel. He held her gaze and it was like being sucked into warm dark mud. 'Did I thank you enough? Really, Valentino, I don't know how to thank you enough.'

He shrugged. 'It's my job. I'm just lucky to have the best job in the whole world.'

'Still…' On impulse she stood and took a step towards him. And then another, until she was standing in front of him. 'Thank you so much,' she whispered. Leaning down, she slid her hands to cup either side of his face, her fingers pushing into the luxury of his hair, and pressed her mouth to his in a brief kiss.

It wasn't meant to be sexual. It really wasn't. It was meant to be grateful and heartfelt. A thank-you kiss from the bottom of her soul.

Friendly.

Quick in and quick out.

But she should have known she was playing with fire. Because her senses were filled with him. His food offerings had awakened them to flavour and aroma and texture and she was experiencing them all—his warmth, the scratch of his stubble and the clean male smell of him—and even though she pulled out of the kiss she was incapable of moving away.

Valentino looked up at her. Her eyes had gone smoky and just before she'd covered his mouth, her baggy shirt had fallen forward and he'd feasted his gaze on her pert naked breasts.

It hadn't been something a friend would do.

He was already hard for her as he reached out and encircled her wrists with his fingers.

Paige looked down at where his thumbs ran a lazy path over her pulse points. There was a brief moment when it was possible to back off, to remember that they'd decided not to do this again. But it passed. And then she was sinking her knees into the leather either side of his thighs, straddling him, settling herself against him.

And then they were kissing. Like the world was about to end. And then her shirt was off and his mouth was on her breasts, sucking her nipples deep into his hot mouth, rasping his tongue around them as they peaked and surged against its boldness.

And then his shirt followed and she was reaching between his legs, unzipping him, touching the hard edge of him, rubbing herself against him as she freed him from the prison of his underpants.

'Oh, God,' he groaned, thrusting himself into her hand. 'Condom?'

Paige slowed.

What?

Condoms? Of course.

Her heart was racing as she tried to order her thoughts.

But then Valentino sucked a nipple into his mouth and she clung to his shoulder as her brain turned to mush.

'Condom,' he said again, releasing her thoroughly worshipped nipple.

Paige sucked in a breath, pushing her hands into his hair. 'I don't have any.'

Valentino groaned into her neck. At home he had boxes of the things. Not that he'd used one of them since coming to Brisbane. They pulled apart and looked at each other, heaving in oxygen, their chests rising and falling, sexual frustration adding to their agitation.

They looked at each other for about ten seconds and then they were kissing again, touching, rubbing, sighing, moaning.

And somehow, Paige wasn't quite sure how afterwards, he manoeuvred her trackpants off and then he was in her, thrusting up as she ground down, and they were panting and calling each other's name and it felt good and right and the consequences be damned.

CHAPTER FIVE

VALENTINO had no idea how long it took for them to bump back down to earth. It was a slow realisation. A creeping awareness of the jut of her hips in his palms, the weight of her head against his shoulder, the slight brush of her lips against his collarbone as her breathing returned to normal.

He shifted slightly and murmured, 'I guess there is one advantage to having a deaf child.' He felt Paige smile against his skin and chuckled.

Paige, malaise heavy in her bones, couldn't move. It was warm and cushioned against his shoulder and she felt as if she'd been stroked all over with a thousand velvet fingers. The fact that they were still joined and he was still hard inside her was another incentive not to move.

Although if she did this…

'Don't do that,' Valentino groaned, clamping his fingers on her hips harder, holding them still. How could he possibly still be so hard?

'What? This?' Paige undulated her hips again and felt the full length of him glide erotically against sensitised tissues.

Valentino felt his breath strangulate in his throat. 'Yes. That.'

Paige smiled again, suddenly getting a second wind. She pushed away from his shoulder, her nakedness on full display. She looked down at herself, at how wanton she was, how not herself.

She'd always hated her breasts. They'd always been small and with her weight loss even more so. But tonight they looked one hundred per cent female, the pale blush of her nipples darkening and puckering like raspberries beneath Valentino's rapt gaze.

She arched her back a little and Valentino pulsed inside her. He didn't seem to find them wanting.

Further down she could see his fingers spread wide against the angles of her hipbones, bronzed against her paler skin. She could feel them holding her firmly, holding her close, branding her. His thumbs circled lazily, stroking the sensitive skin where her hip sloped to her belly.

Lower still she could see where they were joined. Where they became one. The most intimate of connections. It was hot and slick, tingling with the remnants of their joining and the hard hot length of him still buried inside her, and Paige undulated her hips again.

This time Valentino thrust a little and she gasped. 'Hmm, that feels good,' she murmured.

Valentino shut his eyes and nodded, slowly pulling out a little and pulsing back in one more time. 'How about that?'

Paige bit her lip as the fuse sparked to life. 'Really good.'

He opened his eyes and watched as her high breasts bounced a little. 'And this?' He leaned forward and took a nipple in his mouth, his tongue mimicking the torture of the deep slow thrusting down lower.

Paige whimpered and stabbed her fingers into his hair,

grasping a fistful and pinning him there. Her hips moved of their own volition and he thrust up again as she slid down.

Valentino moaned, releasing her breast, his eyes shutting as his forehead dropped to her chest. Their bodies seemed to find a rhythm together and he was powerless to resist the pull of it. They were barely moving at all but she was tight around him, holding him inside, massaging his length with subtle flexions and slow pulsations creating a wonderfully erotic friction that stoked a furnace deep in his belly.

He slid one hand to her naked bottom, pressing her closer, and the other up her back until his hand cupped her nape, his fingers furrowing into her hair. His lips brushed her chest, her collarbone, the hollow at the base of her neck.

She whimpered at the back of her throat and he could feel her trembling. Could feel a corresponding quivering of his own muscles as a climax that had been on a slow burn ignited to full throttle.

When she gasped and threw her head back his hand slid to her shoulder and he pulled her closer still, their joined bodies slick with heat and sweat as they rocked.

'Valentino,' Paige cried, as her orgasm broke and she bucked against him.

'Yes,' he groaned. *'Quello è ritiene così buon.'*

Paige had no idea what he'd just said and neither did she care. It was low and husky in her ear and then she was sucked back into the vacuum where only they existed and pleasure was the only purpose.

Valentino looked up from fixing his clothes. Paige was dressed again and watching him with strands of passion still decorating her gaze like dewy cobwebs. She smiled at him and he realised he could get used to that look.

Kiss it goodnight every evening.

Wake up to it every morning.

His smile faded a little as a frisson of unease crawled up his neck.

Because there was no denying in such a short time he had felt a connection with Paige. Even just today, they'd been through so much. Witnessing McKenzie's reaction to his clap had been incredibly satisfying. And talking about his mother this evening had been…nice. Normal. What couples who dated did.

What couples did, full stop.

Not what he did. He didn't do couple stuff.

Not since…

And then there was what had just happened between them on the lounge. Twice.

What the hell was he thinking?

Paige picked up their bowls off the coffee table, the movement of her thoroughly ravaged body shrouded beneath her baggy sexless clothes.

It was a timely reminder that she wasn't the usual type of woman he did this with. Despite the sexual gratification shimmering in her gaze. She was a single mother with a high-needs child. She had commitment written all over her. She was a couples woman. Or at least she deserved to be.

And this was the second time they'd got naked together. It was starting to feel like something a little more serious than what he usually went in for.

He didn't have a script for that.

Not any more.

'We can't do this again,' he said.

Except all he could think about was doing it again. Stripping those godawful clothes away and doing it in every room in the house.

And then maybe come back and do it all again tomorrow. *No. No. No.*

Paige blinked, setting the dishes down. Okay.

She knew he was right, of course but, deep in her heart a little dent appeared. She shrugged with as much nonchalance as she could muster. 'Of course.'

Valentino blinked. Well, that was easy…

In his experience women didn't usually take those five words all that well. 'I don't really do anything serious,' he explained, not really understanding why he felt the need to clarify things. 'And I think it's a bad idea for colleagues to get too involved.'

Paige suppressed a laugh. He hadn't been too worried about it thirty minutes ago. But he was certainly running now! Looked like the playboy had reached his end game.

Well, that was okay. Or it would be. This had only ever really been one thing. A thank-you kiss that had got way out of control.

Just as well, though, she hadn't expected anything from him. That Arnie had hardened her heart to romantic nonsense and that she didn't have the time or the energy for someone else in her life. How many women had he devastated with that turn of phrase? She could well imagine how some dates would not take it so well.

'I agree.'

Valentino nodded, his hands on his hips, waiting for the *Oh* that usually came in this part of a conversation he was especially good at.

It didn't come.

He decided to explain further. 'I think we're adult enough to accept this for what it was.'

Paige suppressed a smile. 'It's okay, Valentino. I understand. Neither of us do this.' She gestured back and forth between them. 'I can't and you choose not to. It's fine.'

He opened his mouth to protest her assessment but he couldn't. He did choose not to. Since Daniella.

This was what he did. This was what he was used to.

'So…colleagues? Friends?'

She quirked an eyebrow. 'We're back to that again, huh?'

'You think you can't do it?'

'Oh, I can do it.' Did he seriously think she had time to sit around pining after him? She stuck her hand out. 'Can you?'

Valentino regarded her outstretched fingers. Remembered how they'd felt digging into his back. 'But of course.' And he clasped her hand in his and gave it a firm shake. 'I'll see you at the clinic tomorrow.'

Paige followed his broad back to her front door. He seemed to take up all her hallway and as some internal muscles protested her movement she was reminded of how big he was everywhere.

Valentino pulled the door open, paused and turned. 'What if there are consequences?'

Paige regarded his serious face with a sinking feeling. Somehow, even without the dimples, it looked as sexy as hell. She didn't like the direction of his thoughts.

Paige sighed. 'It'll be fine.' She hadn't had a proper period since the twins had been born. She doubted she'd even ovulated regularly the last two years due to her borderline weight.

She probably had the fertility of a panda.

'It's…safe?'

She knew what he was asking and it was an assurance she felt one hundred per cent comfortable with giving, even though they both knew, as medical professionals, no time was one hundred per cent safe. 'Yes. It's safe.' Still, she found it difficult to meet his gaze and she looked out at a point beyond his head, to the darkness of the street.

Valentino reached forward and lightly grabbed her chin, directing her gaze back to his. He fixed her with a stare. One that told her he meant business. 'I want to know, Paige. If…'

The mere thought of it was so painful Paige couldn't even contemplate it. She certainly was clueless to the slight edge of menace in his tone, to the fierce light in his eyes. Even mentioning it without actually saying the word was enough to fracture the surface of her heart and she shut her mind to it, blocked it like a force field.

'It'll be fine,' she repeated, before stepping back, causing his arm to fall by his side.

There would be no pregnancy.

Valentino regarded her for a moment or two longer before delivering a slight bow and disappearing into the night.

The next few weeks flew by. Life was fuller, crazier than normal. Further mapping sessions of McKenzie's implant and twice-weekly speech therapy chewed up her remaining three weeks at home.

But the rewards were amazing. After a few days it was evident that McKenzie heard just about everything and it was like witnessing the world being created all over again, seeing her wonderment of it all.

Instruments in the toy box that had merely moved in the past now made noise. The drumstick did more than bounce off the taut surface of the bongos—it actually bonged. The tambourine did more than shimmy—it rattled. And the sleigh bells tinkled.

But not just that. The doorbell chimed. And the plughole sucked and gurgled greedily as the water swirled away. And the television talked to her. The Wiggles talked to her! Every sound was new and amazing.

In the beginning she'd caught McKenzie just looking at objects that created noise, as if expecting them to get up and produce sound completely unaided. But she'd caught on quickly and no object was safe.

Her speech had also come on. In just a few weeks she already had a handful of words. Paige had never dared hope for the day that she would hear her daughter say 'Mummy'. But she had. And it had simply been the best moment of her life.

McKenzie still signed as she spoke—they both did—and Paige wondered how long it would be before her verbal communication skills were such that they outstripped her signing vocabulary. They would always need to sign as McKenzie was still deaf without her external device so it was vital to keep up their signing vocabulary as well.

And, anyway, being bilingual was such a skill—Valentino being a classic example—it would be a shame to lose it.

Before Paige knew it, it was time to go back to work, which she did reluctantly. Every minute with her daughter as she discovered a whole new world was precious and Paige resented having to surrender any of them.

Sure, McKenzie was in good hands with her parents but that didn't stop the gut-wrenching emotion she felt as she kissed her daughter goodbye three mornings a week. The only consolation was she still got to see McKenzie when she came in for her speech therapy and she made sure she scheduled her daughter's appointments for the days and times she was on the clinic.

There had to be some advantages when you ran the show.

Three weeks in and everything was back running like clockwork. The op had been successful, intensive therapy had been instituted and the care arrangements clicked smoothly back into place. And McKenzie hadn't been sick in months. There was even some roundness to her face for a change, although Paige didn't hold too high a hope for cracking the twentieth percentile any time soon.

She and Valentino had even managed to find a happy medium in their relationship. She'd expected it to be awkward at first, like the day they'd first met again after that fateful night, but they'd both been invested in making it work. And he was great with McKenzie, who had also learnt to say 'Dr Valentino' very quickly.

Finally there'd even been encouraging news with little Ben, who'd been transferred out of Intensive Care and admitted to a specialist acquired brain injury rehab ward.

Things were great for once. All the planets were aligned. The gods were smiling. Life was good.

And then it all went to hell.

The last day of her third week back started as an ordinary day. Nothing remarkable. Until she was standing in neck-to-toe green, masked and hatted, waiting for Valentino to finish drying his hands and gown up, and a strong urge to go to the toilet gripped her bladder.

She frowned as she mentally suppressed the urge. For goodness' sake, she'd already been three times this morning already. Once when she woke up, once when she got to work and just prior to scrubbing up. How on earth could she possibly want to go again?

And, anyway, she couldn't just walk out of the theatre and go to the bathroom. She was scrubbed, sterile. It would require degowning and then rescrubbing and regowning, and with theatre times tight they didn't have the luxury of running on the whims of her bladder.

She gritted her teeth and ignored it, holding the cuff of Valentino's glove open ready for him to thrust his hand straight in.

'Thanks,' he murmured as he repeated the process on the other side.

Paige could tell by the smile in his eyes that his dimples would be flashing beneath the mask. Normally that would be exceedingly distracting, despite their determination to keep things asexual, but today, as her bladder twinged again, it didn't even rate.

She clamped down on the sensation, trying for mind over matter as the three-hour operation stretched in front of her. There was no physical way her bladder could be full again.

She'd had a glass of water with breakfast and that had been it. Years of working as a scrub nurse had taught her not to drink tea or coffee prior to commencing surgery for just this reason.

It wasn't physically possible to have anything in her bladder. Surely?

Maybe she had a urinary tract infection? But no. It hadn't stung or burned at all. Fever? She did feel hot but she was swaddled in a gown, under bright operating lights and holding her muscles so tight she was probably over-heating every cell in her body.

Or maybe it was some kind of delayed cystitis from that night a few weeks ago? Valentino's arm brushed hers and for a sweet second she was back on his lap again.

Ten minutes later, though, she knew she couldn't hold on any more. She was actually crossing her legs beneath her gown. 'Darren can you scrub in, please?' she asked, hoping the discomfort in her abdomen wasn't detectable in her voice. Darren was one of the two scout nurses on for the theatre today.

Valentino, who was just preparing the drill, stopped and looked down at her. 'Everything okay?'

She nodded as she passed him the next instrument. 'Fine.'

The five minutes it took for Darren to wash his hands, re-enter the theatre, dry his hands and gown up felt like an hour as her bladder stretched to painful proportions. 'Excuse me for a moment,' she murmured stepping back from the table and degloving and degowning as quickly as possible without looking like her underwear was on fire.

She made it to the bathroom in record time and had never been more pleased to sit on a toilet in her whole life. So when the sum total of fifteen mils was forthcoming Paige was totally unimpressed.

What the hell?

After a further ten minutes of sitting was no more pro-ductive, Paige finally gave up. She washed her hands in the sink, inspecting her face in the mirror. The hollows beneath her cheekbones seemed more pronounced in the harsh fluorescent light. Maybe she did have a UTI? One that just involved frequency? Or maybe a kidney stone was blocking the neck of her bladder, only allowing a dribble through at a time? A painless one?

Hell, maybe she was the only woman on the planet to be in possession of a prostate gland?

She shook her head and watched her reflection follow suit. Maybe it'd be okay. Maybe it wouldn't happen again. Maybe she was going crazy and she should get back to work and stop worrying about something that was probably nothing.

She hurried back to the theatre, washing her hands again before donning a mask and pushing through the swing doors. Valentino and Darren both looked up as she entered.

'You want to scrub back in?' Darren asked.

Paige shook her head. She didn't want to risk it. 'You keep going. I'll scout.'

Which ended up being a wise decision. Paige spent the entire day in and out of the toilet. She may as well have stayed at home for all the help she'd been. And when the last patient was wheeled out of the theatre to Recovery she'd never been more pleased to clock off in her life.

She changed into her civvies, grabbed her handbag out of her locker and hurried back to Audiology to update the day's operating charts. The department had shut for the day and was deserted, for which she was grateful as she steamed into her office and made a quick phone call to her G.P.

This situation was ridiculous and needed remedying as soon as possible. She was put on hold straight away and Paige tapped her foot.

'I knew I'd find you here.'

Paige startled a little as she looked up to see Nat beaming at her from the open doorway.

'Hi.' She smiled back, gesturing for her friend to enter.

'Oh, sorry,' Nat whispered, plonking herself in the chair opposite. 'I didn't realise you were on the phone.'

'It's okay. I'm on hold. What's up? You look like you just won a million bucks.'

Nat grinned. 'Better. I'm—'

Paige held a finger up as the receptionist came on the other end. 'Just a sec,' she said apologetically. 'Hi, yes, my name's Paige Donald. I was wondering if Dr Mantara could squeeze me in this afternoon?'

Paige listened as the receptionist explained it was impossible and tried not to scream her frustration down the phone. There was no point in shooting the messenger. She took an early morning appointment the next day instead and hung up.

Nat crinkled her brow. 'Everything okay?'

Paige sighed. 'I don't know.' She looked at her friend. They'd been close during school but life had pulled them apart again until the last few years. Paige just hadn't had the time or an excess of emotional energy for the type of friendship most women valued. She didn't realise how isolated she'd become until right now as the urge to unburden took her by surprise.

'I think…' She hesitated, unused to sharing such private matters. 'I think I have a UTI.'

'Okay.' Nat leaned forward, placing her elbows on the desk. 'Why don't you start at the beginning?'

Paige told her about the day and the inconvenient frequency symptoms. 'It has to be a UTI, right?'

Nat regarded her for a few moments. 'You're not…? Could you be…pregnant?'

It took a few seconds for Paige to compute what her friend had said. And she laughed. 'Don't be ridiculous,' she dismissed. And then she sobered as a cold hand clutched at her gut. No way. She couldn't be. Surely?

Nat watched a procession of emotions march across her friend's face. 'Are you sure? I thought you and Valentino might be getting—'

'Quite sure,' Paige interrupted, her heart booming like church bells in her chest.

Nat didn't think Paige looked overly convinced. She reached into her handbag. 'I just happen to have an extra one of these.' She placed a packaged pregnancy test on the desk and pushed it towards Paige.

Paige looked at it like it was a venomous snake. She could not be pregnant. Could not. An image rose unbidden in her mind. Daisy's tiny white coffin covered in pale pink roses.

Even now it had the power to paralyse her.

'You know it's the first thing the GP's going to do anyway,' Nat murmured. 'Might as well save her the effort.'

Paige nodded, knowing Nat was right. She looked at the test again, a sudden thought occurring to her. 'Just happen to have this huh?'

Nat shrugged. 'I bought one of those two-in-ones…in case.'

Paige could tell from her friend's face that she'd already used the first one and was trying really hard to be sensitive to Paige's situation in the face of her own good news. 'Does this mean congratulations are in order?'

Nat nodded and then grinned. 'You're the first one to know.'

Paige grinned back, even though inside she felt bleaker than a Bronte moor. 'That's fabulous, Nat.' She leaned forward and gave her friend a big hug. 'Alessandro and Juliano will be over the moon.'

'They'll be ecstatic,' Nat agreed. 'I've been trying to get hold of Alessandro for the last two hours but he's not answering. I just had to tell someone.'

Paige smiled. 'I feel honoured.'

They chatted for the next few minutes about due dates and morning sickness until Nat's phone beeped with a message from Alessandro. 'He's at home.'

'Well, what are you waiting for? Off you go,' Paige teased. When Nat hesitated she said, 'I mean it, go. I'll be fine.'

Nat stood. 'You will do the test, won't you?'

Paige eyeballed it, remembering the last time she'd done a pregnancy test. The joy. The hope. She looked away. 'Yes.'

'I'm going to ring in the morning and check on you.'

Paige rolled her eyes. 'Yes, ma'am.'

Nat leaned down and gave her friend a quick squeeze. 'I'll see you tomorrow.'

The room seemed preternaturally quiet after Nat left. There was just Paige and the test and her heart beat ticking loudly in the silence like the doomsday clock.

Her fingers trembled as she picked it up and turned it over and over. She couldn't do pregnant again. After Daisy had died she'd vowed to never make herself vulnerable like that again. She couldn't stand nine months of living on the edge, being paranoid about things going wrong, demanding scans every week, thinking the worst should there be no foetal movements for a minute, an hour, a day.

Giving birth in a haze of anxiety, constantly testing the baby's hearing, driving herself insane at the slightest sniffle.

Oh, God. What if it was twins again?

And what about McKenzie? Her child, the one she already had, needed her. There was no time for another.

Certainly not for two. There was no spare time to give at all.

She just couldn't do it again.

'Are you going to take that or just stare at it?'

Paige didn't have to look up to know Valentino was standing there. He sounded annoyed.

He could get in line.

'I have a UTI,' she said, raising her face defiantly.

Even glowering at her from the doorway he looked magnificent and her breath caught in her throat. His hair was all messy from the cap and his top two buttons were undone. In another time and place, having his baby would have made her very happy indeed.

'Is that why you kept leaving the theatre today?'

'Yes,' she said testily.

'So why bother with that?'

She shrugged. 'Just pre-empting my GP.'

Valentino's heart beat a crazy tattoo in his chest. What if she was pregnant? What if his baby was already growing inside her? 'What if it's positive?'

Paige felt her stress levels rise a notch. 'It won't be.'

'What if it is?' he insisted.

'It isn't.'

Valentino wanted to shake her. Years ago he'd known briefly what it was like to have created life before it had been snatched away. He was surprised now at how fiercely he still wanted it. 'So go and prove me wrong.'

Paige swallowed. She should. She knew she should. But at least here and now, with the test tucked safely away in its packaging, she could believe in her denial. Once it was out, once the test had been done, it became a whole different proposition.

She stood. 'Fine.' It had been twenty minutes since she had last gone and the urge had returned with a vengeance. May as well get it over and done with. Then at least she could discount pregnancy and get on with having the right tests done.

Valentino stood his ground as she brushed by. He would not be shut out the second time around. 'I'll wait in the lounge.'

Paige's legs felt like wet noodles as she made her way through the lounge area to the staff toilet. Her hands shook as she undid the packaging and it took her several attempts before she was able to liberate it. Between her nerveless fingers and the vibrations of her heartbeat she was frightened she was going to drop the damn thing in the loo!

She doubted very much that Valentino understood the potential impact of this test. How could a footloose, fancy-free, playboy bachelor understand the full implications? For him it was no doubt a test of his virility. Proof of his manliness.

But for her? It was a whole different proposition.

Still, regardless of that, it did need to be done so she took a deep breath and managed to eke out enough urine to do the test.

And even before the little plus appeared somewhere inside she knew.

'Well?' Valentino asked as she appeared back in the open lounge area.

Paige held up the test, barely keeping upright as the foundations of her world crashed all round her. 'It's positive.'

Valentino stared at the pink plus sign. It was a full minute before the information sank in. He was going to be a father. He smiled. And then he grinned. 'This is the best news I've ever heard.'

Paige wasn't similarly overcome. In fact, a huge block of emotion built in her chest till she thought she was going to pass out from the pressure of it. It stung her eyes and prickled in her nose. She sucked in a breath. 'No, Valentino, it's not. This is the worst possible news. You have no idea.'

And she burst into tears.

CHAPTER SIX

WHATEVER Valentino had been expecting it hadn't been this and confronted with her emotional state, he felt at a loss. 'Hey,' he crooned, stepping forward and putting his arm around her shoulders.

Paige shrugged his arm away and moved back. 'Don't touch me,' she half snapped, half sobbed as she wiped at her face with the heels of her palms. 'That's what got us into this mess in the first place.'

'It's not a mess, Paige,' Valentino said gently. 'I'm really okay with this.'

Paige felt a bubble of hysteria rise in her throat to join the mix of other emotions. 'How lovely,' she said sarcastically.

'I'm just saying—'

'Do me a favour,' she interrupted. 'Don't say anything, okay?'

Valentino wisely followed her advice, standing silently, his fists curled by his sides while tears poured down her face. She was in shock. She needed a little time to wrap her head around it. He understood that. But as far as he was concerned, he'd been primed for this moment for a long time. Ever since his ex-fiancée had come into his hospital half-dead from a botched back-yard abortion.

Yes, since then he'd taken precautions to avoid it but whether it was his Italian pride or his legendary uncle status, he'd always known deep down that he wanted to be a father.

And he would move heaven and earth to make sure this child, his child, had everything it ever wanted.

Paige didn't know what to do with herself. Valentino had sat on one of the lounge chairs and was regarding her with his steady brown gaze. 'How can you be so calm?' she demanded. Her cheeks felt hot and she knew she must look a mess. Her nose was running and her face was no doubt an ugly, blotchy mess.

Valentino shrugged. 'I don't see the point in hysteria.'

Oh, really? As far as she was concerned, this was precisely the moment for hysteria. 'Why?' she asked, raking her hands through her hair. 'Why did you have to come along and ruin everything? I was perfectly happy the way I was.'

Valentino was prepared to talk about it, he was even prepared to argue and to cope with more tears, but he wouldn't sit here and listen to her lie to herself. 'I think we both know that's not true.'

Paige choked on a sob. What did he know about her life? 'Are you calling me a liar?'

'I'm just calling it like I see it, Paige.'

Paige's lips twisted into a bitter grimace. 'Oh? And what do you see? This should be interesting.'

'I see a woman whose world was torn apart. One who's going through the motions but can't get any enjoyment out of life. I see someone who's physically and emotionally starving.'

Paige shied away from the truth that resonated in his words. 'I'm eating,' she said, completely exasperated.

'Great. So your stomach is full but what fills your emotional well, Paige?'

'That doesn't matter,' she dismissed.

Valentino snorted. 'Of course it does.'

'Well, what fills yours, then, Valentino?'

'Vivaldi.' It was sterner than he had meant it to come out but her stonewalling was frustrating in the extreme. He continued in a gentler tone. 'A letter from my mother. The first time a patient hears sound. Children laughing. Bruschetta. The way a woman's waist curves out to her hip. *Swan Lake.*'

Hell, did he think she had time for ballet? 'What? No raindrops on roses?'

'Paige.' This was no time for deflection. 'The point is I can take enjoyment from the world around me. When was the last time you did that? When was the last time you rejoiced in being alive?'

Paige fleetingly thought about those few seconds of dread that she woke with every morning and quickly pushed them aside.

'Oh, for crying out loud,' she snapped. 'I don't have time to get my emotional well filled.' She suddenly felt overwhelmed by everything and sat in the lounge opposite Valentino. 'I'm the sole parent to a high-needs child. I certainly don't have time for another baby. That wouldn't be fair to McKenzie.'

'You don't think McKenzie would like a brother or a sister?'

Paige rubbed her brow. 'I'm sure she would. I'm also pretty sure she'd like a unicorn. Unfortunately she doesn't get a say.'

Valentino chuckled but, as he had just stated, she didn't

find any joy in it. She turned beseeching eyes on him. 'I'm tired, Valentino.'

'I'll be here. I'll help.'

Her gaze turned quickly incredulous. How long would it take an Italian playboy surgeon with an international reputation to grow tired of playing house in little old Brisbane? She hardened her heart to his pretty words. Arnie had also promised he'd help. Promised he'd be here until death parted them.

Obviously he'd taken Daisy's death as a literal translation. Their daughter hadn't even been in the ground a week when he'd left for good. She couldn't go through that kind of heartbreak again. She just couldn't.

'And when London calls? When Harry gets back?'

Valentino hadn't thought that far ahead. 'Then you come with me.'

Paige felt the broken edges of her heart grate together. 'No, Valentino. I won't. This is my home. It's McKenzie's home. And whether you like it or not, we are a package deal. I'm not going to uproot her when she has years of therapy left.'

'They do have speech pathologists in other parts of the world.'

Of course they did but Paige had vowed never to blindly follow a man again, like she had Arnie. 'She trusts the St Auburn's team. Has built a relationship with them.'

He shrugged. 'Children adapt.'

Paige glared at him. Spoken like a true egotist, used only to looking after himself. Not a responsible father who put the needs of a child first. 'So let me get this straight. You want me to up sticks and follow you around the world with your child without any mention of us? Of our relationship? Do you even love me, Valentino?'

Valentino could see the stormy uncertainty in her gaze, the earnestness. He looked away. Love? *Dio!* He was too busy trying to come to terms with becoming a father. 'I don't think that's relevant.'

Paige's head spun at his quick dismissal of the fundamental human emotion. 'How is it not relevant, Valentino? Do you expect me to follow you around like a puppy dog, hoping you can squeeze your child in between your work and dating catwalk models?'

Valentino stood, the scorn in her voice stabbing like a stiletto between his ribs. '*Dio!* No, I have more respect for you than that. We would marry, of course.'

Paige blinked up at him. If that was a proposal, it sucked big time. Not to mention it was utter insanity. 'What?'

He hadn't given any of this much thought but now it was out there he knew it was the right thing to do. 'We'll get married.'

'You just told me that love wasn't relevant and now you want to marry me?' Try as she may, Paige couldn't rid her voice of its high squeaky quality.

It had been a long time since Valentino had thought about love. About those three little words. But he did remember how callously they could be used. How empty they could be. 'Did you love your husband?'

Paige frowned. 'Yes. Of course.'

'How'd that work out for you?'

Paige gasped. If her legs had been feeling remotely solid, she would have stood up and slapped his face.

Valentino could see he'd shocked her. Hurt her. He hadn't meant to be so insensitive. He sat. 'I'm sorry, that was unthinking of me.'

She was sitting hunched forward in her chair and he

reached across the space between them to squeeze her arm but Paige moved back out of his reach.

'Yes, it was.'

Valentino regarded her solemnly for a few moments. 'I don't have all the answers yet, Paige. I'm just saying we can work them out. We have time.'

Except the thought of going through it all again, of growing a baby inside, loving it, wanting it, was just too much for her to bear. Her head throbbed in unison with her heart. It was just all too overwhelming.

She stood. 'I can't think straight any more. I have to get home. Mum will be wondering where I am.'

Valentino nodded. 'Of course. Will you tell them about the baby?'

Paige frowned, her mind too full to think straight. 'Of course. Eventually.'

She shuffled her feet awkwardly for a moment. Valentino's head was downcast. This had no doubt thrown a huge spanner into the works for him too. And even though he'd just made the most preposterous suggestion she'd ever heard, she kind of got where it came from. This whole thing was completely unexpected.

She had the strangest urge to gather him in close and lay his cheek against her belly where their baby grew. Instead, she brushed past him with a quiet 'Goodnight'.

Valentino grabbed her hand as she went by. She looked down at him and he fixed her with imploring eyes. 'You won't do anything…rash, will you?'

His meaning was clear and her first reaction was anger. Did he seriously think she would go off behind his back and terminate his baby? Or that she'd go off riding a wild bronco or throw herself off a cliff with only a bungee cord around her ankle? But there was a plea in his gaze that reached right inside her gut and she realised he was as vulnerable, as unsure as she. He had as much at stake as she did.

It seemed natural then to follow through on her earlier impulse and move closer. She buried her hand in his hair and urged his cheek against her stomach.

'Of course not. I won't do anything without talking to you first.'

Valentino shut his eyes as her fingers sifted through his hair and her aroma filled his senses. Her words were utterly sincere and he didn't doubt her. 'Thank you,' he murmured, turning his face to press a kiss against her belly where his child nestled.

Paige shut her eyes as the innocent gesture constricted her throat and breathed fire into her belly. She wished she could give him what he wanted. But what about when it conflicted with what she wanted?

What about her?

'I need time to think. I have to go,' she said, wriggling out of his hold and striding away without looking back.

After a fitful sleep, Paige woke the next morning with only the craving to eat everything in her pantry trumping the dire urge to empty her bladder. She couldn't remember the last time she'd woken with biological matters taking such urgent precedence.

Usually she had to fight herself out of a thick shroud of grief that seemed to pounce in her sleep, making her limbs weak and dampening her mood, steeling herself to face the day for McKenzie's sake. But this morning she was so hungry none of that registered. She would have eaten the sheets had she been tied to the bed.

The devastating fact of her pregnancy, the thing that had had her tossing and turning all night, seemed to pale in comparison to her hunger. She felt like a grizzly bear coming awake after a long winter's hibernation.

The doorbell rang as Paige passed it and she checked her watch. Seven-thirty. A little early for her parents to be here. McKenzie, unusually, was still sound asleep. Paige had checked on her twice already.

She opened the door to find Valentino standing there. He looked good, even for someone with bloodshot eyes and hair that appeared to have been raked all night. It was on the tip of her tongue to tell him to leave then she spied the brown bakery bag under his arm at the same time a waft of yeasty goodness reached her nose.

'Oh, God,' she said, grabbing the bag, her mouth watering already. 'Come in,' she ordered, turning on her heel as she opened the bag and the warm sweet smell of freshly baked croissants hit her olfactory system.

Valentino blinked as Paige disappeared as quickly as she had appeared. He looked at the space where his offering had been and was now gone. He'd been expecting many things this morning. More tears. More anger. Recriminations.

Certainly not this.

Hunger was a good sign, yes?

He found her in the kitchen, tearing chunks off a croissant and stuffing them into her mouth. She was making short work of it. It was compelling viewing as flakes of pastry stuck to her lips and she made little noises of pleasure at the back of her throat as each morsel hit her taste buds.

In fact, he was rather turned on.

When Paige opened her eyes Valentino was the first thing she saw, leaning casually in her doorway. She wasn't sure if it was the morning light or the sugar rush but he looked pretty good there.

'Do you own anything that's not ten sizes too big?' he mused.

'Sit.' She gestured to the stool opposite, ignoring him as she stuffed the last piece of her croissant into her mouth. She turned and retrieved some plates from the cupboard behind her and placed a croissant on each one, pushing his towards him.

She nodded at the side counter. 'Coffee percolator if you want one.'

Valentino would rather never drink coffee again than settle for the stuff that Australians euphemistically called coffee. 'Not even if I was dying,' he said dryly.

Paige laughed. She actually laughed at the disdain on his face. 'Snob.' And then she tore some off her second croissant and devoured it. 'God, this is so-o-o good,' she sighed, licking her fingers.

Valentino temporarily lost his train of thought. Watching her eat was gastronomic pornography. 'Your appetite has returned, I see.'

She nodded. 'I'm so-o-o hungry. I'd forgotten how good things taste,' she said around another mouthful.

'Pleased I could be of service.' He made a mental note to bring a wider array of tempting goodies every time he called in. Which hopefully would be often.

Valentino watched her choose a third croissant, bringing it to her lips, opening her mouth but stopping before she took the first bite. 'Oh, I'm sorry. This is yours,' she said, placing it back on top of the bag.

Valentino chuckled. 'Take it.'

'No, no.' Paige shook her head even as the flaky pastry called to her like a mermaid luring sailors onto the rocks.

He picked it up and held it out. 'I wouldn't dream of depriving you, *bella*.'

Paige winced and hesitated. 'I'm being a pig, aren't I?'

Valentino shook his head. 'I could watch you eat all day,' he murmured, and passed the croissant slowly beneath her nose. 'Besides, you're eating for two now, remember?'

Paige made a grab for the pastry on his second pass. Not even the reminder of her predicament, their predicament, overrode her stomach's demands. Maybe the decision she'd come to in the wee small hours made everything a little easier.

She sank her teeth in, the flakes of soft, velvety pastry melting as they hit her tongue. 'Mmm,' she sighed.

Valentino waited until she finished, not wanting it to end but knowing they had things to discuss. 'We need to talk.' He pulled a tissue out of the box on the counter top and passed it to her, knowing he wasn't going to be able to concentrate with delicate flakes clinging to her gorgeous mouth.

'Sorry,' she apologised, licking at her lips, desperately playing for time now her stomach was satisfied. What had seemed thoroughly reasonable at 3 a.m. didn't seem so reasonable with Valentino sitting in her kitchen. 'I bet it's everywhere.'

Valentino almost groaned as her pink tongue ran back and forth very thoroughly over her lips, picking up stray flakes. Then she dabbed at her mouth with the tissue like a proper society matron. Like she hadn't just done a good impression of the cookie monster or licked her lips like a porn star.

'So,' he said, trying to wrangle his thoughts and the ruckus in his underpants back under control. 'The baby. You said you needed time to think. I don't know about you but I've thought of little else since yesterday afternoon.'

Paige nodded. This was it. She only hoped he understood. 'I can't have this baby, Valentino. I just can't.' She held up her hand as he opened his mouth to protest. 'Please, just hear me out.' She shifted off the stool. 'I want to show you something.'

Valentino followed Paige into the lounge room, his anger simmering. If she thought he would sit by and let her decide the outcome for their baby then she was sorely mistaken. Despite evidence to the contrary only a minute ago, he felt so impotent. He would not let another woman take from him what was also his.

'Sit down.'

He sat and watched her, his thoughts swirling and brooding inside like a gathering storm. She opened a cupboard beneath some bookshelves and pulled out what appeared to be a photo album. She stood for a moment, running her forefinger over the front cover before turning back towards him and sitting down next to him.

Paige passed him the album, her hands trembling. Her eyes locked with his. Her fingers kept hold of the object, lingering, reluctant to surrender it even when she knew it would help him to understand.

'I've never shown this to anyone before.'

Valentino nodded. He could see her qualms swirling like encroaching fog in her big grey eyes and he felt her resistance when he tried to take the album from her. He could see the struggle and what it took for her to finally release it to him.

'I am honoured,' he murmured.

His gaze fell on the window cut out of the cover. It was a close-up of a tiny baby, eyes closed, crisscrossed with tubes and wires. The only way to even tell its sex was from the tiny pink knitted cap that fitted snugly over its head. The little girl was clasping an adult finger in the foreground. It dwarfed the little babe's arm, giving true perspective to its size.

'This is Daisy, yes?'

Paige nodded. 'Yes.'

Valentino hesitated, even though she'd yielded the album to him. 'May I?'

Paige took a deep breath and nodded. Valentino opened the cover slowly, as if he'd just been handed an incredibly old parchment, and she was touched by his reverence.

Her gaze fell to the pages. There, first up, was a picture of Daisy at four hours old. And three years rushed out at her, sucking her straight back into the tumult. The anguish.

'They were twenty-seven-weekers, yes?'

Paige nodded as he continued his reverent journey through the album. 'Daisy was nine hundred grams. McKenzie was twelve hundred.'

Ah. That explained a lot. Premature babies born under one kilo had the odds truly stacked against them.

'It's a beautiful album,' he commented as each picture chronicled Daisy's battle and ever-increasing medical support. The pages were pale pink and decorated with pretty stickers, silky ribbons and baby-themed cut-outs. Every effort had been made to present Daisy as a baby, a precious gift, cherished and loved.

'My mother made the album for me after…'

Valentino didn't push her to complete the sentence. 'It's a good idea. She obviously took a great deal of care with it.'

Paige nodded. 'Mum's very good at craftwork. She does all her own stationery and cards.'

Valentino flipped the pages over, taking great care to linger over each photo with the reverence it deserved. Towards the end they became more medicalised. There were more tubes than baby.

'She had several chest tubes, I see.'

'She kept blowing pneumothoraxes towards the end. Her chronic neonatal lung disease was so bad she didn't respond to any treatment and they just couldn't ventilate her.'

Valentino didn't say anything. What was there to say? It must have been agony to watch. In fact, it was written all over Paige's face in the photos. The album wasn't just a timeline of Daisy's life but a startling map of Paige's grief.

'They withdrew treatment?'

'Yes. She'd suffered so much.' Paige reached out and traced Daisy's face with her forefinger. 'We couldn't ask any more of her.'

The 'we' soon became evident as Valentino turned to the second last page. A photo of a blond man looking down at Daisy, his hand resting against her ever-present woollen cap, jumped out at him. 'Your husband?'

Paige nodded. 'Arnie.'

'He…left?'

'Two days after Daisy's funeral.'

Valentino gripped the edges of the album. How could he do that? How could he walk away from his grieving wife and his other child? What kind of a man did that? 'Do you have contact with him? Does McKenzie see him?'

Was that one of the other factors that Paige had to consider? Was she still carrying a candle for him? The thought struck deep in Valentino's chest. Surely not?

Paige snorted. 'The only correspondence I've had from Arnie since the day I begged him not to leave me has been through his lawyer when the divorce papers arrived.'

Her voice was laced with bitterness and Valentino knew without a shadow of a doubt that it was Arnie he had to thank for Paige's less than flattering opinion of men, the brick wall around her heart. But at least she seemed well and truly over him.

Valentino flipped to the last page. He felt Paige tense beside him and he could see why. It was a very raw photo, difficult to even look at without feeling as if he had intruded on something truly intimate. A snapshot full of utter human misery. Painfully private.

Paige was holding a swaddled Daisy. She was free of all her tubes, her eyes swollen and closed, pink cap pulled snugly over her head. Her mouth was a straight line, the lips colourless, her skin deathly pale. The caption in stickers read 'Rest In Peace Our Precious Daisy'.

Paige was crying in the photograph as she looked down at her daughter with such anguish, clearly distressed. Like she'd give anything in that moment to bring her daughter back. Trade places even. The look said, Don't go, I haven't had the chance to get to know you yet.

Completely desolate was a good description and Valentino felt it right to his very soul.

'She was just too little,' Paige whispered. It had been a couple of years since she'd seen this photo. Tears burned at the backs of her eyes and then welled up and spilled over.

'She fought the good fight,' Valentino murmured.

'She did. She fought for so long.'

Valentino heard the sob catch in her throat and put his arm around her, tucking her head against her shoulder.

He closed the album and let Paige cry until her tears ran out.

Paige wasn't sure how much time had elapsed when she pulled away from him. She was just grateful he'd let her cry. He hadn't tried to tell her not to upset herself or be brave for McKenzie, as Arnie had. He'd just been there.

She used her baggy sleeve to dry her face. 'Do you see why I can't go through another pregnancy? I can't lose another child, Valentino.'

Valentino knew he had to tread carefully here. That just because Paige's fears weren't necessarily rational, it didn't mean they weren't real to her. 'I understand why you don't want to be emotionally vulnerable again. You've been through a lot in the last few years.'

Paige nodded, pleased to see he understood. 'Don't you see?' she reasoned. 'If there is no baby then there's no chance of what happened to the twins happening again.'

Valentino took her hand. 'But there is a baby, Paige. Do you think terminating a pregnancy doesn't count as losing a child?'

'It's…it's different,' she said defensively.

'No, it's not.'

Paige looked at him sharply. Just when she'd thought he understood. 'Is this a religious thing?'

Valentino's brow crinkled. 'What?'

'You're Italian. I know it's frowned on there…'

Valentino was trying to hold onto his temper but it was fraying rapidly. 'This has nothing to do with religion. It's my child, Paige. My. Child. I have rights too and if you think I'm going to allow you to terminate this pregnancy, you're very wrong.'

Paige was surprised to feel the depth of his convictions

blast towards her. The vehemence in his speech. The fierce light burning in his gaze. But it didn't mean he could dictate to her.

'Why?' she demanded. 'Why do you care so much? This whole thing smacks of commitment, of long term. I'd have thought you'd be running a mile.'

Valentino knew her assessment was justified but it stung anyway. He stood and strode to the glass doors that over-looked the deck.

'You thought wrong.'

CHAPTER SEVEN

PAIGE flinched at the steel in Valentino's voice. But as he continued to stare out of her windows, his hands buried in his pockets, she sensed there was more to his insistence then she knew.

'Is there something you're not telling me?'

Valentino could hear his heartbeat pounding like surf in his head. He hadn't spoken her name in years. But if ever there was a time to open up, this was it. Paige had just shared a part of her life that was intensely private. Maybe it was time to share his?

'There was a woman.' His voice was husky and he cleared it. 'A long time ago.'

Paige stilled. Ah. 'I see.'

Valentino turned. Where did he even start? 'We were in love. Or at least I thought we were. I was first year out, an intern, back home. She was a fashion design student. She was…beautiful.'

It was a surprise how much it hurt to hear him talk about a woman in such hushed, awed tones. And even though he was looking at her, Paige knew he'd gone somewhere far away.

'She was twenty-one and she had all these curves and this gorgeous long hair…'

Valentino stopped and Paige didn't need to join the dots to know the woman must have been a stunner. She suddenly felt plain and unattractive with her short hair and angular frame.

What had Valentino seen in her?

'I was completely besotted. I proposed within two months and she leapt at it. Bought her this magnificent rock because she just had to have it. We went to lots of parties, made the society pages. She bragged about marrying a doctor to all her friends and revelled in the kudos.'

He paused for breath and Paige spoke for the first time. 'What was her name?'

Valentino fought his way back from the past and Paige slowly came into focus. 'Daniella.'

Once even the mention of the name had sent him a little crazy but he was surprised at how unaffected he felt, standing here today.

What on earth had he seen in her? Looking at Paige now, an intriguing woman with depth and layers, he just couldn't figure it out. Daniella had been terribly superficial. Yes, she'd been young but all she'd cared about had been clothes and shoes and the trendy new bars in town. He could admit now that conversation had been terribly dull. He'd just been too in lust to see it.

'Then I took her to meet my parents. The whole sign-language thing freaked her out, I think. And when I started to talk about setting a date and planning a family, she ran a mile. She had a career and a social life. How could she possibly fit into her designer wardrobe or drink champagne at glamorous balls with swollen feet and no waist? What if we had a deaf child?'

Paige heard the bitter edge to his voice. 'Ah.'

Valentino nodded. 'I was devastated.'

'Of course. First love is always the hardest.'

Despite having dated on and off throughout her twenties, Arnie had been her first love. She'd fallen for him hard and married him in a rush. His desertion when she'd needed him most had cut deep.

As, obviously, had Daniella's. Suddenly his playboy rebound love-life made sense. He'd evidently been trying to forget Daniella's callousness. Who was she to judge how he dealt with his loss? Just because she'd withdrawn completely, it didn't mean it was the right way to cope.

Was there a book of etiquette somewhere that explained how you were supposed to act when your whole world fell apart?

Valentino's mouth compressed into a tight line. 'There's more.' He hesitated. How did he say something he'd never truly voiced to anyone before? 'Six weeks after we broke up I was working night shift in Emergency when Daniella was rushed through the doors. She was haemorrhaging heavily. She'd had a back-street abortion.'

Paige gasped. She hadn't expected that. 'Oh, Valentino.' She got to her feet, crossed the short space between them and placed her hand on his arm. 'I'm so sorry.'

He captured her gaze. 'She didn't tell me she was pregnant. She didn't ask me for help or bother to find out what I wanted. She just went and took my child from me.'

She closed her eyes against the anguish she saw in Valentino's. She knew how it felt to have a child taken from you. No wonder he'd been so vehement with her. It must be like Daniella all over again. 'You wanted to keep the baby?'

Valentino gave her a hard look. 'I wanted the choice. I wanted to be consulted. Included.'

Paige nodded. 'That was wrong of her. To act without consulting you.'

'Damn right.'

'She was young and scared,' Paige said gently.

'So was I,' he said. 'But I'm not now.'

Paige sighed and returned to the lounge. She raised pleading eyes to him. 'Valentino, please don't make this more difficult for me than it already is.'

'You want me to make it easy for you? I won't.'

He strode towards her, dropping to his knees beside her. He grabbed her hand and pressed it to her belly. 'Feel that. Inside there is our baby. He lives and he grows. He has a heartbeat and every right to be born. He's going to have my dark wavy hair and your beautiful grey eyes and he's going to be healthy and perfect and we're going to love him.'

Paige shook her head from side to side. Damn him. It was ridiculous to think she could feel the baby move but she could have sworn tiny flutters danced beneath their joined hands. And suddenly she could picture him.

Him! For crying out loud!

Just as Valentino had described him. Perfect in every way. A unique blend of both of them.

And she knew she couldn't do it. Not to Valentino. Or herself. Or the baby. A baby she already loved more than life itself. As she had loved Daisy and McKenzie from the second she'd known about them. Who was she kidding? She could no more deny this tiny life growing inside her than fly to the moon.

And looking at Valentino's tormented face, she knew she couldn't hurt him either. Not like that. Not like Daniella had.

Her gaze fell on the album beside her and she touched Daisy's cheek with heart-breaking reverence. 'Chances of delivering early again increase in subsequent pregnancies.' She glanced at Valentino with huge eyes. 'I'm scared,' she whispered.

'Don't be. I'm not going to let anything happen to our baby.'

And for a crazy moment she believed him.

The next day Valentino arrived on her doorstep, bearing freshly baked blueberry muffins. And an engagement ring.

'Dr Valentino!'

'Well, good morning, young lady.' Valentino crouched down, signing as he spoke. He could just make out the external component of the implant attached to the side of her head and mostly hidden by her gorgeous curls. She was wearing a pink tutu and fairy wings, which looked even sweeter on her diminutive frame.

'*Osservate molto abbastanza oggi.*' Although he spoke in Italian he signed in English so she knew she was looking very pretty today.

'We're having breakfast,' McKenzie signed with a flourish.

'That's good.' Valentino grinned. He opened the bag and let McKenzie peek inside. 'I brought muffins.'

'McKenzie, darling?'

Valentino stood as an unfamiliar voice came closer. It sounded older. Paige was obviously not alone.

'Oh. Hello, there.'

An older woman with Paige's big grey eyes blinked curiously at him. He recognised her from the photo on the television. 'Hi. I'm Valentino,' he said, holding out his hand.

'Oh, yes.' Paige's mother shook his hand. 'You're the surgeon who took over from Harry. You did McKenzie's surgery.'

Valentino smiled. 'Yes.' McKenzie slipped her hand into his and he watched as the older woman's shrewd gaze followed the movement.

'I didn't realise you made house calls?'

Valentino saw the teasing sparkle in her eyes and chuckled. 'Only for my special patients,' he said, grinning down at McKenzie and signing for her benefit.

'I'm Adele, Paige's mother.'

'Very pleased to meet you.'

And he was. Adele was a fine-looking woman. Tall, like her daughter, she'd aged well with graceful laughter lines around her eyes and mouth. But what struck him the most was her aura of contentment. Adele obviously lived well and laughed a lot. She looked healthy and robust and mischief danced in her eyes. She reminded him of his own mother.

'Would you care to join us for breakfast?'

Valentino held up the bakery packet, pleased to have bought a few extras. 'I brought muffins.'

'I'm sure they'll be welcome. My daughter seems to have found her appetite at last.'

She gave him a speculative look before turning on her heel, and Valentino smiled as he and McKenzie followed her.

'Look who I found lurking in the doorway,' Adele announced as she stepped onto the deck.

An older man looked up from several newspapers he appeared to be reading at once. He looked at Valentino over the top of bifocal glasses with a startled expression. Paige looked up from buttering the last slice of toast.

'Valentino!'

She wanted to say this really had to stop but he looked all sexy in his casual chinos and open-necked shirt and infinitely male and his dimples screamed lazy Sunday morning.

But this really had to stop.

Adele could see the indecision on her daughter's face. 'He brought muffins,' she said, digging Valentino in the ribs.

Valentino smiled to himself and held out the bag exactly as Adele had no doubt hoped he would. 'Blueberry,' he said. 'Warm. Just out of the oven.'

Paige relented. How could she still be hungry after an omelette stuffed with mushrooms, cheese and bacon and three pieces of toast? 'My favourite.'

Adele relieved him of the packet, placing it in the centre of the table, and walked around to the empty chair beside Paige and pulled it out for him. 'Sit here, Valentino.'

As a well-adjusted Italian male, Valentino had a healthy respect for mothers and wasn't about to argue with one who would hopefully soon be his mother-in-law. But before he sat he stretched his hand across the table towards the man he assumed was Paige's father.

'Hello, sir. I'm Valentino Lombardi. Pleased to meet you.'

Paige's father half stood as he accepted Valentino's hand in a firm, brief shake. 'McKenzie's surgeon? Don Eden.' He looked over his glasses at his wife as he reclaimed his seat, speculation in his gaze. 'Didn't realise you blokes made house calls.'

Valentino grinned as Adele winked at him. 'Coffee?'

'Valentino would rather eat dirt then drink our heathen

colonial coffee,' Paige said around a mouthful of muffin. 'Is that a fair summation?'

Valentino chuckled. She had crumbs on her lips and it was most distracting. It was sexy, watching her eat with such gusto. He wondered how she'd look eating something gooey, like ice cream. In bed. With no clothes on. 'More than fair.'

'Oh, I don't blame you,' Adele said. 'Nicest coffee we ever had was in Italy, wasn't it, darling? Where are you from exactly?' she asked.

They chatted for half an hour about Italy and travelling and McKenzie's implant. Not that Paige contributed much. After eating two muffins she dropped her head back against her chair and shut her eyes, letting the morning sunshine warm her skin.

She didn't want to encourage him, she didn't want him too cosy with her family. Just because she'd agreed not to do anything rash, it didn't mean they were one big happy family.

Despite his assurances of support, Paige had been burnt before.

It was pleasant conversation but Valentino was charming her parents and it was strangely irritating. As good as he was to look at, as amazing as he smelled this morning— like bakery and sunshine—she wished he would just go.

Valentino found his attention drifting as he chatted with Adele and Don. He was hyper-aware of Paige beside him all loose and relaxed in her chair. She was wearing her usual baggy clothes but whether it was the angle of her body or this particular view he couldn't help but notice how fuller her breasts seemed. How they formed two firm, high mounds against the thin fabric of her shirt and bounced when she shifted in the chair.

He wanted to nuzzle her neck, let his hand drift to one of those very enticing mounds.

Dio!

He came here for one thing and one thing only. He rose, needing desperately to get away and get his mind back on the game plan. 'Excuse me for a moment.' Valentino stood. 'Paige, your bathroom?'

Paige gave him directions and, despite wanting him to leave only seconds ago, she suddenly felt bereft without him. She steeled herself for the grilling she knew was to come.

Her mother went first. 'I like him.'

'You don't know him.'

'I'd known Arnie for two minutes and knew I didn't like him.'

Touché. She glanced at her father smiling at her mother, his dimples blazing. 'You've always been a sucker for men with dimples.'

Adele ignored him and looked at her daughter. 'So have you, darling.'

Had she? When she looked back over her life prior to Arnie the few boyfriends she'd had had indeed all been blessed with dimples. 'Dimples do not maketh the man,' Paige grumbled.

Adele smiled at her husband. 'I would have to disagree with you there.'

Paige shook her head, humbled as ever by her parents' enduring love and affection for each other. 'Well, you would.'

'I'm just saying that I think he's good for you.' Adele reached across the table and squeezed her daughter's hand. 'Isn't it about time you declared a truce on the men of the world? They're not all like Arnie, darling.'

Paige wondered how her parents would feel if they knew that this Italian Lothario they were so enamoured with had impregnated their daughter. Neither of her parents were keen for her to have any more children given what had happened with the twins.

Before she could speak, Valentino's voice drifted out to them and three pairs of eyes sought him out. He'd stopped to talk to McKenzie.

McKenzie had grown bored quickly with the adult conversation and had asked for 'Wigga' and Paige, who didn't like her watching too much television, hadn't been able to refuse. Hearing her daughter say actual words was sweeter than the sweetest music in the world and seeing her dance now she could actually hear the music was endlessly thrilling.

They watched as Valentino took McKenzie's hands and danced around with her. McKenzie giggled as he lifted her off the floor and twirled her round, his dark hair almost black compared to her lighter hues. She clapped as he put her down and said, 'Again.' And Valentino complied, his easy laughter rich and deep.

Laughter you could drown in.

And her broken, fractured, battered, stomped-on heart just about melted in her chest.

'Oh, my,' Adele said, her hand fluttering to her chest.

Paige dragged her gaze away from the endearing sight of Valentino—a large, virile, Italian man his hands dwarfing McKenzie's torso—twirling her daughter—a little pink fairy girl—round and round. It was exceedingly sexy.

She blasted her mother with an impatient glare. So he was good with children. Arnie had been great with kids. Had been over the moon about the pregnancy.

But look how quickly he had turned his back when it had come to the crunch.

'You've won a heart there,' Don commented as Valentino rejoined them on the deck.

Valentino shrugged. 'I have ten nieces and five nephews back home. Children like to dance in any language, I think.'

'That they do,' Don agreed.

'Actually, sir,' Valentino said. 'I'm glad you're both here.' He looked at Paige, who frowned at him. 'My cousin Alessandro tells me its tradition here to ask, permission of the woman's parents to marry her. So—'

'What?' Paige stood up, effectively cutting Valentino off. Had he gone mad? 'I'm not marrying you, Valentino. I told you that yesterday.'

Valentino reached into his pocket and pulled out a velvet box. He opened it and placed it on the table in front of her.

Paige blinked. The simple square-cut diamond nestled in the satin and dazzled in the direct sunlight. It was simple and beautiful and perfect. Every woman's idea of an engagement ring right there before her. And she wanted to put it on her finger so badly it itched. Instead, she reached down and pushed the lid shut.

'I said no.'

Don and Adele looked at the box and then at each other. 'It's pretty traditional to have the woman's consent first,' Don joked, and Adele dug him in the ribs with her elbow as she fought a smile, mashing her lips together hard.

'Which he doesn't have,' Paige said adamantly.

'Paige, I can't allow our baby to be born outside marriage.'

Paige felt the air around her evaporate. 'Valentino!'

Valentino frowned as Adele gasped and turned to Paige.

'Baby?' she demanded.

Valentino raked his hand through his hair. She had said she was going to tell them. 'You haven't told them about the baby?'

Paige shut her eyes and slowly sat down. 'No,' she said, utterly defeated. 'Not yet.'

Adele looked at Don. 'That explains the appetite.' She turned to her daughter and gave her hand a squeeze. 'Are you okay, darling?'

Valentino could see the worry in their eyes as Paige's parents looked at her with concern. They were no doubt apprehensive about their daughter going into premature labour again.

'A little shocked actually, Mum. And ravenous.'

'Maybe that's a good sign?' Adele suggested. 'You couldn't keep anything down with the twins.'

That was true. She'd actually landed in hospital on a drip twice. 'Maybe.' Paige nodded. But the truth was she was still scared witless about the pregnancy. And she didn't have to look at her parents to know they were too.

Valentino observed the byplay intently. He could see the prospect of a second pregnancy for Paige didn't just affect her and him. That her parents had been a major support for Paige and they were understandably concerned.

'I'm not going to let anything happen to Paige or the baby. You have my word.'

Adele gave a sad smile and squeezed her daughter's hand again. 'I believe you. But for now I think we'd better leave you both alone to talk this through. We'll take McKenzie out to the park.'

Paige nodded. 'Thanks.'

Paige's parents rose and Don held out his hand to

Valentino. 'It was nice meeting you. And I appreciate that you want to do the right thing by our daughter.' He dropped his hand after a brief shake. 'It's been a tough few years for all of us. It hasn't been easy as a father to watch Paige go through what she's been through. I trust you understand our less than enthusiastic response.'

Valentino nodded. 'Of course.'

Paige was grateful that Valentino waited till they had all departed before he spoke again. 'I'm sorry. I didn't know your parents were going to be here this morning.'

Paige picked up the velvet box and held it out. 'That didn't seem to stop you.'

Valentino ignored it. 'I'm serious about this, *bella*.'

'So am I.'

'You are carrying my child. It's the honourable thing to do. My duty. My mother would disown me if I didn't do the right thing.'

Duty and honour. Two things that Arnie hadn't been big on. Still, they weren't the words a girl wanted to hear when talking marriage. Arnie had said he loved her and couldn't live without her.

That had worked a treat.

Fortunately she was somewhat more evolved now, her heart hardened to flattery. But there was no way she was making the biggest commitment of her life based on anything other than love. And as she'd vowed to never be so stupid again, she just didn't see how it could work.

Paige placed the box back on the table. 'Listen to yourself. This shouldn't be about what's honourable. About duty. This is a long-term commitment. You are not a long-term guy.'

'I am now.'

Paige gave him a reproving look. 'Are you telling me

that the first time you laid eyes on me you knew I was the girl you wanted to marry?'

Valentino didn't think it wise to tell her exactly what he had been thinking that day at the wedding. Suffice to say it had come to fruition a few hours later. 'Love at first sight is not a sound basis for marriage.'

'Maybe not, but it's a good place to start. What about Daniella? Didn't you take one look at her and know?'

Valentino frowned. 'I was twenty-four. I'm pretty sure I wasn't thinking with anything north of my belt. It was lust, not love.'

Maybe it had been lust with Arnie too? Maybe she hadn't fallen in love after all. Maybe his flashy, blond good looks and his total adoration of her had blinded her to the real man beneath.

'And it didn't work out. Neither did you and Arnie. So maybe approaching marriage like this is the best way to go about it. We don't have to get married straight away, we have time to get to know each other.'

'My mother would say we should have done that first.'

He shrugged. 'So would mine.'

Paige smiled despite her heart pounding in her chest as she prepared to ask the next question. 'Just say I agree to getting married…what happens when you do meet the one and you're trapped in a marriage with me? Do you expect me to be okay with it? Do you expect me to sit back and watch you break our child's heart when you leave me for her? Not to mention McKenzie's heart? Would you fight me for custody?'

'*Il mio dio!* I haven't thought about any of these things.'

Paige tried not to let his avoidance of the answer have an impact on her. 'No kidding!'

Valentino's jaw tightened. 'There will be no other women.'

'What about sex?'

Valentino frowned. 'What about it? I thought you liked having sex with me?'

Paige didn't think her liking it was really the issue. That was a no-brainer. 'If you think I'm going to risk this pregnancy by having sex during it, then you really are crazy.'

Valentino rubbed his forehead. He hadn't thought about that aspect of it. *'No problemo,'* he dismissed.

'You seriously expect me to believe you can go without sex for that long?'

Arnie had cited lack of intimacy as one of the reasons he was leaving and she'd known their defunct sex life had frustrated him. But she had been exhausted, being at the hospital all day and worried sick about the twins, watching Daisy grow steadily more ill. She'd been emotionally numb and physically disconnected from her body, and sex had been the last thing on her mind.

And, besides, it hadn't felt right, enjoying herself while her children were in Intensive Care, fighting for their lives.

Valentino smiled at her incredulity. He should have been angry with her sexist assumption that he was incapable of going without. But he wasn't. 'You don't think,' he said, his voice dropping an octave as his gaze dropped to the interesting mounds he could now make out beneath her baggy T-shirt, 'I'm imaginative enough to be able to satisfy you in other ways?'

Paige swallowed and to her dismay her nipples hardened in blatant response to his ogling. Her breasts had been sore and tight and uncomfortable but they seemed to flower beneath his gaze.

She was temporarily speechless.

Valentino caught her gaze and chuckled as she folded her arms across her chest. Good, he had her attention. 'I don't want to be excluded from the pregnancy, Paige. I want to be around to feel the baby move and kick, to see your belly grow. To help out when you're not feeling well. To get you ice cream and tomato sauce when you wake up with a craving at three o'clock in the morning. I want to get to know McKenzie as well. I'm going to be in her life too.'

Paige wanted to shut her ears to the cosy picture he was painting. A flash of McKenzie and Valentino dancing flitted through her mind, the look of adoration on her daughter's face as she'd clung to his neck crystal clear.

How could she expose McKenzie to him, like he was asking? Have her love and adore him when, try as she may, she couldn't believe he was going to stick around.

Especially if something happened to the baby.

Yes, he was telling her he would but he'd spent the last decade of his life constantly moving on from one woman to another. Did he seriously expect her to believe he could reverse what by now must be fairly ingrained behaviour?

'And what if something happens to the baby—?'

'I told you nothing would happen,' he interrupted.

She held up her finger. 'Just go with me here on this, okay? Something happens and I go into labour again at twenty-eight weeks or even less and the baby dies. There's nothing keeping us together after that—there's certainly not love. Are you going to tell me you're going to stick around? Or will you run when it all becomes overwhelming because, trust me...' Her voice wavered. 'It will. What happens to McKenzie then?' Or to her, for that matter. 'It'll be devastating.'

Valentino ran a hand through his hair. 'It won't happen.'

'Goddamn it, Valentino,' she snapped, banging her fist on the table. 'What if it does?'

'You're dealing in a lot of what-ifs.'

'Yeah, well, I have to, I'm her mother, I have to protect her. That's my job.' To say nothing of protecting herself.

Valentino's jaw clenched. 'I make you a solemn promise. I will not walk away.'

'But it would be easier for you to go if we didn't marry. If there was no wedding ring holding you here.'

It was Valentino's turn to slam his hand down on the table in frustration. '*Dio!* Listen to me. I. Will. Not. Walk. Away.' He punctuated each word with a vicious finger stab at the table.

For what it was worth, she believed him. Right now, at this moment, his conviction was palpable. But Paige knew that life cold throw you curve balls and things could change in a heartbeat.

She also knew this was getting them nowhere. They needed a compromise, something to break the stalemate. 'You want to get to know me? Us? Then let's just do that for now. I'm not going to stop you from being involved in the pregnancy, Valentino. I will include you as much as possible.' She picked up the box again. 'Let's spend some time together first and then…' she pushed it across the table to him '…we'll see.'

Valentino picked up the box. Paige looked conciliatory and certainly a lot less exasperated. It was a good compromise. She was so skittish, so hurt from her ex, he suspected if he pushed too much she'd never agree. Maybe he'd have to play it cool for a bit. Prove to her he could be the man she needed him to be.

'So it's not a no? It's a maybe later.'

Paige nodded, even though she knew deep in her heart she would never marry again. 'That's right.'

Valentino examined the box for a few moments and then put it back in his pocket. 'I'm going to keep asking.'

And she was going to keep saying no. She smiled at him. 'I wouldn't expect anything less.'

CHAPTER EIGHT

AND he did. At the end of every week together he asked her again. And at the end of every week she said no. Then they started all over again.

They fell into a routine. He came for tea one night a week after McKenzie was in bed. Paige insisted they wait till her daughter was asleep. She knew how easily McKenzie loved people and she didn't want her becoming too attached.

On Sunday mornings he joined the whole family for breakfast. It seemed less intimate with her parents there as a buffer to his charisma and charm and Paige had to admit she looked forward to it. If for nothing else than to taste what amazing culinary offering he brought with him.

And, of course, they saw each other at work three days a week. Although Paige and Valentino were scrupulous about keeping it strictly professional. No one in the department had an inkling of their private affairs, which was exactly what she wanted.

Paige had also insisted that they tell no one about the baby, including McKenzie, not until she'd passed the twenty-eight-week mark at least. To her surprise, Valentino agreed. As he had with the McKenzie-in-bed rule. It seemed he didn't want to do anything to upset her.

He treated her with kid gloves. Was attentive and sweet. He fed her tempting, delicious creations at every opportunity and made her laugh. Apart from his weekly proposal he didn't push her into any decisions or even try to make a pass at her, despite how alarmingly she wanted to feel his lips on hers again.

It was an urge that grew with each week of pregnancy into an almost unbearable craving. Forget ice cream with tomato sauce! Her hormones went into overdrive as she entered the second trimester and Valentino looked more and more edible.

But he seemed immune to her vibes. It was like he'd decided her body was a temple for his baby and that she was no longer a woman that he'd kissed and made very thorough love to on two very long nights. She was a mother now. A sacred vessel.

She should have appreciated it. And she did. By and large. But sometimes she just wanted to grab him and smack a kiss on that full sexy mouth so badly she could barely see straight.

When she started to feel the baby move at 16 weeks he came over twice a week for tea and spent all day Sunday with them. Which was harder on the raging libido but involved him more, for which he was very grateful.

And Paige really kept him as involved as possible without them actually living under the same roof. He attended the weekly ultrasounds and all the doctor's appointments. When it came to discussing the best course of action to prevent another premature labour, she involved him in all the decisions and even looked to him for advice.

Dr Erica de Jongh, the obstetrician, was confident that although Paige was at an increased risk of having a second premature labour, it was highly unlikely she would this time round because the risks factors from her first pregnancy did not exist in this one.

For a start, there was only one baby and from the weekly ultrasounds they could see their baby boy was growing normally, unlike Daisy who had always been small for dates and suffered from borderline intra-uterine growth retardation.

Erica saw no reason for intervention, fully confident that Paige would go to full term. It was only the patients who went into premature labour for no apparent reason that she tended to treat more aggressively in subsequent pregnancies.

And even though it was true that Paige would never be entirely relaxed, both she and Valentino had confidence in Erica, who specialised in high-risk pregnancies and were happy with her care and her treatment plan. And each week as their little boy grew and did all the right things and there were no signs of trouble, they were more and more encouraged.

The day she turned twenty-two weeks Paige was joined by Valentino in the scrub room as she was nearing the end of her three-minute hand wash. It was their first case of the day.

'So,' Valentino said, wetting his arms and applying the liquid surgical scrub, 'twenty-two weeks today.'

Paige could see the smile in his eyes and knew his dimples would be dazzling beneath his mask. Still, they'd agreed not to talk about it at work. 'Not here,' she murmured.

Valentino chuckled. 'I'm just making conversation.'

Paige rolled her eyes at him. 'It's a nice day is conversation. We need more rain is conversation.'

'Ah.' Valentino shrugged, his arms soaped to his elbows. 'Blame it on my command of the English language. Subtleties are harder to pick up on.'

Paige laughed. Valentino spoke perfect English. He certainly understood subtleties and nuance just fine. 'Poor Valentino.'

As she ran her hands under the water for one last rinse the baby kicked her hard and high as if he objected to Paige teasing his father. She gasped, the motion of her hands freezing as her breath was momentarily stolen by the strength and suddenness of it. She leaned over a little, her hands still elevated above the sink.

Valentino frowned, his hands also ceasing their activity. 'Paige? Are you all right?'

Paige nodded as the baby continued to tap-dance in her womb. 'I think this baby's going to play soccer for Italy.'

Valentino grinned. 'It kicked?'

'Oh, yeah. I think he's awake and ready to party.'

It took Valentino all of two seconds to decide his next course of action. He abandoned his scrub and reached for her belly, soaped arms and all.

'Valentino!' Paige gasped as his hands made wet imprints on her blue scrubs. She looked over her shoulder. 'They're expecting us inside.'

He ignored her. 'Where?' he asked, shifting his hands around, waiting for the tell-tale movement beneath his palm, desperate to be part of this moment with her. He would never tire of feeling his son move. Her scrubs were an annoying barrier and he ran his hands under the hem until his soapy fingers touched bare belly.

Paige gasped again, quieter this time, her teeth sinking into her bottom lip as she concentrated on keeping her arms sterile and remaining upright while his asexual touch spread sticky tentacles to places lower. Much lower.

He'd felt her belly before. But never skin to skin, always through her clothes. His warm, slippery hands were completely methodical and thorough as he slid them all over her small bump, searching for movement. It was crazy. There was nothing intimate about it at all and yet her nipples hardened and rubbed painfully against the fabric of her bra.

'Valentino...' Even to her own ears it sounded husky and aching. Not that he seemed to be listening, intent on awaiting the baby's next move.

She was about to give him the whole this-is-entirely-inappropriate spiel but then the baby kicked again, another hard jab, right where Valentino's hand was, and he laughed, looking up at her with joy in his eyes, and she forgot about what was appropriate. He turned a few more loops for Valentino's benefit and Paige watched his downcast head, his dark hair visible beneath the semitransparent fabric of his theatre hat.

'This is just the best feeling in the world, isn't it?' Valentino asked, looking up at her.

Paige smiled and nodded. It was hard not to be infected by his enthusiasm. Even though she could only see his eyes, his joy and excitement were plain to see. He held on for another minute, rubbing his hands around the rise of her abdomen.

Paige, her arms having practically drip-dried by now, shifted slightly. 'I think the show's over.'

Valentino's gaze returned to hers. Her grey eyes had gone

all smoky and he became very aware that he was touching her quite intimately. Still, the ripe swell of her felt good beneath his hands. Sexy. Right. He hadn't touched her bare stomach since the night they'd conceived his son and he suddenly realised he missed touching her.

He'd spent so much time trying to distance himself from Paige as a woman that he'd forgotten how good her skin felt. He withdrew his hands as if he was back in fifth grade, being rapped over the knuckles by the nuns.

'Sorry.'

Paige wobbled as his hands left her belly and she ground her clogged feet into the floor to stop herself from pitching forward. She tugged a deep breath into her lungs and nodded at his hands. 'You'd better start again.' Then she flapped her arms to dispel the last drips from her elbows and headed for the theatre doors.

That Sunday Valentino accompanied McKenzie and Paige to the riverside markets and then they met Adele and Don for brunch at South Bank. It had been months since McKenzie had come down with a sniff or a fever and Paige, at the urging of her parents, had decided to risk an outdoors expedition.

And she was pleased she had. The weather was glorious and McKenzie had been in absolute heaven. She'd worn her external device but, unused to crowds, the background chatter combined with the cool river breeze played havoc with the sensitive external microphone and overwhelmed her quickly. Paige removed it after the first ten minutes and she was much happier.

McKenzie had come along in leaps and bounds with her language skills over the last few months and it was a joy to watch her grow and develop now sound and speech were a part of her world.

It was midday as they got up to leave, passing the lunch crowd on their way out. Paige was feeling quite weary from all the walking around and couldn't wait to collapse on her lounge and veg out for the afternoon.

McKenzie tugged on her sleeve and Paige looked down. Her daughter was pointing at the large, white modern Ferris wheel that was a smaller version of the London Eye and could be seen from all over South Bank. Paige groaned. She'd forgotten she'd promised McKenzie a ride.

'We'll take her,' Adele said, giving her daughter's arms a squeeze. 'Valentino, drive her home. She looks exhausted.'

Paige felt torn. 'Are you sure?'

'Of course,' Don assured her.

Paige reluctantly agreed and watched her daughter skip off quite happily with her parents. Then Valentino whisked her away and had her ensconced on her lounge within twenty minutes, including a quick stop at his favourite deli.

'Mmm, that feels good,' Paige groaned as she slipped her shoes off and lay down on the squishy leather.

Valentino smiled at the pleasure in her voice, which he could hear all the way from the kitchen. He arranged a fat slice of tiramisu on a plate and picked it up, along with two forks.

'This is just as good,' he announced as he carried it into the lounge.

He lowered himself onto the edge of the coffee table closest to her head, immediately noticing the way her hand rested low on her belly, emphasising her bump. His baby was just there and he was surprised by the urge to link his hand through hers.

His gaze drifted higher and was drawn to the way her shirt pulled taut across her chest. Her belly wasn't the only thing that was burgeoning—her breasts seemed determined to keep pace.

He swallowed. Up until he'd laid his hands on her belly the other day he'd been doing just fine with keeping his distance. Treating Paige as the pregnant mother of his child. Affording her the right amount of reverence and respect. But that smoky look in her eyes had stayed with him and ever since his thoughts had been less than... reverent.

'Tiramisu for two,' he said, dragging his gaze back to her face.

Paige could smell the coffee and chocolate before he even sat down, reviving her somewhat. 'Mmm, smells delicious.'

Valentino passed her a fork and watched as she struggled into a semi-upright position. It was on the tip of his tongue to tell her to stay put, that he'd feed her, but the images that rose to his mind were far from respectful and he feigned interest in the dessert as things shifted and moved interestingly.

He held the plate forward and watched as she attacked the cake with gusto, loading up her fork and stuffing it into her mouth. Her pink tongue lapped at excess cream on her lips and her sigh of bliss went straight to his groin.

'Mrs Agostino is a goddess,' Paige groaned.

Mrs Agostino wasn't alone there. Paige had put on weight and there was a healthy glow to her fuller cheeks. Watching her eat was a divine experience.

She loaded up again and slipped the airy creation into her mouth. She looked at Valentino to share her bliss and noticed he wasn't eating. 'You're not joining me?' she asked, around a mouthful of cake.

Valentino's gaze fell to her mouth decorated in crumbs and cream. *Dio!* Was she trying to kill him?

Paige stilled her chewing and swallowed her mouthful as the direction of his gaze registered. Her lips tingled beneath the intensity of it. Maybe he wasn't as immune to her as a woman as she'd thought? She felt a surge of feminine hormones power into her bloodstream and arched her back a little. The corresponding rounding of his eyes made the move worth it.

'Valentino?'

Val dragged his gaze away from her breasts. 'Sorry. What? Oh, no, thanks. Here.' He thrust the plate at her. 'You have it.'

Then he shifted off the table and went and sat in the single lounge chair furthest away. It was still a sin to watch her eat but at least he'd removed himself from the temptation of leaning forward and using his tongue as a serviette.

'Mmm, that was amazing,' Paige said a minute later, scraping the last crumbs off the plate before placing it on the coffee table. She should be full but nothing seemed to fill her up these days. She had three years of sparrow appetite to make up for and her stomach was accepting the challenge with gusto.

'Now, if only my feet didn't ache so much, everything would be perfect. Honestly…' she looked at Valentino '…you'd think a theatre nurse would be used to standing.'

Valentino chuckled. 'We walked a lot.' Now she'd stopped eating he felt on a more even keel. He moved across to the end of her lounge. 'Here,' he said, slapping his lap. 'Pass me that moisturising cream. I'll give you a foot massage.'

Paige regarded him for a moment. He looked cool and calm and totally in control again and she wondered if she'd imagined that mad moment when he'd looked at her like she was on the menu. Maybe her hormones were also playing havoc with her eyesight?

Anyway, she wasn't about to pass up a foot rub when her feet were throbbing so she grabbed the cream and handed it to him then shuffled down the lounge till she was almost completely horizontal, her head resting on the arm, and placed her feet in his lap.

Valentino soon discovered there was no such thing as an even keel with her as her heels and her painted red toenails created instantaneous mayhem in his trousers. Praying for strength, he lifted one into his hands and shifted the other to the relative safety of his thigh.

Desperate for something to do other than look at her, he got right on the job, squeezing some cream onto his palms and then smoothing it onto her foot.

'Oh, my God.' Paige's head lolled back against the arm. 'That is so-o-o good,' she groaned as aching muscles responded to his light touch.

Valentino's fingers temporarily forgot their job as her breathy appreciation caused paralysis of everything but the activity in his pants.

'Don't stop,' she groaned, wiggling her toes.

Reaching for sanity, he willed his fingers to continue.

'Maybe you should give up work?' Valentino suggested in a bid to give himself something else to think about other than inching his hand higher up her leg.

Paige lifted her drowsy head. 'Erica seems to think it's okay to continue. She'll let me know if she thinks I should pack it in.'

'I know. I'm just saying you're exhausted and you're only going to get more tired as the pregnancy progresses.'

'I'm fine,' Paige murmured, her eyes drifting shut as Valentino rubbed her instep and her head lolled back. 'Besides, I can't afford to give up work this early.'

He kept his gaze firmly on her toes with the red nail polish. 'I can support you.'

Paige was too chilled out to be affronted. 'No.'

'Paige—'

Paige smiled at the wounded Italian male pride she heard in his voice. 'No. If I need your help, I'll ask.' She lifted her head from the arm. 'Okay?'

Valentino didn't dare look at her. Her voice was all light and husky—he didn't need to see her looking all loose and relaxed and blissed out. 'Fine.'

'Good,' she murmured, dropping her head back. 'Now, please just keep doing what you're doing.'

So he did. The job would have been a lot easier, however, had Paige remained silent. But every time his fingers strayed to a new part of her foot she gave an appreciative moan and it shot his concentration to pieces. He continued through sheer grit alone and steadfastly refusing to look at anything but her feet and what his fingers were doing.

And not thinking about what they'd like to be doing.

Paige hovered on a blissful plane a few inches off the lounge as Valentino's deep steady strokes soothed all the aches away. She watched him through half-closed lids, diligently concentrating on the job. He hadn't taken his eyes off her feet once. Not even when he'd offered to make her his kept woman.

Anyone would think he was a professional masseur, for crying out loud.

Just looking at his bronzed hands on her pale skin was building a fire deep down low. The deep press of his fingers sent streaks of sensation from her foot up her instep to her inner leg and on to her entire body. She was melting into a puddle of desire, a boneless mass of longing.

It was wrong on so many levels. She'd told him this wasn't going to happen. But she wanted him more at this moment than she ever had.

And he was being Mr Professional.

Paige squirmed her body to ease the ache inside and pressed her palm to her belly for some outside fortification. How was she going to get through the next weeks without jumping his bones?

The squirm was his limit. He'd been fine till she'd moved but things jiggled in his peripheral vision and he couldn't stop himself from turning his head and looking his fill.

Her hand rested on her belly in a pose he'd seen more and more often these last few weeks since her tummy had popped out. Her habit of wearing baggy clothes and her baggy scrubs had allowed her to hide it from others, but he knew. He'd felt it.

He knew.

She was wearing a skirt that was too big, its folds hiding her legs all morning, but lying horizontal the folds fell away and the skirt very neatly outlined thighs that had filled out beautifully over weeks of feeding her the most tempting food he could find.

Paige popped her head up. 'Hey,' she protested quietly. 'You stopped.'

Valentino looked down at his stilled hands, surprised. 'I'm sorry.' His gaze returned to her hand splayed down low on her stomach. He wanted to see it. He wanted to gaze on his child growing inside her. 'Can I…can I look?'

Paige's breath stuck in her throat at his intense gaze. He looked so unsure. Valentino, who always looked so sure of himself. She could have no more refused him than have got her boneless body up off the couch. She locked her gaze with his and slowly inched the fabric of her shirt up her abdomen until she was exposed to his view.

Valentino sucked in a breath at the sight of her small round belly. His child grew there. 'You're beautiful,' he murmured. 'May I?'

Paige nodded and watched as his hands left her feet, slid up the sides of her legs, over hips that were less angular these days and onto her stomach. Her muscles contracted beneath his hands as he pushed the waistband of her skirt down slightly and they moved to cradle his child.

Valentino leaned forward and Paige widened her legs to allow him better access, and when he dropped a string of kisses across the swell of her belly her eyes blurred with tears and her fingers speared into his hair.

His tongue found her skin, laving her belly, and she felt the erotic scrape of his three-day growth deep down inside. When he dipped into her belly button she cried out.

Valentino looked up from his ministrations, his chin resting against the rise of her stomach. Her lips were parted and her smoky eyes glazed. Not taking his eyes off her, his hands moved slowly up, pushing her shirt as they went. When they found the lace-enclosed mounds of her breasts she shut her eyes and arched her back and Valentino swiped his thumbs over the taut peaks of her nipples.

Her whimper was soul-deep satisfying and he wanted to kiss her mouth so badly he was moving before he knew it, rising on his knees, looming over her, dropping his head closer and closer to her moist parted lips.

And when she raised her head to shorten the gap there was no holding back. Her mouth was sweeter than he remembered and the moan deep in her throat as she parted her lips widely, inviting him in, mingled with his.

He couldn't get enough of her mouth. Or the curve of her neck or the sweet spot behind her ear. His hands pushed aside her bra cups and she arched her back, pushing herself harder into his palms.

He dropped his head to suck a taut bud into his mouth and her swift indrawn breath was harsh in the silent room. He released it and looked down into her flushed face, her lips moist and ravaged from his ministrations.

Paige's breath sawed in and out of her lungs as she burnt up beneath his incendiary stare. She wanted him in her so badly she could almost feel him.

But.

'We can't…' Actually, technically, they could. Erica hadn't forbidden it at all. But Paige didn't want to risk anything.

'I know.' He nuzzled her neck. 'Move over,' he whispered. 'Lie on your side.'

Paige gave him kudos for having a plan. She was beyond such things. But her body knew what it wanted and eagerly followed his instructions. And then they were on their sides facing each other and Valentino's mouth was plundering hers and his hands were roaming over her breasts and stomach and pushing the waistband of her skirt lower, lower, and repeating the process with her underwear.

Her hands had a mind of their own too as they plucked at Valentino's shirt, pulled at it, lifted it over his head. Then reached for the clasp and zipper of his trousers, making them seem flimsy as she quickly undid them. His erection strained against his underwear and she pushed it aside too.

'*Dio!*' Valentino groaned into her neck, and shut his eyes as her hand enclosed him, squeezed him.

'You feel so good,' Paige murmured, milking the length of him.

'So do you,' Valentino gasped, his mouth closing over a dusky nipple as his hand found its way between her legs.

When his mobile rang it took several seconds for either of them to even hear it over the beat of their hearts and the heaving of their breath.

Valentino lifted his head and Paige pulled him back to her. 'Ignore it,' she whispered.

But Valentino had a separate ring for family members so he knew it was one of his sisters. He did a quick calculation in his head, surprised to find he was capable and also realising with a sinking feeling it was three in the morning back home. He knew they wouldn't be ringing at that time for anything trivial.

He pressed a hard kiss to Paige's mouth and then laid his forehead against her chest. 'I'm sorry. I have to get it. It's one of my sisters.'

Paige almost wept when he rolled away from her, adjusting his clothes and fishing in his back pocket for his mobile. She certainly wasn't capable of movement.

Definitely not capable of fixing her own clothes as her blood pounded like the ocean through her head and the room spun merrily around.

Valentino flipped his phone open and turned his back to her. She looked rumpled, dazed, her mouth glistening, her nipples engorged, her belly round with his child. He could smell her all around him and she looked thoroughly seduced. The temptation to end the call and turn his phone off was far too great.

'*Ciao.*' It was harsher then he'd meant it to come out but, really, his sisters had always had a sixth sense for interrupting at very inappropriate moments.

Paige listened absently to the conversation in Italian she didn't understand. It was brief and something was obviously wrong as Valentino's voice grew urgent and his words quickened.

He snapped the phone shut and turned back to her. Paige was still lying on the lounge, clothes skew, belly on proud display. She looked utterly sexy and he'd give anything to rewind time and delay the phone call.

'I'm sorry. That was my sister Carmella.' He raked a hand through his hair. 'My mother has been in a car accident not far from where we live.' He shut his eyes briefly as his sister's hysteria clawed at his gut. 'They're flying her to Rome for exploratory surgery.'

In the face of Valentino's wretchedness the sexual fogged evaporated and Paige pulled herself together. 'Oh, Valentino!' she gasped, climbing off the lounge, yanking her shirt down and adjusting her skirt. 'Is she all right?' she asked as he opened his arms and drew her close.

'I don't know. No one knows anything at the moment. I…have to go.'

Paige felt the blow to her heart immediately. She pushed away from his chest and plastered a resolute look on her face. 'Of course you must. Go. Go now.'

Valentino was torn. He couldn't believe in a few short months a woman had become just as important as his family. 'Come with me.'

Paige blinked. What the…? Had the haze of lust fried his brain cells. 'I…can't. I can't just up and leave. I have McKenzie and work and—'

'It'll just be a few days, maybe a week, until I know. Your parents—'

'No,' she interrupted, dismayed at his lack of understanding. 'I'm not leaving McKenzie.'

Valentino tensed, taken aback by her rejection and struggling to appreciate her reasons. 'Fine.'

'Valentino,' she said, stepping towards him, reaching for him. How had they gone from the heights of sexual dizziness to this? 'You know this isn't possible.'

A nerve jumped in his jaw and he flinched as she touched him. 'Anything's possible.'

Paige dropped her hands from his chest. 'No. That's what I've been trying to tell you. You can drop things and just leave. Like right now.' Like he no doubt would for the rest of their lives. Would he want to take their baby too? 'I can't.'

Valentino could feel irrational anger simmer in his blood. He grasped her by the upper arms. 'Marry me.'

Paige could feel the bite of his fingers peripherally only. She knew this was coming from a deep well of concern for his mother but it didn't make it any less difficult to deal with.

If only things were different…

But they weren't.

Paige shifted against the restraining bands of his hands. 'No. Go to your mother. Go home.'

It took a few seconds for her words to sink in and he released her, rubbing at her upper arms, smoothing where he had hurt her. 'I'm sorry,' he said.

Paige linked her arms around his neck and gave him a fierce hug. 'It's okay. Now go.'

Valentino pulled back slightly, slammed a hard kiss against her mouth and then turned away.

It wasn't until she heard the front door shut that Paige realised the awful truth. She loved him. Loved a man who didn't love her back. And there was nothing she could do about it but keep it to herself and never let him know.

CHAPTER NINE

Two weeks later Valentino lay horizontal in his business-class seat, wide awake, somewhere over the Pacific Ocean. The lights in the cabin had been turned down low and most sensible travellers were using it to grab some shut-eye. They'd be landing in Brisbane in just over four hours.

But he couldn't sleep.

He was impatient for the plane to fly faster, to get there sooner. He needed to see Paige. To tell her that he loved her.

It was something he'd known the minute he'd walked out of her door that momentous afternoon and had kept to himself for two weeks. Well, not strictly to himself. He'd told his mother about the baby and she'd demanded to know about Paige. She'd asked him point blank if he loved her and he'd been able to say yes with utter conviction.

But he hadn't been able to confirm Paige's feelings for him to his mother. The truth was he just didn't know how she felt at all. She'd been keeping him at a distance, protecting her damaged heart for the entire time he'd known her. Valentino just didn't know if she'd ever allow herself to fall in love again.

Sure, there was something between them. He knew that. There was a strong physical attraction. He sincerely doubted whether they'd ever be able to keep their hands off each other for any length of time. And there would always be their son.

But he wanted to be more in her life than just the father of their child. A part-time parent. Someone to scratch the itch when it got too much to bear for both of them. He wanted to love and cherish her. Introduce her to his family as his bride. He wanted to grow old with her.

He'd come a long way since his infatuation with Daniella. The young love he'd felt for her was lightweight compared to this heavy feeling in his chest. It had been impulsive and superficial. Skin deep.

What he felt for Paige reached right down to his soul. It was complex, multi-faceted. Messy and complicated. Especially in comparison to the easy, carefree time with Daniella. But maturity was a wonderful thing. He now knew sometimes good things didn't come easily. Sometimes they had to be fought for.

And if that's what it took then he'd do it, because he most certainly knew his life would be empty without her by his side.

Paige rubbed her back absently as she sat in her office chair and updated the charts from the day's surgery. It was hard to concentrate when her mind kept drifting to Valentino and the fact that in two weeks she'd received three lousy texts.

One had been to say his mother had undergone an emergency splenectomy and was doing well. The next had come four days later to say she was being discharged and he was staying another week or so. And the last a couple of days ago, which had informed her he'd be back soon.

She'd been worried sick about him but he hadn't answered any of her calls or returned any of her messages. He couldn't have been any clearer about her lack of importance to him if he'd opened his mouth and told her.

And it hurt.

Worse than with Arnie. Way worse than with Arnie. Because she'd been an infatuated, blind fool with him but she'd walked into this one with her eyes wide open and the door to her heart firmly shut, but she'd opened the damn thing anyway. Flung it wide open despite her misgivings. And not just her heart but McKenzie's heart too. She was the worst kind of fool.

Another tightening sensation gripped her belly and she had to stop what she was doing and rub at it. She'd been having irregular Braxton-Hicks' contractions on and off all day, no doubt aggravated by standing in a cold theatre in hard clogs.

She'd panicked earlier in the day when the first one had hit in the break between theatre cases and she'd rung her obstetrician in a state of absolute dread, fearing the start of another premature labour.

Not that it felt like it had with the twins at all, just an occasional tightening, but at only twenty-four weeks and with her history, any little niggle was cause for fright.

After asking succinct questions, Erica had assured her they were Braxton-Hicks' contractions, which were perfectly normal. Not having had any before her first pregnancy had come to a rather early finish, Paige was ignorant to what they felt like, although she'd heard pregnant women and mothers talking about them frequently.

Erica had talked her through the things to watch out for
and by the time Paige had hung up the panic had receded
and she'd got a grip. Braxton-Hicks were a perfectly
normal sign of a perfectly normal pregnancy. They were
a good thing. She was going to have a normal pregnancy
and deliver at a normal time.

She picked up the pen and starting writing again.

'Paige?'

Her hand stilled in mid-word and her heart contracted as
her gaze flew to the doorway. Valentino stood there, taking
up all the space, looking as sexy as ever in a haggard twenty-
four-hour-flight kind of way. Rumpled clothes, jaw heavy
with stubble, bleary eyes and unruly hair.

Actually, he looked like hell.

Good.

She stifled the urge to get up and run to him. No matter
how her arms ached to hold him and her heart bled, she
would not debase herself with him any more. He'd made
it perfectly clear where she stood.

'Valentino,' she murmured, her fingers strangling the
pen. Another Braxton-Hicks came and she frowned as it
gripped her belly hard, much closer and stronger than any
of the others. How long had it been since the last? 'How
is your mother?'

Valentino saw the wariness in her eyes. The frigid
coolness of them. It hadn't been the welcome he'd
expected. Not that he'd known what to expect but the way
they'd left things he'd hoped for a little more warmth.
Maybe even pleasure lighting those expressive grey pools.

Her shuttered look certainly wasn't conducive to con-
fessing his undying love. 'Fighting fit again. Not much
keeps her down for long.'

Paige nodded, her jaw cramped with the effort of keeping her voice evenly modulated. 'Good to know. I'm pleased she came through it well. It must have been worrying for all of you.'

Valentino frowned at her formality. He didn't want this. He wanted to sweep her up and lay her down, see how much her belly had grown in the interminable two weeks he'd been away. Kiss it. Kiss her. Tell her how much he loved her. 'Is everything okay?'

Her shoulders tensed. 'Fine.'

Valentino walked into her office and stood in front of her desk, hands on his hips. He was so tired. All he wanted to do was lie down with her, fall asleep with his hand on her belly. 'You seem…upset.'

A bubble of rage combined with another sharp pain spurred her into standing. She was so angry with him the Braxton-Hicks was secondary. Was he seriously that obtuse? 'Upset? Why on earth would I be upset?' she snapped. 'You don't answer your phone or return my calls. You could have plunged into the ocean days ago for all I knew.'

Paige hated how she sounded. Like a spurned lover, or, in his case, a discarded girlfriend. But she couldn't stop as the pain gripping her belly increased in length and intensity.

She glared at him. 'I was worried sick about you.'

Valentino was unsure whether it was a good thing or a bad thing that she was mad. She'd been worried about him? Did it mean she cared? 'I texted you.'

Paige slammed her hand against the desk. 'Three times! Three lousy times in two weeks? You profess to want to marry me, for us to be a family together, yet you can't even ring me when you get there to tell me everything's okay? You text me?'

Valentino blinked, taken aback by her fervour. It was true he hadn't rung. But that had been deliberate. He'd known that the minute he heard her voice he would have told her he loved her and he hadn't wanted that for her. Not over the phone.

He'd wanted to say the words face to face. So, no, he hadn't rung. But he'd dialled her number a hundred times and listened to her messages over and over again, wishing she was by his side.

And then there was the other side of it. If he'd told her he'd loved her and she'd rejected him or, worse, panicked and run, he would have been a half a world away, unable to do anything about it. At least face to face she couldn't run or hide.

'Nothing to say?' she snapped. 'Damn it, Valentino, I—' Paige broke off as another pain assailed her down low, doubling her over. She gripped the desk with both hands.

Valentino rushed to her. 'Paige!'

Something was wrong. 'Help,' she cried, clutching Valentino's sleeve. That hadn't felt like a normal, natural Braxton-Hicks. That had felt exactly like it had with the twins when her membranes had ruptured at twenty-eight weeks and she'd been eight centimetres dilated. Exactly.

'I think I'm in labour.' And she burst into tears.

Valentino stared at the top of her downcast head, his arm going around her back, supporting her against him.

No.

No, this could not possibly be happening. He'd told her it wouldn't. He'd told her he'd look after her.

Paige turned a tear-streaked face to him. 'I'm only twenty-four weeks. We have to stop it.' She grabbed the front of his shirt. 'We have to.'

Valentino fought a tidal wave of emotions. The woman he loved was in distress, fighting pain and a bunch of demons. And his baby, his son, possibly also in distress, was too young to survive.

But he couldn't afford to let the wave sweep him up and carry him out to sea. She needed him. So did his son.

'We will,' he said, grim determination in his eyes as he swept her up into his arms.

'What are you doing?' she cried.

'Taking you to A and E. I'll call Erica to meet us there.'

Valentino's long strides took them quickly through the lounge and he deposited her gently into the wheelchair they always kept in the department. Paige's anguish tore at his gut but he blanked it out as he pushed her to the lifts, using his mobile to call Erica.

'Have your membranes ruptured?' Valentino asked.

'No,' Paige wailed.

He relayed it to Erica, listened for another moment and then snapped his phone shut. Another contraction hit as they entered the lift and Paige cried harder, reaching back for his hand. 'Its okay, Paige, just breathe. Erica's ten minutes away.'

The ride in the lift was the longest of his life and by the time he wheeled Paige into St Auburn's chaotic accident department he was running on sheer adrenaline.

Nat was the first person they saw. Her initial look of welcome quickly turned to alarm as she took in the situation. She knelt beside the wheelchair. 'Paige! Whatever is wrong?'

Valentino answered for her. 'She's twenty-four weeks pregnant and having contractions.'

Nat blinked. 'Pregnant?'

'Yes,' Valentino snapped. 'Pregnant. Erica de Jongh is on her way.'

Natalie didn't need any more information. She didn't reprimand her friend for lying to her on the phone all those months ago when she had rung to check on her. In thirty seconds a blubbering Paige was in a cubicle and being transferred onto a gurney.

'I'll just get the CTG,' Nat said, ducking out of the curtains.

Paige, who was lying on her side, her back to Valentino, had curled herself into a ball and was sobbing quietly. Valentino couldn't bear to see it. 'Paige,' he murmured, placing his hand on her shoulder and applying gentle pressure to get her to face him.

'Go away,' she choked out, giving her shoulder a violent shrug. 'Just go away, Valentino. It'll save you the effort later.'

Her anguished insult hit him square in the solar plexus. 'I'm not going anywhere,' he said, pulling at her shoulder again.

Paige felt a block of rage like molten rock wedge in her chest as she flung herself back to face him. 'I told you. I told you this would happen again and that I didn't want to get close to another baby, to love another baby.'

She half sat, wiping at her streaming eyes and nose. 'But, no, you said it'd be fine, you said it wouldn't happen. You…' she poked him viciously in the chest '…made me go along with it. You…' another poke '…made me want him.'

Valentino's heart broke at her torment. 'Paige, we don't know what this is yet.'

Paige shook her head violently. 'I do.' She knew deep in her bones. 'I. Do.'

Valentino tried to take her hand but she snatched hers away. 'We discussed this contingency with Erica—'

A contraction gripped her and Paige's gasp interrupted him. She tried to breathe but was crying too hard at the same time. It eventually eased and then Nat came in with the CTG machine and hooked the belt around her bump. She squeezed Paige's hand. 'Erica will be here really soon.'

Paige watched the curtains fall back into place as Nat left. She looked at Valentino, so strong and positive, and felt weary, old beyond her years. 'I can't do this again, Valentino.' Paige heaved in deep breaths. 'Do you hear me? I can't do it. I don't have enough strength for this.'

'Yes, you do, Paige. You are the strongest woman I know.' He brushed at her fringe. Her face was all red and blotchy, her nose and eyes were streaming and he cupped her cheek, using his thumb to wipe at her tears. 'Look what you've been through already. Look how you survived. You're a survivor.'

Paige angled her head and leaned her face into his palm and shut her eyes, two more tears squeezing out and trekking down her face. 'Why can't something just go my way for once?' She opened her eyes and straightened her head. 'You told me it would be okay,' she whispered. 'I trusted you.'

He placed his other hand on her face so he was cupping both cheeks. 'You can trust me. I'm not going to let anything happen. We'll get an ultrasound and if it is preterm labour then you'll go on nifedipine and the labour is going to stop and you're giving up work and going on bed rest and I'm going to support you and feed you and pamper you and this baby will go to full term and then we're getting married because I love you and we're going to Italy for a honeymoon and we're taking the kids.'

Paige was feeling so churned up she found it difficult to follow his stream-of-consciousness speech. She wasn't even sure if she heard him right. But the conviction in his words was strong and she so wanted to believe him.

And had he actually said the L word? She sniffed and said, 'What?'

Then the curtains snapped back and Erica arrived, pushing a portable ultrasound machine and looking calm and efficient and in control. Valentino squeezed her hand and they and their future faded away as the immediate danger to their baby took precedence.

'How are you doing?' she asked both of them as she switched on the machine and fiddled with some dials.

'Lousy,' Paige admitted.

Erica nodded. 'You?' she asked Valentino.

'Scared witless.'

Paige looked at him, startled. He hadn't seemed in the least bit afraid. He'd been commanding and confident and had got her to A and E and arranged for Erica to be here and told her everything was going to be okay. He'd been the epitome of cool, calm and collected, especially in the face of her histrionics.

Erica nodded again. 'Normal, then.' She inspected the graph readout the CTG had traced.

Her face gave nothing away but that just made Paige even more frantic. 'It's bad, isn't it?'

Erica looked her in the eye. 'It's showing regular strong contractions. But the baby's heart rate is steady and there are no decelerations. He doesn't appear to be in any distress. Let's have a look first, okay?' She placed a condom over the trans-vaginal probe and squirted warmed lubricant on it.

Paige grabbed Erica's sleeve. 'Please tell me it's going to be okay.'

Erica glanced at Valentino then back to Paige. She shook her head. 'I don't know yet, Paige. But I will in a second. Let's be sure, okay?'

Paige felt a hot tear escape out the corner of one eye and tried not to tense as she drew her knees up and Erica inserted the probe beneath the sheet. Valentino squeezed her hand and dropped a kiss on her shoulder, which made her tear up even more.

An image flickered on the screen and she shut her eyes tight, turning her head into Valentino's shoulder. She couldn't bear to watch.

After what seemed like minutes Paige couldn't take the silence any longer, convinced Erica was trying to find a way to tell her she was almost fully dilated again. She glared at Erica. 'Well?'

Erica flicked a switch and the sure and steady beat of their baby's heart filled the cubicle. Paige broke down at the glorious sound. It seemed so strong but Paige knew at twenty-four weeks their son was so very, very fragile. Too young to be in the outside world.

Erica removed the probe and switched off the machine. She looked at Valentino, his arm around Paige, who was weeping quietly. 'The good news is you haven't dilated at all.'

Paige clutched at Valentino's sleeve as the news sank in. He kissed her head and for the first time since she'd realised she was in labour, Paige felt a ray of hope.

'But. You are fifty per cent effaced.'

Valentino knew both effacement—shortening and thinning of the cervix—and dilatation were required for the baby to be delivered. 'So, it's definitely preterm labour?'

Erica nodded. 'I'm afraid so.'

Paige was incapable of anything as she went from fragile hope to the walls crashing around her. It was happening all over again. She was going to give birth to Val's baby soon. Too soon. A hundred memories of Daisy and McKenzie when they had first been born floated before her.

And her son was going to be even earlier. A whole four weeks of crucial development time.

'So what's the plan?' Valentino asked.

'Oral nifedipine regime to relax the uterus and hopefully stop the contractions, even if it's only for a few days to give us time to administer some steroids to mature the baby's lungs.'

Valentino nodded. 'And then?'

'Hospital for a few days, monitoring blood pressure and regular ultrasounds to check on the cervix.'

He nodded again. Nifedipine's normal use was as an anti-hypertensive and had only been used regularly in an obstetric drug in relatively recent times. Paige's blood pressure would need close monitoring. 'And then?'

'If we can stop the contractions, home on twice-daily tablets and lots of bed rest. If she makes it to thirty-six weeks we take her off the medication and let nature take its course.'

Valentino's methodical medical mind prioritised and sorted. 'So, the worst-case scenario is that we buy a few days. The best case is we go to term?'

Erica nodded. 'Spot on.'

Paige was taking none of it in. She was numb now. Numb all over. There were no more tears left. Flashes of three years ago bombarded her—the twins on life support,

Daisy's tiny white coffin, Arnie walking away—as she tried to reach a mental place where she could shut down her emotions and deal with the next few days, maybe months if Valentino's child was a fighter.

Juggling McKenzie and watching Valentino become ever more distant.

A sob caught in her throat.

'Paige!'

Valentino's voice invaded her thoughts and the mental place moved further out of reach. She looked at him as if seeing him for the first time.

'Leave me alone,' she whispered.

Valentino could see her withdrawing before his eyes and he wanted to shake her. *Dio!* He would not let her give up. This wasn't a battle he could fight on his own, neither could his son. She had to believe it was going to be okay too. 'No.'

Paige had started to recede again and his insistent denial dragged her back. 'What?'

'I said no.'

Paige shook her head. He truly didn't understand how much of her had died inside her last time. 'Just do what needs to be done,' she muttered. He said he loved her? Then he could do that for her.

Valentino looked hopelessly at Erica. 'What do I do?'

Erica gave him a grave smile. 'What she asked you to do. Do what needs to be done.'

Valentino glanced at Paige, so near and yet so far. 'Okay, then.'

Paige swallowed pills and lay passively as they put in an IV and gave her a steroid shot and took her blood pressure endlessly. She didn't feel the belt of the CTG

Valentino chuckled for the first time since he'd landed. 'Two a day should be enough.'

Paige laughed as Valentino resumed his chair. His chin rested on his hands and he looked utterly exhausted. His stubble was longer still and his clothes more rumpled. His hair looked as if it had been raked to within an inch of its life. 'You should go home,' she murmured. 'You look totally exhausted.'

Valentino rubbed his chin against the sheets and it rasped into the silence. 'I'm not leaving,' he said. 'I'm never leaving.'

Paige swallowed. She believed him. The man had seen her at her lowest ebb and was still here. Arnie had never been good with her tears and hadn't been able to cope with her grief. He certainly would have been at a loss with her withdrawn state.

Valentino had just taken it in his stride.

'I'm sorry about earlier. I don't know where I went...I totally freaked out.'

Valentino slid his hand back to her rejoin hers nestled against her belly. 'You went where you needed to go. It's okay.'

Paige gave him a small smile and yawned as her eyelids fluttered shut.

'Go to sleep,' he urged. 'I'm staying right here.'

Paige nodded but something niggled at the back of her mind as she drifted off. Three seconds later she was wide awake and sitting bolt upright, her heart in her mouth. 'McKenzie!'

Valentino squeezed her hand. 'She's fine. She's with your parents. I've been giving them regular updates.'

'Really?' she demanded, her pulse still racing.

'Really,' he assured her, reaching his arms up to push gently against her shoulders. 'Go to sleep.'

Paige complied as her heart rate settled and her breathing became deep and even, yet still something niggled.

Paige wasn't sure how much time had elapsed since she'd last woken up but she could see a slight pink hue lightening the sky through a gap in the curtains.

Her gaze drifted to Valentino's sleeping face. For the first time he actually looked his thirty-seven years. A lock of his luscious hair had fallen forward and was kissing his eyelid. It was such an endearing picture her heart filled with her love for him. She forgot all about being mad at him earlier.

What did that matter now? He had been her true hero tonight and she loved him completely.

And suddenly she was able to put a finger on that strange niggly feeling from earlier as memories from yesterday afternoon rushed back. He had told her he loved her too. And today, at the breaking of a new dawn, after a night of miracles, she was going to embrace it and choose to be happy.

Paige advanced her finger slowly and gently lifted the stray lock back into place. He murmured and stirred and then opened his eyes.

She gave him time to focus. 'Good morning,' she whispered.

He licked his dry lips and smiled. *'Buongiorno.'*

She smiled back, her toes curling at his husky morning voice and sexy accent. 'You told me you loved me.'

Valentino stilled for a moment and searched her face. She seemed relaxed. Happy even. 'Yes.'

'Did you mean it?'

'Assolutamente.'

Paige smiled, not needing a translation for that one. 'And when did you have this particular epiphany?'

'About ten seconds after I left your house to go to the airport a fortnight ago.'

Paige laughed this time. 'I think that was about when I had mine.'

Valentino's heart stopped briefly before skipping madly in his chest. He slid his hand to her belly. 'Really?' he murmured.

She nodded, holding his hand close. 'Really.'

'It was before that, though. The moment I fell in love with you. I just didn't realise until much later.'

Paige quirked an eyebrow, intrigued. 'Oh? When?'

'That night at the wedding when you looked so confused as to why out of all the women at Alessandro's wedding I wanted you.'

Paige frowned. 'Why then?'

'Because you truly didn't know how beautiful you were and that, my darling…' he lifted her hand off her stomach and kissed it '…was utterly endearing.'

She could feel her cheeks turn pink. 'I think for me it was when you promised me there would be no sleeping.' Valentino chuckled and she grinned. 'That was a great line. You'll have to teach it to our son when he's older.'

Valentino felt his chest expand. Their son. 'So you're not going to fight me any more? You'll marry me?'

Paige nodded vigorously and snuggled his hand back against the swell of her belly. 'And the four of us will honeymoon in Italy together.'

Valentino grinned. It sounded like bliss. 'I brought this with me from the airport.' He reached into his pocket with his spare hand and pulled out the velvet case he'd produced all those months ago. He presented it to her. 'Will you wear it?'

Paige slipped her hand out of his and flipped open the lid. The diamond glittered beneath the dim overhead light. 'Just try and stop me,' she murmured as she freed it from its satiny cushion and slipped it on. 'See?' She turned it around to show him and he rose slightly and pressed a gentle kiss against her mouth.

'Perfect. Just like you.'

'Just like us,' she whispered. 'Just like him.' And her hand rejoined his as she kissed him back.

EPILOGUE

'He's perfect. Perfect in every way,' Valentino mused, peeling back the wad of wrapping in the crook of his wife's elbow to reveal his one-hour-old son Ferdinando Lombardi.

Paige smiled as her little boy slept. She couldn't agree more. She was exhausted from a fifteen-hour labour but somehow still too elated to sleep. Erica had taken her off the nifedepine a week ago and their son, after wanting out at such an early stage, had finally decided to make an appearance seven days later, weighing a very healthy three and a half kilos.

'Can we come in?'

Paige looked up to see her parents and McKenzie waiting impatiently in the doorway.

'McKenzie!' Valentino smiled and held out his arms to her.

She rushed into the room. Don and Adele followed at a slightly more sedate pace. Slightly.

Valentino swept McKenzie into his arms and plonked her on the side of the bed. 'Are you ready to meet your little brother?' he said as he signed simultaneously.

McKenzie squirmed with barely suppressed excitement. 'Yes,' she said.

Paige smiled, still in love with her daughter's voice as she turned her son around.

'This is your brother, Ferdinando,' Val murmured, signing as well.

McKenzie looked at him as if he were a baby unicorn she'd found in an enchanted forest, her eyes big and round. 'Nandi,' she said, and leaned forward to kiss the tip of her sleeping brother's nose.

'Looks like he's already acquired a nickname.' Adele beamed, reaching forward to gently touch her grandson's tiny fingers.

Valentino chuckled. 'I like it.'

Paige made way for McKenzie to snuggle into her side and they all gazed on her newborn son's perfection.

'Thank you,' Valentino mouthed after a few moments, interlinking his hand with hers.

'Thank you,' she whispered back.